Scarlet Wilson wrote her first story aged eight and has never stopped. She's worked in the health service for twenty years, having trained as a nurse and a health visitor. Scarlet now works in public health and lives on the West Coast of Scotland with her fiancé and their two sons. Writing medical romances and contemporary romances is a dream come true for her.

Having tried a variety of careers in retail, marketing and nursing, **Louisa George** is thrilled that her dream job of writing for Mills & Boon means she gets to go to work in her pyjamas. Louisa lives in Auckland, New Zealand, with her husband, two sons and two male cats. When not writing or reading Louisa loves to spend time with her family, enjoys travelling, and adores eating great food.

Also by Scarlet Wilson

One Kiss in Tokyo…
Christmas in the Boss's Castle
A Royal Baby for Christmas
The Doctor and the Princess
The Mysterious Italian Houseguest
A Family Made at Christmas
The Italian Billionaire's New Year Bride

Also by Louisa George

How to Resist a Heartbreaker
200 Harley Street: The Shameless Maverick
A Baby on Her Christmas List
Tempted by Her Italian Surgeon
Her Doctor's Christmas Proposal
Tempted by Hollywood's Top Doc
The Nurse's Special Delivery

Discover more at millsandboon.co.uk.

RESISTING THE SINGLE DAD

SCARLET WILSON

REUNITED BY THEIR SECRET SON

LOUISA GEORGE

MILLS & BOON

First Published in Great Britain 2018
by Mills & Boon, an imprint of HarperCollins*Publishers*
1 London Bridge Street, London, SE1 9GF

Resisting the Single Dad © 2018 by Scarlet Wilson

Reunited by Their Secret Son © 2018 by Louisa George

ISBN: 978-0-263-93349-9

RESISTING THE SINGLE DAD

SCARLET WILSON

MILLS & BOON

This book is dedicated to my editor, Sheila Hodgson.

Thank you for looking after me so well in the past
year, and for being such a brilliant advocate
for the Medical Romance line.

Love you, Sheila!

CHAPTER ONE

CORDELIA GREENWAY RELAXED back into the chair as she tried to ignore the palpitations and light-headedness that had started. She breathed deeply and put her fingers to the side of her neck, massaging gently and closing her eyes as she waited for the manoeuvre to take effect.

Sweat started to run between her shoulder blades—another symptom. People were chatting all around her—no one seemed to have noticed her little 'turn'. And that was just the way she liked it. She hated fuss. She hated being under the spotlight.

So she stayed quiet, gently continuing to massage, and willing her heartbeat to steady. She probably should have glanced at her watch to time this—but she was so used to dealing with it, so used to keeping it under the radar, that it hadn't even entered her brain until now. She'd just gone into self-protect mode.

Her other hand lifted the hair off the back of her neck, where it was sticking. Ugh. But things were finally starting to work. She could almost hear out loud the beat of her heart starting to slow. Thank goodness.

After a few minutes she took a deep breath and rested her head on the cool desk for a second. Better. She tugged at her shirt, pulling it away from her body to let the air circulate. First thing she'd do when she got back home was jump in the shower.

There was a noise to her left. She stuck her head up above her cubby hole. Several of the other researchers were doing the same—they looked like a family of meerkats.

Professor Helier was pacing with his phone. The noise had come from his office. His voice squeaky. She didn't hesitate. She was at the glass door in seconds. 'Franc?'

Now he was nodding, scribbling things frantically on a piece of paper. He looked so pale. He swayed a little. She walked inside and held out her hands protectively behind him, in case he fell over. Professor Helier was the whole reason she was here.

When she'd found out that he was heading up the cardiac research at this lab, she *had* to be here. She would have done just about anything to work with this famed researcher.

But in the end all it had taken had been a few phone calls. She'd been head of the zebrafish research in the UK—leading the pioneering work into discovering their ability to regenerate heart muscle and how that could be transferred to humans. Professor Helier had embraced her interest instantly, inviting her to come and meet him, and asking if she wanted to lead one of his teams. She hadn't hesitated for a second.

The chance to work in Switzerland. The rich, clean air, snow-topped mountains, and a whole host of chocolates she should never touch. When she'd explained her reasons for working in cardiac research he'd just given her a beaming smile, and patted her hand. 'Cordelia, we all have our reasons for being here. That's what makes us all special.' He'd winked. 'That's what gives us all heart.' And the bad jokes had continued for the last three years.

He swayed a little again as he replaced the phone. She felt instantly protective. Franc must be approaching seventy and time hadn't been too kind to him. He always had a kind of frazzled appearance about him, along with his sometimes white coat and mass of grey hair. 'Franc, what is it? What can I do?'

No one knew exactly how old Franc Helier was. Even doing an internet search didn't help. He'd had the same mad grey hair and slim frame for the last forty years. Some of the junior staff joked that he looked like a mixture of Albert Einstein and a mad professor from a time travel movie. But for Cordelia it didn't matter. He was her friend. And she was his. That was all that mattered.

Franc put both hands on the desk. 'It's Emily,' he said a little breathlessly.

'Your sister?' He nodded, his expression a bit glazed. 'That was the hospital in Marseille. Apparently she collapsed at home and needs emergency surgery.'

Cordelia didn't hesitate. She lifted Franc's hat and coat from the hook behind her, thrusting them towards him. 'Go. Go now.' As he took them with slightly shaking hands she walked around his desk and opened his second drawer. She really did know him like family. 'Here. Your passport. Do you want me to book you a flight and arrange a pick-up? I can book a hotel for you too.' She glanced at the name of the hospital written in scrawled script on the note. 'I'll find one near there.'

He blinked. And she reached out and touched his cheek. Franc had no other family. His wife had died ten years ago and all he had left was his sister. 'Go, Franc. Go be with your sister. Everything will be fine here. You know it will.'

He nodded nervously. 'Of course. I trust you, Cordelia. You know I do.'

She pulled up the collar of his jacket. 'I'll email you the details of the flight, transport and hotel. Just go home and pack a few things.'

He still looked a little stunned. Just what had they told him on the phone?

'Is there anything else I can do for you, Franc?'

It was almost as if she'd flicked a switch in his brain. 'The Japanese investors are coming on Tuesday. Drug trials AZ14 and CF10 need to be monitored, with all data recorded by midweek. There are clinics to cover.'

She smiled and touched his arm. 'I've got them. You know I've got them.'

His gaze met hers and it was the first time he'd looked a little more assured. Her illness had led her away from the traditional role of doctor. She'd spent years on wards dealing with her own symptoms, along with patients'. Long shifts and nights and nights of being on call had made her symptoms worse. When she'd finally realised she couldn't do the job she loved, she'd picked the next best thing. Her role here was fifty-fifty. Fifty per cent researcher and fifty per cent doctor in a well-supported, controlled environment. It suited her. It let her be involved in research that could make a difference for millions of patients around the world—herself included.

Franc gave a little jolt. He waved his hand at the chaos that was his desk. 'Oh, and we have a new doctor arriving. I'm supposed to pick them up at the airport.'

Cordelia winced and grabbed her notebook from her pocket. 'Is it Geneva?'

He nodded. She had to check. They had staff flying

in from all around the world, and they didn't always arrive at the closest airport. 'What's the name?'

'Jeanne DuBois. It sounds French but it's American.' Something must have flashed into his brain. 'Oh.'

It was just the way he said it. 'What?' she questioned. 'What's "oh"?'

He pulled a face. 'They're supposed to stay with me. They were kind of a last-minute addition and hadn't managed to sort out accommodation yet.'

Cordelia swallowed, then nodded her head appropriately. She gave a smile. 'You're turning into an old cat lady, Franc. Taking in every waif and stray.'

She shook her head. Her own apartment's ceiling had collapsed last week after a neighbour upstairs had suffered a burst pipe. Franc had been gracious enough to let her stay in his own rambling mansion on the outskirts of Geneva. He often put up visiting researchers. Cordelia waved her hand. 'Leave it with me. That probably makes things easier anyway. It means when I pick them up, I get to drive back home. Oops.' She put her hand up to her mouth as she realised what she'd said.

But Franc just shook his head and gave her shoulder a squeeze. 'My home is your home, Cordelia. It always will be. Here's hoping they take more than a month to fix your ceiling.' He closed his eyes for a second. 'It could be that soon you'll be the only family I have left.'

Her stomach flipped. This was serious. Part of her wished she'd heard that phone call. She reached over and gave Franc a bear hug. He felt so frail. So thin. Had he lost more weight and she hadn't noticed?

She whispered in his ear. 'I think of you as family too, Franc. Always remember that. You need something—I'm here.'

Franc nodded. 'Thank you, Cordelia.' He pulled himself free from her embrace and put on his hat and tucked his passport into his jacket. 'I'll call you.'

She shook her head. 'No, I'll message you. Go home and pack, and I'll arrange the flights and transfers. Head straight to the airport and I'll have things sorted by the time you get there.'

Franc nodded as he headed to the door. 'What would I do without you?' He gave a shake of his head. 'Just glad I don't need to find out.'

Her heart gave a little twist as he headed to the elevators. She'd have to send out an email to let everyone know Franc had been called away for a few days. And she'd do that—just as soon as she'd organised the flights, hotel and transport. She spent the next twenty minutes online then messaged Franc.

A little pink sticky note was sitting in the debris on Franc's desk. She plucked it out and stared at it for a few seconds.

Geneva 20.00

She glanced at her watch. *Please tell me that isn't the flight for the visiting doctor.* She rummaged amongst the papers on the desk. Franc's desk had a notoriety all of its own. Some of the people who worked here thought that messages came to Franc's desk to die. It certainly seemed like that. It was extraordinary. In all his research studies he was fastidious. Meticulous. Cordelia always joked that Franc's desk was the one place he could leave his true mess behind.

Try as she might, she couldn't find any other notes that resembled airport pick-up times. Darn it. She grabbed her purse. She'd barely make it.

The last thing she wanted to do was leave this poor doctor stranded at the airport.

If she hurried, she might just get there in time…

The first flush of passengers exited through the gates to screams and yelps from people waiting. Cordelia always felt a little like a voyeur at these times—intruding on private family moments. The joy on some of the faces was beautiful. There were obviously a few more painful reunions. People embracing and bursting into sobs as they hugged each other. It made her heart ache.

She looked down at her hastily scrawled black letters. Jeanne Du Bois. She didn't even have any idea what age the doctor that was arriving from the US was. The only thing she was sure of was that they would be expecting Professor Helier, not a brunette in her thirties.

She people watched for a while. An elderly couple greeting adult children returning home. A woman dropping her bags and running towards a guy, almost knocking him flat with her embrace. A few tourists, walking out with maps in hand and heading to the taxi rank.

And a guy, complete with cowboy boots and Stetson, wearing jeans and a dark grey T-shirt. He travelled wearing a *Stetson*?

She watched in amusement as he glanced around arrivals. He was tall. He really didn't need the Stetson to emphasise his height. As for those well-fitting jeans… She pulled her eyes away and focused on the door again, waiting to see if Jeanne Du Bois would appear. What would she look like? Probably tired. Most researchers who came from the US had to take two or three flights to get to Geneva.

She leaned against the barrier and tried not to dream of coffee and takeout food. She hadn't had time to eat before she'd left the research centre. Her stomach gave a growl just as the click of the cowboy boots came towards her.

A pair of deep brown eyes fixed on hers as he tipped his hat at her. He gestured towards the sign. 'I think you might be waiting for me.'

She blinked and looked down at her sign as if it might have changed while she wasn't looking.

He was close enough that she could smell his woody aftershave and see his sun-kissed skin. But it was the accent that threw her.

It was a thick American drawl. Like treacle. Or maple syrup. Something that smothered you in gorgeousness and just made you go…whoa.

She frowned as she tried not to let her herself be distracted by those very chocolaty eyes. Why was she associating everything with food? She was obviously hungrier than she'd thought.

'I'm waiting for a woman.' She looked down at her sign again, checking she hadn't been secretly pranked. Nope. It was still her writing. 'Jeanne Du Bois.'

The guy gave a lazy kind of smile and put his hand on his chest. 'I'm Jeanne Du Bois. Except it's G E N E. You know? Like Gene Kelly? Or Gene Hackman?'

She blinked. She still couldn't get over that accent. She wrinkled her nose. It reminded her of her favourite US TV series. 'Are you from Texas?'

He tipped his hat again. 'My mother was French, but I'm a Texan through and through.' He held out his hand towards her. 'Pleased to meet you, ma'am. You've obviously dyed your hair, Professor Helier. And had a sex change,' he added with a wink.

Her brain sparked back into gear. 'Oh, yes. I'm sorry.' She shook his hand swiftly, the warm touch sending a little pulse up her arm. 'I'm Dr Cordelia Greenway, Professor Helier's second in command. I'm so sorry. He's had a family emergency, literally in the last few hours. I asked him who I was collecting at the airport and when he told me Jeanne Du Bois. I just assumed it was a woman.'

The guy shrugged. 'You're in Switzerland. I guess I can live with being mistaken for a woman.'

She wanted to laugh out loud. There was no chance of this guy being mistaken for a woman. Not when he looked, smelled and sounded like that.

She gestured around him. 'Where's your luggage? My car is in the car park just a few minutes from here. I can take you back to Professor Helier's house. I'm staying there too.'

For the briefest of seconds something flashed across his face. 'Oh.' He looked her up and down. 'Right. Yes…that's great.'

She felt heat rush into her cheeks. He was making assumptions. She shook her head frantically. 'Oh, no. No. Professor Helier and I are…friends. He's helping me out too. The ceiling in my apartment collapsed last week.'

Gene's eyebrows rose. 'Oh, no. What a nightmare.'

She nodded and smiled. 'Yip. And my upstairs neighbour is off on a round-the-world cruise for a month. And still doesn't know about her leaking pipe, or the fact the factor had to break down her door to get in and switch her water off.'

Gene glanced over his shoulder, then looked back at her. 'So where does that leave you?'

'Homeless. Wet. With water pouring down my walls and ruining my carpets and electrics.' She raised her hand and shook her head. 'No, really, the water might have been turned off, but until my neighbour is back and

our insurance companies can battle it out together...'
She let her words trail off.

He nodded. 'You're kind of stuck?' He took off his
cowboy hat to reveal short brown hair that he ran his
hand through. 'I guess that means that Professor Helier
doesn't really have a lot of room.'

She held up her hands. 'It's fine. Really it is. Honestly, his house isn't a house—it's a kind of rambling
mansion. It's the kind of place they read you fairy stories about when you're a kid. He has plenty of space.'
She wiggled her hand. 'Not all of it habitable. But there
are rooms next to mine that are comfortable. You'll be
fine.' She looked back at the doors. 'Do you want to
collect your luggage and we'll go?'

He gave her a nod and stuck his hat back on his head.
'Are you okay to help me with the cases?'

She was a little surprised. 'Just how many did you
bring?'

He smiled. 'Just one each.'

She blinked and looked behind him. 'One each?
There's someone else with you?'

A wave of concern swept his face. 'You mean Professor Helier didn't tell you?'

She felt her stomach flip over. She was so looking
forward to getting home, eating something takeout and
climbing into her pyjamas. She didn't need any more
unexpected turns right now. Not when she needed to be
up at six a.m. to prepare for the patients attending clinic
tomorrow. She almost didn't want to say the words out
loud. 'Tell me what?'

'That I wasn't coming alone?' He sounded nervous.

She half expected some beauty queen to emerge from
the arrivals hall with a stunning full-length gown, silver
heels and blonde hair tumbling down her back. After

all, he looked like a guy who would inevitably be dating some kind of beauty queen.

She swallowed. Wine. Maybe she'd have some wine instead of coffee when she got back.

'No.' She tried to sound friendly. 'He didn't mention it.' She looked around him again. 'Is your wife just freshening up?'

He gave her a quizzical glance. 'Oh, he really didn't tell you. It's not my wife. I don't have a wife. It's my son, Rory. He's sleeping. One of the airline staff is minding him while I checked to see if our pick-up was here. I guess that's you.'

'Your son?'

She couldn't help it. She hadn't meant it to sound like that. Of course some of the visiting doctors brought their partners or families when they came to stay. It just wasn't like Professor Helier to miss such an important detail. It just let her know how distracted he'd actually been.

Gene gave her a little frown. 'Is that going to be a problem? I'm happy to call a cab and check into a local hotel. I don't want to put you to any trouble.'

It was the tone of his voice. He was annoyed. And no wonder. He'd been travelling for hours to a strange city, a new job—and she wasn't exactly being welcoming.

She held up her hand. 'It's no problem. If you want to get your son, I can manage the cases.'

For a few seconds he just stared at her, almost as if he was trying to decide whether to believe her or not. But she could see the fatigue on his face. She had a cheek to feel tired when he'd just crossed the Atlantic to get here. No wonder his son was sleeping. Gene Du Bois probably wanted to be sleeping too.

He gave a nod and headed back to the doors. A perfectly groomed stewardess met him with the child in her arms. Gene took the sleeping little figure easily, letting him snuggle into his shoulder, with one arm under his legs. He grabbed a large navy blue case with one hand as the stewardess brought out another—bright green with a lion on front.

Cordelia smiled as she felt a little pang. Kids. She normally managed to circumvent them. Having an on-going cardiac condition wasn't exactly conducive to having kids, and the older she got, the more she thought about it.

She'd learned to distance herself. It was easier that way. There was less chance of seeing what she'd miss out on. Less chance of becoming bitter about what could never be hers.

But she couldn't exactly circumvent a kid in the same house as her.

She hurried over and grabbed the bright green suitcase, trundling it behind her, and tried to keep up with Gene Du Bois's long strides.

'Dr Du Bois, Professor Helier didn't let me know what programme you'll be contributing to. I'll need to make some introductions and ensure everything has been put in place for you. Can you let me know what research you're involved in?'

Gene gave her a sideways glance and slowed his steps. 'I'm beginning to wonder if this was a good idea. I came here because the Reuben Institute is supposed to be at the forefront of cardiac research. I'm here for a month, to take the lead on the cardiomyopathy studies.'

She couldn't help but pull a face. 'Listen, I know this might seem chaotic, but the only thing that's normally chaotic at the Reuben Institute is Professor Helier's desk. Everything else is ruthlessly efficient, I assure you.'

They crossed the road towards the car park. 'What project do you lead on?'

She winced as her stomach grumbled loudly. 'The zebrafish studies.' She opened the car door. 'How about we put aside cardiac studies for this evening? I have to confess to not being much of a cook. Would the little guy eat pizza if I picked some up for us on the way back to the house?'

Gene settled the little boy into the car and strapped him in, with barely a murmur from his son. He ruffled his son's hair. 'Rory happens to be a big fan of pizza. After nearly twenty hours' travelling, I'm willing to do takeout.'

Cordelia gave a thankful nod and climbed into the car. 'Great. We should be home in twenty minutes. Settle in. The scenery is outstanding.'

She paused for a second and couldn't help but ask the question that had been swimming around her head since she'd first seen him. 'So, Dr Du Bois, do you always do full cowboy when you travel?'

He took off his hat as he climbed into the car and gave her a wink. 'What can I say? I'm from Texas.'

Gene wasn't quite sure what to think. He was beginning to regret dragging his little guy halfway across the planet to be involved in this research project. Professor Helier had guaranteed everything would be in place—including a suitable day-care arrangement for Rory.

Gene leaned back in the comfortable seat and closed his eyes for a few seconds. Maybe he should be watching the gorgeous scenery, but twenty hours of jet-lag was rapidly catching up with him. It had already made him more than a little short with his hostess. His momma would be spinning in her grave and slapping the back of his head right now.

No one could believe when his French scientist mother had fallen for a Texas cowboy—least of all her. Moving from Paris to Houston, Texas had been a culture shock for her. And after ten years and still no wedding ring, she'd finally bailed.

So Gene had spent his life between two continents. And he'd considered himself lucky. Flitting between a ranch in Texas and the city of Paris hadn't exactly been hard. As a child he'd excelled in living on two continents. And even though his father had been disappointed his son wanted to study medicine instead of ranching, he knew his dad had still been secretly proud.

The only thing that had really swept the feet from under him had been the message three years ago from the fellow doctor he'd had a fling with at a cardiac conference. Mindy had suffered from congenital hypertrophic cardiomyopathy. Pregnancy should never have been on her life plan. But when she'd found herself pregnant with Rory after a few passionate nights together in Istanbul, she'd chosen to go ahead with the pregnancy.

She'd only contacted Gene when things had got desperate. Everyone had advised her not to go ahead, knowing exactly what the strain of a pregnancy would do to her. Sure enough, soon after Rory had been born, she'd ended up on the heart transplant list.

And when she'd gone into complete heart failure, she'd finally contacted Gene to let him know about his son.

He'd been angry. He'd been furious. But how furious could a guy be at someone who was clearly dying?

His life had turned upside down in an instant. One look at the nine-month-old cheeky little blond baby, pulling himself up on wobbly legs to the side of his mother's bed, had been all the time he'd needed to make a decision.

It didn't help that in the interim since the conference he'd actually met someone. Karen. An anaesthetist at Boston General where he was working. They'd moved in together. Had had tentative talks about the future. He'd even considered buying a ring.

But the unexpected son had been a bolt out of the blue that Karen could never have expected. She'd been shocked—and then walked away. And he couldn't blame her. They'd discussed the fact they might like a family in the future—but Karen wasn't ready to deal with one that had been thrust on her. So after a year of being in a settled relationship he'd found himself alone.

Mindy had died three weeks later. And Gene had immediately set about turning his life around.

A single dad working in a hospital environment wasn't exactly conducive to good parenting.

He'd never considered working in research up until that point. But knowing that his son carried the gene for cardiomyopathy was enough to put his priorities in order. He'd spent the last three years with his dad joking about Gene looking at genes.

But that was fine, because he'd spend the rest of his life looking at genes if it could help his son and any future grandkids.

He smiled to himself. Rory had just turned four. Four. And he was thinking about grandkids. But he was a doctor, he had to plan ahead. And every plan in his life now included Rory.

He opened his eyes and glanced at the woman driving the car. Cordelia Greenway. He was sure he'd seen her name on some of the research papers published by the

Reuben Institute. She'd said she was Professor Helier's second in command.

Gene had learned to take things in his stride. He'd had to. Life frequently threw curve balls. He didn't mind curve balls. What he did mind was feeling as if his son was an unwanted extra. Maybe he was just being too sensitive? Or maybe he was being overprotective. But he was sure there had been a look of… something flash across Cordelia's face when he'd mentioned his son.

It could just be that she'd been taken unawares. But his gut told him something else. His gut could almost sense her take about ten steps back. And he didn't like that. He didn't like that at all.

He wasn't crazy. He didn't expect the whole world to love his son the way he did. Some folks just didn't do kids. He got that. But he would never tolerate anyone making his four-year-old feel unwelcome. Long journey or not, if he had to, he'd jump on the next flight back to Texas. Getting a job was never a problem. Getting the *right* job was more important than anything.

He gave himself a shake as she pulled the car up outside a pizza parlour. She turned around and gave him a nervous kind of smile. 'What's your poison?' she asked. 'This place is great. Everything's fresh and their pizzas are to die for.'

He drew in a deep breath. She was making an effort, and it was clear he made her a bit nervous. He dug into his pocket for his wallet, but she shook her head and waved her hand. 'Don't be silly. You just got here. This is on me.' She bit her bottom lip and nodded towards the sleeping figure in the back seat. 'What about Rory?'

Gene glanced at his son again and felt his heart swell.

This little guy was his life. One look of that cheeky little face could brighten the darkest day.

'Just cheese and ham for him. I'll have whatever the Swiss equivalent of a meat feast is.'

Cordelia gave him a nod and ducked out of the car. 'No problem. Give me five minutes.'

She walked into the pizza parlour and he leaned back in the seat again, watching as she interacted with the servers. She seemed at home here—it was obvious that they knew her. She leaned on the counter, giving him a prime view of her curves visible in her pink fitted shirt and black trousers. He gave a small smile. She'd probably look great in a pair of jeans.

Her fingers toyed with a strand of chestnut-brown hair as she chatted. For the first time he looked at her left hand. No ring. Nothing. She'd said they would all be staying in Professor Helier's mansion. Did she have a partner already there? Or would she be there alone with him and Rory?

His stomach gave a little clench. Maybe that was part of her discomfort. She'd clearly expected a woman to arrive at Geneva airport. Maybe being alone with a strange guy and kid had completely thrown her.

After another five minutes she slid back into the car with the pizza boxes. 'Do you mind holding these until we reach the house? It will only be another five minutes.'

He nodded and started to pay attention to the scenery as they drove through the outskirts of Geneva. The buildings and architecture were stunning, a mixture of Gothic spires and brand-new glass towers. All this with a backdrop of snow-topped mountains against a darkening sky.

The road gradually became a little more rural and

Cordelia indicated and turned through a pair of elaborate iron gates and continued on down a long driveway. Thick green trees lined the driveway, with extensive grounds all around them. After a few minutes a dark house seemed to emerge out of nowhere.

Gene couldn't help but smile. It was like a real Gothic-style mansion—straight out of a Dracula-style movie. Gargoyles adorned some of the dark grey stonework around the myriad thin windows lining the front of the house. A huge, imposing double door, painted black with a large knocker, was right in front of them.

Cordelia pulled up directly outside and turned to face him. It was the first time she'd looked a little more relaxed since they'd met.

She held out her hand towards the house. 'Here it is. And I'll say it before you do. Dracula's mansion. The inside is much more welcoming than the outside. You'll love it.' She glanced nervously over her shoulder towards Rory again. 'And I'm sure he will too.' She shot him a big smile. It only seemed a little forced. 'Welcome to Switzerland, Dr Du Bois.'

CHAPTER TWO

SHE WAS BABBLING AGAIN. It was ridiculous. She was a thirty-one-year-old experienced doctor. She had absolutely no reason to be nervous. But somehow the cowboy from Texas with the blond kid had totally knocked her sideways.

She unlocked the front door and switched off the alarm. Rory was tucked up on his dad's shoulder again. 'Do you want to put him straight to bed?' she asked, praying that the beds in the guest quarters were made up.

Gene shook his head. 'No. I want to wake him up and feed him before letting him sleep right through. I always find it's best to try and acclimatise as soon as possible.'

She blinked. 'You move about a lot?'

He shrugged as he glanced around the wide entrance-way and huge staircase leading to the upper floors. 'I have done. Rory will be going to school next year, so I'll need to have a rethink. But so far he's been in nursery in the US, the UK and France. He seems to have loved them all.'

She gave a careful nod of her head. 'Wow. That's a lot.' She hesitated then pointed towards the rooms to the right. 'The formal kind of sitting rooms are that way. But how about we grab the pizzas and go through to the kitchen? The bedrooms are all upstairs, I'll show you them soon.'

Gene glanced back out to the car. She waved her hand. 'I can grab the cases.'

'No way.' His Texas drawl almost stopped her in her tracks. 'There's no way I'm letting you get them. Let me sit Rory down at the table. He's waking up anyway. Can you get him a drink of water while I grab the cases?'

She nodded quickly and showed him through to the extensive black and white kitchen, with old-fashioned wooden table in the middle, pulling out the high-backed chairs for him to settle Rory.

The little boy watched her with suspicious eyes as she opened the cupboard and nearly pulled out a glass, before changing her mind at the last moment and swapping the glass for a mug. She grabbed a bottle of water from the fridge then filled the mug and sat down next to him. She couldn't help but feel nervous. What did you talk to a four-year-old about? And the truth was she was a little curious about this little kid. Would he have an accent like his father? 'Hi, Rory, I'm Cordelia. I'm going to be working with your daddy.'

She flipped open the lid of the smallest pizza box. 'We got you ham and cheese pizza. Your dad said you'd like that. Would you like some?' She pulled a slice of the pizza free and left it for him to grab himself.

Rory watched her with dark eyes for a few moments. It was unnerving what the gaze of a four-year-old could do to her. She didn't blame him. He'd literally just woken up, and was in completely strange surroundings. And she'd seen those big brown eyes before. Rory definitely had his father's eyes.

She could hear Gene rolling the suitcases inside then

closing the main door behind him. He strode through to the kitchen and sat down next to Rory, ruffling his hair again as he looked at the pizza boxes. 'Which one is mine? Come on. Eat up, little guy. You must be starving.'

Rory stared at him. 'Where's the French fries?'

Cordelia almost laughed out loud—there was a definite hint of a Texan accent, but there was also a little bit more. Gene said they'd stayed in France and the UK too. It seemed the little boy had picked up a little of everything. She stood up and flicked the switch on the kettle and glanced over at Gene. 'Do you want a cup of tea or coffee?'

Gene shook his head. 'I'll stick to water, thanks. I want to try and sleep a little tonight.'

Rory stopped staring at her suspiciously now his dad was back and picked up a slice of pizza. He leaned his head on one hand. 'Where's my bed?'

Gene glanced at her and Cordelia answered quickly. 'It's upstairs. There are two rooms, so you can either go in a room on your own or you can go in with your dad.'

Her stomach gave a little flip. She still didn't know if the rooms were ready or not. Franc had a housekeeper who kept the place tidy. If he'd told her in advance she would have the rooms ready.

'Give me five minutes,' she said, bolting down a bite of pizza and running up the stairs.

She flicked on all the lights as she ran down the corridor, past her own rooms and on to the other guest bedrooms. The door were already open—always a good sign. She checked the first. The bed had been made up in pale blue, with a pile of white towels, some soap and a toothbrush and toothpaste in the bathroom next door.

The second room had been made up in pale green.

There was a teddy sitting on the bed next to the pillow. It was slightly threadbare, but it was something. She sighed in relief. At some point Franc must have remembered—even if he hadn't this afternoon. At least the rooms were ready. She could sort out everything else tomorrow.

By the time she got back down the stairs, Rory was back in his father's arms, a half-eaten slice of pizza on the table.

'Is he out for the count again?'

Gene nodded. 'Everything okay upstairs?' he asked warily.

She nodded. 'Yes, just checking the rooms. Everything is perfect. I was just worried in case Franc hadn't mentioned to the housekeeper about your arrival. But he must have remembered. The rooms are fine.'

Gene followed her up the stairs and laid Rory down on the green bed. He sat for a few seconds, stroking his blond hair and just watching him.

It felt like she was intruding. Watching a moment that should be shared just between a parent and child.

He turned to face her. 'What time are we going to the institute tomorrow? I need to know so I can get us up and ready in time.'

Her brain automatically revised her usual plans. If she told them she was usually there from six a.m. until seven at night they would think she was crazy. Or sad. Or both. 'I normally go in around eight a.m. I like to be available to check on any of the patients involved in the trials before they get started for the day. Would you be okay if we had breakfast just after seven?'

He nodded. 'That's fine. We'll probably be up early anyway. Your morning will be our afternoon.'

She felt a wave of panic. 'Rory—what does he eat for breakfast?'

Gene shrugged. 'Whatever you've got. Cereal, toast, eggs. He's happy with just about anything.'

'If you write a list tomorrow, the housekeeper will get you whatever you need for him. I'm not sure just how many child-friendly foods we'll have in the house right now.'

Gene looked over at her in the dim light. She could see the shadows under his eyes. He must be just as tired as Rory was.

A million questions were burning in her brain. Where was Rory's mother? Why hadn't he mentioned her at all?

There was a hint of bristle along his jawline. She watched as he leaned over Rory and kissed him gently on the head, the muscles on his chest and arms visible beneath the thin soft cotton T-shirt.

Her skin prickled. It wasn't like her to notice things like that. Of course she wasn't blind. Of course she'd had a few relationships in the past. But she'd never been the kind of girl to really notice a guy. To look at his eyes. To look at his build. To notice the way he looked at his son.

She gave herself a shake. She was being ridiculous.

It looked like Gene could be a while, so she backed out of the door into the corridor.

She had work to do. Plenty to distract her in the meantime. Cardiac research could easily stop her thinking about the man with the accent as thick as syrup and his equally cute young son.

She gave herself a shake and hurried back to the kitchen, pulling a stack of paperwork from her bag.

Work. That's where she was always safest. She should concentrate on that.

Rory had snored peacefully all night while Gene had slept fitfully. It always took him a few days to be comfortable enough in his surroundings to sleep well. It didn't help that his mind had kept drifting to the chestnut-haired woman with the bright green eyes.

He still wasn't sure about her. If Professor Helier wasn't going to be around he'd give her a day, then decide if he was staying or not. He'd learned not to waste time in this life.

Rory got ready eagerly, jumping into a pair of bright green shorts and his favourite baseball shirt and hat while Gene showered. He generally liked to dress a little more informally at work, but first impressions always lasted, so he left his Stetson on the dresser and pulled on work clothes more fitting for a cardiac physician.

By the time they reached the kitchen, Cordelia was already there, humming to herself as the coffee percolated and she popped some bread in the toaster. The kitchen table was set with cutlery, some cereals, a jug of milk and some butter, jam and marmalade. She even had a little pad and pen with 'Shopping list' written across the top.

She smiled as they appeared. 'Good morning. Hi, Rory, did you sleep well last night?'

Rory started. It was almost as if he'd forgotten that he'd met her last night. Gene pulled out a chair for him. Cordelia had the sides of her hair pulled back in a clip and she was wearing a red dress and black suit jacket. The dress ended just on her knees and he blinked in surprise at her red baseball boots.

She laughed at his expression. 'I know. I know. I had

a problem with my feet a few years ago. I find baseball boots comfiest.' She pointed to a pair of medium-heeled black shoes at the side of the kitchen, 'But I promise I'll change before we leave.'

'What happened to your feet?' Rory asked immediately, while Gene cringed.

There was the briefest uncomfortable blink from Cordelia then she gave a small shrug. 'A very long time ago I was a ballet dancer. And when you're a ballet dancer you go right up on your tippy-toes.' She opened one palm and put the tips of the fingers of her other hand in the centre. 'But when you do that when you're still young it does damage to your toes.' She pulled a face. 'So my feet are quite ugly. But…' she waved down at her shoes '…it gives me a chance to wear my favourite baseball boots.'

Gene felt a bit warmer. She seemed a little more relaxed this morning. More amenable. Maybe she'd got her head around sharing this house with a stranger and his kid.

Rory stared at her. 'I like them,' he said as he shot a glance at his dad. Gene almost laughed out loud. He knew exactly what was coming.

'I wanted red baseball boots, but my dad wouldn't get me any.'

Cordelia grabbed the toast as it popped and put it on a plate, carrying it over to the table with the coffee pot. She raised her eyebrows and gave Rory a conspiratorial glance. 'He wouldn't? Why ever not?'

She sounded easy. She sounded comfortable around them, but Gene noticed a tiny twitch at the side of her eye. She might be acting as if everything was fine, but she was still a little nervous. Why?

He picked up a piece of toast for Rory and started

buttering it for him, smiling at his son the whole time. 'I didn't buy him a pair of red baseball boots because we already have a pair of blue and a pair of green.'

'You have?' Cordelia ducked her head under the table.

She frowned as she sat up. 'But those aren't baseball boots.'

Rory smiled as he picked up his toast. 'Yeah. I put on my runners today. I decided I might need to be real quick.'

Gene poured some of the coffee into the mugs on the table. 'Why would you need to be quick, Rory?'

Rory bit his toast and chewed for a few seconds before he answered in a whisper. 'Because there might be…girls.'

Cordelia choked at the other side of the table, putting her hand over her mouth, her cheeks getting pinker and pinker. Gene watched in amusement. 'Okay?'

She nodded and jumped up, grabbing a glass for some water. 'Yes. Sorry.' She smiled as she looked back at Rory. 'I just wasn't expecting that one.'

Gene leaned forward on the table, looking between his son and Cordelia. He ruffled Rory's hair again. 'Dad,' said Rory, trying to shake him off, 'stop that.'

Gene pulled his hand back and shrugged at Cordelia. 'Apparently, it doesn't matter what nursery or day care Rory goes to—his blond hair makes all the girls say he is cute.'

'I'm not cute. I'm four,' said Rory quickly.

Cordelia grinned as she sat down again. 'I think four is kind of cute.'

Rory rolled his eyes. 'Oh, not you too.'

Gene pulled a face at her and bent down to whisper

in Rory's ear. 'Watch out, Rory. She might be like those other girls. She might want to kiss you.'

Rory gave a shudder and Cordelia laughed out loud. It was almost as if he could see the knot in her shoulders start to loosen.

They finished breakfast quickly and Gene scribbled a list for the housekeeper. 'Remember red apples, Dad. And 'nanas.' Gene added bananas to the list as Rory stuck his arms into his jacket. He was proud at how articulate his little boy was, but there were still some words that seemed like tongue-twisters to a four-year-old.

He swung Rory up into his arms. 'Ready?'

Rory held up his fist and Gene bumped his against it. It was their move. Their superhero move.

Cordelia's brow was wrinkled as she watched them. She had kind of a bewildered smile on her face as she stood next to the alarm, ready to punch in the code. 'Let's go then, guys.'

For the last week she'd breakfasted with Franc. It had been a much more genteel and sedate experience. This morning had been entirely different.

And it made her feel…odd.

She was getting to the stage in life where most of her friends had kids. Those who knew her best had enough awareness to realise that she occasionally found things tough. It wasn't that she completely avoided kids. Of course she couldn't. She just didn't generally have them under her nose.

So this was different.

And even though part of her stomach twisted and turned, it was also nice. And that was unexpected.

This morning's breakfast had been noisy, chaotic and maybe even a little fun.

They travelled the distance to the institute easily. It was close enough to the city centre for public transport but far enough away to be spacious and have adequate parking.

The institute employed more than three hundred staff. Physicians, nurses, researchers and admin staff. There was also a small day-care centre, which she prayed that Franc had remembered to book Rory into.

Helene, the woman in charge, gave the briefest of pauses when they entered, before putting a beaming smile on her face. 'Ah, yes. Professor Helier mentioned that we might be getting a new recruit.' She gave Gene a questioning smile. 'I think he said for a month?'

Gene nodded. 'Yes, my contract is just for a month.'

It was odd. Cordelia could tell he was a little nervous— but Rory clearly wasn't. He might say he didn't want to play with girls, but he wandered off straight away to go and join a group of kids. Helene walked quickly over to a desk and pulled out some paperwork and a pager. Gene smiled as he took it. 'Haven't had one of these since I was a hospital physician.'

Helene gave him a nod. 'It's just for the first few days. It means I can get hold of you quickly if Rory doesn't settle.' She ran through the paperwork, requesting medical history, allergies, immunisations and any special requirements. Rory was already babbling away in French to his counterparts. The kids in Switzerland spoke a whole variety of languages. It was fortunate that Rory had already spent some time in France.

Cordelia put her hand on Gene's shoulder. 'You okay?'

His eyes were fixed on Rory. He gave a nervous

laugh as his dark brown eyes met hers. 'Sure I am. The little guy never seems to have any problems fitting in. I just worry.'

Cordelia was curious. 'Rory never stays with his mum?'

The look he gave her made her want to pull back the inquisitive words. What was it with her and this guy? He bit his bottom lip and put his head down, completing the paperwork, checking his pager was working and finishing with Helene.

Her skin prickled at the awkwardness of it all. He was new. They had visiting fellows at the Rueben Institute all the time. The institute was renowned. Their last Professor had won a special prize for his research. They had many joint projects with university hospitals across the globe. People wanted to work here. She counted herself lucky that she'd managed to secure a permanent position. If Gene Du Bois was going to be here for a month he'd have to lose a little of his prickliness.

She walked him out across the granite-floored, glass-fronted foyer. Above them was a glass atrium, showing the four floors of the institute.

She ignored the earlier hiccup and held out her hands. 'Okay, Dr Du Bois, welcome to the Rueben Institute. Now that Rory is settled, let me show you around.'

Darn it. For some reason his tongue had stuck to the roof of his mouth and he'd been unable to answer her question. Last time he'd been tongue-tied he'd been around fourteen. This was ridiculous.

But what was even more ridiculous was the thought that had shot into his head when she'd asked about Rory's mother.

He literally had the story off pat. He'd been asked

on numerous occasions where Rory's mom was. It was
a sad story. But lots of kids all over the world had only
one parent. It wasn't the biggest deal in the world.

But this time, when he'd been asked, he'd just frozen. Maybe it was those green eyes. Maybe it was the
shiny brown hair and the way it looked so good with
her red dress. Maybe it was those darned curves in that
red dress that seemed to make a swishy kind of noise
every time she took a step—daring him to look at the
swing of her hips.

Or maybe it was the tiny freckles running across the
bridge of her nose.

Whatever it was, it was something.

He was tired. That was all. Probably jet-lagged too.
Maybe it wasn't a good idea to start straight away. Per-
haps he should have given them a few days to settle in.
But, then again, Rory looked like he'd settled already.
And Gene couldn't help but be proud of the way his son
had naturally babbled away in French to the other kids.

He pulled his eyes away from the swinging hips in
front of him and looked up at the impressive foyer. He'd
seen pictures of the institute before. But he hadn't really
expected this.

Cordelia had walked over to the back of the institute—or what should be the back wall of the institute.
Instead of brick, there was a wall entirely of glass, letting the bright morning light stream in and giving a
picture-perfect view of the Alps in the distance. It was
like capturing a holiday snap. Or picking up a picture
postcard.

The view was breathtaking. And unexpected. She
gave him a nod as she stood alongside him. She sucked
in a deep breath. 'Whenever I get exasperated at work,

or fed up, I always like to remember how lucky I am to work here.'

He stood for a few minutes, his eyes scanning the horizon. It was like taking a chill pill. He'd been on edge, agitated about the arrangements and worried about how they might affect Rory. But standing here, watching this, it was almost as if someone had just put his head on a lavender pillow and told him to relax and calm down.

He'd wanted to come here. He'd wanted to work with Professor Helier. And even if Professor Helier wasn't here, the rest of his team was.

He glanced sideways at Cordelia. She was smiling, drinking in the scenery that she obviously saw every day. 'It never gets old,' she said quietly. 'Every day is a new day, with a world of possibilities.'

He pressed his lips together and asked the question that was burning in his mind. 'You said you're Professor Helier's second in command. What's your background?'

She turned to face him with an amused expression. 'What is this? An interview?'

She gestured towards the glass staircase leading up to the next floor.

'Maybe.' He shrugged.

She nodded her head thoughtfully. 'Okay, then. But it works both ways. Deal?'

He held his hand out towards her. 'Deal.' The warmth from her fingers almost made him shudder, especially as they brushed against the inside of his wrist.

Cordelia walked up the stairs ahead of him. He had to tell himself not to focus on her legs. Or her hips. Or her...

She started talking and broke into his wayward thoughts. 'I'm a physician. I trained in the UK.'

'I take it your speciality was cardiology.'

She nodded. 'Of course. And yours?'

He gave the briefest of smiles. 'The same.'

She hesitated for a second. 'I always had a special interest in cardiology.' She gave a nonchalant wave of her hand. 'Family stuff. So I decided to get into research.' She hesitated once again and he was instantly curious as her eyes went up to the left for a second. Wasn't that supposed to be a sign of thinking or processing?

They reached the top of the stairs and she took them down a different wing of the building. 'This is the research labs.' She gave a little smile. 'This is where I get lost in the wonder of zebrafish and what incredible creatures they are.' She gave a little sigh. 'If only us humans had the power of healing and regeneration like they do.'

He stopped at the front doors of the lab and looked inside. As expected, it was white and pristine. There were several rooms. Laboratories where clinical scientists were processing blood tests. A vast room filled with computers where information was obviously being processed and analysed. In the middle of the room was an unusual spiral-shaped fish tank. Even from here he could see the tiny zebrafish swimming around.

He tilted his head to the side and looked at Cordelia curiously. It was almost as if she expected the question. 'They teach us so much. And they give us hope. Professor Helier thought it was important that people didn't just watch them in a lab. He wanted us all to appreciate them. That's why he commissioned the special tank for right in the middle of the room.'

Gene nodded thoughtfully. 'So many people are against research involving animals.'

'And so many people would be right. Here, we don't harm the zebrafish in any way. But we watch them. We learn from them and their DNA. And we try to replicate what they can do in a lab environment.'

He leaned against the wall and folded his arms. 'I like the ethics here. I knew that before I came. It was one of the things that made me want to be part of the team—even if it is just for a short spell.'

Her phone pinged and she pulled it from her pocket, frowning.

'What's wrong?' Her skin had paled and when she looked up her eyes were kind of watery.

She pressed her lips together. He could tell she was trying to keep it together. 'Professor Helier's sister has terminal cancer. She's his only living family. He's going to stay with her. He's going to look after her.'

Gene felt his heart clench. It was selfish—he knew it. But part of the reason he'd come here had been to work with this man—to learn from him.

'What does that mean?'

She blinked back the obvious tears as she tucked her phone back into her pocket. 'It means that I'll have to email everyone in the institute. Franc—he wants to call you tonight.' Her bright green eyes met his. There was something in them. A wariness, but also a tiny hint of desperation. 'The monitoring of the cardiomyopathy patients is at a really crucial stage. I suspect he's going to ask if you'll take over as head of the trial.' Her voice was a little shaky.

He reached over and touched her arm. 'Cordelia? Are you okay?'

She nodded and brushed the side of her eye. 'Of course I am. I'm just being silly. I'm worried about Franc and how he'll cope with nursing his sister.' She held out her hands. 'This place is virtually his life.' She gave her head a shake. 'I just don't want to let him down in his absence. The work here is so important to so many people.'

It was the way she said the words. Everyone who worked here would be passionate about what they did. But there seemed to be a real emphasis on her words. As if there was something that he was missing.

And he got it. He got it better than anyone. Because the work on cardiomyopathy could end up being a life-line for his son.

He watched her carefully. He could almost see her shaking off the overspill of emotions, tidying them back up and putting them in a box. His stomach roiled a little. It was the weirdest thing, but it was almost the same expression she'd had on her face at one point last night. He just couldn't understand why.

And he definitely couldn't understand why he was so curious.

She licked her lips and looked at him again. 'My turn to ask the questions. I'm sure that Franc knew all this back to front. But I don't. What's your background?'

For a second he felt himself move into self-protect mode. The bit where he only gave the edited version of his life.

But he turned around as she led him back from the research wing and he was faced with the picture-post-card landscape again. The world was so vast out there. He was only a tiny bit of it. Why on earth did he feel he had something to hide?

He stopped walking and his fingers brushed against her elbow. She turned to face him. He almost laughed.

Yip. He was currently in a movie of his life. Cordelia was the heroine in this movie and she was standing in front of a green screen. Because this background was just too perfect to be real.

And as he stood a little longer, she began to look too perfect too. She was sharply in focus. Now he could appreciate the long, dark lashes. Now he could appreciate the smudge of red lipstick still on her lips.

Now…he was definitely losing his mind.

It was almost like hovering above and watching, instead of really taking part.

He shook his head. 'I trained as a physician in Texas but lived my life between France and Texas. My mom—*ma mère*—was a French scientist. Somehow she managed to meet my rancher father and I lived between two continents.'

She tilted her head to the side. 'Wow. That's some childhood.'

He nodded. 'I was lucky. I had barrel loads of love on both sides of the Atlantic. I had friends in Houston and in Paris.'

'So what made you become a doctor?'

They walked along the corridor towards the other wing. 'Oh, I always wanted to be a doctor. Right from when I was a little kid. My dad wanted me to take over the ranch and while I love it, my heart was never in it. Thankfully I've got a stepbrother who has ranch blood running in his veins.'

'Oh, okay.' He could see the obvious question running around in her head. He could avoid it—or ignore it—like he had before. But he had a reason for being here. He was invested in this research. And there was almost an ethical responsibility to say why.

He stopped walking. 'Rory's mom was a fellow doctor I met at a conference. We had a few nights together and then didn't keep in touch. I met Rory when he was nine months old. Mindy had hypertrophic cardiomyopathy. She was already in a degree of heart failure when she became pregnant and was advised not to continue with the pregnancy. I had no idea she was unwell and she didn't listen. And she only contacted me when she'd been on the heart transplant list for a few months.'

Cordelia's eyes were wide. He just kept going. It was easier to have it out there. 'Three weeks later Mindy died. And it's been just me and Rory ever since.' He slowed down as the edges of his lips turned upwards. 'My world.'

She didn't speak for a few seconds, just stared at him. 'That's how you came into research?'

He nodded. 'I was already in cardiology. But, you'll understand, the clinical side is tough.' He hadn't asked her for her reasons for leaving her clinical role, but he'd understood the implication. People who'd spent years training to be a doctor didn't walk away unless they had no real choice.

'It didn't work for me with no real help at home, covering emergencies and on calls with a baby. Research was the natural place. Find out what I needed to know, while still keeping a clinical role—in more manageable hours.'

She nodded as he continued. 'And with the potential for Rory...' He let his voice tail off.

The realisation didn't take long to hit her. She worked in research. She knew exactly what he was getting at. Cardiomyopathy was a hereditary condition.

'Rory has the gene?'

'Rory has the gene,' he repeated.

She didn't hesitate. She reached over and squeezed his hand. 'Oh, Gene. I'm so sorry.'

He drew in a deep breath. 'So am I. But that's life. You'll know the odds. He had a fifty per cent chance of inheriting the gene—and he has. But so far there are no symptoms. No indication that there's anything to worry about. That's what I need to keep inside my head. But it doesn't stop me making this my life's work.'

He didn't need to say any more. She'd know the potential. She'd know that hypertrophic cardiomyopathy was the condition frequently undetected then associated with young sportsmen suddenly dying.

That was why the 'no symptoms' was so important to keep in his head. Because late at night, when he looked at that gorgeous little mop of blond hair, every worst-case scenario in the world wound its way through his head.

Her voice had a sympathetic tone and he could see the understanding her eyes as she looked at him. 'So you're committed. You want to be here. You want to do the work.'

He could tell she was almost relieved. If he'd turned and walked out today because Professor Helier wasn't going to be around, it could have potentially brought the research to a halt. But he'd never do that. He repeated those words. 'I want to do the work. It's important to me. It's important to Rory. And it's important to a whole host of other people all around the world affected by this disease.' He didn't have a single doubt about what he was saying.

She gave a nod of approval and held her hand out towards the next wing. 'Well, in that case, Dr Du Bois, come and meet your fabulous team. And your fabulous patients.'

Her head was swimming as she pasted a smile on her face. Her heart ached for him—literally.

Now she understood—probably a whole lot better than he expected her to.

The thought that his gorgeous little son could have a ticking time bomb in his chest—similar to her own—was heart-wrenching. How must it feel to look at that little guy every day and wonder if at some point he would develop symptoms or become unwell? As a medic, one thing was crystal clear in her head. Parents shouldn't outlive their kids. They just shouldn't. There was something so wrong about that. Unbearable. And she wasn't even a mother.

She'd worked with families who'd lost kids due to cardiac defects and anomalies and there was something so wrong about it all.

They walked down to the east wing—where all the patients were seen and monitored. The Rueben Institute was like many other cardiac research centres. They monitored patients with certain conditions, seeing if small lifestyle changes could have impacts on their lives, along with dietary changes and alternative therapies. They also monitored certain new medicines, making sure that patients didn't have any side effects and comparing the differences between them and the existing medicines. There was no point introducing a new medicine to the world if it didn't really make any improvements for patients.

There were similar institutes all over the world, but in the land of cardiac conditions, with or without any trials, patients' conditions could change in an instant. The staff here were highly trained and the institute well equipped to deal with any emergency. Cordelia showed him from room to room.

'We have twenty monitoring bays for the clinical trials. We also have overnight beds available with monitoring, too, for anyone feeling unwell.'

'Who covers that?'

Cordelia dabbed an electronic tablet next to one of the doors and grabbed hold of one his hands. She pulled up a page and pressed his forefinger to the pad, shooting him a smile. 'As quick as that—your fingerprint will open any of these. It gives a complete list of all patient details, contacts and staff on duty. At any time we have two doctors on—day and night—along with four nursing staff. We never fall under that ratio and are frequently above it.'

He frowned a little. 'Do those numbers include you and me?'

She shook her head. 'Oh, no. We're supernumerary—along with all the research staff. Around fifty per cent of our researchers have a clinical background. And working here helps them maintain their clinical registrations. You'll frequently see our researchers doing the clinical monitoring of patients.' She tried to choose her words carefully. 'Quite often, our clinicians have had to go into research because of health conditions of their own. Working here helps them still have the patient contact that they love, as well as contributing to improving things for patients.'

He nodded thoughtfully. 'So, what will be expected of me while Professor Helier isn't here?'

She tried not to pull a face, hoping that nothing she would say would make him bolt for the door. She really didn't know much about Gene Du Bois at all. He might seem like a stand-up guy, but some people couldn't handle pressure, and he might not like what came next.

'Professor Helier was very hands on. Every morning he would review every patient—usually around twenty, who would be involved in research in that day. The nursing staff would highlight any issues or concerns to him, and he might end up ordering cardiac echoes, ECGs, chest X-rays and listening to chests. He frequently adjusted medications for heart failure, arrhythmias, and so on. We do have protocols for all this,' she added quickly. 'You wouldn't be doing it blind.'

He gave a quick shake of his head and a wave of his hand. 'That all sounds fine. I like patient contact.' He gave a smile and raised his eyebrows. 'Some people might say I even crave it. Just a check, though—what if someone needs an intervention? Do we have links with a local hospital?'

Cordelia nodded and pulled up some more information on the tablet. 'Here's the contact details and private consultants we deal with. If, for some reason, someone had an aneurysm or needed a bypass, we have a red-button service with a private ambulance service here, and our patients would get seen right away.'

She looked at him warily. 'How long since your last cath lab session?'

He pulled back in surprise. 'Two weeks. Why?'

She frowned. It wasn't quite the answer she was expecting, even though she was secretly relieved. 'Why two weeks?'

He shrugged. 'I covered sessions for doctors on annual leave at my last job. It was all daytime, scheduled theatre time, so I didn't need cover for Rory. It worked out fine. Why?'

She smiled and led him to another door. 'Because we have our own cath lab here. It was built for emergencies but has been used on a number of occasions. Our own doctors are perfectly proficient, but it's best if you're up to date too. We also have an anaesthetist on call, and all our usual cardiac technicians are available whenever required.'

He stepped into the white cath lab. All the equipment

was state of the art and practically sparkling. He walked around, taking slow steps, checking it out, running his fingers over the monitors before finally giving an approving nod. He opened a few drawers, looked where equipment was stored and then had a final check, familiarising himself with the contents of the cardiac arrest trolley. 'Emergency code?'

'Code red.' She pointed to a phone on the wall. 'Pick up any phone, say the words "Code red" and an announcement will come over the Tannoy. You don't even need to give your location. It automatically identifies where you are and gives the location in the call.'

He folded his arms as he turned to face Cordelia. 'Everything seems very well organised.'

'I hope that it is.'

He stepped a little closer. 'So, what will you be doing?'

She gave a nod. 'Overseeing the whole place. Dealing with the drug companies and investors. Meeting the Japanese investors due in a few days. All the while mirroring what you'll be doing here for cardiomyopathy in my own department for heart failure and heart regeneration studies. My clinics run in parallel with yours. We have two separate teams.' She rolled her eyes. 'And if I get half a chance, I might even clear Franc's desk.'

He laughed. 'Is it that bad?'

She shook her head as she led him back out of the cath lab. 'Oh, no. It's worse. Now, come along and I'll introduce you to your team. I'll warn you in advance. The secretary for the project, Marie, is the scariest, most organised, ruthlessly efficient human being you will ever meet.' She bent over and whispered in his ear. 'I think she might actually be a cyborg. But that's another story.'

He tipped his head back and let out a hearty laugh. It was the first she'd heard since he'd got there. Her insides had been churning for a little while, hoping he wouldn't say he didn't want to take over Professor Helier's clinical responsibilities. Not everyone would. But Gene Du Bois seemed completely comfortable. It was like water off a duck's back to him. She grinned as she pushed open another door.

'Don't let it be said we're not welcoming.' A delicious smell met them. 'This is the coffee lounge. Or the tea lounge. Or the natural fruit water lounge. Whatever your preference is—we'll have it. And if we don't? Let us know and we'll order it in. We like staff to be comfortable. And well nourished. If you have dietary requirements—or if Rory has dietary requirements in day care—just let the kitchen staff know. They aim to please.'

He looked around at the comfortable red sofas, the TVs mounted on walls, the work stations with computers, and the large white tables and chairs for dining.

Cordelia kept watching him. 'We like people to be comfortable,' she reiterated. 'Not everyone thrives in an office environment. Professor Helier doesn't care where people work—just as long as they do.'

Gene nodded in approval and put his hands on his hips. 'This sounds like a good work ethic. I could get comfortable here.' Little crinkles appeared around his eyes as he smiled and she felt a little warmth spread throughout her belly. He was happy. Good. She wanted things to go well while Professor Helier was away. The last thing she wanted to do was phone him with some kind of disaster.

Gene strolled over to a glass jar stuffed with tiny

sweets wrapped in gold foil. 'And what are these? Some kind of treasure?'

She smiled as she joined him and stole one from the jar. 'Gene, you're in Switzerland. What are we famous for?'

He wrinkled his nose. 'Alps. And the Geneva Convention.'

She shook her head and rolled her eyes. 'You Americans. Chocolate, Gene. That's what Switzerland is famous for. Chocolate.'

She held up her little sweet and started to unwrap it. Within a few seconds the dreamy cocoa milky smell had reached them both. He even started to lean a little towards it.

His eyes started to glaze. 'Is this really a good idea for a place that specialises in cardiac research?'

She gave a broad smile. 'That's why they're tiny. Just enough to give you the magical sensation of chocolate hitting every taste bud, without sending your blood glucose spiralling and your weight out of control.' She gave her best intelligent nod. 'You know, research has proved that if you just take a little of what you crave, it makes management much easier.'

He made a grab for the chocolate. 'I'll take your word for it.'

For some reason, even though she wasn't entirely sure of Gene, there was something very amicable about him. She felt quite safe around him. And while that might not be what some guys would want to hear, it was important to her.

She was very used to erecting walls around herself. But, after his initial reaction of ignoring her question about Rory's mother, he'd told her—in his own time—what had actually happened. Most people probably felt sorry for him. He could easily take on the widower persona. But he didn't. Not at all. Instead, he'd been straight about his story. There had been no great love between him and Mindy. He hadn't even really had the chance to be angry with her. Cordelia didn't have a single doubt that most guys would have been totally blindsided by all of it.

But Gene seemed to have taken the news about his son well. He loved his son. And whilst she was sure he wished he could change his genetic heritage, he seemed to have accepted it for what it was.

She met a lot of patients who hated what their genes meant for them. Something they could never control. Her own were the same. And she'd long since known that accepting what you couldn't change was the biggest part of the process for some people.

Like her. Like Gene. And, eventually, hopefully like Rory.

She gave him a sideways glance as she led him down towards the offices for the clinics.

'Maybe I should have recommended that you take a handful of chocolates to get you through the next part of the day.'

He gave her a suspicious glance. 'What do you mean? Aren't I just reviewing the patients and taking care of the clinic work and trial?'

She licked her lips and gave a little sigh. 'You make it sound so simple.'

He stopped walking. 'Isn't it?'

She couldn't help herself. She winked at him as she reached the doors. 'Oh, Dr Du Bois, you have a lot to learn. Welcome to the Reuben Institute. Now, come and meet your master.'

* * *

Gene was sprawled across the sofa. Rory was also sprawled across him, sleeping, with his mouth open and drool landing on Gene's shirt. He hadn't even had a chance to change since they'd got home.

Cordelia appeared and took in the scene, leaning against the doorjamb and crossing her arms. At some point in the day she'd changed back into her red baseball boots. He couldn't get over quite how quirky and cute she looked with her business-style dress and jacket, coupled with flat red baseball boots.

'You survived?' she asked.

He raised his eyebrows and held out his hands. 'If I could jump off this sofa right now and chase you down, I would.'

She shook her head. 'That's fighting talk.'

He nodded. 'It is. But now I've met your lethal weapon—Marie.'

Cordelia couldn't pretend not to laugh. 'I did try to warn you.' Then she shook her head, 'And, oh, no. She's not mine. She's yours. I did tell you might need chocolate to see you through.'

'But you didn't tell me why,' he quipped.

She sighed and shook her head. 'No, I didn't. You'd just lulled me into what could be a false sense of security. You'd told me you would stay. I didn't want to frighten you off.'

'You just left that to Marie?'

Cordelia laughed again. 'What can I say? She's chewed up tougher guys than you.' She walked over and perched on the edge of the sofa, her eyes on the sleeping figure of Rory. 'I'm sorry. But Marie has been at the institute since the day it opened. She's almost like the institute herself. She knows every patient. Every trial. She has the scariest but most brilliant encyclopaedic brain in the world.'

He nodded. 'She certainly doesn't let anyone get around her.'

Cordelia nodded. 'And it's not worth the energy even trying. And whatever you do—don't use her mug. It's the one thing that will absolutely tip her over the edge.'

He wrinkled his brow. 'Seriously?'

She nodded. 'Completely.'

'Then thanks for the warning. What mug is hers?' She could see him picturing the jam-packed cabinet in the staff kitchen.

'Why, Dr Du Bois, couldn't you tell just by looking?'

He narrowed his gaze. 'I'm going to like this, aren't I?'

She nodded again. 'It's Glinda. The Good Witch from the *Wizard of Oz.*'

His shoulders started to shake and he lifted his hand to the sleeping Rory on his chest, trying not to disturb him. 'No way. It should be Darth Vader, or at the very least the Wicked Witch.'

Cordelia smiled. He seemed to have settled. On a few occasions she had actually been worried that Marie might chase some of the visiting doctors away. Her manner was…brusque, to say the least.

'I agree. Now, what would you like for dinner?'

He placed his hands on Rory's back and swung his legs around so he was finally sitting up on the sofa. 'It's my turn to sort out dinner—you bought pizza last night.'

'But you've got your hands full.'

He shook his head. 'But that doesn't mean I can't take a turn.' He looked down and gave Rory a little shake. 'He's worn out from day care today. But, thankfully, he loved it.'

'That's great. I thought he would.'

He nodded again. 'And you'll see the hire company dropped off a car for me so you don't need to ferry us around. I didn't want to be an extra burden to you this month when you have an institute to run.'

She waved her hand. 'It was fine. It was no problem.' But secretly it was. She was glad he'd been thoughtful enough to hire a car. It meant she could head in early to the institute, or stay late if she needed to.

He looked up. 'Why don't you let me get changed and I'll take us all to dinner. I'll drive. You can suggest somewhere that suits.'

She looked down at her baseball boots. 'I should change too. Shouldn't really go anywhere dressed like this.'

'Don't. You look great.' It came just a little too easily and she felt heat rush into her cheeks.

Rory started to wake up. 'I'm hungry,' he murmured.

Gene set him down on the floor. 'Then it's decided. Let's go for dinner. And…' he gave Cordelia a cheeky smile '… I may even tell you how I plan to conquer the mountain that is Marie.'

An hour later he was dressed in jeans and a T-shirt and sitting in one of the local restaurants that Cordelia had recommended. 'The staff are great and there's a good kids' menu. It always seems to be full of families.'

That was recommendation enough for him and the service was quick.

She hadn't changed. She'd kept on her red dress and her baseball boots. And even though he noticed a few raised eyebrows, Cordelia seemed immune to them.

She was comfortable in her own skin. He liked that about her.

He could tell she was still a little wary around Rory. But that was fine. She didn't have any kids of her own and some people just weren't natural around kids. It wasn't as if she ignored him. Or didn't bother. It was just he could almost sense her nerves. They almost seemed to jangle when she had to interact with the little boy.

It almost felt as if there was something he just couldn't put his finger on.

But tonight things were fine. They'd eaten dinner and, as he'd offered to drive, Cordelia had drunk a glass of wine. As they waited for Rory to eat his ice cream, he gave her a nod. 'I know how to win her around.'

She wrinkled her nose. 'Who?'

'Marie.'

He could tell she was instantly amused. Marie was a hard nut to crack. From what he'd heard, Marie had broken more than a few researchers who'd dared to challenge her on something.

She folded her arms across her chest. 'And how, exactly, are you going to win Marie around? Tell me. I'm fascinated.'

His eyes twinkled. 'It's simple really. She loves my accent. She's told me more than once.'

'But that still doesn't mean she likes you.' She ran her fingers up and down the stem of the wine glass.

He gave a conciliatory nod. 'No, it doesn't. But she will.'

Now she looked really intrigued. 'How?'

'I have a secret weapon.'

For a second she didn't say anything but her eyes rested on Rory, who was busy almost examining the bottom of his ice-cream bowl to make sure he hadn't missed any ice cream. 'Is that fair?' The tone of her voice was a little strange.

He didn't push her on the tone. He just leaned back in his chair. 'I'm bringing out my secret weapon. I'm going to go full cowboy on her.'

'What?' Several people in the restaurant turned around at the rise in her voice.

He laughed 'Yip. I'm wearing my Stetson tomorrow. Probably the boots, maybe even the jeans. What do you think?'

'You're serious?' She had the strangest expression on her face.

He leaned forward a little, catching a whiff of her orange-scented perfume. 'Of course I'm serious. What did you think I meant?'

She gave a little shrug but she didn't meet his gaze. 'Oh, I don't know. I thought you might have been using Rory.' She pointed across the table. 'I mean, one look at his gorgeous little face and...'

Gene followed her gaze across the table, where by this point Rory had ice cream on his face, his hands and his T-shirt. But you'd never know, because he was still concentrating so completely on the tiniest bit of ice cream at the bottom of the bowl.

'Everyone's a sucker,' he finished for her.

His heart squeezed. Even though she wasn't that easy around Rory it was clear she could see the appeal that made him thankful every single day that he'd found this little boy.

He turned to Rory and lifted the bowl away from him. 'Give me that before you start licking the bowl.' He wiped Rory's face and hands with a napkin. 'Time to go home, champ.' He raised his fist and Rory bumped his against his dad's.

'What is that?' asked Cordelia.

'The fist bump? That's just us. That's our move.'

'Your move?'

Rory wriggled out of his seat and Gene followed, picking up the bill from the table. 'You know, everyone has a move, or a saying, something like that.'

She put her hands on her hips. 'They do?'

He nodded. 'Of course. Don't you?'

She frowned for a second. 'I don't think so.'

He nodded as he settled the bill. 'Leave it with me. I bet you've got one. I'll figure it out.'

They walked out to the car and Gene strapped Rory in before making a grab for something in the back seat before Cordelia had even managed to climb in.

His Stetson. He plonked it on his head with a cheeky wink. 'Is that fair? Going full cowboy on her? Like I said, I'll even wear my boots and jeans if you think it will help.'

Cordelia laughed out loud. 'You really are going to wear that to the institute tomorrow?'

He tipped his Stetson towards her. 'I told you, it's my lethal weapon.'

He watched her suck in a breath as his eyes connected with hers. He was joking. Of course he was joking. So why had his heart rate just quickened? Ridiculous. It was like being a teenager again.

He shook his head as he took off his Stetson and climbed back into the car. He was only here for a month. He had work to do. And a child to look after. He couldn't afford any distractions.

But as Cordelia hitched up her dress to climb into the car, he had a distinct flash of toned, tanned leg.

And try as he may, he couldn't get it out of his head on the drive home.

CHAPTER THREE

CORDELIA SIGHED AND leaned against the wall as she checked the chart again. One of her patients was failing. Truth was, most of the patients in the heart failure study were failing—that was why they were here.

But Jonas Delphine was one of her favourites. He was an old sea captain, eighty-six, and had smoked for forty years. His chest complaints, along with his cardiovascular disease and heart failure, made him a difficult candidate to manage.

Some trials only wanted 'perfect' candidates. Ones who had no other health complaints but who had unhealthy lifestyle issues that could be changed and monitored then assessed to within an inch of their lives. But the Reuben Institute didn't work with unrealistic patients. What was the point of that? More complicated patients meant more bias for the trials. Some people didn't like that. Some drug companies definitely didn't like it. But Professor Helier had always been clear. The institute was here to help *real* patients. Not perfect ones who didn't really exist.

Now, after listening to Jonas's heart and lungs, she'd just ordered another chest X-ray and echo cardiogram.

'Something wrong?' Gene's voice made her jump.

She couldn't help but grin at the sight of him. He'd

been a man of his word and had come to the institute this morning full cowboy.

The patients loved it. The staff loved it. The Stetson, cowboy boots and jeans had certainly made their mark. Even the normally frosty Marie had seemed to like his unusual appearance.

Gene was still wearing his Stetson and tipped it towards her. 'Cordelia?'

She held up the electronic tablet. 'Nothing that a new heart won't cure.' She straightened up. 'Actually, now that you're here, you can give me a second opinion on someone.'

He held up his electronic tablet. 'Great minds think alike. I was just coming to get you to do the same.'

A tiny surge of pride welled in her stomach. She was pleased. Pleased that he'd came to her for a second opinion on one of his patients. Hopefully, that meant he thought she might be a good clinician.

They swapped tablets. 'You tell me yours, and I'll tell you mine.'

'Aryssa Maia, forty-seven, hypertrophic cardiomyopathy. She's had unsuccessful ablations for atrial fibrillation and she can't tolerate the usual drugs. She also has a permanent pacemaker in place. I've checked her previous scans and just listened to her chest. I think her ventricle is getting to the stage it is barely functioning. She's symptomatic, breathless and tired, with swollen extremities.'

She nodded. 'I have a similar case. Jonas Delphine is eighty-six, with existing COPD and chronic heart failure. I think I'm going to have to take him off the study and put him on IV steroids and diuretics. In the space of one day he's gone downhill fast.'

Gene nodded slowly. She knew he understood. The

patient's welfare was always their prime concern. But the regulations for any research study were strict. They didn't want any findings skewed. If they used certain other drugs on patients then they were taken off the study programme. It was important that any improvement in a patient's current condition was only attributed to the drug being studied—not to any other intervention made.

Cordelia sighed as she looked at Aryssa's chart. 'She was doing so well,' she said sadly. 'I really thought that this might be the one drug that could make a difference for her.'

Gene ran his fingers through his hair. 'I get that. But my gut is telling me that something else is going on. I almost feel as if her pacing wire has moved. Her heart just isn't functioning the way it should be.'

He glanced at Jonas's chart and smiled. 'Why do I feel as if this guy could teach me everything I need to know about life?'

'He probably could. I'm not ashamed to say I love him and have a completely unnatural bias towards him.' She lifted her hand. 'That's why I'm checking for a second opinion. I need someone who can just look at the clinical signs.' She gave a slow nod and handed back Aryssa's notes. 'And as for your patient, I agree, she needs an ECG and a cardiac echo. I suspect her pacing wire has moved too. That's what fits the symptoms, rather than anything happening within the trial.'

He gave a nod. 'I ordered the tests. Just wanted to double check.' He kept a hold of Jonas's tablet. 'Now, let's go meet your patient, while mine has her investigations.'

Things moved so swiftly here. He was secretly pleased that Cordelia had come to him for a second opinion. By the time he'd sounded Jonas's chest and looked at his hands and ankles, the nurse from his part of the clinic had brought along Aryssa's ECG. It couldn't be clearer. The pacing wire definitely wasn't capturing, meaning Aryssa's heart rate was erratic and low. Both he and Cordelia nodded.

'I'll come back and speak to her. But can you attach her to a portable cardiac monitor in the meantime and ask them to put a rush on that cardiac echo?'

The nurse gave a nod. 'I'll take her for the echo now.'

He gave Cordelia a nod and walked through to the treatment room. 'It looks like we're both about to lose patients from our trials. Jonas needs some IV steroids and diuretics.'

Her eyes were downcast for a moment. It probably wasn't what she wanted to hear. But he knew she would always put the patients first. That's the way it should be. Research work always brought these challenges and any medic who worked on the trials knew that.

She looked back up, nodding and opening the drug cupboard. 'I'll draw them up. Can you prescribe them on the tablet? Thanks.'

He gave her a nod and checked the bottles with her as she drew up the medicines. He couldn't pretend not to notice the slight shake of her hands. 'How about I do this for you? You can distract Jonas and persuade him this is a good idea.'

She sucked in a deep breath and let her hands rest back down on the counter top. 'Do you know what? I'd like that. Thank you.' She gave him a small smile and his insides clenched. He got the distinct impression that Cordelia Greenway didn't normally let anyone help her. But from the way her jaw had been clenched and the shake in her hands he knew she was emotional about this. He knew she felt connected to this old guy. She'd worked here for four years. She might even have known him that long.

It was hard not to get attached to patients you saw on a regular basis, let alone nearly every day. It was harder still if those patients condition got worse—which inevitably frequently happened to doctors.

He understood. He'd been there and felt it himself. For the last few years he'd moved from place to place. All of his emotional investment had been in Rory. That's the way it had to be. He'd had to learn to be mom and dad to the little guy. He'd always done a good job by his patients, but he hadn't been around long enough to form lasting relationships.

And he missed that. He couldn't pretend that he didn't.

He moved his hand to lift the tray with the syringe and Venflon but Cordelia's was still there. His first instinct was to pull away, but instead he put his hand over hers and left it there as she gave a little sad sigh.

She didn't object. She didn't jerk away. The heat of her hand filled his palm in a way he hadn't expected.

It had been a long time since he'd touched a woman—held a woman. Of course he touched patients every day. But relationships in the last three years just hadn't been possible. He didn't want to be the guy who introduced Rory to a new girlfriend every few months so it had been easier just to let that part of his life slide.

So…this was different. Not new exactly, but just different. And up until this moment he hadn't realised how much he'd missed connecting with someone.

She gave the briefest nod of her head and he knew it

was time to pull away. He lifted his hand and let hers slide out from underneath his, picked up the tray, and gave her a conciliatory nod. 'Let's go and make Jonas feel better.'

It was the little things that made you realise how thoughtful someone could be. Her insides had twisted and turned at the thought of being the person who would deliver the treatment to end Jonas's time on the trial. She knew it was essential. She knew it was the right thing to do. But part of her had ached, knowing she would have to be the one to do it.

The thought of not seeing him five days a week made her sad. After four years she was sure Jonas still had a world of stories to tell her. His cheery nature in the face of his heart failure made her feel more positive about her own condition.

She had to have hope. She had to feel as if one day her Wolff-Parkinson-White syndrome wouldn't cause some odd arrhythmia that would send her heart into a whole host of problems. For some people with her condition it could lead to death.

Five years ago her physician had sat her down and given her the news she'd known would be coming. She should look at a permanent contraception choice. Her Wolff-Parkinson–White syndrome was progressing. Her condition was unpredictable. What was certain was that the extra stress and increase in pressure of a pregnancy would cause huge strain on her already struggling heart. Pregnancy was out of the question. She'd never have a family of her own.

She'd been living with a fellow researcher then. Han. They'd been working together in London and their relationship had just developed slowly. She'd liked that.

He'd known about her condition and had helped her through difficult spells.

But the news from the consultant had been a turning point. Han had backed off, slowly but surely. Never with malice. But his plans for the future included a family. And as he'd drifted away she'd felt more and more hurt. More and more like less of a woman. Less of a partner.

She'd had to learn to accept that a family wouldn't be in her future. She'd had to accept that any potential relationship would have to be one where she had that difficult up-front conversation. The one where she'd have to admit she was unsure what the future with her cardiac condition would look like.

In the meantime, she'd thrown herself into work. Her almost safe place. But every now and then, when a patient's condition worsened at the clinic, it always brought home to her the fact that one day that could be her.

So she was grateful to Gene for the offer. And he'd been true to his word. He'd charmed Jonas and given him time to express his sadness at having to leave the trial before graciously accepting the other treatment that he needed. Gene kept him distracted with cowboy-type stories as he slowly administered the medicine to Jonas.

They'd just finished up when one of the other nurses came rushing in. 'Dr Du Bois? We need you now. Aryssa has become unwell during her cardiac echo.'

Both of them moved at once, walking down the long white corridor rapidly. Gene reached the room first. He moved swiftly around Aryssa and examined her, taking in her vital signs. 'She's bradycardic,' said Cordelia, moving to the other side of the bed.

The sonographer was pale-faced next to the bed.

'She just seemed to fade while we were doing the echo,' he said.

'What did it show?' asked Gene.

The sonographer gave him a serious look. 'What you expected. The pacing wire has moved.'

Gene frowned as Aryssa's eyes flickered open. 'It's odd. That's unusual. A pacing wire shouldn't move.'

Cordelia put her hand on Aryssa's shoulder. 'Aryssa, how are you feeling?'

The heart rate on the monitor seemed to rise for a few seconds. 'Not good,' she whispered.

Cordelia nodded. 'Don't worry. We'll look after you. But has anything happened in the last day or so that could have dislodged your pacing wire?'

Aryssa lifted her hand to her chest. 'I had an accident in the car on the way to the institute this morning. It was only a small bump, but the airbag exploded.'

Gene shot Cordelia a look. 'Did the airbag hit you?'

Aryssa winced. 'Yes. But I got more of a fright because of the noise. And the powder.' She closed her eyes again, obviously exhausted just answering those few questions.

They moved outside into the corridor.

Gene didn't hesitate. 'That's enough for me. We need to insert a new pacing wire. She's too symptomatic to move her elsewhere.'

It was the weirdest feeling. All of a sudden she almost felt as if she were a spectator instead of part of the situation. As if she were dangling up somewhere in the corner of the room, watching everything.

She couldn't remember the last time there had been an emergency in the clinic. Not like this anyway.

Everything she'd ever learned at medical school decided to fly out of her head in an instant. She couldn't tell a clavicle from a femur, or an atrium from a liver lobe.

Crap. She'd never panicked as a medical student. She'd always been one of the calmest in the class. While others had fainted at the sight of blood, or any other body fluid, Cordelia had just wondered why on earth they wanted to be doctors.

So what was wrong with her now?

One of the clinic nurses appeared at her side. 'Are we pacing?'

Simple words. And that was all it took. Her brain shifted gear.

Gene walked into the next-door cath lab. His actions were automatic. It was clear he'd dealt with this situation before. He pulled over a trolley and set out the equipment. He nodded to the nurse. 'Can you bring the patient in, please, and we'll explain what we need to do.'

Cordelia moved over to the sink and started scrubbing her hands. A temporary pacing wire wasn't performed in a traditional operating theatre, but the cath lab was as good as it got around here. The wire went straight into a central vein, and everything had to be done aseptically to protect the patient from infection.

The nurse wheeled Aryssa in. She was lying on her back, her face pale and sweating. She was already attached to a portable cardiac monitor showing her very slow heartbeat and low blood pressure.

Gene gave Cordelia a nod. He moved over and took Aryssa's hand. He mouthed one word to her. 'Cold.'

Cordelia pressed her lips together. Cold extremities meant that the blood flow just wasn't getting enough power to circulate properly. She dried her hands and held them out in front of her to where the nurse was holding out a disposable surgical gown. Next came the gloves then she checked the equipment on the trolley.

'Percutaneous sheath, bipolar pacing catheter and bridging cables and pacing box.' She murmured the contents out loud, mentally ticking them off in her head.

Gene spoke quietly to Aryssa. 'Aryssa, I know you might be feeling light-headed. We're sure that your pacing wire has moved. We're going to insert a temporary pacing line to get your heart back on track. You'll probably be a little woozy until we get this sorted. But trust us. We've got this.'

Aryssa's eyes were closed but she tossed her head from side to side. 'But I'll be flung off the trial. I don't want that. The drug is the only thing that's worked for me.'

Gene met Cordelia's gaze. Her heart gave a little flutter inside her chest and that made her freeze. *Oh, no. Not now. Not here.*

He spoke smoothly. 'Aryssa, with a heartbeat of around forty we couldn't let you stay in the trial. We've got to keep you healthy. This isn't something we can debate. You need this procedure.'

A tear trickled down Aryssa's cheek and Gene clasped her hand tightly while looking at Cordelia. It was awful. Aryssa had been doing so well on the trial. The new drug seemed to be having a good effect on her. Her symptoms had diminished over the last few weeks and up until the last day her heart function had looked a little better.

Hypertrophic cardiomyopathy could throw up a whole host of problems, depending on which part of the heart was most affected. Right now, they had no way of reversing the condition, but this drug had actually looked as though it could slow and stabilise the condition, optimising the output of the heart.

Gene looked so conflicted. She could almost see what he was seeing—Rory on the bed instead of Aryssa. It must be breaking his heart.

For a few seconds his dark brown gaze intersected with hers. He wasn't a doctor right now, he was a parent. It was like seeing the window to his soul. His hopes and fears all tumbling over and over. She gave him the briefest nod of acknowledgement and it was almost like flicking a switch.

His doctor face fell back into place.

'What site?' asked Gene.

Cordelia breathed deeply, focused and ran her eyes over her patient as the sonographer appeared. She gave him a grateful smile and a nod as he moved into position without even speaking.

She looked at Aryssa's neck. There was a small white scar at her neck—obviously the place of the last insertion. The right internal jugular vein was the preferred option due to the ease of positioning the wire into the right ventricle. But since it had already been used there was a risk of scar tissue. She wanted this procedure to go smoothly.

She could see Gene's eyes following hers. 'Looks like the left subclavian is our best option,' she said.

The nurse gave a nod and eased Aryssa's gown down from her left shoulder, giving easy access to her left clavicle and covering around the area with sterile drapes. Cordelia picked up a swab and cleansed the area, feeling with her fingers for the identifying features. She then nodded to the sonographer, who placed his probe just under the clavicle, allowing her to identify the artery and vein on the screen. As the artery and

vein were so close it was important to familiarise herself with the patient's anatomy.

She waited until the arterial wave form was shown,
to differentiate between the artery and vein, then in-
jected some local anaesthetic into the site.

Gene's voice was low and reassuring in the background. He talked to Aryssa the whole time she lay
with her eyes closed, keeping a soft grip of her hand.

Cordelia threaded the dilator into the catheter, at-
taching it to the needle and inserting it, waiting for the
flash of blood, before continuing. She held the needle
steady while advancing the wire into the vein. She then
removed the needle, made a little cut with the scalpel
and inserted the sheath, with the dilator in place, over
the wire.

'Almost done,' she said quietly to Aryssa. 'I'm just
removing the wire and testing the balloon on the pacing wire.' That only took a few minutes then she completed the procedure by inserting the wire into Aryssa.
The wire was attached to the pacing box and it turned
on. They watched on the screen as the balloon allowed
the wire to be positioned. A few seconds later the pacing spikes appeared on the monitor, showing them that
the wire was in the correct position.

Cordelia still marvelled at the technology they had
these days that allowed them to do relatively complicated
procedures in such a quiet and controlled environment.
They waited another few minutes, watching the monitor
for any potential changes. It only took a few seconds for
Gene to smile and nod and for Aryssa's cheeks to start
to pink up. Her heart rate was now sitting at around seventy beats per minute. The pacing wire was doing its job.

They held steady. Waiting to ensure that everything
was in place.

That was when it started. The noise like horses' hooves in her ears. That feeling of a runaway train in her chest.

No. Please, no.

She stared down at her gloved hands, wanting to lift one to her neck. But she couldn't. This was a sterile procedure.

She tried to take some long, slow, steadying breaths. But it was useless. She knew that. She'd dealt with this condition too long.

She kept her voice as steady as it could be. 'Dr Du Bois, would it be possible for you to stitch the line in place for me, please?'

The nurse next to her turned her head in surprise, and Gene looked up. He gave her the strangest look. Stitching only took a matter of minutes—minutes that she didn't feel like she had right now. It seemed odd to ask another doctor to scrub and get sterile. It would take him longer to do that than it would for her to do the stitching. But her head was starting to swim. She had to get out of here. Now.

She didn't wait for his answer. She just turned to the nurse next to her, who was already gowned and wearing sterile gloves. 'Could you hold this for me until Dr Du Bois is ready, please? I need to get a little air.'

The nurse moved swiftly, sliding her hands over Cordelia's so there was no change in position. Cordelia didn't hesitate. She turned and left as the thudding in her chest threatened to overtake her. She heard someone call her name. But she couldn't afford to wait.

Her legs were shaking almost as much as her head. Heat swamped her and she tugged the sterile gown from her throat and sterile gloves from her hands as she staggered the last few steps to her office.

It was like a sanctuary. She didn't even have time to close the door but slid down the wall, automatically putting her fingers to her neck to start massaging.

It was all she could think about. All she could concentrate on. Every molecule in her body had to think about those fingers. It was her own fault. She'd never left it this long before. She always dealt with the arrhythmia as soon as she'd felt it. As soon as she'd had symptoms.

She counted in her head. Slowly. One...two...three. It was impossible. Counting wouldn't slow her heart rate. Or stop the wooziness in her head. Or the tightness in her chest.

She pictured something else. Green meadows. For as far as the eye could see. Flat green meadows. Dotted with daisies and dandelions. She sucked in a long, slow breath.

This was the place she liked to see when she needed to. It normally helped to centre her. Keep her calm. Keep her feeling in control, even though her body revolted. But this time there was a difference. This time something else was in *her* place. A blond-haired kid. And a broad-chested father. Smiling, laughing together. The father picking the kid up and swinging him in the air and the little guy screaming with joy.

It startled her. She'd never visualised things like this before. Her hands slid from her neck.

Her heart rate had slowed and she hadn't even noticed. She put her fingers on her wrist and counted her pulse. Old-fashioned but effective.

She let her head sag back against the wall. The tightness in her chest eased. Thank goodness. She pulled her shirt from her body. Cold sweat was uncomfortable. She'd need to change. Just as soon as she checked on Aryssa.

Her stomach clenched.

Patient. She had to check on her patient.

Gene was dumbfounded. Had she really just left?

The nurse met his gaze. 'She was paler than Aryssa,' she whispered in a voice only he could hear.

He nodded and swapped sides, moving to the sink to scrub. Another nurse appeared, holding out a disposable gown for him. Within a matter of minutes he was scrubbed and gloved and talking away to a much more alert Aryssa as he placed a couple of stitches to hold the pacing wire in situ.

If the rest of the staff thought it strange that Cordelia had left in mid-procedure they didn't say anything. But she hadn't really left in mid-procedure. He was being hard on her. She'd completed about ninety per cent before she'd bailed. But it still didn't make him feel any easier.

He kept talking, finished up, all the while keeping an eye on Aryssa's ECG readouts before asking the nurse to keep her on the monitor for the next few hours. It was routine after a procedure like this and Aryssa already looked better. They would transfer her to another facility later. The pacing wire was only a temporary measure. She'd need a new permanent pacemaker in the next few days.

She reached over and touched his arm. 'Thank you, Dr Du Bois. I feel much better. But I can't pretend to be happy about getting flung off the trial. I'd finally found a drug that had actually improved my other systems, and probably my heart function. I feel as if— even though you've given me a new pacing wire—it will go downhill from here. I'll miss the effects of that drug.'

He understood exactly what she was saying. 'Cardiomyopathy is a complicated disease. Even when you have the gene, things can be different for every patient. You think the drug might already have helped. And those effects might last.'

Aryssa shook her head sadly. 'I don't think so, Doc.' She sighed and leaned her head back against the pillows. 'I'm just sorry this happened. All because some stray cat ran on the road in front of us.'

He wanted to tell her she could stay on the trial. He wanted to tell her there was a way around this. She'd had a pacing wire from the start. Who needed to know it had been replaced?

But Gene was far too ethical for that. The trial conditions had to be strictly adhered to. Trials were always strict—for good reason. They had to be absolutely crystal clear that any side effects or changes in a patient's condition were caused by the new trial drug and not by anything else.

He put his hand over Aryssa's. 'I'm sorry, Aryssa. You know there's nothing we can do about the rules of the trial. We have to follow them.'

A million thoughts were racing through his brain. This could be a drug that could help thousands of cardiomyopathy sufferers throughout the world. This could be the drug that could one day make a difference for his child.

He had to push all his personal feelings aside and think purely like a doctor, purely like a researcher. It was like being a coin, balancing on its edge. One tiny push could see him campaigning to keep Aryssa on the trial. And even though every professional bone in his body knew that was the wrong thing to do, the parent in him would always wonder if he should.

Aryssa was wheeled out to Recovery and Gene pulled off his gown and washed his hands again, running his fingers through his hair.

Cordelia. He had to find her. He had to ask her what on earth was going on.

He walked down the corridor towards her office, trying to play down the whole host of emotions currently circulating in his head. She was standing in front of the mirror, pulling her hair back into a ponytail. It looked a little damp. And she'd changed. She was wearing a green shirt instead of a pink one.

'Everything okay?'

She jumped at the sound of his voice, spun around to face him and glanced down, pulling at her shirt to straighten it.

'Have you quite finished titivating yourself?' He wasn't quite sure where the words had come from.

Her face fell, then he saw a sweep of anger flare in her eyes. 'Titivating myself? Is that what you think I'm doing?'

It had been a poor choice of words. He knew that. But now he'd started, it seemed like he couldn't stop. It was almost as if his mouth went into overdrive. 'Well, what *are* you doing? You were in the middle of a procedure on a patient. I had to finish for you. I think I have a right to know.'

A scowl creased her face. Her reaction was immediate. 'No. You don't have any right to know anything. The pacing wire was in place and Aryssa's heart rate had improved. I stepped out because I felt unwell for a second. That's all. I got changed because I was uncomfortable.'

It was a plausible enough explanation. But for some

reason he just didn't buy it. He was an experienced doctor. He knew when someone was hiding something from him. And that's exactly how he felt.

She took a deep breath. 'How is Aryssa? I was just about to come and see her.'

He spoke carefully, trying to maintain a hint of the composure that had already slipped. 'She's fine. I completed the stitches and she's in Recovery. She is still upset that she can't stay on the trial—just like Jonas was.'

Cordelia nodded solemnly. 'I'll talk to them both.'

'Shouldn't you sit down or something if you didn't feel well? Maybe you should eat something. Or drink something.' It was snappy. He knew that. But he also sensed she wasn't being up front.

She paused for a second. And he knew she was searching for something to say. It made his insides coil. Cordelia didn't strike him as someone who would be untruthful. And if she wasn't being untruthful? Then she was definitely hiding something from him.

'I'm fine,' she said quickly. 'I feel better now.'

He couldn't help himself. 'So quickly?'

She nodded and picked up some papers from her desk. 'Yes. Thank you for finishing up the procedure on Aryssa. I appreciate it. Now, if you'll excuse me, I have some work to do.'

She gave him a smile.

And somehow he knew she was resisting the temptation to say, 'As do you.'

She was second in command at the institute and he'd do well to remember that.

She swept past and strode down the corridor in front of him and he couldn't help but watch.

What did a woman like Cordelia Greenway have to hide—and why did he care?

CHAPTER FOUR

SHE'D JUST FINISHED pulling on her pyjamas when her bedroom door opened.

A little mop of blond hair appeared at the edge of the door. 'Rory? Is something wrong?'

'Want some milk,' he murmured.

She looked behind him. Gene wasn't in the corridor. 'Where's your dad?' she asked.

'He's in the shower. But I want some milk.' Rory walked tentatively into her room, holding a dog-eared book in one hand.

'Okay.' She nodded. 'I can get you some milk.' She looked at his bare feet. She wasn't quite sure where his slippers were, and didn't want to go into Gene's room to find them. Things had been a little tense for the last few days since the incident at the institute. He'd clearly been annoyed with her when he'd come to speak to her afterwards. She'd tried to make excuses but somehow she knew he hadn't really believed her.

Gene Du Bois was curious. He didn't like being fobbed off, and that's exactly what she'd tried to do.

It felt like they'd spent the last few days purposely avoiding each other and staying out of each other's way. It was almost like some carefully choreographed dance—but, then, she hadn't danced since she'd been a teenager and she'd no intention of starting again now.

She lifted Rory up onto her bed. 'Why don't you sit here for a minute while I go downstairs and get you some milk?'

'Okay,' he said, as he sat on her bed and looked around the room. She almost laughed out loud. Somewhere inside this four-year-old was a little old man waiting to get out. She could see him eyeing the clothes she'd thrown across a chair and her two pairs of shoes lying in one corner of the room.

Thankfully they had plenty of cold milk in the fridge downstairs so she poured some into a mug and carried it back up with her.

She walked around to the other side of the bed and climbed up alongside him, handing him the mug and praying he wouldn't spill it.

'I like your pyjamas,' he said as he took a sip of milk.

Her light jersey nightwear was bright pink and covered in tiny teddies. 'Thanks very much. I like yours too. Are they space rockets?'

He nodded. 'And planets. I was going to be an astronaut. But Dad says I might not be able to do that. So I'm going to be the scientist that presses the buttons and sends the shuttle into space.'

Her skin prickled. He was just a little guy but his vocabulary was so good. And his comprehension. But just because he sounded older than he was, it made her a little wary.

'You know, I think they get thousands of people who apply for every job as an astronaut. It's tough.'

He shrugged. 'I don't care. I'd get through.'

He said it with the confidence that only a child could

have. She liked that. She wished she still had that herself. The fearlessness. The expectations.

Nowadays, if you could bottle and sell something like that you would be a millionaire.

She lay back on the bed and looked out at the dark night sky. She hadn't remembered to close the curtains yet. She pointed up at the stars. 'Don't you think it might be a bit lonely up there?'

Her heart was giving a few little flutters in her chest. Not because anything was wrong but because somewhere along the line she figured that Gene must have had that general conversation with his little boy about doing certain things and getting certain jobs.

Hypertrophic cardiomyopathy was a tricky disease. The advice frequently said that children and adolescents with HCM should refrain from competitive high-activity sports to prevent the risk of sudden death.

Anyone with the HCM genes would never get on the space programme. Never be a deep-sea diver. Never be able to do certain other jobs. But did Gene really need to tell his kid that now?

She turned to face Rory as he took another sip of milk. 'But I wouldn't be lonely up there.'

'Why not?'

'Because my mom's up there.'

Her breath caught somewhere in the back of her throat. From the mouth of babes. She opened her mouth to speak but he kept talking, 'And I would take my girlfriend with me too. She's new. I met her today.'

Cordelia's brain was still dealing with the first statement. But she couldn't help but smile at the second. 'You have a girlfriend already? Who is she?'

He looked at Cordelia in surprise. 'I always have a girlfriend. Her name is Jana.'

Cordelia knew a lot of kids in the nursery and she frantically tried to remember which one was Jana.

'Blonde hair? Curls?'

Rory gave her a wide smile. 'That's her.'

'You've only been at nursery for a week and you've got a girlfriend already?'

He wrinkled his nose. 'Don't you have a boyfriend?'

She felt herself blushing. 'No. Not right now.' She gave a casual wave of her hand. 'Boys are too much trouble.' Then she rolled her eyes. 'And too messy.'

His dark brown eyes looked between her, her untidy pile of clothes, then back at her again. He didn't even have to say the words out loud.

Cordelia decided it was time for a quick subject change. 'Do you think your girlfriend wants to be an astronaut?'

Rory took another sip of milk and nodded his head thoughtfully. 'I'm not sure. Didn't you want to be an astronaut?'

She loved the way he asked her. As if every person on the planet wanted that job. She shook her head. 'Nope. I want to explore the pyramids. Or build a pirate ship and paint it red. Whatever came first.'

Something swept over his little face. 'Is that where your mom is?'

She almost felt her heart fold over in her chest. She couldn't help herself and did the most natural thing in the world. She sat up and put her arm around Rory's shoulder. 'No, honey. I'm very lucky. My mom is still here. She's quite old, but she lives by herself now.'

His brow creased and he looked up at her. 'Oh. My dad doesn't have his mommy any more, and neither do I.'

She wasn't used to kids. And she wasn't quite sure

how to frame her reply. She'd had lots of life and death conversations with patients over the years—and with grief-stricken relatives. But this was a kid. Way out of her range of expertise.

'I heard that. And I'm sorry. But you've got a great dad. And I bet he does everything with you that a mom and a dad would do.'

Rory seemed to think for a few seconds then took another big glug of milk, resulting in the cutest milk moustache she'd ever seen.

This little guy could tear the heart clean out of her chest. It didn't matter that she felt as if she were treading on eggshells. It didn't matter she was so far out of her comfort zone it was scary. He had a way about him. An aura that just pulled her straight in.

'I might get a new mommy one day.'

She swallowed and spoke carefully. 'You might.'

His wide brown eyes looked up at her. 'Do you think she'll like me?'

She pulled him up on to her lap. 'Rory Du Bois, I think anyone who could be a mommy to you would consider herself the luckiest woman on the planet. Of course she'll like you. She won't just like you. She'll love you. Just as much as she loves your dad. That's how these things work. Your dad wouldn't marry anyone who didn't love you just as much as he does.'

She was probably way overstepping here. But even knowing Gene for a few days made her know that would be true.

Rory's big brown eyes were fixed on hers. He blinked. Just once, and put his head back down, leaning on her shoulder. 'That's okay, then,' he murmured.

She reached over and picked up the picture book.

Strangely enough, it had a picture of a space rocket on the front cover. 'Want me to read this to you?' she asked.

Rory nodded and climbed off her lap and settled himself back under her arm. She didn't even want to acknowledge how that made her feel. The way that a tiny part of her that been tightly coiled up in her stomach for so long was slowly starting to unravel.

Or the fact that it made her realise just how much she was missing.

Gene wandered out of the shower and into an empty room. For a second his heart stopped.

He started to walk out into the corridor and stopped. He was naked. And he was a guest in someone else's house. He roughly towelled himself off and yanked on his jeans. The water was still running down his chest as he walked to the door and started to towel-dry his hair. 'Rory?'

The corridor was empty.

His heart rate quickened. He opened his mouth to shout again and then he stopped. And listened.

He could hear murmuring voices. There was only one other person in this house apart from Rory. Cordelia.

His curiosity was piqued. He took a few steps towards the door to Cordelia's room. It was ajar and he could see Rory sitting up on the bed next to Cordelia, drinking a glass of milk.

He put his hand on the door to push through and apologise but the words stopped him dead.

'My mom's up there.'

Gene winced as his stomach clenched.

The one thing he couldn't control. Just how much his son missed his mother.

It was normal. It was natural. Rory had attended a few nurseries and seen lots of other kids being picked up by their mommies. Gene always kept a photograph of Mindy around. He told Rory that was his mom and that she'd loved him very much.

Rory asked questions sometimes, but not often. Maybe he hadn't spoken about Mindy enough? The trouble was, there was no one else to tell Rory about Mindy, and what Gene knew wasn't really that much. He wasn't really into embellishments. But that looked like the only solution he had left.

His son had just told a perfect stranger that he wanted to be an astronaut because his mom was up in the stars. It was a story that families the world over told little kids. That someone they missed or loved who had died was up in the stars, watching over them.

Rory had long held a fascination with the planets and stars. But he'd never mentioned his mother. Gene had no idea that was the way he'd been thinking.

He was frozen. His feet rooted to the floor. But the woman who'd been prickly at their first meeting seemed to be managing around Rory.

In normal circumstances he would walk in and take over. But was that really best for Rory right now?

Rory had just told Cordelia Greenway something he hadn't shared with his dad. That made Gene's skin prickle. Was he failing his child? Wasn't he being the best dad that he could be?

His mouth felt dry.

He kept listening, watching through the gap in the door.

It felt like prowling. And he certainly wasn't doing that. Rory was safe.

And right now he was seeing a side of Cordelia he hadn't noticed before.

He could see she was dedicated to her work. The staff at the institute appeared to both like and respect her.

It almost made him want to push what had happened the other day out of his head. But he couldn't. It sat there, churning away in his mind, making him wonder what he was missing.

He could hear Cordelia still talking softly to Rory. Occasionally there was a little tremor in her voice. But she also sounded reassuring.

He closed his eyes for a second. Could he imagine Karen ever doing something like this? The truth was, no. He'd been hurt when she'd walked away. She'd been clear that she couldn't see herself taking on someone else's child. And that had hurt. Because Rory had been like a bolt out of the blue to him too. But he couldn't walk away. He would never have dreamed of it.

But here was sometimes prickly Cordelia being sweet to his son in a way he would never have expected.

When Rory asked about getting a new mommy and if she would love him, Gene's stomach clenched so hard it felt like it was made of lead.

Cordelia's answer seemed so simple. And completely and utterly true. He would never be with someone who couldn't love his son as much as he did. They were a package deal.

His heart squeezed in his chest. The woman he'd been angry with a few days ago got that. She had got that about him straight away. And as he watched she settled Rory under her arm and started reading him his favourite story book.

Now his heart gave an unsteady flutter. Rory looked so comfortable there. His little body had adopted the slumped position it normally did just before he fell asleep. Sure enough, like clockwork, only a few pages into the book Rory's eyelids started to droop.

Gene took a deep breath and collected himself, willing that he'd look as if he'd just appeared this second.

He stuck his head around the door and whispered, 'Cordelia?'

She looked up and stopped reading. Her eyes widened as he realised he still hadn't put a shirt on.

He almost hesitated, then dismissed it. She was a doctor, she'd seen more than enough naked torsos in her line of work. He walked over to the bed. 'Apologies,' he whispered. 'I was in the shower. Rory hasn't really grasped the concept of patience.'

She looked down at the mop of blond hair and ruffled it with her fingers. His head was completely sagging now. He was fast asleep.

'I'm not too good at the whole patience thing myself.' She looked up and met his gaze. The sincerity in her green eyes made him catch his breath.

'I'm sorry. I was in the shower,' he repeated. Crazy. He'd already said that. What was wrong with him?

'So I can see.' A smile danced across her lips as her eyes fixed on his bare chest.

He held out his hands and smiled back. 'What can I say? I didn't have time to put all my clothes on. I came out of the shower and realised I was missing a child.'

She shook her head. 'Poor excuse. You never got paged when you were in the shower when you were working as a resident?'

The hours and workload of resident doctors were notorious. By the time every doctor had finished training they had dozens of stories to tell.

She tutted and shook her head. 'I can't believe you

don't know how to do the ten-second soaked-to-fully-clothed dance.'

There was a gleam in her eyes. She was teasing. Of course she was.

He shook his head and slid his arms under Rory's body. 'I can assure you I'm a professional.' He winked. 'I can do it in eight. Give me a sec, let me put Rory to bed.'

He kissed Rory on top of his head and walked back through to their room, putting him into the double bed and pulling the cover over him. He grabbed a grey T-shirt and tugged it over his head. She was standing at the door with her arms folded over her chest. She tilted her head to the side. 'If you can do it in eight, then how come you didn't manage?'

He stepped closer. He hadn't even realised she was wearing a pair of cute pink pyjamas. Now she was standing up, even though every part of her was covered, he could see the way the jersey hugged her curves.

He gave a shake of his head and held up his hands as he kept his voice low. 'Clothes aren't really required when you're missing a four-year-old.' He rubbed his hands on his jeans. 'Just be glad I put on these.'

She started to laugh then put her hand up to her mouth and stepped back. 'Sorry, don't want to wake Rory.'

'Oh, don't worry. You won't wake Rory. Once he goes to sleep, that's it. Nothing—not even a freight train—could wake him.'

She smiled again. 'Sleep's a funny thing. I could sleep within a few seconds when I was resident, but I was always on alert, waiting for the next page. But as soon as I got home? That's it. I was out like a light—

just like Rory. I once slept through guys drilling on the road outside.'

Gene felt something wash over him. Completely un-expected.

'I used to do that.' The words came out almost on autopilot.

She met his gaze. 'And you don't any more?'

He glanced at the sleeping figure on the bed. Rory's head was resting on the pillow and he was curled into a ball. When Gene sucked in a breath he almost juddered. 'I haven't slept like that since Rory arrived.'

She blinked. And for a second he thought he'd made her feel uncomfortable. But she just gave a gentle shake of her head. 'I can't imagine how it must be to hear out of the blue that you've got a child. And that his mom was so sick. But whatever you've done over the last few years, it's worked. He's a gorgeous kid. Bright, articu-late, intelligent and…' she smiled '…very, very sweet.'

For a second he thought there was a flash of sad-ness across her face. But as quickly as it had appeared, it vanished again.

She pulled up one of legs behind her, catching her foot by the ankle and letting it click loudly. 'Sorry, aches and pains. I get that way sometimes. Must be my old dance injuries—or my age.'

He put his hand at the back of his neck. 'Mine too. But it's an old football injury.'

She gave a smile. 'Well, I can't claim any kind of sport injuries. My biggest sport these days is how quickly I can read a book.'

He didn't quite believe her. She was only wearing thin pyjamas and although she had a few curves, there was no hint of heaviness in her frame.

'Did you recognise that book that Rory made you read? You seemed to relate easily.'

She laughed. 'It's a book. I always relate to books. When I was a kid you were only allowed four books with your library card. I tried to pretend to be another kid and get an extra card so I could check out eight books at a time.'

'Did your plan work?'

'Are you joking? My disguise was very flawed. I only took my outdoor jacket off.'

He couldn't help but laugh out loud too. He was watching the easy, casual way Cordelia was chatting— as if it were completely normal to be chatting to someone she didn't know that well in her pyjamas.

But that was the life of a doctor. Running around in scrubs permanently wasn't that different from pjs.

She reached over and touched his arm. It was just her thumb that came into contact with his still-damp skin, but he could almost hear a hiss. Even in the dim light her bright green eyes seemed to draw him in.

Female contact. When was the last time he'd had some?

He didn't even want to think about that. And certainly not now. In a semi-dark room with a woman with chestnut-brown curls resting on her shoulders.

'I think I'm going to go downstairs and make some toast. Want some?'

He could sense it. That tiny hint of breaking the ice between them again. Things had been awkward these last few days and he had to admit he didn't like it. This was the first time they'd been face to face again. And the dim lights and thin layers of clothes made things seem much more…intimate.

He glanced back at Rory, whose little chest was rising and falling deeply. He was sound asleep.

It must only be around nine o'clock. He couldn't pretend to be tired so he nodded and followed her down the staircase to the kitchen.

Cordelia moved with ease, putting on the kettle and popping wholemeal bread into the toaster.

'What can I do?'

She waved her hand. 'Sit down. It's only toast. What do you want? Low-fat spread, butter, jam or marmalade?'

He leaned back and met her gaze. He wanted to talk. He wanted to talk so badly it almost made his stomach ache. He wanted to ask her about Rory, what she thought about what he'd said, if it meant that Rory was disappointed in him, if he just wasn't enough on his own?

But he couldn't do that. Cordelia might be nice. She might be a fellow doctor. She might be dedicated to her work and respected by her patients. And she might have been good with Rory. She might also be extremely attractive—a fact he was trying very hard to ignore.

But he couldn't forget his instincts. There was something he just couldn't quite put his finger on.

Cordelia Greenway was keeping secrets.

It was there. In every sideways glance. Every careful answer.

The toast popped and he realised he hadn't answered her question. He jumped up and walked over to the fridge, pulling out what he needed. 'I love the way you guys call it jam when it's really jelly.'

She wrinkled her nose. 'No way. Jelly is the stuff that wobbles—that you have with ice cream.' She raised her eyebrows. 'And I've seen how much Rory loves ice cream.'

She buttered the toast quickly as the kettle boiled and she set down the mugs. He still couldn't stop smiling at the thought of Rory with the ice cream.

She sighed as she sat opposite him and leaned her head on one hand. It was the first time he'd noticed how tired she looked. Of course. Not only did she have two unexpected house guests, she also had the whole responsibility of the institute on her shoulders. It must be tough.

'So,' she started, 'how do you feel things are with your part of the trials?'

He'd been holding his breath, wondering if she'd mention what had happened between them a few days ago. And he looked at her steadily, sure that his eyes were asking the question that wouldn't quite form on his lips.

There was something in her return gaze. A determination and stubbornness that he expected had been there for a long time.

He licked his lips and tried not to smile. They weren't going to talk about it. Even though they had complete privacy.

Fine. He could do this. He could play this game.

'I think the trial is going well. Apart from what happened with Aryssa.' He had to say it—her exclusion would be detrimental to the trial. 'From a review of the case notes and bloodwork it looks as if around sixty-five per cent of the trial candidates are showing clear signs of improvement. That's really impressive for a trial.' He gave a wry smile. 'Of course, things are complicated by the range of comorbidities suffered by the patients. But that's what makes them real. And that's what makes these studies more worthwhile than others.'

Cordelia gave a slow nod. 'Sometimes I love the

studies—sometimes I hate them. I get lost in the zebra-fish studies. They're such remarkable creatures. If only our hearts could regenerate the same way. Then we'd have no heart failure, no tired and worn-out cells.' She gave a sad kind of smile. 'Maybe a chance to create better pathways for some.'

It was cardiac-speak. Only a fellow cardiac specialist would understand it. But it struck a little chord in him.

She was drumming her fingers on the table but looked up and met his gaze. 'It sounds like your study is doing better than mine.' She hesitated for a second then reached over and squeezed his hand. It was an unexpected move that took him by surprise.

That was a few times now. A few times when her skin had just brushed against his and...

'I'm glad. I'm glad for you, glad for Rory, and for all the other patients who might get to lead an easier life.'

He could see it. The shine in her eyes. The truth. The sincerity. And it was confusing him. That, and the tingles shooting up his arm. He couldn't quite get a handle on what was happening.

She pulled her hand back and wrapped both of them around her mug of tea. 'The research can be hard. Some find it soul-destroying because there are no fast answers, no magic cures out there. But it never gets old. So I try to remember that every day is a new day, with a world of possibilities.'

Her voice was quiet, soft with a distinct edge of hope.

'That's your thing,' he said quickly.

'My what?' She frowned.

He couldn't help but smile. 'I asked you the other day what your "thing" was. You said you didn't know.'

She was still frowning and looked totally confused.

She shook her head. 'But we didn't do that weird fist bump thing.'

His smile widened. 'No, that's my thing. Mine and Rory's. But that's twice now I've heard you say it. *It never gets old. Every day is a new day with a world of possibilities.*' He lifted his hands and shrugged his shoulders. 'There. It's official. It's your thing.'

She tilted her head to one side and looked thoughtful. 'I didn't think I had a thing.'

He lifted his mug towards hers. 'Well, you do. To things.'

She laughed as she chinked her mug against his. 'Okay, then, to things.' She glanced over her shoulder. 'How about some more toast?'

CHAPTER FIVE

'How about a bit of fun?'

She turned sideways. Was he talking to her or to Rory? The other night had been a weird mixture of feeling the most relaxed she'd been since Gene and Rory had arrived, and a crazy spin cycle of other emotions. One minute she was thinking about the relationship Gene had with his son—how it made her ache inside and gave her strange pangs of envy. The next minute she was trying to fight the crazy, stupid waves of attraction she was feeling to the handsome Texan.

It was ridiculous. He was a short-term colleague—albeit a very handsome one. And there wasn't the slightest chance he was attracted to her.

Except...

That sometimes she caught a look, a sideways glance that made her heart trip over itself. Or there was the fleeting tingle when their skins connected and her senses flipped into overdrive. Maybe she was going crazy. Maybe she was finally losing her mind, because she never did this. Never.

Something washed over her. She'd never even had these crazy mixed-up feelings about Han—and he'd been in her life for a few years, not a few weeks. She couldn't deny that when he'd left she'd been shattered and hurt. But was that all really over Han, or had it been about the gradual sinking in of the news from her consultant that she shouldn't have kids?

The truth was she hadn't really given herself time to think about it all. It had been much easier just to immerse herself in work up until now…

She wasn't the kind of girl to fall head over heels for some totally unsuitable guy. She'd always been far too practical for that. Why should it change now?

But for the last few days things had been much more relaxed around the workplace and at home, and she liked that.

She'd liked the vibe and warmth that seemed to emanate both from Rory and Gene.

'Cordelia?' The voice broke into her thoughts. 'How about a bit of fun?'

Gene was standing at the kitchen doorway, leaning against the jamb with his arms folded.

There was something about the look on his face. Had he been reading her thoughts? Fun with the Texan cowboy?

Her heartbeat gave a little flutter and she ducked her head as heat rushed into her cheeks. She pushed the ridiculous thoughts from her head as she turned to face him. 'What do you mean?'

There was something about this guy. He just had to give her *that* look. The one where his eyes twinkled and she wanted to dig underneath and see what mischief he was hiding. It was so easy to be pulled in.

He raised his eyebrows and held out his hands. 'Apparently, we're in Geneva. One of the most beautiful cities in the world. I haven't had a chance to see any of it. And I've no idea what's suitable for kids.' He stepped towards her. 'You don't need to work today—I've checked. How about you show us around a little?'

His chocolate-brown eyes fixed on hers. A little shiver ran down her spine. He'd checked her schedule. He'd made sure she was free. It could just be that he wanted someone to show him around—someone who was familiar with the territory. But the butterflies in her stomach were hoping it was something else entirely.

How stupid was that? He was a colleague. He was here on a temporary basis. She wasn't in a position to think about anything else. So why was she?

But something inside gave her a little push. The words were out before her brain had any more time to think about it. 'Sure, why not?'

Geneva. The most gorgeous city in the world. Of course he'd want to see it. When she'd first got here she'd been in awe of its beauty—from the Alps to the lakes. But where to take a kid?

There was so much to see in the city. A museum of natural history. The cathedral, and the Jardin Botanique. But Rory was too young for most of that yet.

She wrinkled her nose for a second as she scanned her brain, stopping at the biggest thing she could think of. 'Do you trust me to find something that a kid will like?'

Gene tipped his head to the side and looked thoughtful for a second. 'Isn't everyone really a kid at heart?'

There was something about the way he said it. As if it was the most natural thing in the world. She felt a little tug inside her. And she knew exactly where to take them. She picked up the phone to call a taxi.

'Get your jackets.' She smiled. 'And be prepared to get wet.'

* * *

They headed towards the city. Rory was excited already. He was chatting as he was sandwiched between them in the taxi. Gene hadn't heard the instructions Cordelia had given the driver, and he'd expected the driver to head towards the city centre, but instead he circled the outside and took them in another direction. After twenty minutes he realised they were skirting the edges of Lake Geneva.

'We're going to the lake?' he asked.

Cordelia nodded as the taxi pulled up to drop them off. 'What do all kids love? Water. Just wait until Rory sees just how many boats there are here.'

As the sun was warm, Gene carried their jackets as they walked to the lake shore. Rory let out a little gasp at the wide expanse of Lake Geneva. He turned to Gene with big eyes. 'Daddy, is this all ours? Do we get to play here?'

Gene laughed out loud. He reached down and grasped the little hand, bending towards the excited face. 'Yeah, but we have to share it with other people.'

'Come over here.' Cordelia was standing next to a telescope that looked out over the lake. She slid some coins into the slot as he held Rory up to the foot stand. 'Just how big is this place?' Gene asked.

She waved out her hand. 'It's forty-five miles long— the largest body of water in Switzerland, crescent-shaped and is shared between Switzerland and France.'

She gave a little smile as she looked over her shoulder. 'And it has the distinct advantage of being surrounded by mountains.'

He looked over at the snow-topped Alps behind the body of water. It really was one of the most picturesque places he'd ever seen.

He gave a nod. 'I'll give you a ten for the view.' His eyes ran up and down her body. He didn't mean to. It just happened. Cordelia was wearing well-fitting jeans and a long-sleeved red top. Her hair was tied back off her face, but the brisk breeze from the lake still made stray strands whip around her face.

She leaned down next to Rory and pointed out all the types of craft on the lake. It was littered with mainly white boats—pleasure cruisers, luxury yachts, a rescue craft, even an old replica paddle steamer. She pointed to some smaller yellow vessels. 'These are *mouettes*. They'll take us across to the other side of the lake. There's something special over there.'

'Can we, Daddy? Can we go?' Rory was jumping up and down at the thought of getting on one of the small ferries.

Gene could see them crossing the lake in a regular manner. They were obviously well used. 'Sure, why not?'

Cordelia led them to a boarding station and they climbed aboard one of the *mouettes*. The boats were covered and sat low in the water. They picked a seat near the front. Within a few seconds Rory was laughing as the air rushed in his face as they crossed the lake.

Cordelia sat in the seat next to him, her arm casually resting on Rory's shoulders as she pointed out other things as they crossed the lake. Ten minutes later they reached the other side.

'This is the west bank,' she said as they climbed out. 'There's lots to do here. But the first thing is this.' She grinned as she pointed straight ahead. 'Jet d'Eau is the world's tallest water fountain.'

Gene frowned as he looked towards the stone jetty. Was this some kind of trick? 'What are we looking at?'

She grinned as she glanced at her watch and she grabbed Rory's hand and stuck one finger in the air. 'Let me check the wind direction. We could get drenched any second.'

Gene had no idea what she was talking about. Something flickered in his brain. Something about a soccer championship. There was a rumble underneath them. Like a train passing beneath their feet. People had gathered around, everyone glancing at their watches. Rory was bouncing. He could feel the excitement in the air.

Seconds later it happened. A huge rushing noise, and water seemed to explode out of the lake, shooting more than a hundred feet into the air.

The effect was instantaneous. Everyone surrounding the area jumped back automatically—even though they were far back from the jet of water.

Tiny droplets started to shower down around them. Gene held out his hands in wonder. 'What on earth is it?' he said above the roar of water.

Cordelia was grinning, her eyes firmly fixed on Rory. 'I told you. It's Jet d'Eau. The largest water fountain in Switzerland.' Her eyes were gleaming.

'And what? They just switch it on?'

She nodded. 'It's been here for more than a hundred and thirty years. It was further along at first—originally as a safety valve for the hydraulic power network— but they realised how much people loved it, and they moved it to here.'

She held out her hands and pointed to the stream of water. 'We have to be careful. If the wind changes we could be drenched in seconds.'

Gene was shaking his head in wonder at the sight. People were crowded around, attracted by the sudden gush of water. He laughed at Cordelia as she grabbed

Rory's hand to stamp in the puddles that had appeared around their feet. 'Five hundred litres of water a second,' she shouted over her shoulder to Gene, 'at about a hundred and twenty miles an hour.'

'Isn't it great, Daddy?' yelled Rory as his baseball boots started to get darker and darker with the water.

Gene swept him up under his arm. 'Hey, buddy. Do you want to have wet feet all day?'

He looked down at Cordelia's equally damp red baseball boots. 'I did warn you.' She grinned. She shook her hair and showered him in tiny droplets of water. 'Come on, we'll head into the left bank. It's fun.'

She led them through the picturesque medieval streets towards a beautiful garden. It was full of families and street performers, and she took Rory by the hand towards the middle of the park where a large feature clock made of brightly coloured flowers was situated.

'It's huge,' breathed Rory. 'Does it work?'

Cordelia nodded. 'The hands move. And the flowers change colour depending on the season. So, it's red, pink and orange now. In a few months it could be yellow and purple.'

Cordelia chatted easily, guiding Rory next to a mini train station, which, of course, he loved. The train was old-fashioned, bright red and they climbed aboard easily. She leaned over next to Gene and whispered in his ear, 'This takes around thirty minutes. It goes along the edge of the lake and takes us to another park.'

He slung his arm around Rory's shoulder and relaxed into the ride. For someone who'd seemed a little uncomfortable around kids, Cordelia seemed to have warmed up. She chatted to Rory as the PA system on the train pointed out the UN buildings on the other side of the lake and all the other tourist attractions. Her scent drifted over towards him as she kept bending down to talk to Rory. He couldn't help but keep watching her. Her skin was bright and clear, her eyes sparkling, and there was only a hint of lipstick on her lips. He almost didn't notice as the train pulled up next to a sandy beach with a massive play park.

'Want to get off?' asked Cordelia 'This is the baby *plage*—the children's beach. There's loads here for kids to do.'

Gene looked around. The beach and surrounding area was already full of families and kids and looked perfect. The kids' area was equipped with a lawn, a sandy area and an unusual set of climbing equipment under a shady tree. Rory was buzzing instantly.

'I want to try that!' he said, pointing at the equipment.

Gene nodded and climbed out of the train, holding out his hand for them both to follow. There were swings, climbing frames, and a mini rope bridge between two big tree branches, all in a safe, secluded area where children could easily be supervised. Water buoys marked the shallow area of the lake where kids could paddle safely. Cordelia and Gene sat on the beach together while Rory had a ball, instantly making friends with the international array of kids around him.

Gene leaned back on his hands as Cordelia's eyes flitted from one kid to the next. 'Isn't it interesting?'

'What?'

'The language of kids. They're all chattering away to each other in different languages. But it's almost like they understand each other.'

'If only adults could do the same,' said Cordelia wistfully.

He turned to her and smiled. 'We get so caught up

in languages. I only speak two. But sometimes I feel as if I really need to speak them all.'

Something flicked into his head. 'The Japanese investors. You're meeting them on Tuesday, aren't you?'

She nodded and brushed some hair from her face. 'They pushed their visit back so I've had some more time to prepare.'

'How are you feeling about it? Are you okay with that?'

There was only a flicker of hesitation. 'Yes, I've met a few of the investors before. Franc always shows them around the entire institute and invites them to talk to staff—even patients if they want to.'

He paused for a second, not wanting to step on her toes. 'But you've never had to meet them on your own before?'

She bit her bottom lip and shook her head, pulling her knees up to her chest. 'Nope.'

There were no further words—and that told Gene all he needed to know. 'If you want, I can make sure I'm around—to answer any questions they might have on the cardiomyopathy study.'

He didn't want her to think he was trying to push his way in. Cordelia would know more about the institute than he could ever hope to. But before he'd even contemplated taking the job here, he'd pored over their research study. He was confident he could cover any questions they might have, and wanted to take the pressure off her a little if he could.

She gave a thoughtful nod. Her eyes were still fixed on Rory on the climbing frame. 'That would be great, thanks. Another person to answer questions on the studies would be great. I know the zebrafish stuff back to front. The cardiomyopathy study—I've never taken the lead on that. I'd like it if you were available.'

Her head rested on her knees and she looked sideways at him. The shade from the trees cast a shadow over her face but still let him focus on her bright green eyes framed with thick dark lashes. She had virtually no make-up on today. Her cheeks were tinged pink from the fresh breeze from the lake. The breeze carried her scent over the short distance between them again, something tinged with a hint of rose and orange.

Just the smell and the intensity of her gaze sent a little pulse rushing through him. His brain was taking in the words 'I'd like it if you were available' to a whole other place. He spoke quickly, to try and stop his thoughts going anyplace else. 'Anything to help out. After all, we are invading your home.'

His voice was quiet and she lifted her head and leaned forward a little. It was odd how glad he felt about that. How he liked the fact he could see a freckle at the base of her neck, or the way a strand of hair was coiled around her ear.

She gave a soft smile. 'You're not invading my home. It's Franc's. In fact, we're both home invaders.' She closed her eyes and let out a breath. 'I'll need to talk to the insurance company again. Things seem to have ground to a complete halt.'

'Daddy, Daddy.' Rory ran over, his cheeks flushed. 'Can I have some juice?'

He was breathing heavily, his eyes bright with excitement. Before Gene had a chance to speak Cordelia pushed herself up and dusted off her jeans. 'I have an idea. How about ice cream? There's an ice-cream cart just a little further along, next to an old-fashioned merry-go-round. Why don't we head in that direction?'

Rory jumped up and down. 'Ice cream, yeah!'

Gene smiled and glanced at his watch. 'Sure, why not.' Cordelia held out her hand towards Rory and he eagerly slid his little hand into hers.

The walk was a pleasant stroll around the edge of the lake. The old quarter surrounding them was quaint, with winding streets filled with unusual and quirky shops. The vintage merry-go-round had a little crowd around it and Rory laughed as he clambered on the biggest blue horse he could find, bobbing up and down merrily as the ride slowly went around.

Cordelia waved every time Rory passed and Gene got out his phone to snap some pictures. Rory was having a great day. His cheeks glowed and eyes sparkled. He gave a shout whenever he circled around again and Gene felt his heart swell with pride. 'Daddy! Delia!' Rory shouted.

Gene laughed at the shortened version of Cordelia's name. Her cheeks flushed as she laughed too. 'Only my old nana used to call me Delia. I haven't been called that in years.'

The merry-go-round started to slow and Gene reached forward to grab Rory. He swung him up onto his hip. 'What kind of ice cream would you like?' he asked his son.

'Chocolate!' shouted Rory.

'Chocolate it is.' Gene smiled as they walked over to the ice-cream cart.

Five minutes later they walked in the sunshine along the edge of the lake. The sun was bright and the ice cream quickly ran down their arms.

He'd asked Cordelia this morning on a spur-of-the-moment thought. It had seemed wrong to explore the city without her when he knew she was free. But even though he was curious about her, he'd never expected to enjoy himself quite so much.

Cordelia was definitely an attractive woman, but the more time he spent in her company, the more he found herself attracted to her.

They'd been here two and a half weeks. His contract was only for a month. This was a bad idea. He knew that. So why wasn't his brain listening?

Rory was still hyper. And he was a pleasure to be around. By the time they wandered through the old quarter streets and looked in the windows of all the quaint shops, he finally started to tire. Time had marched on and Rory was up in Gene's arms, snuggled into his shoulders.

Gene smiled as he adjusted Rory's position. 'He's not quite as light as he looks. How do you feel about grabbing an early dinner?'

Cordelia nodded. The day had been so nice. She really didn't want it to end. She looked around. 'Sure, why not? Do you have a preference where we go?'

He shook his head. 'Just somewhere that I can put Rory down on a seat.'

They walked a little further through the streets until they came to a friendly-looking German restaurant. A woman was trying to usher tourists in from the streets. She waved them over when she glanced at Rory. *'Anglais? Français?'*

Cordelia smiled. *'Anglais.'*

'Come, come.' The woman gestured. 'I find you somewhere for little one.'

Gene grinned and raised his eyebrows at Cordelia. 'What do you think?'

She shrugged and nodded. 'Why not?'

The woman's smile was broad as she showed them into a booth with leather seats on either side. Gene hesitated for a second. 'Do you mind if I put Rory down on one side and let him lie flat?'

'Of course not.'

Rory didn't even make a sound as his father laid him down—obviously the excitement of the day had all been too much for him.

Within minutes they had menus and drinks—a beer for Gene and a glass of wine for Cordelia. The restaurant was informal and friendly. Their waitress gave them her recommendation from the menu: *sauerbraten* over *spaetzle*—a marinated pot roast served with a buttery *spaetzle* pasta and spicy red cabbage—and they were soon eating heartily.

'So, what do you do normally on a day off? Have we ruined things for you?'

Something inside her gave a little buzz at his interest in her. 'Of course not. I've had a great day.'

She leaned towards his ear and whispered, 'I'll let you into a secret. I've always secretly wanted to go on that merry-go-round.'

'You should have said something. You could have gone on with Rory—he would have loved that.'

She laughed. 'And how would I have looked—a thirty-something woman sitting alongside all the kids?'

He raised his glass of beer towards her. 'I think you would have looked good.'

It was the expression in his eyes as he said it. The little flirtatious glimmer. Or was she imagining it?

There had been several times today that their gazes had meshed and she'd felt…something. A connection.

A connection she kept wondering if she really was experiencing.

Because, if she was, it was completely messing with her brain.

Gene's long legs were stretched out beneath the table alongside hers. His head was facing her, leaning on one hand. The fingers of his other hand stroked the outside of his beer glass.

Her thoughts immediately went elsewhere, making her skin tingle. What on earth was wrong with her?

She picked up her wineglass and took a gulp. There was an amused expression on his face as he watched her through heavy lids.

'What?' she asked as she glanced over her shoulder. 'What is it?'

He gave a small shrug. 'I don't know. Every now and then, just out of nowhere, it's like you have a flash of panic.'

She knew exactly what he was talking about. She was feeling the flash of panic right now—all entirely related to him.

'No, I don't.' She tried to sound casual.

He straightened a little, still looking amused. 'Yeah. You do. I can see it in your eyes. I can always tell when you're about to change the subject or walk away.'

She bit her bottom lip for a second and tried to stop the instant throw-away remarks that circled in her head.

She looked down at those long legs again. Nope. Not helping.

She stared back at those brown eyes. Darn it. Why did they have to look so deep? Like something you just swirl around and get lost in?

'Well, I haven't walked away now. Or changed the subject, have I?'

His shoulder brushed against hers. 'No, you haven't.' He looked over at Rory. 'But now we're away from work, and little ears are sleeping, how about we have some adult chat?'

Heat rushed into her cheeks like some kind of race car zooming around a track as she shifted on the bench seat. 'What do you mean?'

He still had that darned sexy smile on his lips. He gave another shrug. 'I mean, let's talk. I share a house with you but I feel as if I don't really know much about you.'

'You know that jelly is jam, I like chocolate, and red baseball boots are my favourite footwear.'

He tapped his fingers on the table with a determined glint in his eyes. He wasn't going to be put off. 'Okay, then. I've told you about Rory's mom. Do you have a secret husband or boyfriend stashed away somewhere?'

She shook her head. 'Nope. Not right now. I've had a few boyfriends. But nothing lasted more than a year.' She gave a laugh. 'I'm not deliberately antisocial but I guess for the last while I've just been so focused on my work.'

'That's understandable. Okay, so I know about this work—at the institute. But where did you work before?'

'I trained in London, then worked in cardiology. I worked at the Royal Brompton and King's College.'

He gave an appreciative look. 'But you decided to have a change?'

She'd answered questions before about her career change. And she didn't like telling lies. But she wasn't quite sure she was ready to share about her condition—particularly when he'd been annoyed with her a few days ago. They were back to a place that she liked. She didn't want to do anything to spoil that. 'Yeah, I decided I wanted to work in research. I loved clinical care, but I've always had big-picture thoughts. About where I can do the best work, to help the most people.'

She was almost holding her breath—hoping it sounded plausible.

Gene glanced over at Rory. 'I feel like that about this work. My brain knows the processes of research...' he gave a rueful smile '...but the inner me is impatient. I wish I had a magic wand and could just know everything now. I sometimes want to jump a hundred years into the future so I don't need to wait to find out what improvements we can make, and what difference all the research does.'

She swallowed the lump in her throat. She understood, but she didn't feel quite ready to share why. 'But you have a really good reason to think like that.' She was glancing at the mop of blond curls at the other side of the table. 'If Rory were mine, I'd think like that too.'

She turned to face him. 'You want to make the difference now. For Rory. For the patients.' Her voice dropped a little. 'For people like Mindy.'

He ran his fingers through his hair. 'I think about that a lot. If Mindy's condition hadn't been so severe she would still be here. Rory would still have his mom.' He looked off into the distance and his voice cracked a little. 'Maybe I wouldn't even have met my son.'

He put his hands back on the table and she could see the tiny shake. That was all it took. She gently rested her hand over his and gave it a little squeeze.

He turned to her with pain in his eyes. 'What if things had been different?'

There was a whole world of possibilities there. If

Mindy had lived. If Rory hadn't been affected by the gene. If only...

His other hand reached over and stroked along her arm. It was clear it was an automatic response for him, his mind looked a million miles away.

Her heart was thudding in her chest nearly as loudly as the sound in her ears. Her skin was on fire. It was almost as if her insides were twisting around. She knew she had to ask a question, even if it wasn't the right thing to do.

'What would you have done—if you'd known Mindy was pregnant?'

She could almost see the tiny hairs on his arms stand on end. A pained expression crossed his face. He shook his head and ran his fingers through his hair. 'How can I answer that? It's impossible.' He shook his head again. 'And how do I answer—as a parent or a physician?'

'You're both, Gene. Answer as you.'

His lips pressed together tightly and he put his hand on his heart. 'No. I can't. I just can't. Maybe if you'd asked me before...maybe if I'd known Mindy had hypertrophic cardiomyopathy. Would I really have asked a woman I'd only known briefly to put her life at risk to have my child?'

She could see the pain on his face. A deep frown creased his forehead. 'What kind of egotistical maniac would I be to do that?'

She understood. She understood what he was saying. As a physician, if he was presented with a patient with Mindy's condition who was newly pregnant, he would have to consider a very serious conversation with her.

He let out a long sigh. 'Everything's different now. Rory is real. He's here. He's not a maybe. He's just my whole life. I can't imagine for a second not being his

father.' He closed his eyes for a second. 'I'd met someone. By the time I found out about Rory I was actually
living with someone.'

Something rushed through her. 'Who?'

He shrugged. 'Karen. She was…nice. But when she
found out about Rory…' He shook his head. 'And that
was before she even knew that he had the heart condition.'

'She left?' It was odd. Tears sprang to her eyes. He'd
had someone who'd left. Just like she'd had. She and
Gene were more similar than she'd ever admit to.

Gene nodded. 'Yeah, she left.' He gave a wry smile.
'I can't admit it didn't sting. But do I really blame her?
We'd only known each other less than a year, and all
of a sudden an unknown kid appeared out of nowhere.
It wasn't fair. I know that. But at the time it didn't just
feel like a rejection of me. It felt like a rejection of the
kid I didn't even know yet.'

Cordelia nodded slowly. She was still watching
Rory. The odd little flare of jealousy she'd felt there
had quickly subsided and she was struggling to understand it. But she could understand the rest. The feeling
of rejection. The hurt.

She shook her head too. 'But look what you've got,
Gene. Isn't he worth a million broken hearts?'

Gene caught her eye and smiled. It made her catch
her breath. A connection. An understanding. 'You're
right. I put Karen behind me a long time ago. I had
too much to think about. Too much to learn and too
much to do.' He sighed. 'I'm still on that learning curve
every day.'

She smiled again. 'Doesn't every parent feel the
same?'

He gave a thoughtful nod. 'I guess they do. But,

then, there's the rest of it. His condition. His future.' There was the tiniest crack in his voice. 'And I struggle enough trying to think about the things I can't control with his condition.' He took a deep breath and met her gaze. 'So the sad truth about me is that now, if you asked me if I would have told Mindy to put her own health first, the honest and selfish answer is, no. I wouldn't. Because I wouldn't want to miss out on the joy that is my son.'

She could feel herself holding her breath as he continued to speak.

He looked away from her. 'Does that make me a bad person? Does that make me a bad doctor? Because it feels like it does. I guess the real answer is that I'm glad I didn't have to find out. Rory is the light of my life. I can't imagine what life would be like if he wasn't in it. The fact that I know he will have the same condition as his mom makes me appreciate every second that I have. It makes me work harder because I know that I could lose him—and that terrifies me more than anything. If only life could be simpler. If only there could be a magic cure.' He sighed. 'If only our genes didn't define us.'

A chill swept through her body. She understood better than he would ever know. Maybe she should tell him? But then what? That would be like revealing a part of herself she wasn't quite ready to share. She'd only known them a few weeks. She didn't want his pity or his sympathy—even though she understood his feelings of rejection. The responsible part of her felt that, as a fellow medic, she should tell him, just in case she should ever feel ill at work again. But the emotional part of her just couldn't do that. She didn't want him to think of her as a patient. Her brain spun around. How did she want him to think of her?

She was so confused right now. As for how she felt about Rory?

He was the best kid she'd ever met. She reached over and grabbed Gene's hand.

'I know you don't think it, but I understand better than you can imagine. Rory is fabulous and you're a brilliant father. Don't doubt that for second. You've done a brilliant job. Anyone can see that.'

His chocolate-brown eyes met hers. Their gazes meshed. She didn't want to look away—not for a second. The world was moving around about them, but right now she could swear they were the only two people on the planet. If only she could capture this moment in time. Her heart squeezed in her chest.

The way he was looking at her made her skin tingle. It made her heart miss a beat. The corners of his lips edged upwards. His voice was a husky whisper. 'I'm glad we met, Cordelia Greenway.'

He leaned forward and pressed his forehead against hers. She could feel his warm breath dancing across her skin. Smell the hint of beer on his breath, mixed with the tang of aftershave.

His fingers intertwined with hers.

And he left them there.

So much was spinning through her head right now.

But she said the thing that was in her heart. 'I'm glad we met too, Gene Du Bois.'

He had no idea. No idea how much that made her insides twist around.

With hope.

With regret.

With affection.

And with the wish he was staying a whole lot longer.

CHAPTER SIX

GENE LOOKED AT the results in front of him. His heart sank into his shoes. No. Please, no.

A new collection of patients were being screened for their suitability to take part in the next trial. He'd met all of them over the last few days, all at varying stages of disease with their cardiomyopathy. All patients required extensive workouts, medical history and a whole array of tests before they could be accepted on the trials.

Lea Keller was a Swiss national in her twenties. She'd been lucky. She'd played professional sports and her condition had been picked up in her teenage years.

But staring at the test results meant that Gene was going to have the difficult conversation he'd spoken with Cordelia about just the other day.

He gestured to Marie. 'Can you call Lea Keller in, please?'

Marie took only a few seconds to pick up on the expression on his face. 'No problem, Dr Du Bois. I'll get her straight away.'

Lea appeared in his office a few minutes later. She gave Gene a wide smile. Cardiac patients were generally very smart. 'Don't tell me, I'm anaemic again?'

Gene kept his face impassive. Anaemia would be easy to deal with—this was not.

'Take a seat.' He gestured to the seat opposite him.

He could see the flicker across Lea's face. She perched on the edge of the seat, her hands clasped nervously on her lap.

He sat opposite her and put his hands on the desk. 'Lea, I have some test results we need to discuss.'

'What is it? Heart failure? Thickening?'

He shook his head. 'No, no. It's something quite different.'

Every female of child-bearing age who was a potential candidate for the research study had a whole battery of tests completed—including a pregnancy test. These were new medications, and even though they had been thoroughly researched, there were very strict rules about suitability of patients. No research study wanted to expose a growing foetus to a new type of untrialled medicine. The risks were just too high. Gene took a deep breath and kept his voice steady. 'You're pregnant.'

'I'm what?' Her voice sounded small. Almost squeaky.

For most women this would be one of the greatest moments in their life. But for Lea this had so many more repercussions.

'You're pregnant.' He said it again, keeping his voice as steady as he could. 'Obviously I'm not your normal cardiac physician, neither am I an obstetrician, and the best advice I can give you right now is that you need to speak to both.'

'I'm pregnant.' She said the words out loud again as if she was trying them for size.

Gene stood up and walked around the desk, leaning against the other side and putting his hand on her shoulder. He gave her the best supportive smile he could.

He had no idea what was spinning around in her head right now.

She looked up with pale golden eyes. 'How pregnant am I?'

Gene spoke calmly. 'I can't tell you for sure. Like I said, I'm not the expert in this, but the test results indicate around six weeks.'

She sucked in a shaky breath and he watched as a tear snaked down her cheek. She shook her head. 'I had no idea. I'm on the injection. I don't have periods. I didn't think I would get pregnant. I am always so careful—' her voice shook '—because I know the risks. I know what this can mean.'

Her hand went automatically to her stomach. 'How can I be pregnant and not even know it?'

He spoke carefully. 'Lea, you'll understand that some women don't get diagnosed with hypertrophic cardiomyopathy until they're pregnant—it doesn't get picked up until then.'

She raised her eyebrows. 'But that's not me. And I already have symptoms, I already have disease progression.' *Just like Mindy had.*

The words were instantly in his head. But he couldn't say them out loud. They wouldn't be useful right now. 'That's why you need to get some better advice. We've just done a whole range of tests on you that we are happy to share with your cardiac physician and your obstetrician.'

He hated the fact that he almost knew what they might say. Some women with hypertrophic cardiomyopathy could tolerate pregnancy. But Lea had some severe symptoms—it was why she was being considered for the research study. The blood flow through the left ventricle of her heart was extremely restricted. Could her heart really cope with the extra work that a pregnancy would entail?

That, on top of the life-threatening arrhythmias that could occur during pregnancy, would make the advice she was given at this stage crucial.

A tear slid down her face and Gene knelt in front of her. His own heart was squeezing in his chest. Right now he felt like the worst person in the world to be dealing with this. He had so much personal bias. He'd always known that through the course of his research he would likely come across patients who were pregnant with hypertrophic cardiomyopathy. He'd intentionally steered away from the studies where it seemed most likely. Not because he felt awkward but more because he wanted to always try and remain impartial, to ensure the validity of any research.

And right now? He felt anything but impartial, and that was wrong.

He reached over and put his hand over Lea's. 'I'm sorry that I had to tell you like this. And I know that for most people news of pregnancy can be a celebration. But I understand what this means for you, and I understand how much you need some advice and support right now.'

Lea stood up. It was almost as if she'd switched onto autopilot. She glanced at the notes on his desk. 'My file, can I take it for my physician?'

He nodded and picked it up. Within the institute they stored most things electronically. He'd only asked for Lea's results to be printed because he thought she might ask for the information. He followed her to the door. 'Please, ask them to get in touch. Or, if you need any help, phone us. We're happy to be of assistance.' Even he could hear the edge of desperation in his voice.

Her pale face turned towards him. 'I guess it goes without saying I'm not a candidate for the study now?'

He gave a wry shake of his head. 'I'm sorry, but no. Pregnancy excludes you from the study. We wouldn't want to risk giving you any new drugs when we have no idea what effect they could have on a growing foetus.'

She met his gaze for just a second. 'If—'

His heart almost stopped for fear of what she might say. But as soon as she started she stopped again, before she turned away and walked down the corridor.

Cordelia was walking down the corridor towards them, her bright green dress swinging as she walked. She gave a bright smile to Lea as she passed then moved swiftly over to Gene. 'I was just coming to find you—' Her words stopped abruptly as she followed his gaze to Lea's retreating figure.

'What? What's wrong?'

He shook his head and walked backwards through the door to his office again, hardly able to take his eyes from Lea's back.

Cordelia followed him. 'Gene? What is it?'

The door swung shut behind them and he leaned forward, running his hands through his hair in exasperation. 'I feel like I just let her down.'

'Who?' Cordelia glanced back over her shoulder, but at this point the only view was of the door. 'The patient?'

He nodded. 'Lea Keller. I just finished her screening for the research study.'

Cordelia's brow crinkled. 'Is something wrong? How could you let her down?'

The words were stuck somewhere in the back of his throat. He hated feeling like this. He really did. All he could think about was what might happen to Lea.

'She's pregnant.'

'Oh.' Cordelia's response came out suddenly. Quickly followed by another 'Ohh…' as she started to understand. She sucked in a deep breath. 'She's like Mindy, isn't she? Hypertrophic cardiomyopathy.'

'Hypertrophic cardiomyopathy.' Gene repeated the words. He even hated the way they sounded right now, even though he'd used the term repeatedly throughout his career, and even more so in the last four years.

'And she didn't know she was pregnant?'

Gene shook his head. 'She was on the contraceptive injection every three months. She didn't have periods and she's had no pregnancy symptoms.'

Cordelia leaned against the wall next to him. Her expression was a little glazed. 'Poor woman.' She frowned and looked at him. 'What did you tell her? '

He shook his head. 'I told her she needed to get some advice from her cardiac physician and an obstetrician. I gave her the test results and told her we were happy to help. Then I had to tell her she'd be excluded from our study.'

'But of course she will be. We can't give a pregnant woman untrialled medicines.'

He closed his eyes for a second as Lea's face flashed before him. 'She'd been quite symptomatic before. She was so keen to be part of this trial. She was hoping the new drugs would help her symptoms and improve her cardiac output.' He put one hand up to his face. 'She looked at me for just a second—and I wondered if she was going to say…'

He didn't say the words out loud, he just let them tail off.

Cordelia put her hand over his. 'You wondered if she was going to suggest she didn't continue with the pregnancy? You wondered if she was going to ask if she could still be part of the trial.'

He hated that she'd said those words out loud. He hated how they made him feel.

'What kind of doctor am I that I couldn't have that kind of conversation with her? That I couldn't allow her to think for herself, and make a decision that was right for her? It's her choice. Her decision. I know that. So why didn't I reinforce that?'

Cordelia intertwined her fingers with his and gently pulled his hand down. She stepped forward and rested her forehead against his. It was the closest they'd ever been. She spoke softly. 'Because it's not the conversation for you to have. That's for her cardiac physician—or her obstetrician. We're just the research institute, Gene. We're the temporary caregivers. For some patients we offer temporary solutions—like a sticking plaster. For others, we don't give them any benefit at all. The drugs don't work. Or they get a placebo.'

His other hand lifted up gently and rested at the back of her neck as she continued to talk.

'This isn't our conversation to have. We can't influence things like that. And you didn't. You told her to seek advice. That's exactly what you should have done.'

His voice was hoarse. 'But maybe I wasn't supportive enough. Maybe I should have been more in tune to what I felt she wanted to say. But my head was just full of Rory—and what my life would be like if Mindy had made that decision. If she'd decided not to have him—and I'd never even known about his existence. When Lea paused for a second and looked at me, that was all I could think about.'

'Stop it.' Her words were so quiet they were barely a whisper. Her warm rose-tinted scent filled his senses.

'Don't second-guess yourself. Don't put thoughts into her head that might not have been there at all. You don't know what she was thinking. And of course that might have flooded her mind for the briefest of seconds. You might be a good doctor...' her mouth curled up in a smile '...but you don't have mind-reading skills.

'She might have been wondering what to say to her partner. She might have been wondering how soon she could get an appointment to have a discussion with her cardiologist. That tiny glimmer of a second that you *thought* you saw?' Her fingers brushed against his cheek as his gaze met hers. 'It could have been nothing. It could have been nothing at all.'

She blinked and her dark eyelashes brushed against his cheek. They were *that* close, his lips less than an inch from hers. And he didn't want to move. Not for a second.

All of a sudden those glints of attraction were rolling into a giant ball that was threatening to knock him off his feet. Those cute baseball boots. The conversation with Rory on her bed. The swing of her dress. The way she sometimes bit her bottom lip as she pondered what to say next. Or even the way her dark hair had partly covered her eyes on the beach the other day.

He froze.

The touch of her fingertips was like an electric current on his skin. Those green eyes were pulling him in.

She hadn't moved an inch. For a woman who'd at first been a little uneasy around him, he couldn't help but admire how comfortable Cordelia was in her own skin. She could have stepped back. But she hadn't. She'd moved closer and reached out.

He had to believe that she felt the same spark of attraction that he did.

He didn't want to think about it any more. Didn't want to analyse it. He didn't want to think ahead.

She was looking straight at him. He murmured gently, 'Someone once told me that research has proved that if you take just a little of what you crave, it makes management much easier.'

Her lips curled into a smile. 'I wonder who that could have been,' she breathed. 'I think I might agree with them.'

He didn't hesitate for another moment, just leaned down and captured her lips with his.

For a second he held his breath, waiting to see if she would object. But she didn't. He could almost sense her smiling again as they kissed, her lips matching his. The rose scent surrounded him as his hand slid up from the back of her neck and through her silky tresses. Her hand stayed on his cheek as they kissed, her touch light as her other hand lay on his chest.

She tasted of strawberries and sunshine. He pulled her closer and her warm curves pressed against the hard planes of his body. They were at work. Anyone could open the office door at any moment. He was just a visiting researcher. This job was Cordelia's life.

She let out a little sigh and it was almost his undoing. He wanted nothing more than to walk her backwards to the desk behind them and push her on to it.

But Cordelia would never be that kind of girl. And he wasn't really that kind of guy. As other parts of his body started to respond he took a deep breath and pulled back. He couldn't help the smile that plastered its way across his face. His breathing was hard. Her hands rested on his shoulders.

'Wow,' came the quiet voice.

'Wow,' he echoed.

* * *

For a second they just stood there, then a nervous kind of laugh bubbled up inside her, and she made herself step back out of his embrace, her breathing a little stuttered.

He raised his hand, but she shook her head. 'Don't. Don't say anything. We both know that you're only here for a month, and that Rory has to be your priority.'

Confusion swept over his face. 'But—'

It was the oddest feeling. She spent her life trying so much to achieve control. In her work life. In her personal life. And in all other aspects.

The arrhythmias were the only thing she'd partly accepted as not being within her control—but that didn't stop her trying her absolute best to keep a handle on things. She hated that it might affect her work. She'd prefer people at work didn't know about it. Didn't need sympathetic glances. And she really didn't want her fellow professionals constantly asking her about living with the condition.

Her reasons for her research were her own.

So this didn't help. This wave of emotions threatening to overcome her made her want to run a mile.

How could one kiss do this to her? Or was it one kiss, and the near miss the other day?

Or was it everything? Living under the same roof as Gene and Rory. Watching the relationship between father and son. Or was it being exposed to such a gorgeous, sweet-natured, fun-loving child? Realising that she would never have that relationship with a child. She'd never have that gift.

Or was it all just pure Gene—pure cowboy? Taking one look at a sexy Texan with the form-fitting jeans, broad chest and come-to-bed eyes?

She started. Where had that thought come from? Heat rushed into her cheeks.

Gene touched her hand and she flinched, then almost cringed.

She couldn't pretend not to see the flicker of hurt on his face. 'Maybe I should go,' he said throatily. 'I guess I read things wrong. I'm sorry if I did.'

The lump in her throat was the size of a tennis ball. But she couldn't let him walk out here like that.

They were still living under the same roof. She still had to see him every day at work.

'You didn't.' She held up her hands, not quite sure of was the right thing to say. The last thing Gene needed was her whole heap of rambling thoughts.

Her feet seemed rooted to the spot. The words bumbled around in her head. This was where she should say something really smart. But her brain refused.

He'd moved closer to the door, the hurt look still on his face.

She struggled to find the words.

'You didn't,' she repeated, then held out her arms. 'It's just…it's here. It's work. I just don't feel comfortable doing this at work.'

He blinked. Then hesitated, then nodded. 'Of course.'

But he didn't smile. He opened the door. 'We can talk later.'

He nodded and walked out.

Awkwardness and relief hit her at once.

She'd just experienced the best kiss in her lifetime.

With the sexiest guy she'd ever met.

She should be shouting from the rooftops.

But all she could think about was how this didn't feel right. *She* didn't feel right. She didn't want to start something that had the potential to be wonderful.

Not when she was keeping secrets.

Not when her heart felt so at risk.

Control was rapidly slipping through her fingers—a sensation she wasn't familiar with.

But, if that kiss was anything to go by, the one thing she truly knew was that by the time she reached home tonight all bets were off.

CHAPTER SEVEN

THE CALL CAME at seven p.m., just as he was about to leave work and pick up Rory from an outing with the institute nursery. He frowned at the phone number, thinking the last few digits were familiar. But this was an international call. Who would be looking for him?

'Gene Du Bois?'

'Gene? It's Franc. Franc Helier.'

'Professor Helier?' It was odd. But Gene naturally defaulted into Franc's professional title. Although they'd spoken on many occasions before he'd got the job, he'd never actually had the pleasure of meeting Franc. And Gene had been brought up strictly—he couldn't quite bring himself to call the professor by his first name.

'Yes, yes, it's me.'

'How are you? How are things with your sister? I was sorry to hear that she was unwell.'

There was silence for a second. Then a small sniff. Gene cringed. Maybe it would have been better not to say anything, but it seemed rude not to acknowledge Professor Helier's family issues.

'Yes, yes...well, not really. Things aren't particularly good. I'm going to have to stay a bit longer—maybe a lot longer.' There was a deep sigh. 'In fact, I have no idea at all how long I need to stay. It could be days, it could be months. All I know is I have to be here.'

He could hear the stress and strain in Franc's voice. 'Of course, Professor, of course you have to stay. What can I do to help?'

His offer came out automatically—just the way his mother would have expected.

'Actually... I know it's a terrible imposition. And I know you have family commitments. And I know your contract is only for a month, but—'

Gene cut in. 'But you want to know if I'll stay.'

He could hear the whoosh of relief. 'Yes,' said Professor Helier quickly. 'Would you be able to?'

Normally, when faced with a decision like this, Gene would think carefully, consider all the options, and take into account all his plans—for himself and for Rory. But for the first time in his life he really didn't need to think for long—it only took a few seconds.

'I will. The truth is I love the research I'm doing here. I think there's a real chance of making a difference for patients with cardiomyopathy. I'd love to stay here for longer and continue with the studies.'

'You would? Really?' The excitement and relief was clear in the professor's voice.

'I would,' said Gene with a nod of his head. He meant it. He really did. Rory seemed happy. He liked the institute. He liked the work. He liked the people. Probably one in particular...

He gave himself a shake. 'What about Cordelia? Have you discussed this with her?'

The professor gave a little cough. 'I'm just about to. But I wanted to ask you first if you would consider staying. If you'd said it was impossible, then I would have had to ask Cordelia to advertise for a replacement. I'm so glad I don't have to do that.'

Gene gave another nod of his head. 'You don't. I had tentatively accepted an offer to work elsewhere. But that can be changed. I don't have any commitments back at home for a few months, when Rory is due to start at school.'

'So there could be more flexibility if needed?' Professor Helier's voice was a little high-pitched.

Gene took a deep breath. He wasn't quite ready to set down roots, but he could only imagine the stress Professor Helier was under. His sister was clearly very sick and couldn't be left. So Gene did what his mother would expect him to do. 'There can be. Let's talk again in another month.'

'Thank you, Dr Du Bois. I can't thank you enough for this. I'll phone Cordelia now and let her know the change in arrangements.'

Gene's heart gave a little lift in his chest as he finished the call.

It really was odd. Normally, something like this would have made him consider all his options, look at all things carefully. He didn't usually ever make snap decisions like this. Today he hadn't had to do that at all. Not for a second.

Something was changing. And he had a sneaking suspicion he knew why.

By the time Gene had manoeuvred Rory into his pyjamas and into his own bed the small boy had woken up again.

Rory had been exhausted after the outing with the nursery and had fallen asleep in the car on the journey home. Gene had been glad of the quiet to contemplate what he'd just done—and the effect it might have.

The buzz between him and Cordelia was so intense he could swear he could almost see the electricity in the air. There was no denying it—just looking at her made him smile, then within a few seconds look away again because his mind was filled with a wave of attraction so strong he might want to act on it.

All he could think about was that kiss today. Things had been left a little awkward, with that whole aspect of what might come next.

And he couldn't wait to find out what that might be.

By the time he'd walked out the shower, Rory had wandered through to Gene's room, rubbing his sleepy eyes.

Gene quickly dried himself with a towel then picked Rory up and sat up on the bed with him. He felt a pang of frustration. And it made him angry with himself.

Angry for being a normal human male and realising whatever he might have hoped for in the next hour or so had probably just been curtailed.

He'd kept Rory so separate from his love life that he'd never had to think like this before. On the rare occasions he'd dated, he'd always had safe and reliable arrangements in place for Rory. His father loved having his grandson and showing the little guy around the ranch. And he'd also encouraged Gene to get out there and find someone. 'You can't stop living. Yes, you can be a great dad and prioritise your son. But that doesn't stop you having relationships.' He'd even winked at Gene. 'I'd actually prefer it if you did, means I get to see more of my grandson.'

But there were only a few people Gene would trust with his son. His dad, or his brother and his wife, and one of his mother's best friends in Paris. It wasn't easy to plan dates around Paris and Texas, so this was the first time he'd actually been put in a position where he wanted to actually meet someone and spend some alone time with them, but couldn't do it.

He hated feeling like that. He really did.

'Dad?'

At this point Rory was huddled underneath his arm. 'What is it?'

'At nursery, Pim got a new mom.'

The hairs on his body bristled. Where on earth had this come from?

'You found this out today?'

'No, yesterday,' came the far-off little voice.

Gene swallowed. Had this been preying on his son's mind?

'What do you mean—Pim got a new mom?'

'Pim's mom went away. But now he's getting a new one. He doesn't like her. She smells funny.'

Gene's stifled his automatic reaction to the kid's words. From the mouths of babes. Rory twisted under his arm and looked up with his sleepy dark eyes. His voice was quiet. 'If I get a new mom, can I pick her?'

Gene's heart squeezed in his chest. 'Of course you can pick her. A new mom is a big deal. It's really always just been the two of us. We'd have to think long and hard before we decided if we wanted a girl to join us.' He knew he probably shouldn't make light of this conversation, but how did you have this kind of conversation with a kid this age?

He'd always told himself he would be as open and honest with Rory as possible. He wanted to think that in future years Rory would feel as if he could talk to him about anything. But the truth was, it was harder than he'd ever figured.

He squeezed Rory under his arm as the little head lay down on his belly. 'We're a team, sport, we're in this together—a package deal.'

'Good,' murmured Rory, ''cause I pick Delia.'

Gene froze, his stomach tensing. Had he just heard correctly?

Goosebumps appeared on his skin. It was like a million little caterpillars stomping all over his chest.

Almost instantly Rory was semi-snoring.

His breath had hitched itself somewhere inside his chest. He blew it out in one long slow moment.

He'd been so wound up about himself, about his attraction to Cordelia that he'd failed to notice something with his son. Rory was growing attached. He'd never really had a mother figure around him. Was he starting to imagine Cordelia in that role? Because this wasn't exactly where Gene's brain had been.

He tried to put himself in his four-year-old's mind. Another kid had just said he was getting a new mom and didn't like her. That was a big deal. Huge. So Rory had thought about the first female he'd actually formed a sort of relationship with—and liked. Cordelia. Was that really such a big deal?

He was blowing this out of proportion. He was taking a four-year-old's glimmer of appreciation, along with the child's simplistic view of picking a new mom. He needed to stop and think sensibly.

This wasn't really about Rory. This was about his unexpected attraction to Cordelia.

This was ridiculous. He was a grown man. True, he was experiencing his first real attraction in a long time. True, this wasn't ideal circumstances or timing.

He ruffled Rory's hair. His son would always be number one. His priority.

But did that mean he had to ignore everything else? He was in charge of his own destiny. The attraction was mutual. He wasn't dumb. And he wanted to act on it. *Really* wanted to act on it.

He took another breath and slid Rory gently to the side, arranging the covers around him.

He kissed him on the forehead and pulled on some clothes. 'Wish me luck,' he whispered as he headed for the door.

Cordelia found herself pacing around the kitchen. She'd showered, washed her hair, then hovered around her doorway, wondering what to do next.

That kiss four hours ago had put her on edge. What next? Was Gene having the same thoughts she was?

He couldn't be. If he was, he'd have turned up at her door.

She flicked the switch on the kettle, changed her mind and pulled out a wine glass instead. Her fingers slipped on the wine bottle as she tried to push in the corkscrew. 'Darn it,' she murmured. A few seconds later a pair of hands covered hers, and she felt a warm body behind hers. She shivered.

'Let me help you with that,' said the husky voice.

It was like music to her ears.

His hands were deft, bare arms next to hers as he popped the cork from the wine, then let a hand slide around her waist as he moved to the side.

'So, are we having wine?' he asked as she pulled another glass from the cupboard.

She licked her bottom lip as she turned to face him. She could almost hear her heartbeat thudding in her ears. 'I wasn't sure if you'd join me.' The words were simple. But it was the boldest thing she could say.

He lifted the bottle and poured the wine achingly slowly into both glasses, before lifting his towards her. 'I guess I wondered if I should.'

Her stomach knotted tightly. But he continued, 'I've never really taken things further when Rory is around. He's never met anyone that I've dated.'

'We're dating?' She picked up the glass and took a sip before smiling at him. It was ridiculous. She was standing in her satin nightdress, short nightgown, and very bare legs. She felt a flutter in her chest. No way. Not now. Not here.

But after a second she realised it was nothing.

She almost laughed out loud. She was normal. Her heart was just skipping a few beats—the way it did for the whole world over when they were swamped with hormones and adrenaline.

He gave her a sexy kind of smile. 'I think we could almost call today our first date.'

'Is office kisses the kind of date you normally go on with women?'

His brow wrinkled as his fingers spread out a little at her waist. If she didn't know better, she'd think he was going to pull her closer.

He gave a soft laugh and met her gaze. The look he gave her almost took her breath away. Open, sincere and sexy as hell.

'Okay. Let's call the day out together our first date then. I think I've just started a new form of dating. No one I've dated has met Rory before. I like to keep those two parts of my life separate.'

She moved forward, letting her body press against his. She tilted her head to one side. 'And now?'

He nodded slowly and set his wine glass down, running the fingers of one hand through her hair. 'I guess it's time to try something new.'

She licked her lips again. 'I hear that you're staying.'

A smile danced around his lips. 'I might have been persuaded to stay.'

She raised her eyebrows. 'Persuaded? By what?'

He raised his eyebrows too. 'Maybe it's not a what. Maybe…it's a who.'

Now he pulled her towards him, the hard planes of his chest against her soft breasts, his lips at her neck as he whispered in her ear, 'Now, this something new. Want to try it with me?'

She set down her glass before it fell over and let her head tip back, exposing her neck to his lips. He didn't need any more of an invitation.

If the kiss in the office had been passionate, this one was different. This one was slow, taunting and teasing her, his lips almost tickling her skin, making her arch towards him and beg for more.

Her arms closed around his shoulders, tightening their grip on him. 'I guess we all should learn something new,' she whispered, her voice barely able to form the words. 'Didn't I tell you before? Every day is a new day, with a world of possibilities,' she breathed.

He laughed. 'I like the sound of that.' He bent down and swept her up in his arms. 'My room is taken.' He grinned cheekily at her. 'Looks like it'll have to be yours.'

She couldn't stop the smile. 'What are you waiting for?' she urged as the kitchen disappeared behind them.

CHAPTER EIGHT

THE NEXT FEW weeks passed in a blur. Cordelia had never really been quite so happy. The research was going well. They were moving closer and closer to being able to replicate the abilities of the zebrafish. Everything at the institute seemed to be running smoothly.

And everything at home seemed to be better than she could have possibly hoped for. The truth was, her apartment had now been fixed and she could move back anytime she wanted.

But she didn't want to.

She was enjoying staying at Professor Helier's house with Gene and Rory. They'd fallen into some kind of easy routine. She knew it wasn't permanent but that didn't seem to matter too much.

All that mattered was, for the first time in for ever, she actually felt happy. She was getting to enjoy the experience of developing a relationship with the sexiest guy she'd ever met, and the cutest little boy.

Every day that she sat at the table, buttering toast for Rory and drinking coffee with Gene, made her happy, and a tiny bit sad.

Professor Helier's sister was deteriorating little by little. No one knew when she would die—only that at some point it would be inevitable.

And at that point he would return to the institute and
Gene and Rory would leave. That made her insides twist
in a way she didn't like.

Gene appeared in the doorway at her office just as
she was trying to contemplate how quiet things would
be for her once they had gone. 'Are you ready?'

She smiled but frowned. 'Ready for what?'

He shook his head, folded his arms and leaned on
the doorjamb. 'Marie and I actually had a bet that you
might forget.'

She stood up quickly. If he'd been talking to Marie
it must be something about work. She started riffling
through some of the papers on her desk.

'Watch out,' came the playful voice. 'You're in danger of turning into Professor Helier with a desk like
that.'

She looked down and laughed. 'You're right. But
I'll have you know that *his* desk and office is immacu-
late. I've tidied it up but...' she blew some hair from
her face '...transferred the stuff I've still to deal with
to my desk.'

Gene walked towards her. 'Anything interesting?'

She bit her lip for a second, wondering how much to
say. 'Well...yes.' She picked up two folders, one green,
one blue. 'There are two really interesting research pro-
posals for next year.'

Gene was instantly interested. 'What are they?'

She had a pang of regret. Chances were he was hoping it was another cardiomyopathy research trial. It was
likely there would be one, but neither of these fitted the
bill. She didn't have anything in her hand that might
persuade him to stay.

She spoke quickly. 'One is around Marfan syndrome and the impact on the aorta and heart, and one

is around Wolff-Parkinson-White syndrome, heart re-generation and renewal pathways.' The pang plucked even deeper. Franc hadn't discussed this with her. He knew how much she would want to campaign for this study—even if she wasn't directly overseeing it.

'Those sound great, really interesting. What stage are they at?'

He bent over to take one of the files from her hand. He had no idea which would be which, so she was relieved when he took the blue file and started flicking through it. He read for a few moments then looked up, nodding thoughtfully, 'I can see where Franc's made notes about the research study, the ethics and practicalities.' He wrinkled his brow. 'He couldn't have had a chance to send his notes back.'

He tucked the blue folder containing the proposal regarding Marfan's syndrome under his arm. 'Tell you what, why don't you let me send Franc's notes back to the proposer for this study, and you do it for the other one. It will probably take them a few weeks to gather all the extra details needed.' He gave a broad smile. 'Let's not leave them hanging.'

She nodded quickly. 'Sure, why not? That seems fair.'

He was still smiling at her.

'What?' she asked.

'You have forgotten, haven't you?'

He walked around the desk towards her and slid an arm around her waist.

'Is this work-related?'

He shook his head. 'Look at your watch.'

She glanced down and looked at her watch. 'What?'

He sighed. 'I'm beginning to think you're playing hard to get.'

She slid her arms around his neck and kissed him.

'Me? Hard to get with you? I think we can safely say that's not happening.'

He glanced down at her baseball boots. 'Cordelia Greenway, we might get into the cinema with those boots, but if you want to go to that fancy restaurant, we might be in trouble.'

The penny dropped. 'Of course!' Her hand flew up to her mouth. 'That's today?'

Because Gene was reluctant to leave Rory with anyone he didn't really know, they'd both agreed to have a day date instead of an evening one. That way Rory could stay in the institute nursery with staff that he knew and they could catch a movie and have an early dinner together. It was unusual. Most of the time they'd been together, Rory had been included in all their plans, but Gene seemed to be keen they have a little adult time too—and not just in the bedroom.

She cringed. 'Sorry, I've spent all day thinking this was Tuesday.'

He was still smiling, his hands on both her hips. 'Nope, it's Wednesday all day today.' He whispered in her ear, 'Get your coat, you've pulled.'

She burst out laughing. They'd spent the day before talking about bad pick-up lines. 'Okay.' She looked down at her red baseball boots. 'I have a pair of heels under my desk. I can take them with me for our early dinner.'

Gene proffered his elbow towards her. 'Come on, then, Cordelia. Let's go be grown-ups for a while— because by the time we get home tonight, it will be dinosaur movies all the way.'

She was dedicated to her work. He admired that in her. So he hadn't been the least bit offended that she'd forgotten their date.

Ten minutes later she was ready, heels in her large bag that seemed to hold the entire contents of the world. They walked the picturesque road from the institute hand in hand. For the first few days Cordelia had been a little shy about letting anyone know about their relationship. But she'd gradually relaxed—which was just as well, since it had only taken a few days for the rest of the staff to work it out.

He swore she almost glowed right now. Her steps seemed lighter, her mood brighter, and what made him happiest was how hard she worked to include Rory in everything. Even though she'd been a little awkward around him initially, the hesitancy had left her and she seemed to have almost warmed to her role around Rory.

She'd mentioned she didn't have brothers or sisters, so she had no nieces or nephews. Maybe she just hadn't had much exposure to young kids? Whatever it was, it was gone now. And for that Gene was grateful.

'What's it to be? Are you an action fan? Sci-fi?' She gave a laugh. 'Or what about romance? Everyone loves romance.'

They were approaching the large cinema complex adorned with multiple posters advertising a wide range of movies. Gene stopped in front of the first advertisement. It was a hopeless romance. He turned to Cordelia, 'Okay, so you know that I like you, don't you?'

She rolled her eyes in the cutest possible way. 'Like? Okay, I'm about to go all teenager and stomp off.' There was a real twinkle in her eye.

He let out a mock sigh as he slung his arm around her shoulders and pulled her close. 'Okay, so *more* than like. But no matter how much I more than like you, we're not going to see that movie.'

She laughed as she put her hand on his chest as she

looked up at the poster. She shook her head. 'That's fine.' She pointed to the hero. 'He's not my favourite, anyway.'

Gene raised his eyebrows. 'Just as well.' He kept smiling as they walked along to the next one. An action movie about racing. He shook his head. 'Not much story in this one.'

The next one looked more promising. 'So, Dr Greenway, how do you feel about a little sci-fi?'

Cordelia looked thoughtful. 'An adventure set in space with a kick-ass heroine?' She nodded and held out her hand towards him. 'I think I can be persuaded.'

Three hours later they emerged from the cinema into the still bright afternoon sunshine. Gene's lips were almost numb. He'd spent a good part of the movie kissing the woman in his arms. It was like being a teenager again. Ridiculous.

They headed to the French-style restaurant he'd booked earlier that week and Cordelia leaned on his shoulder as she quickly changed her shoes and straightened her skirt and blouse to make herself look more respectable. She looked up at him with bright eyes. 'How do I look?'

He leaned forward and kissed her red lips. 'Perfect— like always.'

She laughed as he held the door open for her and entered the restaurant.

Although it was early, the lights were dim, setting an ambience that was just right.

They ordered some wine and took the recommendations from the maître d'. The restaurant was quiet and he liked it that way, because it gave them some privacy.

'How are you feeling? You look a little pale.'

She wrinkled her nose. 'Do I? I guess I am a little tired, but nothing else.' She gave a grin. 'Maybe it's the unexpected late nights.'

He nodded. 'Could be. Rory seems to like it here. He's settled really well.'

Cordelia winced a little. 'How will that be when you move on?'

He couldn't help but raise an eyebrow. 'Trying to get rid of us?' He hated the way his stomach gave a flip.

She shook her head. 'Of course not. I like having you here.' She picked up her wine glass. 'Or maybe I just like having Rory.' She laughed. 'He's definitely more obedient.'

The waiter brought over their entrées.

Gene hesitated for a second. He was curious about Cordelia. He still had the impression there were things he didn't really know. For a start, she was one of the smartest, prettiest doctors he'd ever met. He couldn't help but be surprised that some other guy hadn't swept her off her feet.

'I'm glad you and Rory have hit it off,' he said carefully as he picked up his knife and fork. 'It kind of makes me wonder whether you'd ever considered having a family of your own? Would you consider kids in your future?'

It was bold. It was downright nosy. But he was finding himself more drawn to Cordelia every day. He'd accepted the chance to stay here easily. Would he consider staying longer? What if Professor Helier decided to work on both of those new studies next year? He would need assistance—a lead researcher for each. Would it really be such a hardship for him to consider some other form of cardiac research besides cardiomyopathy?

He looked up sharply as Cordelia gave a little cough, as if she'd choked on her chicken entrée. Her face had paled.

'Cordelia, are you okay? Do you need some water?'

She shook her head sharply, hand at her throat as she looked down at her plate. The paleness disappeared quickly as colour rushed into her cheeks.

She waited a few moments before she answered the earlier question. 'I've never really considered having children. It's never been on my radar. I haven't met the right guy and all that,' she added dismissively.

There was a strangeness in her tone. Something decidedly forced. It sent a prickle down his spine.

It was every woman's right to choose if she wanted to have children or not, but somehow her answer wasn't that convincing. 'Children weren't on my radar either, at least not until I knew Rory existed. I guess at some point in the distant future I thought I might have a family. But sometimes life has other plans for us.'

He looked up into her green eyes. She blinked sharply, her eyes glassy.

'Yeah,' she muttered. 'I guess life does that.'

He probably shouldn't pursue it. But every part of his curiosity was spiked. 'So you never met the right guy, huh? No one you ever wanted to engaged to or married to?'

She pulled her shoulders back. 'That's an awfully traditional view. Does a woman have to be engaged or married? Can't she just be happy on her own?' She sounded remarkably defensive—almost as if she'd taken offence at his words.

'Are you happy on your own?'

She bristled. 'I've managed to get through the last thirty-one years on my own. It's amazing how self-sufficient we women can be.'

Gene cringed. This wasn't at all how he'd wanted the conversation to go. He'd been trying to sound Cordelia out about her plans for the future, not to make her instantly annoyed and defensive.

He paused. 'I don't doubt your self-sufficiency, Cordelia. I would never question that.' He hoped his tone was softer than before. 'I just wondered if you had any plans for the future.'

She paused again. He could almost swear she looked as if she had tears in her eyes. How on earth could he cause so much upset by just asking a basic question? Wasn't it normal for people who were dating to have this kind of conversation after a while? He'd kind of hoped that Cordelia might eventually want the same kind of future that he did. She seemed to get on well with Rory. Had he imagined that? Was it so wrong that he might a picture a future he could spend with the woman he loved, his son and maybe another child?

Something twisted inside him. It seemed like everything was going wrong here.

Her expression was pained. 'Of course I have plans for the future. There's new research and—'

'I wasn't talking about work.' He knew he'd cut her off, but she was about to start babbling. She hadn't really done that since they'd first met.

'What exactly were you talking about, then?' she snapped.

His appetite gone, he pushed his plate away and reached across the table and took her hand. 'I was talking about us, Cordelia. I wondered what might happen next.'

He stared at her shocked expression.

'But you'll have to leave. You've said that yourself.'

He nodded. 'I know I have. But if Professor Helier is

taking on new projects, he might be looking for someone to lead one.'

'But neither of the new projects is to do with cardiomyopathy.'

He pulled one hand back and ran it through his hair with a sigh. 'I know I said that I only wanted to look at cardiomyopathy because of Rory. And I suppose I do. But now I guess I'm considering if I want to widen my interests in cardiac research.'

She blinked. 'Because of me? Because of us?'

He took a long, slow breath. What he'd hoped might be a light conversation that might help him sort out the thoughts in his head had turned into almost a declaration of his intentions. Was he ready for this?

Cordelia's reaction hadn't been what he'd expected. Why so defensive? Maybe he was completely misreading the situation.

'Maybe,' he replied. 'I'd always intended to take Rory back to Texas or Paris to start school—mainly because I have people there that I trust with my son. I never really thought about any alternatives.'

She wasn't saying anything. She wasn't giving him any reason to think he should stay.

Her voice came out in a squeak. 'And now you are?'

Frustration was building in him. The waiter appeared and removed their plates, his mouth twisting once he saw how little they'd eaten.

Gene leaned back in his chair. The words *I was* ran through his brain. But he could hardly say that out loud now.

'I guess I just wanted to know if you had plans for the future.' He waved his hand. 'For all I know, you might have decided you wanted to leave the institute and work someplace else. You might have decided you don't want to be a researcher any more and have plans to move to the jungle in Borneo and study plant life.' He knew how ridiculous this sounded, but it wasn't just about him, it was about Rory too, so he had to put it out there.

He sighed and looked at her. There seemed to be an air of panic about her. He hadn't expected that—not after how well things had been going between them. 'I don't want to uproot my life and my son if you can't see any plans with us in them.'

It was the most exposed Gene had felt since Mindy had died. Since Karen had walked out.

It was out there. He'd said it. He'd put his cards on the table. The waiter reappeared and put down their main courses, fussing around them until Gene almost snapped.

Cordelia still hadn't spoken.

When she did, her voice wavered. 'Well, I've no plans to go to Borneo—or anyplace else for that matter. I've always thought about my future being here at the institute. When I got here, it just felt like home.' Her fingers twiddled nervously with a bit of hair. 'I've had a few other tentative job offers, but I've never even considered them.'

She wasn't meeting his gaze. She was looking everywhere but at him.

'This was a bad idea. I shouldn't have said anything.' What he really wanted to do was push his chair back, stand up and leave. The light, airy restaurant was suddenly feeling claustrophobic.

Her voice was quiet. 'No. You should have.' She gave a half-smile. It was first time he felt as if her barriers fell a little. 'I guess I just wasn't quite prepared for it.'

A wave of sadness washed over him. He felt like some high school guy who'd just asked out the popular

girl and been turned down. 'Well, if you weren't prepared for it, I think we're both in different places. I'm
sorry if I put you on the spot. I'm sorry if I made you
uncomfortable.'

His insides were curling up and dying.

But Cordelia shook her head quickly. 'No. No. We're
not really in different places. I just... I just hadn't contemplated that you might change your plans. I kind of
thought they would be set in stone. You're so clear about
what you want for Rory. I never hoped or imagined you
might change your mind.'

It was first flicker of hope that she'd given him. Had
he really seemed so single-minded?

She put her hand up to her chest and kept talking. 'Of
course I was delighted when you stayed a little longer.
And I know Franc will come back, but I also know he's
getting older. He needs more help, more support. I think
he'll always want to be Head of the Institute. He loves
the place. It's his life. But if he could have me lead on
one side, and someone else like you lead on the other?
It would be such a weight off him.'

She was babbling. But this time he didn't stop her.
He needed to hear what she had to say.

She looked around, as if checking to see if anyone
was listening to her, as she leaned across the table towards him. 'Gene, I love having you around. I love having Rory around. I haven't been this happy in...well, for
ever.' She gave a sad kind of smile. 'But in my head I
never hoped you'd want to hang around because of me.
I just thought that wanting any more would line me up
for heartache.'

Now he was getting somewhere.

Neither of them had said the other word. The one that
was like an elephant in the room. And Gene wasn't sure

he was ready, even though he couldn't deny his brain and heart were walking down that path.

'You think I could cause you heartache?' His teasing tone lightened the tense mood a little.

She threw down her napkin. 'Phew, I bet you were the regular heartbreak kid in Paris and Texas while you were at school. It's practically written all over your face.'

He almost laughed out loud. 'I might have had a few girlfriends at school.'

Now she shook her head. 'A few!' she mocked. 'You were the kind of guy that girls wrote about on bathroom walls.'

He leaned forward, stretching out his fingers to touch her hand again. 'Have you written about me on any bathroom walls?'

This time their gazes meshed. All he could see were her bright green eyes, clear skin and shiny dark hair. 'Not yet.' She smiled. 'It's a work thing. You know, it's hard trying to resist defacing the walls of the women's bathroom in the institute.'

The waiter hovered around them, looking at their almost full plates disdainfully.

'We're fine,' said Gene quickly. 'Can you give us some more time, please?'

He sucked in a deep breath and lifted up his glass of wine. 'How about we agree to see how things develop. I don't want you to feel as if I'm pushing something. I just wanted to be honest. To put my cards on the table.'

She nodded and lifted her glass to his. 'That sounds good. That sounds…nice.'

He raised his eyebrows. 'Nice?' The possibility of their relationship developing was nice? Should he run for the hills now?

She clinked her glass against his. 'What can I say? Too many people around.'

But the smile she had on her face told him all he really wanted. She looked happy. The tension had left her neck and shoulders. She finally looked as relaxed as she had earlier.

But somewhere inside his stomach gave a little flip.

He'd started the day so positively, and now? He just wasn't sure.

Gene wanted to stay. He wanted to stay because of *her*.

While that made her heart swell in her chest, it also made her feel sick.

She hadn't been honest with him. She hadn't told him about her condition. It wasn't that she'd really meant to hide it. It was just that she was quite a private person. And at first she hadn't been sure how long he would be here, and hadn't wanted him to feel sorry for her.

But now…it was something else. It was a secret. Something she hadn't shared. And she felt slightly dishonest.

He was looking to the future. Would he want to have a relationship with a woman who had a cardiac condition? Particularly one that had ruled out the possibility of children?

Because that's what he'd been asking. He'd been asking her if she'd contemplated having children.

Had she contemplated it? She'd done more than that. She'd ached with loneliness and cried long, hard tears after realising that getting pregnant could put herself and her baby at risk. She'd already had one man leave her because she couldn't have kids. She certainly couldn't take the heartbreak of another. Because this time it was different. She hadn't felt this way about Han.

Their relationship had been sweet. Comfortable. But her heart hadn't skipped in her chest when she'd heard his voice, or felt his touch. Not the way it did with Gene.

As for having children? For a few years she'd been obsessed. The whole world around her had seemed to be expecting a baby. Friends, workmates and old university colleagues all seemed to be simultaneously pregnant.

Accepting what was for the best had been hard. She'd moved into self-protect mode, taking cautious steps away from friends who rapidly had one baby after another, and throwing herself into her work.

She couldn't pretend it hadn't stopped her forming new relationships. She'd really never wanted to have that conversation out loud. To finally say the words *I'm sorry, I can't have children*, and be met with a look of disappointment. In her head it would inevitably lead to the breakdown of any relationship, and she just didn't want that. She didn't want to feel as if she lacked something.

And she always knew she would never do that to someone she loved—ask them to give up the thing she longed for too. It wouldn't be fair.

So she'd tried to take herself out of those equations. And now?

Gene had the most adorable little boy on the planet. But it was clear he was interested in having more.

She would have to tell him. No matter how much she didn't want to.

But the truth was, a little part of her heart was still singing. Singing at the part of life that had led them to meet. Had put them under the same roof, and let her meet this gorgeous Texan and his son.

He thought she was worth it. Wasn't that what he'd

implied? That he'd consider changing his plans and stay here with her?

A single tear snaked down her face as she towel-dried her hair in the bathroom. They'd picked up Rory and come home to spend the evening together. Rory wanted to be a couch potato. So they were all putting in their pyjamas and getting ready to watch the latest kids' movie with cowboys and spacemen.

Part of her wanted to stay in this bathroom and cry. She'd made a mess of things today. He'd asked her about plans for the future and all the words she should have said had jumbled around in her brain and completely stuck in her throat.

She knew what she should have said.

But her brain just couldn't go there.

Part of her heart had been leaping around in her chest—threatening a WPW attack any moment. But deep down in her soul she was pining already.

Pining for this gorgeous man and his son.

She couldn't pretend they could be a family together—not when Gene seemed to have hopes to expand their family.

At some point in the near future she'd have to tell him the truth—that she had Wolff-Parkinson-White syndrome. That her symptoms were so severe her cardiologist had strongly advised against ever considering getting pregnant. She knew there were a lot of women with the condition who tolerated pregnancy without too many complications. But everyone was different.

And she was different from most.

She brushed the tears away from her face and tugged a comb through her hair roughly. Gene had been here six weeks ago. He could be here much longer. Was it so wrong to keep pretending? To have a little of the life she really wanted?

She might never get this chance again. To love someone. To be loved.

She pressed her lips together. If he mentioned staying again—if he started to make plans—she could tell him then.

She wouldn't let him find out from anyone else. But she could have a few weeks. A few weeks of the almost perfect life.

A few more weeks of the most gorgeous cowboy and his adorable son.

She loved the sideways glances from Gene when his mouth said one thing but his eyes hinted at a whole lot more. She loved the way Rory flung his arms around her neck and bear-hugged her. She wanted it to last just a little bit longer.

If she told Gene, and he considered still working at the institute, then she would deal with that. It was highly likely he wouldn't want to continue their relationship.

But that didn't mean he would disappear to Paris or Texas. He liked it here. Chances were that Franc would need the support they'd discussed. Franc had already been impressed by Gene's résumé. He might well offer him a permanent position.

But if he stayed, could she watch Gene fall in love with someone else and build his family?

It didn't bear thinking about.

She shook her head, demanding the tears forming in her eyes disappear.

She was taking this time. She was taking it.

The next few weeks were hers. She wanted to laugh. She wanted to enjoy.

And if she lost her heart in the process, to not one guy but two?

Then it was a cross she would just have to bear.

CHAPTER NINE

HER GAZE FLICKERED to the view outside. On the path outside the institute a woman was walking with a stroller. The little girl in the stroller had a mass of dark curls and was wearing a bright red coat and a pair of black patent-leather shoes. It reminded Cordelia of a photograph of herself when she was around two. Who knew those curls would tame into poker-straight hair?

A wave of unease crept down her spine and she swallowed uncomfortably. Something sparked in her brain.

She reached for her bag as she hurried inside the institute and fumbled to find her hand-held diary. It had to be in here somewhere. Pens, her mobile phone, receipts, credit-card wallet, umbrella and foldaway bag, along with the odd chocolate all ended up dumped on her office desk.

She didn't stop to repack. She flicked through the pages quickly as the prickle of unease spread like the march of a legion of soldiers over her skin.

She pushed her wheeled chair closer to the wall, where there was a large calendar. Her head flicked between the calendar and her diary.

No. No.

Her hand went to her throat, her mouth instantly dry. Her period was late. Her fingers flicked through the pages again, as if they could find a mistake. Cold sweat broke out on her skin. She leaned back in the chair, staring out the windows towards the snow-topped Alps.

Had she been careless? No. She hadn't. Years ago she'd accepted what pregnancy could do to her body and she'd always been meticulous about her method of contraception. Her IUD had been securely in place for a while. She hadn't been sick. She hadn't been taken antibiotics. Nothing had changed. Everything should be fine.

She let out a groan. Of course everything had changed. Gene was here, and for the last few weeks he'd been in her bed.

She'd been under more pressure at work while Franc was gone, she'd been…distracted, to say the least, with her change in personal circumstances.

Bile rose in the back of her throat. Right now she could be sick all over her shoes. She'd need to tell him. She'd need to tell him about her WPW condition and what this could likely mean.

The implications had always been there for her. She'd known about them right from the start. But Gene? He knew nothing about this and, what's worse, he'd already been through this once.

What kind of a person was she? Why hadn't she spoken to him right at the start?

Now it wasn't a prickle of unease. Now it was heading towards a full-blown panic attack.

As if in penance for her behaviour, her heart started beating erratically. She pulled her chair over to the desk. Now she wasn't in an office with other people. Since Franc had left, she'd been using his office at times. She leaned her elbows on the desk and lifted her hand to the side of her neck, closing her eyes as she slowly massaged the area. Her heartbeat drummed in her ears.

You should have told him. You should have told him. He'll never want this. He'll hate you.

The drum seemed to magnify—almost as if it were mocking her.

She tried to take long, steadying breaths. How long had it been since her last attack? There was no way this could be pregnancy-related. It was far too soon.

Pregnancy hormones couldn't affect her this quickly, could they?

Her brain was churning around a thousand thoughts. She needed to find out more. She needed to find out what happened next. What tests would she need? Could she do them in secret?

Her stomach flip-flopped over in protest.

The echo in her ears was finally quietening down, the pulse under her fingertips slowing. She leaned forward and put her head on the desk for a few seconds.

Part of her wanted to put her hand on her stomach— and part of her couldn't bear to. Her biggest dream and worst nightmare all rolled into one.

A baby she might probably not live to see.

A trickle of cold sweat slid down her back.

She was in a clinic. They did pregnancy tests in here all the time.

She could find one, and check right now. These days pregnancy tests could be positive from the first day of a missed period. She was nearly a week late.

She stood up quickly, grabbed her white coat and walked along the corridor towards one of the clinics. A few staff passed and nodded at her. It was like having a giant sign on her back.

Look at me, pregnant when I shouldn't be.

Her stomach twisted as she remembered how hard
Gene had taken it when he'd had to break the news to
Lea Keller about her pregnancy. It must have brought
back memories and, from what he'd relayed, a hint of
underlying sadness and mixed emotions. Did she really
want to be the person who did that to him?

By the time she reached the white treatment room in
the clinic her heart was thudding again. Only the drug
cabinets were locked so she opened the supply cabinet
and pulled out a pile of pregnancy tests, stuffing them
in the pocket of her white coat.

It was pathetic. It almost felt as if alarms were going
off around the place to let the world know exactly what
she was doing.

One of the nurses came in at her back and she
jumped. 'Hi, Cordelia,' the nurse said casually as she
picked up an electronic blood-pressure monitor and
walked back out.

Cordelia pressed her hands to her face. Yip. Her
cheeks felt on fire.

She turned on her heel and walked smartly back
down the corridor. The office had a private bathroom.
She could do this in a matter of minutes.

But even though she felt ready, it had never been so
difficult to pee on demand.

She sighed as she realised they often asked patients
to do this, and plied them with water until they could
manage.

Finally, she squeezed a few drops onto the stick and
tried to breathe.

Two minutes had never seemed so long.

She washed her hands then, as the bathroom was
large, slid down the wall at the other side, keeping her
eyes on her watch.

A picture of Rory laughing the night before danced into her head. A bolt of pain caught her. She'd just started being part of the little guy's life. He and Gene were the perfect partnership. How on earth would Rory understand? She wasn't clear how much he remembered Mindy—but he had mentioned the fact he thought she was in space in the stars above.

What if Gene had to tell him the same thing had happened to Cordelia? How much heartache could one kid take?

She leaned her head back against the cool, white tiles. What would she tell Franc? He had enough to deal with. He didn't need this too. The thought that she'd let him down made her feel sick to her stomach. The man who'd always had her back had known and understood about her illness. What would he think of her now?

Physicians shouldn't get 'accidentally' pregnant—particularly when they had a condition that could cost them their life. It was beyond stupid.

Maybe this pregnancy wouldn't be as taxing on her body as her cardiologist had always warned about. Maybe she could reach the end of a pregnancy and get the unbridled joy of holding her baby—their baby—in her arms? Couldn't she at least hope for that—no matter how unlikely it seemed?

The tap at the sink was dripping. It was almost like a countdown clock.

She glanced at her watch again. Her two minutes were up.

She closed her eyes, stood up and turned over the test.

Breathe. Breathe.

She opened her eyes.

Negative.

She blinked, then blinked again.

Negative. Negative.

She wasn't pregnant at all. Her period was just late.

Nausea hit her like a tidal wave and she leaned over the sink and retched, grabbing her hair with one hand. Her legs quivered beneath her. She wasn't pregnant. She wasn't going to die. Her baby wasn't going to die. Gene and Rory weren't going to have face losing a child and sibling, along with its mother.

She gripped the edge of the sink tightly, her knuckles turning white.

Relief. That's what she should be feeling right now. Pure and utter relief.

She could breathe again. She could forget about this.

But what if the pregnancy test was wrong? What if she was actually pregnant?

She stared at the word again. It was quite clear. Negative.

Her insides churned. So why wasn't she quite as overjoyed as she should be?

She leaned against the tiled wall again and let her legs slide her back down the wall to the floor.

She pulled her knees up to her chest and wrapped her arms around them, leaning her head on her knees.

For just a few minutes she'd actually *wanted* a baby. She had. She knew pregnancy would likely kill her. She knew her baby would be at risk. She knew the heartache it would cause both Gene and Rory but, still, a tiny selfish part of her had wanted it. She had. To hang with the risks.

What kind of a selfish monster was she?

Angry tears spilled down her cheeks.

'I thought I was past all this,' she murmured. 'I was.' She shook her head.

'Children aren't on the plan for me.' She said the words out loud, vainly hoping she could convince herself.

She leaned her head back against the hard tiles.

She might have convinced herself she was past it. But she'd never had a pregnancy scare before. She'd never been in a place where she thought she was actually falling for someone. She'd never had someone actually come out and ask her about her plans for the future.

And that's what she had now. The chance of a future with a gorgeous man and his son.

But she hadn't been honest with him. No, she hadn't been honest with *them*.

Because if she was going to tell Gene she was sick, she had to tell Rory too. She had to think about teaching a kid to dial the emergency number if she didn't wake up. She had to think about how her condition might progress and deteriorate in the future.

She could potentially become a mother figure to Rory. Would he eventually have two graves to visit?

It was horrid. It was decidedly morbid. But somewhere in amongst what seemed like fanciful thinking she needed a reality check.

There was a noise outside. Footsteps. 'Cordelia? Are you around?'

Gene. Her bag was lying on the floor next to the desk. He would know she was close. She quickly turned the tap on at the sink, hoping the sound of running water would give her a few more minutes' thinking time.

She splashed some water on her face, pulled her hair back into a ponytail, rinsed out her mouth and washed her hands.

There was no point even checking what she looked like in the mirror. She was pretty sure she already knew.

She stared at the test, sitting on the sink edge, the word 'Negative' still clear.

She picked it up and sighed.

The most difficult conversation in the world had to start somewhere.

She'd left this too long already.

CHAPTER TEN

WHERE WAS SHE? Her bag was there, as well as her heels, which were lying sideways on the floor.

There was the sound of running water, followed by a few sniffs. He stood off to one side. He had to talk to her. He had to let her know what the research was starting to show. Things were looking good.

There had been significant progress in one of the trials. Even though the data still had to be thoroughly analysed he had a really good feeling about it. It gave him hope. A large percentage of the patients on this trial were showing signs of improvement. Their cardiac function had improved, their blood results were stable and they had few—if any—side effects. This could be a turning point in the progression of cardiomyopathy. And he wanted to share it with the person who shared his enthusiasm and passion most—the woman he wanted to share everything with.

'Cordelia?' he called again, a little more cautiously. Was she all right in there?

The bathroom door opened. The bright light shone behind her, highlighting her pale skin and the dark circles under her eyes. She looked...drained.

He stepped forward immediately, putting one hand at her elbow. 'What's wrong? Aren't you feeling well?'

She didn't speak, even though her mouth opened. It was her eyes. The expression in her eyes. As if something terrible had just happened.

'Cordelia?' he said yet again, this time more concerned. Maybe something had happened to Professor Helier.

Then he looked down. He'd been a doctor for a long time. He recognised a pregnancy test at twenty paces. It was dangling from her fingertips.

He stepped back as his mind leapt to a thousand possibilities and his brain tried to control his words.

It took less than a second for his heart to start racing in his chest. Thrill. Wonder. Excitement. Then just as quickly he realised that the expression on her face didn't match the thoughts in his head.

'Cordelia, are you pregnant?'

She shook her head as a tear trailed down her cheek. He lifted his finger instantly to brush it away. She held up the test so he could glance at the word. *Negative.*

It was like something inside him sagged. He pulled her into a hug. She still hadn't spoken but he could feel her body tremble.

'It's okay. Did you think you were pregnant? Don't be upset. I know we didn't plan anything. I know it's soon. But it wouldn't be the end of the world, would it? That's the kind of thing I wanted to talk to you about. I guess we should have that chat now.'

He kept holding her, feeling the shaky rise and fall of her chest against his. She hadn't hugged him back; her hands still hung limply by her sides.

He reached up and stroked her hair, pulling her head back a little so he could see her face. He kissed her forehead then her nose. 'Talk to me, honey.'

Something didn't feel quite right. He could understand she might have been a little shocked at thinking she was pregnant. But right now he couldn't quite figure if she was devastated at *not* being pregnant or devastated at *thinking* she might be pregnant.

Right now his brain was focusing on that initial feeling of elation. Another baby. A brother or sister for Rory?

He'd always thought he might like to have more children under a different set of circumstances. But up until a few seconds ago he hadn't realised just how much.

He was disappointed Cordelia wasn't pregnant. *Disappointed.*

And that made him catch his breath at all the implications that went along with that.

A new relationship. Potentially a new home. A new life. A life with a partner for him, a new mom for Rory and maybe—in the future—a new baby.

Cordelia stiffened in his arms. She stepped back, holding up her hands in front of her. She shook her head and he watched her trying to catch her breath.

'This…this…' She was still holding the pregnancy test. 'It can't happen, it can't… can't…happen.' She shook her head more fiercely. *'Ever.'*

Every tiny little hair on his body stood on end at the way she spat out that final word. He stepped back too.

'You don't want kids?' Was that what she was telling him?

She flung up her hands and let out an exasperated whimper. Her jaw clenched and her voice shook. 'It's not that I don't want kids. It's that I *can't* have kids. Not if I want to keep living. '

Now he was completely confused. She'd thought she was pregnant. So she must be able to have kids. She must be able to get pregnant. If she couldn't, why did she need a pregnancy test?

'You're not making any sense.' His brain couldn't quite compute.

She threw the test in the trash can next to his feet. 'Why do you think I work here? Why do you think I work at the institute?'

She was angry. She was angry at him and he couldn't understand why.

'I don't know. You said you wanted to, you loved it.' Why did he feel as if he was the only person in the room who didn't have a clue what was going on?

She leaned forward and poked him in the chest. 'You work here because of Rory. You do cardiac research because, ultimately, you want to find a cure for your son.'

He nodded warily. 'Yes, and I've been up front about that from the start.'

She let out a wry laugh. She shook her head and pressed her hand to her chest. 'I work here because of Wolff-Parkinson-White syndrome. I work here because my condition meant that I could no longer work on the wards. My symptoms got so bad, I couldn't be in a clinical area full time. You think I wanted to leave clinical work? You think I spent all those years training as a doctor not to actually *be* one?'

It was like a chill over his skin. A cool, prickling breeze.

Pieces of the jigsaw puzzle started to slot into place in his brain. The way she'd evaded a few questions. The day she'd been sick.

He opened his mouth. But the words were stuck. She'd known. She'd known about her condition for how long? And she hadn't mentioned it to him. Not at work, not at home and not in bed.

His brain was still trying to process this as he spoke out loud. 'Why didn't you tell me?'

She laughed. She actually laughed.

She threw up her hands again and started pacing around the office. 'How do I tell you that? What part of the conversation starts with "Wait till I tell you about my medical condition"?'

His answer was sharp. He could feel anger rise in his chest. Another woman with a cardiac condition who hadn't told him. A different cardiac condition but one that had risks. Risks he hadn't been told about. 'That's not fair and you know it. You've had more than one opportunity you could have told me about this.'

He frowned. 'Women with Wolff-Parkinson-White have babies. Some people don't even know they have the condition when they get pregnant.' He was just saying what he knew out loud.

'Not me. My cardiologist warned me years ago about the severity of my condition and what pregnancy could do. He knows me. He didn't sugar-coat it.'

He opened his mouth to respond but she stopped pacing for a second, hands on her hips. Her hair had become unravelled from its normally groomed style and was mussed around her face. She gave him a sideways glance.

That little flare of anger ignited again. It was almost as if she wasn't giving him permission to speak.

Her voice was low and laced with anger. 'How could I tell you, Gene? You'd just told me about Rory and his mother. How could I tell you that I've got a condition that means I should never get pregnant? You've been down that road. It's not one you'll want to walk again.' She closed her eyes and he could see the tremble along her jawline. It was almost like she was speaking the words that were currently racing around in his brain. Her words came out with force.

'I didn't know anything would happen between us. You were only supposed to be here a month.' She opened her eyes and gestured with one hand. 'I didn't even know about Rory.'

'And when you did?' Gene stepped right up close to her. His anger was starting to make sense in his head now. He was a parent. He was Rory's only parent. Rory was his first and foremost priority.

Maybe the magic of the Geneva setting had messed with his mind? Something certainly had.

This time her voice wasn't quite so strong. She breathed in, in awkward jerks. 'I probably should have kept my distance. I struggle around young kids.' She looked over at the trash can. 'I thought I'd come to terms with things a long time ago.'

He couldn't describe the feeling swamping over him. Disappointment. Disillusionment. It was like watching a bright balloon he'd been holding slip from his hands and float out over the nearby mountains.

He couldn't quite work out how he felt about all this. 'You have a condition that could kill you if you get pregnant. And you didn't tell me. You were sleeping with me—but you didn't tell me. You're a doctor. You knew the risks. And you didn't think to share them?'

She turned on him. 'Don't say it like that. You think I wasn't careful? Of course I was. I've always taken care of contraception. I've never wanted to be in a position like this.'

'So what happened?' He couldn't help the strangulated sound that came out as he walked away and ran his fingers through his hair. 'We'd been talking about having a future together. We'd been talking about possibilities. If I'd known about this—'

'You'd what?' she snapped. The words came out like a challenge.

'I'd have worn a condom!' he shouted back. 'When there's a high risk, two types of contraception are better than one.' It was just as much his responsibility as it was hers. Inside he was cringing. Yes, he'd asked her. Yes, she'd reassured him.

But shouldn't he have taken matters into his own hands anyway—even without any risks?

'What if the test wasn't negative, Cordelia?' His stomach was churning now. It had leapt at the thought of another child. He'd actually had a few seconds of pure joy at the thought of bringing another child into the world with a woman he actually loved.

'What if we were standing here right now, and you were telling me you'd just given yourself a death sentence?' His voice almost cracked. 'And I'd caused it?'

Her head dipped but her voice was clear. 'That's why I'm telling you now, Gene.' She walked over to the glass wall and put her hands on the glass, staring out at the backdrop that was normally behind them. Her head bent forward, resting against the glass.

'This can't happen again,' she said, her words almost a whisper.

'You're right. It can't.'

It came out before he could think straight. What she'd just thrown at him was enormous. He'd never really considered a partner before in terms of health.

The Mindy thing had sideswiped him completely. He knew what being completely unprepared felt like.

He never wanted to feel like that again. And he certainly didn't want to expose his son to that.

Her green gaze met his. It was almost as if she'd built a shield over her eyes. They were glassy and detached-looking.

He straightened himself up. 'You should have told me about your health condition. I'm assuming that Professor Helier knew?'

She gave the briefest of nods.

'Then in his absence you had a responsibility to tell me too. We are living under the same roof, working in the same clinic. Treating patients clinically.' He closed his eyes—just for a second. 'That day in the cath lab. You had an attack, didn't you?' He didn't even wait for a response. 'You should have been honest.'

'I was. I told you I had to step outside.' There was an air of desperation in her voice.

He moved closer to her. 'Not. Good. Enough. If the doctor I'm working with has a condition that can affect her patient care at any point then I need to know about it. I need to know to look for the signs and intervene if need be.'

She flinched and he could tell she hated those words. Hated the fact they were right. Hated the fact he'd said them out loud.

'Don't tell me what I can and can't do.'

He turned to walk away. 'I'm not. I'm taking responsibility for your condition. Something that you clearly haven't. I have no interest in being your cardiologist. But I do have an interest in the welfare of the patients in this clinic. Don't do any procedures without another physician present.'

'I never have.'

'And if you don't tell your colleagues, I will.' He headed for the door. 'This isn't over, Cordelia.'

He felt betrayed, both personally, and professionally.

The future he'd dared to imagine in his head for the first time in four years had just disappeared in a puff of smoke.

And he had no idea what to tell his son.

CHAPTER ELEVEN

By the time she'd picked herself up at least an hour had passed.

The little white stick in the trash can had unearthed a whole host of feelings she hadn't been ready for, or prepared for.

A few days ago she'd dared to hope the life she'd always dreamed of might actually come true. A life with Gene and with Rory.

And that had been enough. That had been more than enough. More than she'd ever hoped for. A gorgeous man who loved her as much as she loved him, and a beautiful child she could love just as much.

A few days of hope. A few days of bliss.

And now it had all come crashing down around her.

All because of a moment of madness. A tiny possibility that had made her realise how much she'd been hiding from herself.

That a child of her own *really* was never possible.

But she hadn't shared that with Gene. She hadn't let him decide to love her despite the fact there would never be any more kids.

Something deep down inside told her that could have been a possibility.

And instead of taking the time and chance to sit

down with him and let him know, she'd gone in completely the wrong direction.

Of course she wasn't pregnant. But because the seed had been planted in her head, she'd realised how much she wanted it.

It was like stepping back ten years—when her cardiologist had first spoken to her about the severity of her disease and its implications.

She pressed her head against the glass. It didn't matter how picturesque the setting. How fabulous her workplace.

Everything was falling apart around her.

She pressed her hand to her chest. How ironic that the one time she felt so exhausted and stressed was the one time her WPW didn't kick in.

She sucked in a breath. It almost felt like someone was sitting on her shoulders, weighing her down to the floor.

Gene had looked so angry. She'd seen that first little flicker, that hint of a smile and flash of delight in his eyes at the thought of a pregnancy.

It had sparked off every wrong emotion in her. Every spark of anger, regret and disillusionment. There had never been a moment in her life where she'd felt quite so inadequate. That tiny smile and glimmer of excitement had let her know that she could never give Gene those things. She could never build a family with him, share a pregnancy. And the emotions had just all tumbled from there.

Now he was angry. He felt deceived and betrayed by her.

She didn't blame him.

The person she was most disappointed in was herself.

She sucked in another deep breath and glanced at her watch.

How could she go back to the house? There was no way she could live under the same roof. She couldn't bear it, and she was sure neither could he.

If she left now, she could make it back to the house and empty her things—take them back to her apartment in Geneva.

She'd overstayed her welcome in Professor Helier's home.

It was time to move out.

He didn't see her for the rest of the day.

He didn't want to see her.

His head was still full of a million questions that just seemed to churn around in his mind.

By the time he picked up Rory at nursery his head was starting to throb.

'Can we play hide and seek, Daddy?' Rory asked.

'Maybe later. We need to get home and fix dinner. Then it will probably be time for bed.'

Rory frowned. 'But I want to play hide and seek. I've found a new hiding place at home. I want to hide there.'

Gene sighed. 'Not now, Rory,' he snapped, then instantly regretted it as Rory winced.

He'd managed to avoid Cordelia at the institute but it would be much harder to avoid her at home. Maybe he should take Rory out for dinner to help prevent any awkward scenes back at the house? Maybe he should look for an alternative apartment to rent? Anything would be better than avoiding each other at home. How on earth would he explain that to Rory?

But two minutes after they reached the house with takeout food he knew something was wrong.

Rory rushed up the stairs then came running back down. 'Something's wrong with Delia's room.'

'What do you mean?' When her car hadn't been outside he'd just assumed Cordelia was working late.

Rory wrinkled his nose. 'Nothing's there.'

Gene turned from where he'd been about to cut the pizza, closed the takeaway box again and climbed the stairs in long strides.

Somehow he knew what he was about to find. And his stomach clenched in the most horrible way.

Cordelia had left in a hurry. The dresser drawers were still slightly open. The wardrobe doors not closed properly. The bathroom had been emptied and wiped down and the bed stripped.

Rory was still frowning. He turned to face Gene and shook his head. 'Where's Delia, Daddy?' He picked up the pillow on the bed. 'Her teddy-bear jammies are gone.'

Gene sat down on the edge of the bed. 'I guess she must have decided to move out,' he said hoarsely. 'This isn't her real house. She has another place she can stay.'

It took Rory a few seconds to speak. 'But why wouldn't she want to stay with us? And why wouldn't she tell us she was going someplace else?' Gene's heart squeezed in his chest. Rory's voice sounded shaky and his eyes looked a little glazed.

Gene reached over and pulled Rory up onto his knee. He chose his words carefully. 'Sometimes adults have a difference of opinion.'

'What?'

Gene tried again. 'They sometimes fight.'

'Did you fight with Delia?'

Gene sighed. 'Maybe.'

'Then just say sorry, Daddy. She'll know you mean

it. And she'll come back. She'll play hide and seek with me. We can all play together.'

Gene pressed his lips together and tried to find the right words.

Pieces in his head started to slot together.

He'd been so angry earlier. So indignant about things. Thinking about himself and about Rory—about how Cordelia's condition could impact on them all.

He hadn't thought about *her*. Hadn't thought about how devastated she'd looked when she'd gripped the pregnancy test in her hand.

He hadn't thought about what *this* might feel like. This…emptiness. This feeling of complete loss.

He loved her. He completely and utterly loved her.

It had kind of sneaked up on him. Taken him unawares.

And now that he realised just how much she meant to him, it completely terrified him.

It was official. He was heartbroken.

How could he possibly be? He hadn't even told Cordelia that he loved her yet. He hadn't even realised that he loved her yet.

But the emptiness of the creaky house—the way that every noise they made seemed to echo down the corridor and bounce off the walls—just seemed to magnify the feelings in his heart.

Of course he loved Rory. That was always going to be a given.

But the last few weeks, spending time with Cordelia, had really opened his eyes. Neither of them were permanent residents in this house, but being here with her had made this place feel like a home instead of a house.

Now he understood her initial reluctance around Rory. She had been trying to protect herself. But watching how their relationship had blossomed and grown had been…special. It was clear she'd liked spending time with Rory, and Rory, in turn, had loved being around her. He couldn't deny it. Having a woman in his life was clearly good for Rory. Gene had always been clear in his head that he could be mom and dad to his little boy. But it was clear that Rory found different qualities in Cordelia than he found in his dad.

Part of Gene hated that. Especially now.

Had that affected how he felt about Cordelia? Sure. He and Rory were a partnership. He could never be with someone who couldn't love his child. But Cordelia? She was already part way there—if not the whole way.

He ran his fingers through Rory's hair. The little head was resting on his shoulder. 'I don't think Cordelia wants to play hide and seek right now, honey.'

Rory lifted his head and narrowed his gaze. 'You don't want to say sorry, do you?'

Every muscle in Gene's body tensed. Children could be so astute sometimes. 'I don't know,' he said.

Rory's face fell. He looked as if he could cry. 'But I asked if I could pick. I pick Delia. I told you that, Daddy.'

Gene wrapped his arms around his son's body. There was so much more to this than he could explain.

'I thought I'd picked Delia too, honey. But I'm not sure that Delia wants to be picked. I'm not sure that she's ready to pick us back.'

As he said the words out loud he realised how true they were.

Yes, he was angry.

Yes, he was hurt she hadn't told him the truth.

Yes, he'd had a glimmer of hope at the thought of her being pregnant.

But with hope came despair.

If she'd been truthful and given him the chance to choose, he would have chosen her over having any more family.

Yes, he would choose someone with a chronic condition—one that someday could kill them.

He knew the risks. He knew ultimately she could go into heart failure or need a transplant.

But these were all ifs.

Next year he could have cancer. Next year he could have a stroke.

He might think he wasn't at risk—but what did anyone really know?

So much was going through his mind.

And he didn't have a clue what to do next.

CHAPTER TWELVE

FOR THE FIRST time in her life, Cordelia Greenway didn't want to go to work.

Every minute at work meant trying to avoid Gene. It was awkward. Impersonal. And totally against what she wanted to do.

There was so much she should sit down and talk to him about. She wasn't stupid. She knew she owed him an apology.

But that could result in something that would ultimately make her feel a million times worse than she currently did.

That could result in him telling her that he didn't want to see her, he didn't want to spend time with her, and he certainly wouldn't be building any kind of life with her.

Why should he pick someone who was broken when he could easily find someone who was whole? Someone without any disease in their heart, someone who could help him fulfil his dream of expanding his family.

Finding out she couldn't be with the man and child she loved and adored would feel like the final nail in the coffin.

She'd always felt as if she fell a little short. It was

odd that parts of her body she had no control over could do that to a person.

There was a world of psychological research that told her these feelings had been studied the world over. She wasn't the only human being who felt like this.

But the research didn't matter to her.

The only thing that mattered to her was the here and now.

Her condition could remain the same for the next ten years. Or this time next year she could end up on the heart-transplant list.

Did she want Rory to see her sick?

Something washed over like a black storm cloud.

Did she want to see Rory sick?

Because that was just as likely to happen.

Her reaction was instantaneous. She wrapped her arms around herself and started rocking. It was her worst nightmare.

Of course she would want to be there. Of course she would want to by Gene's side so they could hold Rory's hand and stroke his forehead.

No matter how much she hated herself right now, she couldn't picture her life without these people.

She loved them.

She loved them with every part of her being. Every breath that she took. Every fibre in her body, and every beat of her imperfect heart.

Her hands shook as she sucked in a breath.

She reached for her jacket and car keys.

It didn't matter that she didn't want to go to work. It didn't matter that she was scared.

It didn't matter that this could all blow up in her face.

All that mattered was that she try.

CHAPTER THIRTEEN

HE PICKED UP the phone as soon as it rang—half hoping it might be Cordelia.

'Dr Du Bois—Gene, how are you?'

It took a few seconds to recognise the husky voice.

'Professor Helier? Is everything okay?'

The old man cleared his throat. 'How are things at the institute? How is the research project? I was very interested in what you sent me.'

Gene pressed his lips together. In his excitement the other day he'd forwarded the preliminary research findings on to Professor Helier. He knew the timing might be wrong, but this work was Professor Helier's life—and he'd asked to be kept up to date on all progress.

Gene nodded. It was really the only piece of good news that he had.

'I'm so glad you've had a chance to look at it. The provisional findings are promising. This could be the start of something really significant.'

'It could. It really could. In fact, that's why I'm calling you.'

'It is?' He was curious, but his insides were churning. He would have to be honest with Professor Helier. He would have to let him know how things were between himself and Cordelia. This research was so important. He didn't want to compromise it in any way.

'It is.' Professor Helier cleared his throat. 'I have something else I have to ask you.'

The hairs prickled at the back of his neck. Gene kept his voice steady. 'What is it?'

Professor Helier sounded hesitant. 'My sister is obviously very unwell. And knowing I don't have much time left with her has made me re-evaluate a few things. I'm old, Gene. And I don't have as many years left as I might wish for. I need to plan for someone to take over from me at the institute.'

'But that will be Cordelia surely? She's your second in command.'

'Yes, you're right. It will be Cordelia. She's my natural choice. But…'

His voice tailed off for a second as he seemed to choose his words carefully. 'I think it would be best if she had someone she could share the workload with. Someone who is equally passionate about the work we do here as she is.'

Gene closed his eyes for a few seconds. It was clear Professor Helier knew about Cordelia's condition but wasn't going to betray her trust. He respected her that much—just like Gene should.

'I'd like you to be that person, Gene. The truth is, I've watched the work that you'd done over the past few years and was delighted to get the chance to invite you here. I'm sorry we've not had the chance to work together, but circumstances—'

'Of course. I understand,' said Gene quickly.

'I'd like you to consider what I'm offering you. Everyone at the institute is very impressed by your work.'

'Not everyone,' he said quietly.

'What?' asked Professor Helier.

Gene breathed in, 'Have you spoken to Cordelia yet?'

'No. But I'm sure she'll be delighted. Over the last few weeks she's been very complimentary about your work.'

Gene ran his fingers through his hair. Somehow he didn't think so.

'There's a lot to think about.'

'I know that. That's why I called you first. To give you some time to consider my offer. I'll still remain as Head of the Institute. But I'd like you and Cordelia to lead the two research teams, to work together.'

Gene let out a sigh. 'Professor Helier, things might be a little more difficult than you think.'

'Why? Don't you like the institute? Or is it Geneva?'

Gene breathed deeply. 'I love the institute. And I love Geneva. But…' he knew he had to say the words out loud '…there's someone else that I love more. And the last thing I want to do is make her feel uncomfortable.'

There was silence at the end of the phone. It was the longest pause, and he could almost hear Professor Helier's brain ticking.

'This her? Is this…a mutual acquaintance of ours?'

Gene cringed. Most of the staff at the institute knew that something had been going on between him and Cordelia. It was likely that Professor Helier would eventually hear too.

'It could be,' he said hesitantly.

'Dr Du Bois, it doesn't matter how wonderful a researcher you are. It doesn't matter what the possibilities for the future work could be. You need to know that my loyalties will always lie with Cordelia. She's worked tirelessly for me over the last few years. She's the most dedicated doctor I've ever worked with. She's family to me.'

Gene felt like some teenager being told off. But he had to admire the loyalty that Professor Helier had for Cordelia.

Professor Helier continued. 'Maybe I was wrong to offer you this position.'

'Maybe you were,' Gene finished for him.

'Let's take the job and the institute out of the equation—even though I was flattered by your offer. I can't do anything to make Cordelia unhappy, and me working here might make things difficult. Let me talk to her. We need a chance to work things out together. I need a chance to convince her that I, and Rory, want to be part of her life.'

'In that case, I will leave things with you. Good luck, Dr Du Bois.'

Gene hung up the phone. Rory was in nursery. He'd checked on all the patients this morning—there was no one he currently had concerns about, except Cordelia.

It was time to be true to his heart.

He could lose Cordelia. He could lose her now. He could lose her in a few years because of her condition or he could spend the next thirty years with her.

No one on this planet knew how long they had.

Not him. Not Cordelia. And not Rory.

Was it wrong to put Rory in a position where he could love Cordelia then lose her? He'd asked himself this question so many times in the last few hours.

He shook his head. It was time to stop asking what if.

It was time to stop second-guessing.

It was time to follow the lead from the most important organ of the body.

His heart.

CHAPTER FOURTEEN

SHE SCANNED THE NURSERY. There was no familiar mop of blond hair. Panic hovered just above her chest. She'd been through the whole institute and there was no sign of Gene. No one could tell her where he was. A few people had seen him earlier but were not quite sure where he'd gone next. Would he actually leave without telling her?

Then a brainwave had hit her. If Rory was here, Gene must be close by. The nursery. The place she should probably have tried first.

She gestured one of the nursery staff over. 'Is Rory Du Bois in today? I can't see him.'

Emma rolled her eyes. 'He's in a bit of a mood today.' She pointed to the corner of the nursery floor. 'He's been in the playhouse for the last hour, refusing to talk to anyone. We've all been in there and tried to persuade him to come out. But Rory is one determined little guy.' She gave Cordelia a sympathetic smile. 'Be my guest.'

Cordelia breathed a sigh of relief and hurried across the floor to the brightly coloured plastic playhouse. She paused at the red door and gave it a knock. 'Rory? Rory, are you in there? It's Cordelia. Will you come out and see me?'

'No,' came the firm little voice, then, after a pause, 'But you can come in.'

Cordelia looked down and hitched up her skirt with her hands. Thankfully, she hadn't changed out of her baseball boots this morning, so she pushed the door open with one hand and crawled inside.

Rory was sitting in one of the corners. All the blue shutters on the windows were closed, his arms were folded across his chest and a frown was on his face.

'Hey, little guy. What's up?'

He stuck out his bottom lip.

She tried to pull herself completely inside the cramped playhouse. 'This isn't like you,' she said as she adjusted her position, pulling her legs up to her chest. 'You always play with the other kids.'

'I'm not talking to anyone,' he said crossly.

Cordelia tried not to smile. She'd felt a bit like that herself yesterday.

'Okay.' She nodded. 'Why not?'

He glared at her. 'I picked you.'

Her breath caught in her throat. 'What?'

Rory's brow was so furrowed she could barely see his eyes. 'I picked you. And Daddy picked you. But he said you didn't want to be picked.'

Cordelia shook her head. 'What do you mean—you picked me?'

Rory held up his hands as if it was the most obvious thing in the world. 'I picked you to be my new mommy.'

Cordelia choked. 'What?' Her brain started to spin and tears pricked the corners of her eyes.

Rory looked at her again. 'I picked you to be my new mommy. And Daddy said he'd picked you too.' He scowled at her. 'But you didn't want to be picked.'

Cordelia put her hand up to her chest. 'Who said that, Rory? Who said I didn't want to be picked?'

Rory looked puzzled now. 'Daddy. He said he didn't think you wanted us to pick you. Why don't you want us, Cordelia?'

A tear slid down her cheek as she shook her head fiercely. She wrapped her arms around Rory and pulled him close. 'Oh, I want you, honey. You've no idea how much I want you both. Us grown-ups are complicated. We get mad at each other. We do stupid things. And we say even sillier things. Don't think for a second that I don't want you, honey. Of course I do. You and your dad are the best people I've ever met. I would pick you a million times over.'

There was a noise at the door and a red-faced Gene appeared. He looked into the cramped playhouse. It was pretty clear he must have heard what she'd just said.

She swallowed, her mouth instantly dry as their gazes met.

She'd come here ready to fight for them both. She regretted what she'd said. She so regretted not being truthful. But would she get a chance to say any of that?

'Room for one more?' Gene asked. 'I heard there was a party going on in here.'

Cordelia bit her lip. 'I think we can squish up a bit.' She shifted over next to Rory as Gene's long jeans-clad limbs tried to clamber into the plastic playhouse.

By the time he got inside, Gene's knees were practically up to his chin. His arms were against Cordelia's and their heads close together.

Once he was settled he gave her a sideways glance. 'I was looking for you.'

'You were?'

He nodded. Her heart started that crazy irregular

beating again. But this wasn't a WPW attack. This was just pure and utter hope.

'I was looking for you too.'

His head tilted to the side and he gave her a curious stare.

'I wanted to apologise,' she said quickly as she looked at Rory. For a second she tried to think of a particular way to say things. A way that Rory might not understand. But she quickly realised that was wrong. She wanted both of these people in her life and it was time to be honest with them both.

'I wanted to say sorry that I didn't tell you about my condition. I should have trusted you. I should have told you.'

'What's your condition?' asked Rory innocently.

She nodded her head slowly and turned to the little boy. She pointed to his chest. 'You know how things can be wrong with people's hearts?'

'That's what Daddy does.'

She nodded again. 'I know. Well… I have something wrong with my heart too. Sometimes it goes too quickly and I have to try and slow it down. It can make me a little sick sometimes and I have to be careful.'

Rory wrinkled his nose. 'Is it dangerous?'

The million-dollar question. Gene's dark eyes were fixed firmly on hers. Would he want her to stop at this point? Maybe she had no right to tell Rory the truth.

But the look in Gene's eyes made her skin tingle. There was nothing but pure and utter support in his gaze.

She gave the slightest nod. 'It can be. Or it could be in the future.' She reached over and squeezed Rory's hand. 'None of us know how we will be in the future. I could get sick, or I could be fine. I just can't say for sure.' She swallowed and tapped her chest again with her other hand. 'There are some things that I do know, though.'

'Like what?' You couldn't beat a child's curiosity for cutting to the chase.

She kept her voice steady. 'Like, for me, it wouldn't be a good idea to have a baby.'

'A baby? Why would you want to have a baby?' Rory looked over at Gene. 'I don't want a brother or sister. I've seen some of the diapers in the nursery.' He scrunched up his face. 'Yeuch!'

Cordelia laughed as her heart swelled in her chest. 'I guess I don't need to worry, then.' She lifted her eyes warily to Gene, trying not to let her voice shake. 'Unless, of course, your daddy wants to have more babies.'

'Oh, no,' said Rory quickly as he waved his hand between him and Gene. 'We're a team. It's just us. There's no room for babies.'

Cordelia bit her bottom lip. 'No room for anyone?'

'Oh, there's room for you. I told you. I told Daddy. I picked you. You can be in our team.'

She blinked back the tears and looked at Gene as Rory slid his little hand into hers. 'What do you think?'

She was holding her breath. Everything depended on what came next. Was it really possible to hope this much?

Gene put his hand on Rory's soft hair. 'Oh, we talked. We talked about how much we loved having you around. We talked about how much we wanted to see you every day.' His voice changed a little. 'We talked about how empty the house seemed without you there. We missed you.'

His gaze didn't waver from hers. 'We don't need any more kids. We're happy just as we are. I have a feeling that Rory might keep us busy for the next thirty years.' He raised his eyebrows. 'If you're up for the job, that is.'

She was still holding her breath. She'd heard a little word in amongst all that. Was she brave enough to use it? She looked at the tiny weathered lines around Gene's eyes. The expression of love on his face. Even now, his gaze flickered between her and Rory. His work shirt was completely crumpled, halfway tucked into his jeans. His brown cowboy boots were only half in the playhouse, because those longs legs were struggling with the cramped space.

She took a deep breath. Now she couldn't stop her voice shaking as she let out a nervous laugh. 'I am *so* up for this job. I love you guys. I really do. I never expected to meet people like you two, and feel like this.' She nodded her head and looked down at Rory. 'You don't know how special it makes me feel to know that you've picked me. But you need to know, I picked you too. I absolutely want to see you every day.' She took another breath. She was willing to do just about anything to make this work. 'If that means I need to move someplace else to be near you guys, then I'll do that.'

Gene cleared his throat. 'Franc called.'

'He did?'

Gene nodded. 'I might have let him know that something was going on. He asked me to stay.' He paused for a second. 'For good.'

'He did?' She repeated it again.

He gave her a smile that sent a million little sparks flying across her skin. 'I told him I couldn't say yes until I'd spoken to you. I didn't know what you might say. I didn't want to compromise your working environment if you didn't want us around.'

She shook her head fiercely, 'Why on earth wouldn't

I want you around?' The tears started to flow freely. 'Of course I want you both around.' She slid her arm around Rory's shoulder and held her hand out towards Gene. 'I want you both around always.'

Rory blinked and gave a small smile. 'Did you bring the present we bought a few days ago?' he asked his dad.

Gene laughed. 'I did.' He looked around, and gave a smile as he shook his head. 'But we might need to get out of here first. I don't know if a plastic playhouse is where we really want to give this present.' He bent down and whispered in Rory's ear, 'We're supposed to be cool.'

Cordelia's stomach was still in knots. But this time, instead of dark twisty knots, the knots were more flutters of excitement. Gene crawled out of the playhouse first, followed by an excited Rory. She tried to tug her skirt back down as she crawled out behind them. Gene's hand came down and he pulled her up into his arms.

There was something so reassuring about being back in his arms. 'You're really okay with not having any more kids?' she whispered.

'We already have the best kid on the planet.' He smiled. 'Why would we need any more?'

He reached over, his thumb brushing away the tear on her cheek. 'No more secrets, okay? You heard our kid, we're a team. We can do this.' He smiled again. 'Someone pretty important once told me we have a whole wide world out there. Let's go and live this life— together.'

She reached her hands up around his neck and smiled. 'I wonder who that might have been?'

He gave a nod, kissed her cheek, then stepped back. 'Give me a second.' He took a few long strides and picked up a plastic carrier bag sitting near the nursery entrance. He came back with a twinkle in his eye. 'I want you to know just how hard it was to find this in Geneva. And it had to be the right colour—Rory insisted.'

She stared at the large shape in the plastic bag, trying to decipher what it could be. Gene's voice was low. 'I know it's not an engagement ring. We'll get to that later. Or maybe we'll even skip it and just go for the wedding.'

'We will?' She smiled.

He put his hand in the bag. 'And we have something special for you to wear on our wedding day. Because we all have to match. I have mine. Rory has his. And now you…' he pulled something from the bag '…have yours.'

She laughed out loud as the large bright red Stetson—that matched her baseball boots—was put on her head. It nearly covered her eyes.

'You bought me a Stetson?'

He pulled her into his arms and dropped a kiss on her lips. 'Of course I bought you a Stetson. Haven't you heard? You're just about to marry a cowboy?'

And she wrapped her arms around his neck and kissed her cowboy, with the backdrop of the snow-topped mountains, surrounded by a gaggle of rowdy toddlers.

Things couldn't be more perfect.

* * * * *

REUNITED
BY THEIR
SECRET SON

LOUISA GEORGE

MILLS & BOON

CHAPTER ONE

HE WAS LATE.

Finn Baird was never late—not any more. These days he always gave himself extra time to navigate the traffic, negotiate the car park and be in his clinic with plenty of minutes to spare. Mainly so he could both impress the boss and be mentally prepared for the day. But also so he could make readjustments to his leg before he started work.

He just hadn't anticipated the readjustments would take so long today. Or hurt so damned much.

Which was more than a little irritating because now he was rushing, and the more he rushed the slower he seemed to get, not to mention the more frustrated.

Two months into his new job as paediatric physiotherapist at St Margaret's Children's Hospital—Maggie's to the locals—and he'd made sure he had a reputation for having all the time in the world for his patients. Hell, they deserved it. A lot of them had challenges worse than his and most of them grinned their way through treatment. Through all the pulling and pushing and straightening and bending he made them do, through all the pain, through all the mind-numbingly repetitive exercises, he tried to make them laugh. Tried to make them believe they could achieve anything if they tried.

He definitely needed to take a leaf out of their books.

Trying to smile and hurry along the corridor while gritting his teeth against the pain, he reached the reception area at the same time his boss did. Neither of them looked at their watches. Neither of them acknowledged Finn was late.

And hell, if that was preferential treatment he didn't want it. 'Sorry I'm late, Ross. Won't happen again.'

'Good morning, Finn. Don't worry; I know you'll make it up.' Ross Andrews, Head of Physiotherapy, threw a pile of paper folders onto the reception desk and looked up. 'You always stay later than everyone else anyway.'

Because he needed to stay on top of everything. Needed this job to work out, and everything took longer these days. 'Just want to get the job done properly.'

'And you do. So you're forgiven for being a few minutes behind. Great run yesterday. Feeling it a bit today? I certainly am. I think I twinged my back.' Ross put his palms on the small of his back and stretched backwards. 'I've got to fix that overpronation.'

'You want me to take a look?'

'Later, if we get a chance. One of the perks of being a physio, eh? Treatment on tap. I'm so impressed with your race time, Finn—you did great. Really great.'

The minutes were ticking by but Finn could hardly snap at the boss and head to his first patient, so he took a deep breath and promised himself he'd be doubly efficient today without hurrying the littlies.

'Let's be honest—I ran a woeful time. I'm just glad I made it to the finish line.' There had been a time when he'd completed the ten-mile Great Edinburgh Run in under an hour; this time he'd been lucky—and utterly exhausted and hurting on both his good leg and his gone

one—to finish half the distance in the same time. He rubbed his left thigh, still sore and tight, but nowhere near as painful as just below his knee where the stitches had been and where the friction was always most intense. 'Still, I stayed upright—that was a bonus. I'm aiming for a faster time next year.'

'Don't push yourself too hard—you'll get there. You just need a little incentive…if you know what I mean. Someone to run towards.' Ross's eyes grew wider as he nodded.

Finn grinned, remembering seeing Ross overtake him on the home straight, having run twice the distance, right into the arms of his new wife. She'd been so proud of him even Finn hadn't been able to stop smiling as she cheered and screamed her husband's name as he went over the finishing line. And then there'd been the kisses; the poor man had barely been able to catch breath.

'A special someone to cheer me on at the end, right? I'm going to be running a long, long way before that ever happens.'

His boss laughed. 'Well, you'll never have it if you don't even ask a lassie out. Greta's sister said to drop a huge hint about a double date. She's single too—?'

Ugh. Not another date set-up. He was starting to regret getting to know his boss a little better out of work. Seemed Finn was surrounded by loved-up couples these days who wanted him to have a piece of the happiness they had. If it wasn't Ross and Greta it was his brother Callum and his new family down in New Zealand dropping hints at every available opportunity about seeing him paired up. The thing none of them understood—or downright ignored—was the issue of his leg. Or lack of it. If he'd struggled to come to terms with it, then what chance did any woman have? How could he give them what they wanted? 'Thanks, but no. Really, no.'

Ross shook his head, undeterred as a matchmaker. 'I never understood why you turned down lovely Julia, the Pilates instructor. Or Molly-Rae from the café… she was definitely dropping big hints to go for a drink. Even I could see that.'

Finn dug deep to keep polite. He dredged up a smile. 'I mean it, boss. No.'

'Or there's the speed dating night every Thursday at the Tavern?' Ross shrugged. 'A bit lame, I know. But it's always a laugh. I went there a few times before I met Greta. As you know, we met at salsa night—oh. Well… Yes…' He glanced at Finn's leg and shrugged again. 'If you can run, you can dance.'

Dancing was a whole lot more than just moving forward in a straight line. 'Really. I'm fine. Thanks. I'm not looking for anyone. Please tell the lovely Greta I'm fine on my own.'

Even as he said it he knew it sounded hollow. But there it was. Before the accident, Finn had taken his looks and raw physicality for granted and enjoyed them, celebrated them with the best and the most beautiful women he could find. He'd paraded around like a prize chump, all cocky and sure of himself, a peacock on show. He'd had a host of women who'd wanted what he'd wanted: a night of fun and drink and mindless sex. Then his charmed life had started to unravel and the last thing he'd wanted was to attempt dating again. Couldn't do it, but it didn't stop them asking. Or his friends trying to set him up.

Most of those women were a blur to him now. All except one…the one who'd not got away, not exactly. The one he'd purposefully let go after he'd fallen from grace, fallen from a great bloody height and broken both his dreams and his body.

Now? He didn't need anyone. Didn't want anyone. Didn't want anyone to see him like this, not after who he'd been before. Not after he'd changed so damned much he was barely recognisable inside or out. 'If I change my mind, Ross, you'll be the first to know.'

'Aye, well, I was like you once—thought I was better off being a lad—but there comes a time in every man's life when he has to settle down. Get serious.'

'I've a long way before I go to those extremes.' Finn laughed. 'I'm pretty serious about myself these days and that's about all I can manage for now.' He'd had to relearn how to do pretty much everything and was still learning. He changed the subject, jumping into work as always. Because work made him focus on the possible, not the impossible, like having a woman who even liked the look of him, let alone could fall for him and see a future. 'I'm going to be running very late, so I need to get on. Who've we got today?'

'Some regular follow-ups from your predecessor and a couple of new referrals. Nothing too taxing. You're doing just fine. Don't rush. They'll understand.' Ross looked meaningfully again at Finn's left leg.

'I prefer it if the leg doesn't come up in conversation.' Finn whipped round to peer at the computer for details of his first client, twisting his leg in the prosthetic. A searing pain ran up his knee. He inhaled sharply, clenched his teeth and waited for the pain to subside. 'Okay. Okay. Let's go.'

'You all right? You need a seat?' Reaching out to steady Finn, Ross peered at him, all concern and questions.

Damn. The last thing he needed was a father figure…scratch that, a *brother* figure. He already had one of those and even twelve thousand miles away he still managed to be overbearing and overly concerned about Finn's welfare. All. The. Time.

The whole point of taking this job and being this new person in a new city, putting the past well and truly behind him, was to live a normal life. He didn't want people to keep asking if he was all right. And yes, he knew they cared and were just being nice. But he didn't want to be treated any differently to everyone else.

He counted to ten under his breath as the pain faded. 'Yep. I'm fine. But even after more than two years I keep forgetting.' And it wasn't just the physical pain that assailed him, sometimes out of nowhere. 'Still, I'm good to go. And now I'm really late.'

Four hours later and his leg was no better, neither was his mood, although the kids always made him smile. A missed appointment meant he could catch up. All he had to do now was finish these notes and then he could lock his door, slip off his prosthesis and the silicone liner and relax for a few minutes.

As he sat in his office—the closest to Reception so he wouldn't have to walk far, apparently—he heard a kerfuffle in the waiting area.

A woman's voice, soft and apologetic. Breathless. 'I'm so, so late. I'm sorry. Really sorry. Lachie had a meltdown at home which delayed things a bit… you know what it's like…he's hit the terrible twos six months early. Then I couldn't get a parking space and then there was something wrong with the pushchair— I think it might be one of the front wheels; it's wanting to go in the opposite direction to all the others.'

The talking stopped. Finn assumed it was for the woman to draw breath. He heard the receptionist sigh.

Then that soft voice again. 'I know you're all busy. I'm so sorry. Please, if anyone could see us I'm happy to wait as long as it takes.'

Their receptionist was renowned for running a tight ship. 'I'm sorry but we have a full list today and there's no wriggle room to fit you in. I can make another appointment for Lachie?'

'He really needs to be seen today. I know it's not relevant, or shouldn't be, but I've taken the day off work as holiday just so we could get here. I'm fast running out of holiday days…' Desperation laced her words. 'It's his boots, you see—they're rubbing and he hates wearing them. That was the trouble this morning—when I took them off after he'd worn them all night he threw them across the room.' A pause. 'Please.'

Finn stretched his left knee. Yeah, he knew all about rubbing. About the tension before you put the damned thing on because you just knew it was going to be sore. He knew how hard that was for a grown man to get his head round, never mind a…what did she say?…eighteen-month-old. He sent an urgent message to the receptionist's screen.

I'll see them. Just give me a few minutes to finish these notes.

A message flicked back:

Thanks. The good karma fairy is looking down on you.

'Okay. One of the physiotherapists will miss his lunch for you. Please take a seat.'

The softly spoken woman's voice wavered. 'Oh.

That's very kind. Thank you. Thank you. Lachie? The nice man will see you soon.'

Finn walked through to the waiting room and was just about to call out the boy's name when he was struck completely dumb. His heart thudded against his ribcage as he watched the woman reading a story to her child. Her voice quiet and sing-song, dark hair tumbling over one shoulder, ivory skin. A gentle manner. Soft.

His brain rewound, flickering like an old film reel: dark curls on the pillow. Warm caramel eyes. A mouth that tasted so sweet. Laughter in the face of grief. One night.

That night…

A lifetime ago.

He snapped back to reality. He wasn't that man any more; he'd do well to remember that. He cleared his throat and glanced down at the notes file in his hand to remind himself of the name. 'Lachlan Harding?'

'Yes. Yes—oh?' She froze, completely taken aback. For a second he saw fear flicker across her eyes then she stood up. Fear? Why? Because he'd never called as he'd promised? 'Finn? Is it you? It's Finn, yes?'

There was little warmth there; her mouth was taut in a straight line. No laughter. Not at all. She was still startlingly pretty. Not a trace of make-up, but she didn't need anything to make her any more beautiful. His gut clenched as he remembered more of that night and how good she'd made him feel.

Too bad, matey.

The fear gone, she smiled hesitantly and tugged the boy closer to her leg, her voice a little wobbly and a little less soft. 'Wow. Finn, this is a surprise—'

'Sophie. Hello. Yes, I'm Finn. Long time, no see.' Glib, he knew, when there was so much he should say to explain what had happened, why he hadn't called, but telling her his excuses during a professional consultation wasn't the right time. Besides, she had a child now; she'd moved on from their one night together, clearly. He glanced at her left hand, the one that held her boy so close—no wedding ring. But that didn't mean a thing these days; she could be happily unmarried and in a relationship.

And why her marital status pinged into his head he just didn't know. He had no right to wonder after the silence he'd held for well over two years.

They were just two people who'd shared one night a long time ago. There was no professional line to cross here. He was doing her a favour by seeing her son. If things felt awkward he could always assign her to a different physiotherapist for the next appointment.

'Yes. Wow. It's a small world.' He infused his manner with professionalism, choosing not to go down Memory Lane. He was a different man now. Although he couldn't help but notice as he turned that his left leg was shaking a little more than usual. In fact, all of him was. It was surprise, that was all. His past life clashing with his present. He concentrated hard on being steady and not limping in front of her, because for some reason it mattered that she saw him as whole. 'Right, then, so this is Lachie? Come on through.'

Good karma? No chance. Judging by the way Sophie was looking at him, the good karma fairy had gone on her lunch break.

Finn.

Wow.

Sophie put her hand to her mouth and followed him into the examination room. Tried to act calm while her heart hammered against her chest wall. So many questions.

Finn. She hadn't even known his surname. *Geez*. It was on his badge. Finn Baird. That information would have been immensely useful a few years ago.

Wow. Here he was, after all this time. After everything. She gaped at him, wanting to rail at him, to put her fists on his chest and pound. Hard. Wanted to ask him where the hell he'd been and what the hell he'd been doing. But she did none of that and instead she smiled, fussed around her son and pretended being here with the man who'd no doubt forgotten her the moment she'd left the hotel room was no big deal at all.

The most important person in the room was Lachie, so both she and Finn needed to rise above any failed promises from a long time ago. 'This is Lachie. He's eighteen months old. He's got bilateral talipes. He's been treated with the Ponseti method and now we're just keeping the feet straight with boots and bars at night.' She paused and tried not to sound as rattled as she felt. 'Thanks for fitting us in. I'm sorry we missed our appointment with Ross.'

'He's got a meeting across town, otherwise I'm sure he'd have waited for you.' *Oh. Okay. So no chance of a reprieve, then.*

Finn lifted his eyes from Lachie's notes and met her gaze. She couldn't tell in those Celtic blue irises what the hell was going on in his head, but she knew by the complete lack of concern in his demeanour that he had no idea. No idea at all.

'So this is his routine check-up? How's he doing with the boots and bars?'

'Not well, I'm afraid. He's pretty grumpy about it all.' She picked her son up and popped him on the examination couch and tickled him. Pretty much guaranteed to bring a smile to his face. Because right now she couldn't cope with another tantrum. Right now she wanted to rewind the clock to this morning, have a different start to the day and make her appointment with the other physiotherapist on time. 'Grumpy, aren't you? Mr Monster?'

Her boy threw his head back and giggled. It was such a delicious sound and always made her world a lot better when she heard it. She looked over and saw Finn watching her. Was he doing the maths?

Her heart contracted in a swift and urgent need to protect her boy. She put her arms around him and held him close. But Finn seemed completely oblivious to what was right in front of his face. 'You're still working, Sophie? I heard you say something about it at Reception. A nurse—that's right?'

So he'd remembered that at least. Had he remembered anything else? How right it had felt? How crazy it had been to find someone who *got* you in a city the size of Edinburgh, a country the size of Scotland? That was what she'd thought then. Now she could only think of curse words. She bit them back. 'Yes. I'm a Health Visitor now, though. I work out of Campbell Street clinic.'

'Ah. A nine-to-five gig?'

'More like eight until eight most days. But yes.'

'You like it?'

What did it matter to him? What did any of her life matter to him?

It was hard to believe she was here having a conversation about minor stuff instead of the conversation they should have been having. But not here, not in front of Lachie. 'I don't want to take up more of your time than I should. Let's get on, shall we? It's all in the notes but I'll précis for you. It'll be quicker. Lachie had eight castings to make his feet straight and a tenotomy to loosen the heel cords, which hurt but he tolerated. He wears the boots and bars only at night-time and for his afternoon naps now. I try to make sure he has them on close to twelve hours a day.' She took the offending plastic boots out of her bag and gave them to Finn. 'He hates them.'

Finn's eyes widened but he nodded. If he was rattled by her he didn't show it, at least not to Lachie. For that she was grateful. Finn grinned down at the boy. 'So, Mr Monster, eh? Cool name, buddy. The rest of us get stuck with boring ones like Finn. That's me. Finn.' He stuck his hand out towards Lachie, who was staring up at him with his wide—Celtic blue—eyes. 'You want to shake hands? No? How about a high five? That's right, my man. High. Low…' Finn brought his hand up high then down low then right back to meet Lachie's little palm. 'Ah, you got me. You're too quick.' He looked down at Lachie's feet and asked, 'Is it okay if I look at your feet? Can you take your trainers off? Atta boy.'

Sophie's heart was bursting with pride as she watched Lachie rip the Velcro on his trainers with a huge grin. Then even more as he hit them on the examination trolley until they flashed. 'Flash.'

'Whoa.' Finn raised his palms and looked very impressed. 'This is superhero territory.'

He leaned his hips against the couch and stamped his right foot. Then wobbled minutely and grabbed the gurney, glancing for the tiniest of moments over to Sophie and then back at Lachie. Which was a little strange.

Was he checking if she'd seen him wobble? Or just checking if she was watching his examination? Some health professionals were spooked if they had to treat other medics, in case they were being judged.

Finn shrugged. 'See? Mine don't flash at all. I need a pair of those. If only you could wear the flashing ones at night instead, eh? But they are for daytime adventures and these…' he picked up the clinical plastic boots and showed them to Lachie '…these are for night-time adventures. I know, I know you don't like them but they'll give you even more superhero powers if you keep them on. Right, let's have a look at those toes. Ten? You have ten toes? Excellent. I won't tickle, I promise. Well, not if you don't want me to.'

'Can you see the redness?' She knew she was starting to sound rude but being in here was suffocating. The pride in her son mingled with sadness and anger in Sophie's chest. Finn should have called as he'd said he would. He should have damned well called. She tried to hurry him up. 'There, at the back of the heel.'

'Well, the feet are nice and straight so that's good. But yes, there is some redness. The boots seem to be the right size. Have you tried putting Vaseline in? That helps.'

'Yes. But he's so wriggly when I put them on it's like a game of Twister, all arms and legs. I think he's scraping his heels against the plastic when he tries to scramble his feet out while I try to squeeze them in.'

Finn nodded. 'Yes, it's a common problem. I'll give you some second skin plasters; they should help. It's often easier to have someone else around to give you a hand putting the boots on at bedtime. Either that or become an octopus.'

'An octopus?'

'Eight arms.' He grinned at his little joke.

She didn't. 'Well, we'll just have to manage because…' She didn't want to say it, not to him, but it was the truth. She'd lost her beloved grandmother—her main cheerleader her whole life—before she'd even met Finn. Her parents had barely been in the same hemisphere as her for twenty-odd years. And she'd been too busy being a working single mum to raise her head over the dating parapet. '… There is no one else.'

Finn's head shot up from examining Lachie. 'I see. Okay. Well, listen, Mr Monster, could you be a good boy and sit very still when your Mummy puts your boots on every night?'

Lachie nodded, open-mouthed.

'I've got some superhero stickers for you. Every time you sit still for Mummy you can have a sticker. Deal? And you can put them on your night-time boots and make them fit for a superhero like you.'

'Yes.' Lachie nodded and laughed. 'Dickers.'

'Stickers, honey. St…stickers. Thanks, er, Finn. That's a great idea. We'll try them.'

Typical. Every night was a battleground lately and, no matter what she'd done or said or promised, Lachie had fought her about those boots. Now he was nodding, all big-eyed at Finn.

Yes, life would have been immensely easier if there'd been two pairs of hands throughout her pregnancy and the birth and the endless hospital appointments for Lachie's feet. Two parents to ease the strain. Two brains to work out how to deal with his problems and work out a shared timetable instead of it all being on her, juggling everything. Two hearts to love him. Because he deserved that, more than anything.

She pressed her lips together and stopped a stream of bad words escaping her mouth. At least the man was taking time out of his schedule to see them. He wasn't all bad.

There had been many times, usually during one of Lachie's sleepless nights, or more recently during his tantrums, when she'd thought the opposite. She really needed to talk to him.

Finn grinned. 'Let's see you walking, shall we? Just bare feet.'

'He started to walk at fourteen months, and he's met all his other milestones. I had him treated as soon as we could and I've been pedantic about making sure he's wearing the boots and bars. The staff at Nursery know what to do and snap the bars on every nap time too.' She looked at the thin plastic boots and the metal bar they snapped into to hold his feet at the correct angle, for over half of his short life, and her heart pinged again. It hadn't been plain sailing.

'Well, it's definitely working. Look, the feet are just a little splayed out and that's what we want for now. Perfect.' Well, the guy definitely knew his stuff; she couldn't fault him on that. Finn lifted Lachie to the floor then he walked to the far end of the room.

Interesting. He definitely favoured his left leg as he walked. A subtle limp he hadn't had that night. Knowing him, it was a rugby injury; he'd mentioned he played. That had accounted for the body she'd enjoyed so damned much. She watched him now, the way he moved with less finesse but with a body that sung with the benefits of hard-core exercise. Beneath his navy polo shirt she saw the outline of muscles, the hug of short sleeves around impeccable biceps. His perfect backside in those black trousers. Her stomach contracted at the thought of what they'd done in that hotel room, the way he'd treated her with reverence, the way he'd slowly undressed her and caressed her. The taste of him.

She swallowed hard and pushed a rare rush of lust away. She had no right thinking like that. He'd let her down. Let her son down.

She appraised the simple facts; he was a man who knew a lot about keeping a body fit, that was all. A physiotherapy student, he'd said he was, and a rugby player for some club or other; she hadn't ever followed the sport so it had meant nothing to her.

Knowing him. Well, she didn't, did she? Not at all. She'd liked him. A lot. They'd clicked. At least she'd thought so.

Turned out they hadn't. When he didn't call she'd tried to find him but it was hard to find someone when you didn't know their surname. She'd Googled. Scoured social media. Even checked out the physiotherapy departments in every Scottish university, but he'd disappeared into thin air and in the end she'd had to give up. The guy really hadn't wanted to know her at all. Or her child.

His child.

CHAPTER TWO

THERE IS NO one else.

Sophie's words had been going over and over in his head since the consultation yesterday. No ring. No partner. And each time she'd appeared in his brain his gut had jumped at the thought of her being single, then taken a dive as he registered the reality of his situation.

But something was bugging him about the boy and her story, like a jigsaw puzzle piece that didn't fit. He couldn't put a finger on it, but her demeanour had been off. She'd been in a hurry to leave. She'd kept the boy close. As if…as if what? As if she didn't trust Finn with him. Why the hell not?

Shaking his head, he punched the boy's name into his work computer and waited for Lachie's file to appear.

'Hey. Put the work down. It's past six and I'm parched.' Ross appeared in the doorway to Finn's office, briefcase in hand and coat on. 'Fancy a drink at the Tavern? I'm meeting Greta and some of the gang from here are coming down too.'

Oh-oh, that spelt trouble. 'It's not some sort of blind date thing, is it?'

'You really are dating-shy, aren't you?' Ross was all pretend offended as he put his hand on his heart. 'Would I do that to you?'

'I don't know.' Finn thought back to yesterday's conversation. 'Yes. Probably.'

'I can one hundred per cent assure you that I have not arranged for any single women to be in the vicinity of the bar tonight. Although I can't vouch for Greta; she's a different kettle of fish altogether, she's keen to see you settled. But not tonight, I promise. All I can offer is beer, maybe some greasy chips and a steak pie. Come on. You missed the last team night out.'

Because he'd been new to the job and hadn't wanted to answer a zillion questions about the accident. But, with a sigh, Finn relented. It was about time he started to extend a hand of friendship to his colleagues. If this new life was going to work out it would have to involve social stuff too. 'Sure, I'll come over when I'm done here.'

Ross walked into the office and looked over Finn's shoulder. 'Problem?'

Searching for Lachie was veering on the personal and not suitable for work. He'd have to look tomorrow to try to solve the puzzle. 'No. Just checking I wrote the notes on an extra I saw yesterday.'

Ross squinted at the screen. 'Ah, little Lachie Harding. Good kid. Mum's pretty cool too. She's worked hard with him. I wish every parent was like that. Although she missed her appointment yesterday, which isn't like her. I wondered if she turned up eventually. You saw them?'

'Yes. He's doing fine, but the boots are rubbing. I think he's getting to the age where he wants what he wants and makes sure everyone knows about it. We talked through some remedies.' Why he had such an interest in the boy he didn't want to admit. He certainly couldn't tell his boss.

I had a one-night stand. I liked her. A lot. I thought there could be something, but then I couldn't get over my big, fat, broken ego to call her.

He had a sudden thought which made his gut plummet. What was Lachie's date of birth again? Finn had been too bamboozled seeing her again he hadn't taken much else in.

Hot damn. The boy was eighteen months old, if he remembered correctly.

Which meant he'd been born… Finn did some maths and inhaled sharply.

They'd used a condom. Hadn't they?

Of course they had. He always did.

His head started to buzz with questions as he tried to clinically reimagine what they'd done that night. But, since the accident, events from around that time were very hazy.

'Earth to Finn.' Ross tapped his foot. 'Come on, beer awaits. Get a move on.'

'Sure. I'll just grab my stuff.' Finn slung his messenger bag over his shoulder then grabbed his stick and leaned heavily on it to stand up. Ross was just about the only person he could do this in front of, even if it smacked of weakness. When he'd applied for the job he'd had to be upfront about what he was capable of and what he couldn't do, but Ross had taken him on with no hesitation.

'Still sore?' Ross glanced down at Finn's leg, taking his role as mentor and supporter very seriously.

Finn shrugged as the pain subsided. What he needed was real time off the stump. 'Just aching after the race. Nothing to worry about. I just thought I'd take a bit of pressure off with this.' He waved the folding black stick with a carved Maori *tiki* handle his brother had sent from New Zealand.

'I thought you hated using it.'

'I do.' Because it made him feel less. Made him look different to other guys his age. And yes, he was all for standing up for diversity issues, but it didn't mean he had to like the fact he only had one leg, or flaunt it, and he definitely never expected to be treated any differently to anyone else. 'Don't think for a minute it gives you an excuse to start being nice to me.'

Ross shrugged. 'Okay. Well, the last one to the pub gets the first round. And if you're going to be all equal opportunities then I'm not giving you a head start. Better get yer hand in your pocket.'

'That's right. Exploit the disabled, why don't you?' Finn laughed, glad to be treated as nothing unusual, and hurried after his boss, letting the stick take the strain for once. He'd hide it away in his bag just before they hit the pub.

Edinburgh was starting to thaw after a long cold winter but the air was still tinged with the promise of snow as they stepped outside. Finn inhaled deeply and walked down the ramp to George Street. This was good. Yes. Beers with friends. A little like old times. He smiled to himself…almost the same and yet a million times different.

Worry crept under his skin, pushing aside the smile, as his mind bounced back to Sophie. They'd used a condom. Right?

It couldn't…he couldn't…the boy. Surely not?

Not now. Not when he could barely look after himself. Not when this new life of his was hard enough to deal with.

'Finn?' A voice from the shadows of the hospital entrance made him jump.

He whirled around, almost losing his footing, but leaned more on the stick to right himself. 'Hello?'

'Finn. It's me, Sophie.' She stepped out from behind a huge stone pillar. Her eyes were haunted. Her skin completely devoid of colour as her top teeth worried her bottom lip. She had a thick red scarf tied under her chin and tucked into a long dark coat but, despite the layers, she looked frozen through. For the briefest moment he thought about wrapping his arms around her to warm her up. Then he remembered his leg. Remembered he'd let her down by disappearing without a trace and not living up to his promise to call her. The likelihood of her wanting his arms around her was less than zero per cent.

Idiot.

He glanced at Ross up ahead, just about to disappear round a corner and oblivious to Sophie's presence, thought about calling after him in case she wanted to chat about her son's issues, but she'd said *Finn*. Not Ross.

In another life he'd have been flattered to have a beautiful woman accosting him as he stepped out of work, but she'd seen him with his stick and his limp and they had a history. His stomach tightened. *Damn. Damn. Damn.* Not a great start. But he had a feeling, judging by the way she was looking at him, things were only going to get worse.

'Hey, there. Are you okay, Sophie? You look…upset.'

She shook her head, eyes brimming with tears. 'No, I'm not okay. I can't stop thinking about it and I need to talk to you.'

Thinking about what? He tried to stay calm but the thunder in his chest kept rumbling. 'Sure. Of course. Here?'

'No. Somewhere warm.' She looked down at his stick and her eyes widened. 'Are you okay to walk? What happened?'

'I'm fine.' He felt exposed and caught off guard as he flicked the stick into thirds and shoved it in his bag. Now she'd see him as something less too. 'There's a bar across the way. Or the café in the hospital?'

'Whatever's nearer. I can't be long; I had to get a friend to watch over Lachie while I came here.'

He walked back up the ramp and inside the hospital, his heart now thundering almost out of his chest. 'Coffee?' Banal but necessary. Anything to fill the void in the conversation.

She almost flinched at his question. 'No. Thanks. Just water.'

After a few minutes they were facing each other in an otherwise empty café. Outside, the street lights cast an eerie glow. Inside, the strip lights were too bright, too clinical. He wrapped his hands around his mug of steaming coffee, bracing himself for what he'd already worked out. At least he thought he had. It was hardly rocket science. Just a bit of sex and some maths.

Only it hadn't been just sex; it had been mind-blowing. Intimate. The most intense, the most sensual he'd ever had, and he would have called her if he'd ever stopped feeling sorry for himself. 'Okay, Sophie, I'm guessing this is more than just a telling-off for not calling you?'

She nodded. 'I wish it were that simple. Believe me, I can most definitely deal with rejection and I would have chalked you up to experience and forgotten all about it.'

He guessed that was supposed to hurt him. Surprisingly, it did, a little. 'But...?'

'That night... I thought... I thought you were okay, you know? I thought we might, well, at least see each other again. You certainly seemed keen. But you just went cold. Was I just a one-night stand to you? Was that it? Because that's not what you said at the time. That's not how it felt. But then, I was pretty cut up about my grandmother's death, so I was easy prey to someone like you.'

Ouch. Someone like you. He didn't know exactly what she meant by that but he could see how it would have looked to her: single guy picks up grieving beautiful woman. Takes advantage. Doesn't call. 'It wasn't like that. I liked you. It was...' Special. Different.

'What was it, Finn? To you?' She twisted her hands together and took a deep breath. Her nostrils flared and her jaw tightened and the deep breathing didn't seem to be helping. She looked up at him and glared. 'Whatever. Forget it. It doesn't matter now; what you felt doesn't matter. Except... Actually, you know what? I'm so angry at you because everything could have been a damned sight easier if you'd just picked up the phone.'

'I lost it. Down a mountain.' Along with his self-esteem, his stupid decision-making and, for a long time, his positivity. Thankfully that was clawing its way back.

He wasn't going to tell her that he'd left his phone down there on purpose, that he'd made sure all his contacts were erased. That the ones in the Cloud were too. That he'd drawn a line between before the accident and after and given his brother instructions to hide as much information about Finn as he could from everyone.

Her eyebrows rose as if to say *lame excuse*. 'You know, I've thought about what I was going to say to you, so many times. I've rehearsed it over and over and now I'm here I don't actually know what to say.'

She was hurting and he didn't think it was from rejection; it was from those hard years of being pregnant and a single mother. He took a breath and jumped. 'Lachie's my son. Right?'

He prayed she was going to say *Wrong*. But why the heck else was she here? She wouldn't come this far just to berate him for not following up on a date almost two and a half years ago.

She gasped. 'I tried to find you. So hard you wouldn't believe. I always wanted you to know. It's your right, and his. But now...' Her eyes darkened. 'I don't know what it's going to mean to you—what *he's* going to mean to you—so I don't want you to know because you might go cold again and he doesn't deserve that. He deserves a father who wants to know him, who's interested and in it for the long haul and I'm not sure you're that guy.'

Wow.

She continued, 'But you have to know, everyone says so, and I feel like I have to tell you, otherwise it's on my conscience. So, yes, my gorgeous little Lachlan Spencer Harding, that beautiful, funny, clever handful, is your son.'

Finn closed his eyes and tried to control the emotions, ones he wasn't prepared for, tumbling through him. He didn't want to be a father. He didn't want to have the responsibility of it all. He wasn't ready. Would he ever be ready? He had one leg, damn it. He could barely walk. He couldn't turn round quickly and catch a falling child. He couldn't teach him how to kick a ball or run around in the park like he'd dreamed his own dad would do, but never did. He couldn't protect himself from hurt, never mind an eighteen-month-old.

He wished they'd never had that night. He wished he'd kept in touch with her. He wished he hadn't fallen hundreds of feet down a mountain in a blizzard and made himself an invalid when now…now he needed two legs more than ever in his whole life.

He nodded, feeling the same kind of sensation he'd had that wintry night when he'd stepped into thin air… as if he was falling into a nightmare. And yet, cushioning the landing, was a bright shining kernel of something good. He had a son.

Whoa.

A giggling, wriggling superhero with two club feet who most definitely deserved the very best of fathers.

He'd had a son for one and a half years. He'd missed so much already.

And he knew all about being that kid with no dad. About the dreams of him turning up one day and being like some sort of king. About watching the other kids get to play, work, laugh with their fathers and wonder what you'd done that was so bad yours didn't want to know you. He knew how that felt and he wasn't going to let his son go through that.

He opened his eyes and looked at Sophie, who was watching him with a hand pressed to her mouth and a frown on her forehead. God knew what she'd been through. He imagined the names she'd called him. Imagined the sleepless nights, the endless worry. Then the righteous anger at his silence. It was time to man up. 'I'm so sorry.'

'Sorry?' Sophie was lost for words. She'd expected him to deny his child, demand a paternity test or be angry that she'd come here and told him. She hadn't expected this. Was it a trick?

'Yeah. I blew it. I messed up. I should have called but…' He ran a hand across his dark hair and shrugged. 'Circumstances meant I wasn't in a position to call for a while. Then I just thought… Well, to be honest, I didn't think at all.'

'Clearly. You lost your phone down a mountain, but you can retrieve information from backup online; everyone knows that.' She had nowhere to focus the anger she'd stored up for so long and he was stripping it away from her with one word. *Sorry.* It seemed as if he really was, but it wasn't enough. 'There are lots of ways to find information if you want it badly enough.' Although wanting hadn't helped her.

'I couldn't. I just couldn't, okay? I didn't know you needed me. And, if I remember rightly, the name you'd tapped into the phone was Sexy Sophie so I couldn't have looked for you anyway. We didn't do the surname thing.'

'Yes, well, I presumed we'd get to that on the second date.'

He'd said she was beautiful, called her sexy as hell, and she'd laughed and told him he was clearly drunk. But he hadn't been and neither had she. He'd been funny and caring and enigmatic. He'd stroked her back when she'd cried about her grandmother. He'd listened when she'd told him about the hole in her life without her and he'd told her about how cut up he'd been over his mother's death, how he felt responsible, how much he understood Sophie's grief. They'd been honest and open. Which was why she'd been so confused when he hadn't called.

He leaned forward and caught her gaze. 'Sophie, I

didn't intend for this to happen. I was going to call. I don't usually—'

'Sleep with someone after just meeting them? Me neither. Ever.' She hadn't had so much as a first date with a guy for over two years. 'You were my first and only. Didn't work out like I imagined.'

'And now I have a son.' He looked as if he was struggling to keep a lid on his emotions. He pressed his lips together and they sat in silence for a few moments, both absorbing this life-changing information. He looked bereft and yet animated at the same time. His fingers rubbed his temple, pushed into thick dark hair that was so much like his son's, and those eyes—the exact same blue. Lachie had inherited her nose and mouth, but there was so much of him that belonged to his father. Finn shook his head. 'So what do I do?'

'About…?'

'About Lachie. What do you want? What does he want?'

Where to start? Two parents who were available and around and attentive, unlike the childhood she'd had. 'Lachie's pretty easy to please. He's a toddler; he wants attention, ice cream and more of those stickers you gave him yesterday. Tomorrow he'll want something else.'

'He likes them? Are they working?' Finn smiled and his face was transformed, and she was spun right back to yesterday when he'd made Lachie laugh. Right back to that night when he'd done so much more than make her laugh. There was something about him that still intrigued her, attracted her, if she was honest. He was still insanely good-looking and, with the cocky edges rubbed off, even charming.

But she couldn't trust him, not with her heart or her son's. She needed to tread carefully. 'He's too young for star charts really, you know. It's probably just novelty value that made him sit still last night.'

'Oh. It works for other kids.' Finn looked as if he'd been stung. 'But you're probably right. What do I know? I only met him yesterday; I have no idea what would work for him.'

'I'm sorry, I didn't mean that the way it came out.'

'You know him, I don't. I have a lot to learn. I don't know where to start.'

He really did look lost and she felt fleetingly sorry for him. He had a lot to take on board. Her son—their son—was a mini hurricane and Finn had no idea about the chaos a child could cause to his life. That was why she was worried about getting him involved with Lachie at all. How could she risk her son's happiness by introducing him to a potentially absent father? Finn hadn't exactly showed 'stickability' or reliability, but he had a right to get to know his boy. She was struggling here between her conscience and her son's needs.

'You learn as you go. I didn't know everything the minute he popped out. It was a huge learning curve that doesn't look like it's going to flatten out any time soon.'

He shook his head. 'So how do you see this working? I have to confess I'm struggling here. Only, if I have a son I will do my best by him. No hesitation.'

'I need to know you're committed to him. That you're not going to randomly bounce in and out of his life and hurt him.'

Shock rippled through his gaze. 'You've got a pretty poor opinion of me. I know we don't know each other very well, but you need to know I wouldn't do that.'

They didn't know each other at all, really. They'd made a baby but all she knew was that he was beautiful and completely unreliable. 'I'm sure you believe you'll be the best of fathers but I'm not willing to take a risk on you spending time with Lachie if you're going to disappear when something else comes along.'

His eyes darkened to navy as anger started to rise again. 'I have a right to get to know him. I'm sure there's a law or something.'

That was the last thing she needed: some kind of injunction to add to being a working single mum and surviving each day. It was in all their interests to work this through smoothly. 'I know. I know you have. But let's just do it slowly.' Then she could assess his impact on Lachie's life and flight risk. 'Baby steps.'

Finn glanced down at his leg and his whole body tensed as if he'd just remembered something. He looked back at her with a bleakness that tugged at her heart and raised so many more questions. 'I don't know if I'm even capable of that.'

CHAPTER THREE

'WHAT HAPPENED?' As Sophie followed the line of his gaze down to his leg, she lost the straightened back and tight jaw and softened into everything he remembered from that long-ago night: concerned, gentle, compassionate. Colour had come back into her cheeks and her eyes were warmer now as she looked back at him. Her head tilted to one side and she smiled. Just enough to make his gut tighten.

It made him want to tell her everything. But he stuck to the medical details; she'd be able to find them easily enough if she looked him up on the health board database. Unethical, but possible, if she felt the need. 'It wasn't just the phone that fell down the mountain. I went with it.'

'Wow. That must have been scary. But you're alive, that's something. Thank goodness.' She looked at his leg again, then at the rest of him and it felt strange to be scrutinised by a woman who'd seen him at his physical best. 'How badly were you hurt?'

He wondered what she was expecting him to answer when he numbered off his injuries. 'A broken pelvis. Cracked spine. Dislocated shoulder. Displaced collarbone. Head injury. Frostbite. Hypothermia…' He waited for all that to sink in, watched her eyes widen.

He looked for pity, thought he might have seen it mixed in with her shock. 'And my pièce de résistance…lower left leg amputation.'

'Oh,' she gasped. He searched for revulsion now but didn't see that. 'I'm so sorry—that must have been hard to get over.'

Was an understatement. 'I'm still on that upward climb.' He armoured himself against the inevitable. 'So this is where you leave, right? After all, a useless father is worse than none at all.'

She frowned, taken aback. 'Are you for real? Is that what you think? I've had a useless, absent father myself, which is why I don't want that for my son, and I work with enough broken families to see how much damage half-hearted and selfish parents can wreak on a child's life. I just want him to have a dad, Finn. One leg or two, I don't think he'd care so long as he was around on a regular basis.'

But Finn cared, and because of that he was having second thoughts about getting involved at all. What kind of pride would shine in his son's eyes when his dad lost the fathers' race at sports day or needed a chair to watch him play football because standing too long hurt too damned much? None.

He felt a tight fist of pain in his gut. And how could he protect his son from hurt? He didn't exactly have a good track record on that front. If he'd been a better person, been more reliable and less self-focused, his mother might still be alive and he might have had two legs instead of one.

No. Much better that he took some steps back and didn't get involved. 'Maybe it would be better if I stayed out of the picture. Stay in touch, obviously. I'm invested here, and I'll pay what's necessary and more. I imagine I owe a lot in child support.'

Those caramel eyes burnt hot. 'What? You think this is about money? You think I want anything from you? I've managed by myself and can keep on doing that if you don't care enough to see him.'

He thought about the little kid he'd met yesterday, the grumpiness that he'd clearly inherited from his dad. The sunny smile he'd got from his mum. Something fierce bloomed in Finn's chest. 'I care enough to not see him. I don't want him to be ashamed. That's a lot to live with for a child.'

'For God's sake, Finn, listen to yourself. He needs love. He needs a dad in his life, someone who is emotionally available, but if you're not up to it we'll be just fine without you.' Sophie scraped her chair back and stood. She tugged a piece of paper out of her bag and thrust it at him. 'I've written some details down for you, just in case you lose your phone again. It's all there: date of birth, weight at birth, milestones, medical issues. Likes, dislikes. I thought you might want to know. And he drew you a picture on the back.'

He had his first picture. From his son. *Holy hell.* That gave him a jolt of pride right in the centre of his chest.

Sophie was shaking her head, her ponytail swinging, eyes blazing. So utterly at odds with the woman he'd shared the night with. This was a lioness protecting her young. She was vibrant, strong and determined. This was what parenting did to you and even though he'd only known about his child for a matter of minutes he felt the stirrings of that inside him. 'He drew me a picture?'

'Don't worry; I just said it was for the nice man at

the clinic. I didn't mention your real connection, just in case—'

'In case I didn't want to know?' Shame flooded through him; of course he wanted to know. How could he not? How could he deny the boy this right? Deny himself the dreams he'd had growing up? He picked up the paper, which had some of the superhero stickers on it and brown and yellow crayon squiggles. His heart contracted. 'I won't lose it, I promise. Thank you. Please sit down; let's talk this through.'

Her eyebrows rose. 'No. You need time to think and I have to go; it's bedtime and I don't want to wear out my friend's generosity.'

'I imagine things have been difficult for you. To get time for yourself.'

She stiffened. 'I manage.'

He didn't want her to go and told himself it was because he needed to sort all this out today. 'We could both go to your house now and talk, work out a plan.'

She took a step back, palms raised. 'Whoa. No way. A minute ago you wanted to stay away, now you want to see him this minute. Like I said, Finn, we need baby steps and we need to draw up some rules. Have a think about it all and email your expectations through to me. I'll do the same. Then we can talk further. Then, and only then, can you meet him for a supervised visit.'

'Supervised visits? You've pulled out the big words for this.' He knew why. He hadn't exactly proven himself, not just once but repeatedly. He'd wavered from promising he'd be the best father in the world to shying away from the realities of his missing leg and his limitations. But proper unconditional love overrode those things.

She shrugged. 'I don't know you and I'm damned

sure I won't let you hurt my child. I'm just protecting us all.'

If she was intending to rile him it was working. She was clearly very protective of Lachie, and he admired that, admired how she'd brought up a good kid on her own. But her lack of faith in him stung.

'*Our* child, Sophie. I'm his father; I won't hurt him.'

She shook her head and he could tell she was not going to give in easily. 'You provided some DNA, Finn. Let's just see how much of a father you can be.'

'Hi, I'm back! Thanks so much for having him for me.' Sophie bundled through the door of her late grandmother's house and found her friend Hannah sitting on the sofa in front of a blazing coal fire, playing with Lachie and a digital tablet. Her heart squeezed as he looked up and grinned. Her boy. Just hers for a few precious months, really, and now she was having to share him… Was she doing the right thing by letting Finn in?

She didn't really have a choice if she was going to be able to live with herself, one way or another. Time would tell.

She let all the anger and irritation and the surprising jolt of attraction go—the guy had been through a lot and yet he was still gorgeous, still capable of being serious and yet funny. Still hot enough to make her heart race and her palms itch to touch him. He was all the things she'd promised herself not to get involved with. She needed to be just a mother now. 'How's my boy been?'

'Very good—eaten all his supper and had a nice play.' Hannah wriggled out from Lachie's grip, planted a kiss on his head and grabbed her coat and bag. 'Bye-bye, Lachie! Be good for Mummy.' She leaned close to Sophie and whispered, 'I thought I'd leave the torture device to you. I'm not brave enough to tackle that. I want him to like me.'

'The boots and bars? Hush now. They're for his own good.'

'I know. I just don't like conflict.' Hannah wandered towards the door and waited for Sophie to join her. There was a teasing light in her eyes and Sophie's heart fell. Because, knowing Hannah, she wouldn't be allowed to get on with the evening without an interrogation. 'How was the dad?'

Gorgeous. Enigmatic. Inspiring. Probably useless.

'Shocked, but I think he'd worked it out. So I'm glad I fronted up and told him.'

'Does he want to be involved?'

Sophie put down her bag and went to stoke the fire, absentmindedly answering her friend. 'With Lachie?'

'Of course with Lachie.' Hannah glanced over to the little boy on the sofa swiping pages and telling himself the story he knew off by heart, and then back to Sophie. 'You didn't think I meant involved with you…' Her eyes grew. 'You don't want…do you? I mean…you did like him once. Enough to sleep with him, and that's not like you at all.'

'Hush! No. Of course I don't want to be involved with him.' She didn't. She really didn't. 'I can't trust him as far as I'd throw him. My heart's not part of the deal, nor my body. I told him Lachie needed a father; I didn't mention anything about a family.' Which was ironic, really, given all she'd ever wanted was a proper family of her own. But she had that now. Her and her boy.

Hannah seemed to have other ideas. 'Still eye candy though?'

'Outwardly, yes, gorgeous. Inwardly, a little hung up. He had an accident and I think it's shaken him up.'

But hell, losing a limb would have an effect on…everything. 'You know it's not about how good-looking he is; it's about what he can bring for Lachie. I really wish you'd never got that eye candy information out of me.'

Hannah winked. 'What's a best friend for?'

'Babysitting?'

'Any time. I love that boy. *Ciao bella*. Love you too.' Then she darted out of the door, blowing a kiss. If it hadn't been for her, Sophie would never had stayed sane over the last couple of years.

Closing the door behind her friend, she took a deep breath and tried to get rid of the strange feelings she'd had since seeing Finn. Through two and a half years of silence she'd been downright annoyed, then frustrated, then, to varying degrees, angry all over again. Eventually the simmering anger had faded into…nothing. She'd had no feelings about him at all. Until yesterday, when her ire had risen again, punctuated with the annoying fluster of being with someone who she'd been too honest with.

And then there was the giddy heartbeat and the uplift in her gut just to be around him and the little tug in her belly—stirrings of something she'd forgotten she was even capable of: attraction.

Damn him for appearing just as she was getting her life into some kind of routine after the craziness of childbirth and learning how to be a parent, especially when she'd had little blueprint for that from her own parents. She looked over at the only male she wanted in her life and her heart softened. 'Okay, gorgeous little man, it's time for bed. Come on, let's get that bath run.'

After much splashing and then warm milk he was just about ready for bed. 'Right, let's get on and do your superhero boots.'

'No.' Lachie waddled to the other side of his bedroom and hid in the wardrobe. 'No.'

'Hey…don't forget you'll get the stickers. That nice man, Finn, at the clinic said you could have stickers.' This was always wearing. The fight, the fight, the fight. She crawled over to the wardrobe and opened the door, found him sitting on the floor, his mouth set in an expression she'd seen on Finn earlier. *God, they were similar.* She'd pretended she hadn't noticed before, but it was stark now. She put her hand on his leg and tickled. 'Come out, Mr Monster.'

'No. No boots.' The kid had started to string two words together now and she'd be so proud of him if he hadn't learnt the word 'no'.

'I'll get the stickers and you can have one if you come out. You can have more if you sit still.' She crawled back across the floor, opened a drawer in his cupboard and took out the stickers. Then she put on her sing-song voice. 'One sticker for Lachie. One sticker for Lachie. Oh, this is a good one. Lachie's favourite.'

After five minutes or so of playing this game to herself her boy eventually crawled out of the wardrobe, too nosy to be able to resist. 'Dicker.'

'When you have the boots and bars on.'

He shook his head.

She nodded and held the boots out. 'Let's put them on now. Now, Lachie, or no stickers at all.'

He didn't make eye contact but he sat on the floor and put his feet out. She tugged him onto her lap and showed him the boots with yesterday's stickers stuck on. 'One sticker for one foot and one sticker for the other.'

She didn't want to admit it, but the stickers had been a great idea.

Her mind did a leap from her son's feet to his father's.

It was the first time she'd allowed herself to really think about Finn's leg. She'd managed to keep her face straight when he'd told her about the amputation, but she couldn't imagine how terrible that would have been for him. How hard that would have been to get over for a physical guy like him. And then there'd been the rugby...losing a leg would have been an absolute game changer for his sport, and it would have meant he'd have had to redefine himself.

That took guts. A lot of guts. There he was walking, working, giving. Coming up with solutions to help her—and yes, it was only a tiny thing, but it changed the dynamic between her and Lachie; it gave them something fun and rewarding and it worked...and for that she was grateful.

She felt a catch in her throat as Lachie sat still. She wiggled both feet into the boots and then snapped on the bars.

Your dad would be proud.

Whoa!

Where had that come from?

An hour later she was sipping a glass of red wine, staring at a book without seeing the words and trying hard not to think about Finn when her phone beeped.

Hey. This is Finn

Typical, just as she was starting to relax. Her heart tripped and she ignored it. He was not going to get under her skin this time. She was tempted to write *Two and a half years too late* but didn't and instead texted back:

Oh. Wow. This is a first. You didn't lose your phone, then?

Almost immediately he replied:

Ha-ha. No. Never again. Listen, I don't need time to think about this. I'm in. 100%. When can we meet?

It was, if she was honest, a little hurtful that he hadn't texted her after that night but was texting her now she had his son. But at least she knew where she stood; she was the mother of his child and nothing more. Good. That was what they needed. What she needed.

She texted him back:

Rules first.

Again, the reply came almost immediately:

Scary lady. What kind of rules? I won't give him whisky, or let him play with knives, or drive my car.

She laughed to herself. If only it was that simple.

Gah! Where to start? He needs boundaries.

Don't we all?

Judging by the way she was smiling to herself and imagining Finn reclining on that hotel bed, hair all dishevelled…naked…she was the one needing boundaries the most.

He needs lots of love and rewards for good behaviour.

Again, don't we all? Does he get treats for being a good boy?

She laughed.

He's a child, not a puppy.

Oh, aren't they the same thing? Do I scratch his ears and rub his tummy and teach him tricks?

She flicked back at once:

Not if you want to keep me happy.

A message was back in seconds:

Of course I want to keep you happy.

It's because I'm Lachie's mum, nothing else.
But hot on its heels another message arrived:

Sophie, I'm sorry about…everything.

Her throat felt suddenly raw. She'd judged him and hadn't known what was happening in his life.

Please stop being so nice. And I'm sorry about your leg.

I have another one, it's okay. ;-)

She knew it wasn't. How could it be? How could he have dealt with losing a limb and the self-esteem issues that came with it and still be funny? But she knew the one thing he didn't need was her pity. She didn't really have any; if anything she was amazed by his resilience. Although she remembered his mental wobble when he'd briefly thought he wasn't fit to be a parent.

And I'm sorry about your collarbone and pelvis and spine and hypothermia and... I can't remember the rest of the injury list.

Just start at the As and work your way through the alphabet, basically.

He'd needed rebuilding, on the outside *and* the inside, probably. No wonder he was gruff at times. He was probably still in physical pain—those kinds of injuries didn't just heal and stop hurting.

I can't imagine how that would have been for you. If I remember, you played rugby or something...?

Ah, yes...my glittering rugby career. You'd never heard of the Swans, right? Top of the Scottish league. I was their best player. And then I wasn't. Stuff happens. So, anyway... Can we meet? If we both have a nine-to-five maybe we could do something at the weekend? The three of us? You can see if I'm suitable.

I know you're suitable.

She had no choice. He was Finn's dad and he'd been through so much she couldn't deny him the chance to get to know his child. If anything it could be healing, give him something other than his broken body to deal with—something positive. And now she was starting to feel sorry for him.

No more messages came through for a while, and she thought the conversation was over until halfway through another glass of wine when she received another one.

It was a good night, Sophie.

She'd lived in Edinburgh ever since that night and had never again stepped inside the pub where they'd met. Had always skirted her path away from the hotel they'd spent the night in. But that hadn't stopped her thinking about it. Thinking about the way he'd kissed her and the need she'd felt for him. She'd never felt so connected to someone, so wanted. And, whatever else he'd done or not done afterwards, she knew he'd felt the same, at least for a few hours. Her body prickled with the memory, a hot rush of need. And, despite everything, they'd produced the love of her life.

She typed on her phone and sent a message back.

It was. A good night...

Then she tapped quickly and sent another message before she had the chance to second-guess herself.

We're going to the butterfly centre on Saturday. Meet us there at two o'clock.

Wouldn't miss it for the world. I'll stick to the rules, don't worry.

She threw the phone onto the cushion next to her and her mind started playing the him-naked-on-the-bed images over and over, and this time she didn't try to stop them.

Truth was, it wasn't him she had to worry about breaking the rules. It was her.

CHAPTER FOUR

FINN DROVE INTO the butterfly centre car park, his heart thudding as he saw Sophie standing at the entrance with Lachie in a navy blue pushchair, waiting. His hands tightened around the steering wheel, but he managed to unglue one to wave to them.

Lying awake in the dark last night, he'd gone over and over how he should act, but none of his imaginings seemed the way Finn Baird would be.

How would he be? He had no idea. How did a father act? What to say? To do? Should he be a little stand-offish? Indulgent? Funny? An educator, grabbing every moment to teach his boy about the world? All he knew was that he didn't want to be like his own father—absent. Not if he could help it.

Sophie peered at the car, nodded and raised a hand, her long hair whipping around in the breeze, then she leaned down to speak to the boy. She was wearing skinny blue jeans and a thick pale blue woollen jumper that hid the body Finn remembered. Skin that had been silk under his fingers. Just the right amount of curves. He wondered how being pregnant had changed her and felt a sharp pang of regret that he hadn't seen her heavy with his baby.

There was so much about her and his son he had

to learn. For a start, it seemed she was even more of a stickler for punctuality than he was; they had ten minutes until the allotted meet time and he'd planned to be there waiting for them so they didn't have to witness his ungainly exit from his car. *Too bad.*

He parked quickly, bundled himself out as best he could without falling over and walked as fast as his sore leg would allow to get to them. Trying to look normal, act normal while feeling anything but. Spending a day with his boy was giving him more palpitations than debuting for the Swans in front of twenty-two thousand screaming fans.

'Hi. Am I late? Sorry.'

'No. We just needed to get out of the house. He was getting a bit stir crazy.' She looked as nervous as Finn felt, but smiled and her eyes were warm. 'You were right; having a toddler is like having a puppy: they need regular feeding and watering and lots of fresh air and exercise.'

'And tummy rubs? Don't forget those.' He smiled to himself ruefully. And regretted saying something so lame. This was worse than a first date and even less predictable. Should he kiss her cheek? *No. Oaf.* He stuffed his hands into his pockets.

'Of course—who doesn't like tummy rubs?' She laughed, her eyes shining, her whole face lit up. *Hot damn, she was pretty.* For a fleeting moment he had an image in his head of the three of them laughing together, tangled up on a sofa. A family.

He shut that idea off straight away. He had no right to think like that. He focused on Lachie: the only reason they were here. Last time, he'd paid little attention to the boy's features, but this time he drank in as much as he could. A shock of dark Baird hair that his mum had obviously tried to tame with a brush, and failed. He could have told her there was no point; the hair did what it wanted. Blue eyes the same as the ones Finn looked into every morning as he brushed his teeth. Cute nose, like Sophie's.

On his mum's bedroom chest of drawers there'd been a photo in a silver frame of Finn at this age and Cal a couple of years older. On a beach somewhere, digging to Australia with plastic yellow spades. The toddler in that photo was the spitting image of this one in front of him. If he'd had even the slightest doubt that Lachie was his son, just looking at him was proof enough.

It was incredible. This boy had his DNA. A Baird in everything other than name.

His chest constricted. He took a deep breath and blew it out. What a responsibility. 'Right, let's get going. Should we let him out of the pushchair for a run around?' Then he realised he had no idea what to do with a child. With this child. With any child, really; he just winged it and tried to make them laugh. And he usually did, but this…he had to get the tone right from the beginning. 'I mean, whatever you think.'

'He's still very slow and unsteady so it'll take us a while to get round. But okay, let's wear him out so with a bit of luck he'll manage the nap he's been fighting for the last hour.' She bent to the buggy and unclipped Lachie's straps like an old hand. She picked him up out of the pushchair and held him in her arms. There was a natural ease between mum and son; they didn't have to think about what to do or what to say to each other—they just knew. Not knowing made Finn's heart ache.

Sophie's smile eased the pain a little. 'Hey, Lachie. This is Finn. You remember him? From the clinic; he gave you the stickers.'

'Hi there, Mr Superhero.' Finn looked over and grinned, noting Lachie had his flashing trainers on rather than the boots and bars. He'd be able to run and walk and chase and catch.

He'd be overtaking Finn in all those endeavours soon enough, leaving his old man behind in his slipstream. For a moment Finn felt bereft and definitely wished he had both legs.

But then he gave himself a talking-to. Didn't every kid overtake his father at some point? It was the natural way of things. It wasn't just about the physicality; parenthood was so much more.

So much Finn wasn't convinced he could give, or even knew how.

The little boy looked up at Finn with disinterest and tapped Sophie's shoulder. 'Flies. Flies.'

'*Butter*flies.' Sophie's voice deepened. 'Lachie, say hello to Finn.'

Lachie shook his head and tapped her cheek. 'Flies. Flies.'

'Oh. Okay. We'll just skip the introductions.' Finn laughed. So meeting *Dad* wasn't a biggie for the boy.

Sophie's hand was over her mouth as she laughed too but her eyes were apologetic. 'Sorry—he's far more interested in the butterflies than silly old adults.' But then she grew serious. 'It's how they are. Don't feel like it's a reflection of anything at all. He doesn't understand what all this is about. You're just the guy from the clinic. Come walk with us and let him get used to you.'

Time minus three minutes and it hadn't been a rip-roaring success so far. But what had he expected? To be accepted with open arms? He was just some guy. One who needed to earn his son's trust. And he needed to earn Sophie's too.

He still wasn't sure he was doing the right thing being here, but as the weekend had drawn nearer he'd felt lighter and lighter, excited at the prospect of seeing them; Lachie because he was a good kid who was part of Finn now, and Sophie because... He shifted his mind from her smile and her soft body and glittering eyes, the memory of her moans and the taste of her.

Because she'd borne enough of bringing up a child on her own.

He refused to believe he was excited to see her for any other reason. They had rules now, after all. He had his own too.

They wandered through to the large greenhouse, walking very slowly as Lachie stopped to investigate every little flower, butterfly, stick. Finn ached to hold his son's hand, but it was very firmly gripping Sophie's. He watched as they walked and chatted, how she explained things, took her time pointing out the caterpillars and the transformed butterflies.

He watched too, as she absentmindedly tugged her hair into her hands and let the soft weight of the curls fall down her back. Watched the way her mouth had no end of smiles for her son, how her eyes brightened when he laughed, how she seemed so at ease with him. He remembered that night and the way she'd been the same with him and the stark difference in her manner towards him now. Friendly, but not overly. Tolerating because she had to.

When she had a moment to focus back on him he asked her, 'So where are you two living these days?' He had the address—she'd written it on the back of the picture Lachie had drawn—Finn just craved more details so he could imagine them there.

But he saw the ease disappear, replaced with a guarding in the straightening of her mouth, the dulling of her eyes. She was here because she had to be and nothing more.

'In Drumsheugh Gardens. I inherited my grand-mother's house and was going to sell it, but then found out I was pregnant. It's perfect for children; there's a park round the corner and a great nursery and school a short walk away. All the things you have to think about with a little one…' She shot him a look that said *Not that you'd know about all this*. 'Suddenly you have to be in the right catchment area for high schools and buying sterilisers and cots. My life has turned out very differently to how I imagined it would.'

And his life had turned out very differently to the trajectory it had been on too. 'What were you going to do, Sophie? After you sold your grandmother's house?'

Her eyes followed a butterfly fluttering from one leaf to another, never still for more than a few seconds. There was something wistful in her look as she watched it flying freely. 'I was going to put the money into a savings account and travel. I had a volunteer job at a charity in India. Then I was going to travel around the world before I settled down. Which was going to be somewhere exotic where I could sip cocktails beachside and dig my feet into warm sand.'

'Scotland's exotic to some people.' He grinned. 'At least, we get a lot of tourists.'

'Cold sand, though. And midges.' She shook her head, her eyes settling on him, the honey-brown of her pupils darkening. 'It's about being somewhere else, Finn. Doesn't matter how much everyone loves this place, I wanted to escape.'

So he'd stolen her dreams too. Every topic he brought up led them down a path towards her disappointment in him. 'You could still travel. Plenty of people do with a baby in tow.'

'It's not just about the practicalities; it's about time off from work and…well, money. We have a trip to Whitby for a fortnight this year in a caravan, if I'm lucky and work hard and save up. Portugal next year if the stars are aligned and I win the Lottery.' She shrugged. 'It's a slow way to tick my bucket list off, but by the time I'm two hundred and twenty I might have visited all the places in the world I want to see.'

'It's my fault. I should have called, shared the load.'

She came to a halt. 'Yes, you should have. But you didn't so we got on with it. Besides, having you here wouldn't have made a jot of difference. I was pregnant. I was going to get fat and have a baby and have no more seconds to myself, never mind hours or days or years to travel.'

'And you said you had no one else to help.'

She bristled, her chin lifting. 'I have lots of friends, Finn.' But she relented. 'Of course I can't keep asking them to help me out. We do reciprocate, though, as much as I can with a full-time job.'

'And your parents?'

'They're in Dubai. They love their life there and wouldn't give it up easily just to help me out with their grandchild.'

'Why the hell not?' He needed to stop taking this personally, but a rejection of Lachie was personal. He glanced over to make sure he was safe, but also because he couldn't get enough of looking at him. *His child. Wow.* It was surreal. 'He's their grandchild.'

'It's not how they're made. They've spent their lives travelling—maybe that's where I get the bug from. Just thought of that.' She looked a little pensive for a moment. 'I try hard not to be like them, but clearly there's more to personality than nurture. Dad's an engineer. I was born in Africa, spent my toddler years in Hong Kong then boarding school in Kent. Which I hated. They didn't want me getting under their feet in...now, where were they then? Abu Dhabi...yes. Hard to keep up sometimes. But my grandma took me in and basically brought me up.'

'Which was why you were so cut up about her death.'

'She was my mum in every aspect except name. Yes. She was my family.'

Blinking quickly, she started to push the pushchair behind Lachie as he wove his way slowly through the huge subtropical glasshouse. Butterflies of every colour flitted between the leaves of thick lush plants bordering the walkway. A pond bifurcated the hothouse and the sound of trickling water had Finn looking out for any danger traps for his boy. Shortly they had to cross a small stone bridge with open fencing either side and he kept his eyes trained on Lachie as he wound from one side of the bridge to the other. This parenting thing was all-encompassing.

Finn couldn't help but call out to him, 'Careful, Lachie. Walk in the middle. Good lad.'

Sophie grinned. 'He's fine. The gaps in the fence aren't big enough for him to fall through.'

'I don't know how you manage to stay so calm.'

She laughed. 'And I thought it was just the mums who were overprotective.'

'You should know—being a Health Visitor, you must meet a few.'

'Oh, we get all sorts, all walks of life. Scared mums, nervous mums, earth mothers. Some who can't manage at all…poor things.' She wrapped her arms around her body and rubbed her arms.

And he had a sudden urge to wrap his around her too and hold her tight and rewrite the last two years. But he didn't. 'What happens to the ones who can't manage? Are they the ones whose children end up in care?'

'At one end it's just a case of teaching basic parenting skills and giving them help and confidence that they can do it. Timelines and organisation suggestions, that kind of thing. At the other end we sometimes do have to intervene. We go a long way for a long time and give them the benefit of the doubt before we have to do anything serious. We put specific plans in place and work with social services and the police. Neglect and abuse usually stem from deeper issues: addiction, psychological problems…' She shuddered. 'Why are we talking about this?'

'I don't know.' He'd learnt about all this in a module at Physio school, but she was at the coal face. She had an emotionally demanding job and had brought up a good kid on her own. 'I guess not everyone's as capable as you, Sophie. You've done amazingly well. For some people parenting isn't innate or straightforward. Lucky I'm a fast learner.'

She eyed him sideways and smiled, cheeks a pretty deep pink. 'Is this your charm offensive starting again?'

'Me?' He pretended to be affronted. 'I'm all charm and rarely offensive.'

Laughing, she shook her head. 'Could have fooled me.'

'You just need to get to know me.' The conversation about her grandmother had been lost somewhere and he didn't want to bring the sadness back to her eyes by going there again. It was hard to converse openly while distracted by a toddler, but he'd have to get used to it. 'Have your parents ever met Lachie?'

'They made a flying visit when he was about ten weeks old.' She smiled grimly. 'Mum's used to having staff do everything for her so she wasn't exactly a help. *Make me a cup of tea, darling. Gin and tonic, heavy on the gin.*'

'And you did.' He'd had the impression Sophie was strong and independent, but clearly she had issues with boundaries and her parents.

'Oh, I made the first one. She was a guest after all. And the second. Then when she asked for a third I told her to make her own and one for me too. She wasn't impressed. She took photos of Lachie to show off to her friends then went back to her hotel, flew out the next morning. To be honest, it was a relief to have them gone. Less work all round.'

So no problems with boundaries then. Every time he learnt something new about her she went up in his estimation.

Her family life had been so different to his experience. His father had never been around, but his mother had lavished him and his brother with attention. She'd never had much money but made up for that with her time. His heart lurched at the thought of her, that she could well still be alive if it hadn't been for him and his selfishness. He had a lot of making up for his stupid self-absorption when he was younger. Starting here.

'So what can I do to make it up to you? To you both?'

She peered at him, looked at his hands and shook her head. 'No. I can't see a magic wand there.'

'Ach, I'm hiding it. I only bring my wand out for very special people. Play your cards right…' *Geez, what the hell was that supposed to mean? What was he doing?*

Making her laugh and that in itself was magical. Her body lit up and her cheeks reddened. 'Finn Baird, I do not know how to take that.'

Neither did he. 'I'm sorry, I have no idea where that came from.'

'Can't help it, eh?' She looked up at him from under thick dark lashes. Her smile was just outside the friend zone boundary, nudging into flirting, and he was surprised at how that made him feel. How, despite everything, there was a pull to her that he couldn't explain. She tutted. 'You really do know how to spin a line, but don't think I'll be taken in a second time. Not for a minute.'

'Too bad.' He raised his shoulders and smiled, trying not to be over friendly but wanting to be all at the same time. There was something about her, with her lovely smile and bright eyes and soft manner, that tugged at his heart and his gut and, yes, at his resolve. 'But really, Sophie, there's no line. I know where we stand here. Seriously. I just like to make you laugh.'

Her eyes widened and she blinked. 'Well, it has to be better than the way you've been making me feel for the last few years.'

'Blamed for something I didn't even know I was doing.' This time he laughed too. 'So, seriously, how can I make things better?'

'You can't do anything, Finn, except be here for Lachie now and in the future.'

'At least now I understand why you're so adamant he has a father who stays around. Something you didn't have.'

She shook her head. 'I probably shouldn't have told you all of that. They're Lachie's grandparents after all; I don't want to turn him against them.'

He imagined she'd never said a bad word to Lachie about his absent father either; that was the way she was—gentle and undemanding, as if she didn't feel she had a right to complain or ask for things for herself. 'It's okay. I won't say anything about them. Not my business.' He nudged her gently. 'Families, eh. Who'd pick them?'

'Some are okay. Most, actually. What about yours?'

Ah. Yes. 'One meddling brother who I sent off to the other side of the world because he was far too involved in my life.'

Her eyes glittered as she looked at him and laughed again. 'You didn't! You sent him away? How did you manage that?'

'He was all cut up because he thought my accident was his fault. I couldn't get a moment's peace without him interfering in treatment, rehab…what I ate, what I drank. So I concocted a plan to have him go on a course for three months to get him out of my hair. Worked a dream. He's met a woman over there and wants to settle down. Couldn't have worked out better.'

She'd pulled up short and was looking at him, greedy for more information. 'And was it? His fault? How did it happen?'

Not going there. How to say that politely? *Hedge. Talk about something else. Misdirect.* 'Ach—'

'Lachie! Don't touch!' In a flash Sophie had moved towards Lachie, who was reaching out to a hatchling butterfly hanging down from a plant at toddler level. 'He's not exactly gentle.'

Saved by his son. He had a feeling it wouldn't be the last time. Relief flooded through Finn. He didn't want to have to revisit that night, the state he'd been in. Although he knew Sophie would be understanding, she'd try to talk him into believing something different about himself. That he was ultimately good. What did she know? He refocused on the boy: the one truly good thing Finn had ever done.

'He's just interested and doesn't realise how fragile they are.' But Lachie was still reaching perilously close to the butterfly.

Sophie's eyebrows rose. 'But he does need to learn. Lachie, love. Be careful. Good boy. These are just babies. Gentle. Gentle.'

They both reached out to stop him from tearing the delicate wing off, their hands meeting as they touched Lachie's arm at the same time. As his fingers touched Sophie's skin a frisson of something stirred deep in his gut. She laughed softly as she pulled her hand away, clearly not feeling the same weird sensation Finn had. 'Little devil. He needs watching every second.'

Finn caught her gaze and for a beat the laughter died, replaced with something else. The sensual sweep of attraction, the sweet scent of pheromones swimming languidly between them. Suddenly he was back to that night, reliving the raw desire he'd had for her that had sprung from her easy laugh and the depth of the connection they'd shared.

Then Lachie started to grizzle and she turned to their son and breathed out deeply.

Finn's gut started to free fall and he looked away. Nothing good could possibly come of any attraction, particularly on his side. He had a child, but he wasn't about to take on a family. And not a woman like Sophie, who deserved so much more than he could give.

CHAPTER FIVE

SOPHIE PULLED HER hand back from Finn's as quickly as she could, spooked by the tingles shooting over her skin and the stirrings deep in her belly, like something waking up after a long, long sleep. It hadn't just been the touch of his hand, or his citrus and leather scent that sent shivers of memory through her and teased her hormones into life; it had been the easy way she'd been drawn into flirting with him.

She knew what he was like. Knew she had to keep her distance. But knowing wasn't anything like feeling. And she definitely had felt the rush of excitement as she'd talked about his...magic wand.

Charmer. She smiled inwardly. He hadn't lost his appeal. And just for a moment it had been fun to think about something else other than bars and boots and nappies and work.

Trouble was, it had reminded her of what she'd been missing...or avoiding...for so long. She swallowed, bundled a grumpy Lachie back into his buggy and changed the subject. 'Right, let's go see the snakes. They have feeding time soon and we can get to touch one. And a tarantula too.'

Next to her, Finn shuddered, back to his teasing normal self. 'I did not know you'd brought me to Hell.'

'Scared?'

'Not of spiders.' He feigned nonchalance, but his wide eyes belied him.

'Snakes?'

'No.' He shuddered again, this time with enough drama to make her laugh along.

'You want to say that with a little more certainty?'

'No.' He laughed. 'We are genetically programmed to be scared of snakes and spiders. I'm just reacting exactly as my DNA dictates.'

'Oh, a textbook human?' She played along. 'It's not as if you're out in the wild, man against beast, though, is it? You'll be able to hand him back to the keeper if it gets too much for you. You should face your fears, right?' Just like she was—taking a risk on Finn and some sort of shared parenting future.

But Finn faced his demons every day, she knew. It took a lot of guts to face what he'd lost and come out with a smile for his clients. For her. He shrugged. 'You wouldn't let me live it down if I didn't, right?'

'Not a chance.' She winked and turned to go, all the better to keep a distance from him. From the intoxication of his smile.

They wandered out to a large decked area outside the snake house where a handler was doing a show-and-tell with a huge gold and black python wrapped around his neck. Above them birds squawked in the clear blue sky and there was a reassuring scent of earth and animals. Sophie inhaled and tried to stay grounded as she once again unclipped Lachie from his pushchair and lifted him out so he could see the action. He was groggy and curled his arms around her neck and refused to look at the snake man or Finn. She squeezed her son against her chest and smelt his little boy scent, feeling the weary weight of him in her arms. He laid his head on her shoulder and she felt him give in to the pull of his afternoon nap.

These were the moments she loved—the total trust of a toddler who didn't want to sleep without the comfort of his mum. Hearing the heavy sighs as he fell deeper into slumber, breathing in the sweet smell of him. The feeling of absolute unconditional love in her heart, in her body. These were her moments. Moments, she realised with a sharp pang, she didn't want to share with anyone.

Would things change between her and Lachie now his father wanted to be in their lives? And how long would he be here? Long enough for her and Lachie to fall for him? Long enough to take a piece of their hearts and then what? Once he got to know them would he want to hang around? Or would he do what her parents had done and flit off for his own adventures without her. Or her boy. Would he even turn up when he said he would?

She knew well enough how sitting around waiting for parents to fulfil their promises—and then failing to—made your heart hurt.

So she didn't want to share if it meant shifting the equilibrium or losing her power. Didn't want anyone driving a wedge between her and the boy who had been her world for so long. Didn't want to stand on the doorstep and watch them head off to have fun without her. To hear about their adventures and not be a part of them, to watch her boy grow under the guidance of a father.

She glanced over to Finn, who was recoiling from the offer to touch the snake and looking at her and laughing…then stopping as he caught sight of her cradling Lachie.

There was something in his eyes that was shaped for her boy. Something she could see swelling and growing as Finn interacted with Lachie.

Sharing was so hard, but she did have to try. She had to at least make an effort, for all their sakes. Because Lachie deserved someone else to look at him the way she did.

'Getting heavy?' Finn's eyes flicked to Lachie's sagging body and then back to her. He looked torn, as if he hungered for something but didn't know how to ask for it. The man was trying. He was here at least, which was more than some men would be when presented with a child. He hadn't run away. He hadn't been difficult.

That was part of the problem, besides the charm and the fun and the gorgeous deep blue eyes that seemed to enchant her all over again—he was a decent man. She dug deep. Tried to share a little of the wonders of being a parent.

'You get used to it and your carrying muscles just grow at the same rate the babies do. But yes, I'm going to have arms like a weight lifter by the time he's four. Do you want to hold him?'

'Won't he wake up?' But Finn's whole face lit up at the offer.

'No. Once he's asleep he's completely out of it.' She looked down at Finn's legs and realised he'd probably need help to do that. *Damn. Inconsiderate.* 'Would it be better if you sat down and I put him on your lap?'

His eyes flashed dark. His jaw clenched. He lifted his chin, snapping back at her, 'I'm not an invalid, Sophie. I can stand up and hold my child.' Fighting. Proving himself. The first time she'd seen that side of him. And she understood. Understood he wouldn't want to be seen or treated as different to anyone else. Even though he was, in so many ways.

She wondered what his leg looked like, what he was like now underneath those clothes. Then pushed that thought away. You didn't judge a person on how they looked, although no doubt Finn was still one hundred per cent Sex God despite his scars.

And she so shouldn't be thinking like that.

'I didn't mean you couldn't manage. I was thinking sitting down would be more comfortable; it usually is. He gets heavy. Now it's my turn to say sorry.' She bit her lip and her hands shook as she handed Lachie over, cradling his head with one hand and wrapping her other arm under his bottom. She watched as Finn mirrored her arms, took all his own weight on his right leg and cradled the boy onto his right shoulder. It looked incongruous but stable. He was a grown man, he knew his limitations; she had to trust him at least about that. She lowered her voice so as not to wake Lachie during the transition. 'I'm just a bit…well, nervous about all this. Not you. This. Playing families.'

As he registered that, Finn's shoulders dropped and he found a small smile. His head touched his son's crazy curls and Finn's whole body seemed to soften and yet solidify with pride all at the same time. For a moment she had to look away as her heart ached with something she couldn't describe, but she was drawn back by Finn's voice. 'It's all a bit sudden and a bit of a surprise, right?'

At least he understood a bit of what she was going through, though she doubted he'd ever fully know what it was like to feel so abandoned, so alone and then to dig deep and survive. Pouring everything she had into the boy she'd carried in her belly and her heart. And now she was having to let go a little of that symbiosis she had with Lachie, for a man she wasn't sure fully deserved it. 'I'm trying to get used to it. It's just weird, sharing him with someone else. No one else carries him usually… I just needed to be sure… I'll get used to it.' She had no choice now; she'd opened the door and let all these obstacles rush in at her perfectly imperfect life.

Finn nodded. He closed his eyes briefly then opened them and caught her gaze. She liked him when he made her laugh, but God, he was impressive when he was fighting. 'I hadn't thought about it like that. You're giving up a lot for me. I shouldn't have snapped at you. And…don't worry about being gentle around me… I hate fussing—it's what my brother does and it drives me mad…as if he thinks I can't decide what's best for me.' He shrugged the shoulder that wasn't supporting Lachie's head. 'I'm an adult, Sophie. I might not like having been dragged into being one, but there it is. I can drive a car. I can ride a bike. I can even ski…badly. And, yes, everything I do now is slower than I used to do it. But holding my child is a no-brainer. I'll tell you what I can and can't do, okay?'

'Yes. Okay.' She had to let him lead on that, for sure. He wasn't an invalid and he'd hate to be thought of as that. The father-son moment she'd been hoping for, for Lachie's sake, had been damaged by her thoughtlessness. She needed to find something to make things better, so went for humour. It had been the way they'd got together in the first place in that bar. A shared joke that had led to a shared bed and now this shared child. 'I bet you're only holding Lachie so you don't have to hold that snake.'

'You got me.' Finn's irises lightened to the colour of the sky on a rare Edinburgh summer's day. 'Any excuse not to come into contact with that, but feel free to have it wrapped round your shoulder. In fact…' He raised his free hand and got the attention of the snake handler. 'We have a volunteer right here.'

'Finn Baird—I can't believe you just did that.' She flung her fists to her hips and scowled at him.

He grinned as the snake handler brought the coils closer. 'Now we'll see what you're made of.'

She took a deep breath and let the man drape the snake around her shoulders, making sure to act as if she was taking it all in her stride. 'Wow. It's heavy. And warm and dry. I always thought snakes were slimy or something.'

Finn tried to gently jostle Lachie awake, tickling him gently and whispering, 'Hey mate, you're missing the action. Have a look at Mummy.'

But Lachie just sighed and turned his little sticky head away. Finn shrugged. 'Doesn't want to look at a snake. Smart kid. Clearly the boy has my genes.'

'Er… I think you'll find he has my brains,' she volleyed at him, surprising herself at the lightness and the flirting in her voice. '*That's* why he's smart.'

'My sense of humour, though.' Finn laughed. He caught her gaze again and the laughter melted away. His eyes burnt bright with a longing that tugged at her belly, at her reserve.

'He's got your…' She couldn't take her eyes off Finn. Nothing to do with the way he shared genes with Lachie and everything to do the raw sex appeal that hummed around him, curling between them and tugging them closer. The breadth of his shoulders she knew she could cling to and they'd hold her tight until she wanted to let go. The kick up of his top lip when he smiled. The glittering eyes that changed colour depending on his mood. Right now they were dark and rich like luxurious blue velvet flecked with gold. 'Er…sticky-up hair.'

'Poor bugger.' Finn laughed. 'And he's got your looks, Sophie…beautiful…'

He paused, seemed to grapple with what he was going to say next. His hand cupped her cheek and his thumb ran slowly over her bottom lip. A shiver of desire lurched through to her core, swirling deeper and tighter and lower, and she leaned towards him. His face was inches away. She could feel his warm breath on her skin, discerned the hitch in his breathing. She saw the desire in his eyes as he kept right on looking at her. And looking. And she felt the same need deep inside her. Her whole body strained for his touch. Voice low, he said, 'I just wish—'

'Wish what?' Her heart began to hammer hard and she had a sudden urge to reach to him. To tiptoe and press her lips to his, to taste him again. To search out that deep physical and emotional connection they'd had and rekindle it. To kiss him.

God, she wanted to kiss him.

But that couldn't happen, definitely not here, with a child in his arms and a snake looped round her shoulders, in front of strangers. It couldn't happen at all. They both knew that. But that didn't stop the ache.

'Nothing.' He turned away. There was something in his manner that changed, as if the enormity of the situation was finally falling into place for him. Or was it something else? What did he wish?

Was it the same thing she'd been feeling and kept pushing away? The tug of attraction. A wish that things had worked out differently? That things could be better? Good even, between them?

The handler interrupted the moment; he had a huge

camera and was pointing it at the three of them. 'What a lovely family. Come on, Dad, give us a smile. What's the matter, Dad? Too close for comfort, right?'

'Yes. A little.' Finn's shoulders were up round his neck and he blinked. Swallowed.

She didn't know whether he meant he was too close to the snake, or if he'd wanted a kiss too. Next to her, Finn's body tensed. And Sophie was pretty sure it had nothing to do with the snake getting ever nearer to him.

In Finn's arms Lachie stirred. For a couple of seconds he rubbed his head back and forth across his father's chest then stopped abruptly. Sensing something different, he looked up at Finn and his features folded.

Uh-oh. Meltdown time. Huge tears filled his baby-blue eyes and a noise erupted from his throat as if his whole world had ended. Then, wriggling and kicking, he reached his arms towards Sophie. 'Mama. Mama.'

She shook her head and smiled as reassuringly as she could. 'Hey, sweetie. This is Finn, remember? He's nice.'

Finn's eyes grew wider and he swayed from side to side—given the heavy lean on his missing leg it was costing him physically—he fixed his jaw and nodded, ear close to Lachie's. 'Hey, buddy. Hey, it's okay. You were asleep. And now, look, Mummy's wearing a snake.'

'No!' Little fists tightened into balls and Lachie hit them at Finn's chest, frowning and arching his whole body towards his mother, away from his dad. 'No!' he shouted. 'No. Mama.'

The contented smile faded as panic and confusion swirled behind Finn's eyes. He held Lachie away from his chest. Arm's length. The peace Sophie had never imagined could ever happen between them immediately shattered. 'Here. You should take him.'

'I'll take Hector.' The keeper helped unwrap the snake from Sophie's neck, although the heavy weight didn't seem to lift from her shoulders. 'Okay. Okay, little one. Mummy's here.' She didn't want to take him. She wanted Lachie to get used to Finn—she wanted father and son to develop something precious and everlasting but it wouldn't work when Lachie was like this. She took hold of her boy and he nuzzled tight against her neck but she kept her eyes on Finn. He seemed to have folded into himself. 'Hey, don't take it personally. He's always cranky when he wakes up.'

'Okay. Sure.' His voice was haunted as he spoke. 'I should probably go.'

'You don't have to.' She tried to make a joke of things. 'Stay a bit longer; we can go see the tarantulas.'

He didn't bite. 'I think it's for the best.' He stuck his hands deep into his pockets. 'I guess he needs to get used to me.'

'Yes. Yes, he does. We all need to get used to each other. It's been a huge step forward but we can't rush it and suddenly bridge the two-year gap in one afternoon.' They needed space to keep their emotions in check. At least she did. 'Stay for the photo at least. Then, yes, we should all go.'

So he found a smile and posed for the camera, then he watched as she laid Lachie back into the pushchair and clipped him in.

Finn seemed suddenly in a hurry. 'Okay. I have to go.'

'I know. It's okay. It's been a big day. Why don't we—' *Try again next week?*

But he wasn't listening and before she could finish

he'd turned tail and was heading for the exit. Taking all the good vibes with him and leaving her heart aching, not just for how things had turned out but for the feel of his skin on hers again.

For one kiss.

CHAPTER SIX

BACK AT HOME, Finn collapsed onto the sofa, removed his prosthetic and rolled off the silicone liner. He breathed deeply as the cool air bathed the irritated and red skin. *Freedom. Relief.*

Too much activity and not enough rest. He had to remember to give himself a break.

And yet… If only… So many if-onlys. Too many.

He forced himself to look at it, at the lumpy skin, the still pink stitch marks. The space where a calf and a shin and a foot should have been.

Forced himself all over again to accept it. This was who he was now. No point in wishing otherwise. Although he did. Every day. *God*, how he wished things were different. Not for the way he looked—he was coming to accept that too; there were thousands of people like him around the world, many more who were much worse off—but for the things he couldn't do. He couldn't hold his son without Sophie thinking he needed supervision. He couldn't be seen as capable. At least, not by Sophie.

More, it was a frank reminder of who he was and the stupid, self-centred, immature mistakes he'd made that had, literally, cost his mother's life. If he could barely be trusted to hold his child securely, he most certainly shouldn't be trusted to keep him safe and well. Protect him. Protect Sophie, which seemed to be an innate need, deep in his DNA.

He traced his fingers over the joining fold, the place where they'd taken the smashed and frostbitten lower leg away and meshed together his skin. Massaged gently until some of the friction pain was rubbed away.

If only he could rub other kinds of pain away too.

His kid didn't like him. Sophie was trying hard to make it happen, but it wasn't the sort of thing that could be forced. His kid didn't like him.

And Finn really liked Sophie—in good ways and over-the-line ways and there wasn't a thing he could do about it.

The heavy beat of a rock song interrupted his thoughts. Cal. He had a dedicated ringtone so Finn could choose, or not, to answer without having to limp around trying to find his phone. It was the middle of the night in New Zealand but Cal was working the para-medic night shift. Which meant he could ring in the quiet moments. As he did, all too regularly, to check up on his brother's progress.

He hesitated to pick up, but then relented; because he'd only call later and again and again until Finn answered. He flicked the screen and his brother's ugly mug appeared in front of the white sterilised walls of the ambulance station. His phone was propped up on a table and the angle caught his brother's jaw and face close and his voice was loud in the stillness of the Southern Hemisphere night.

'Hey Cal, how's things?'

'Good time? Bad time?' Cal scratched his chin and sat back in his chair, settling in for a long talk.

Uh-oh. 'I've just got in. And I've got a ton of stuff to do.'

'Oh? Tell me more. Where've you been?' The thing about Cal was that he tried hard to be relaxed around Finn but sometimes it was too hard. And it was the trying that got to Finn the most. 'A date? The game? Where?'

'I haven't been to a game of rugby since the accident and I don't think I ever will.'

Cal's eyebrows rose. 'It might be good therapy for you. Facing your demons and all that.'

Geez, everyone seemed to want him to do that these days. 'I don't need to go out of the house to do that; all I have to do is look down at my feet. Foot. And please stop telling me what might be good for me.'

Cal shrugged and slumped back into his chair. Tiredness drew dark circles under his eyes. 'I'm sorry.'

'You look terrible.'

'Trying to fit my sleeping schedule in with the baby's naps isn't exactly working.' He rubbed his face and yawned. 'But, anyway, you should try the rugby... or dating or something. You need a focus.'

Well, boy, did he have one now. 'I know it's because you care, but we've been over this. I'm a grown-up now; I make my own decisions about what I do.' Which meant he had to take responsibility.

So he should probably tell big brother about Lachie.

Finn took a deep breath and tried to work out exactly what to say, how to say it. No doubt feeling similar to the way Cal had felt only six months ago when he'd fallen in love with a woman who was having another man's baby via surrogacy. Now, that had been confusing, but there they were, all those miles away, happily settled. And if he was going to be a good dad he needed to find someone he could get advice from. The only man he knew who was a father was his brother, Cal. 'Listen, I have something to tell you. Something big.'

Cal immediately frowned, jerking forward, on alert. 'What? Is it trouble?'

'I don't know.' Because that was the truth of it.

'You okay? Still taking your meds? Because depression can hit you any time out of the blue.'

'Stop fussing, Cal. I'm fine… I'm over that now. I know what I have to do, what signs to watch for. I was down because I lost my leg…anyone would be, right? But I'm over it now.' And finding out about Lachie and Sophie had his heart leaping, not sinking. At first anyway. Now he had to get over a zillion hurdles to make it all work. And he had to own this. 'Okay.' He swallowed. It wasn't every day you made this kind of announcement. 'I've just found out I have a child.'

'What? Are you for real? A child?' Cal's head tipped back and he laughed. 'Copycat. You always did the sibling rivalry thing well. I get a child so you get one.' Then he got serious. 'Is it a good thing?'

Was it? Finn had had sleepless nights going over and over what to do, how to be. How things would pan out. 'Yeah. It's good. He's good. He's eighteen months old and he's called Lachlan. Lachie.'

'Wow, Finn. This is a lot to take in. A lot for you to deal with. Are you sure you're okay? You need me to come over?'

'Geez, man. I'm fine. Stay there with your own family. I just wanted to let you know. You're an uncle.'

His brother's eyes widened. 'So I am. Uncle Callum— who'd have thought? Wow, no babies for years then two come along at once. I hope the poor little mite's got his mother's looks and not yours.' His eyes narrowed. Not a good sign—he was homing in, scrutinising. It was his OP as the big brother who'd saved little brother's life. 'Who is she, the mother?'

'Sophie. She's…' This was where things got murky for Finn. He'd never been one to believe in all that love-at-first-sight stuff, but it had definitely been attraction at first sight, and then things had got complicated.

Cal filled the silence. 'One of your famous conquests?'

'No, she was not.' So he'd had a reputation of loving and leaving. He'd been young and immature. But a lot had happened between then and now… In fact, Sophie was the last woman he'd slept with. He didn't know whether to feel sad or proud about that. Proud, actually. 'It wasn't like that. Not at all.'

'Finn Baird, you used to be like that. You had women lining up. You probably still do, knowing you. So what's so special about this one?'

'I didn't say she was special.' But she was and he'd wanted to kiss her in the butterfly garden. He wanted to kiss her now too.

But then, he'd wanted to kiss a lot of women in the past. Had kissed them. But Sophie? He had a feeling kissing her would mean a lot more than he wanted it to.

Cal was watching him, eyebrows furrowed, but with a wry smile. 'You don't have to say anything, mate. It's written all over your face. Well, this is interesting. She's a keeper?'

He couldn't keep anyone. Didn't Cal know that? 'Tell me, why did I bother picking up when you called?'

'Because you love me.'

He did. He owed him a lot too, if he was honest. But if Cal could step a little back sometimes that would be awesome too. 'You're no help, man. I'm not looking for a keeper or anything else. I just wanted to ask—how do you be a dad? A good one? What do you do?'

Cal settled back in the chair and grinned. 'I'm no expert. Far from it, Grace is only six months old. But I'd say you just do what feels right.'

Kissing his son's mother felt right. Holding her. Making love to her. And he couldn't do that, any of it. Not if he wanted to make things right for his son. 'He doesn't like me.'

'Ach, how could he not love such a bright, bubbly guy like you, Finn?'

'Quit the sarcasm. I mean it. You should have seen him trying to get back to his mum when he woke up and found himself in my arms. He almost screamed the place down.'

Cal's face softened. He quit the jokes. 'You've got it bad.'

'Aye. I think I have.' The fierce helplessness when Lachie had squirmed away from Finn still hung around in his gut. And he wanted to erase it with his kid's giggles. Giggles Lachie only seemed to have for his mum.

Sophie. At just the thought of her his whole body prickled with heat. Even though he'd only seen her twice since the clinic and both times had been blurred with revelations and relearning, and nothing she'd said or done had given any cause for hope that she might want him in any other way than being a father to their child.

He was going crazy. This wasn't some youthful lust thing going on—it was more than that.

Cal was still stuck on Lachie. 'You want to be part of his life? Hands-on? Not like our deadbeat father?'

'I do.' *More than anything.*

'Then do it. Be there. Make sure you're around. Stick-ability wins out. Wear him down, mate. Win him over.'

He made it sound so easy, but then he hadn't seen the panic and fear and pure upset in Lachie's face when he realised he wasn't nestled in his mother's arms but in some almost stranger's.

'What about Sophie?'

'That's her name? Right. Win Sophie over too, with the wit, charm and good looks you got from your brother.'

'That's the highest mountain I'll ever have to climb.'

Finn didn't trust himself, so he couldn't expect her to trust him. And now the most important question of all. Not for the first time, he opened his fears up to his brother.

'Cal, what if I can't do it?'

His brother didn't need to read between the lines. He'd been there when Finn had fallen into thin air, had kept him alive through that dark, icy night, had been there—sometimes supremely annoyingly—for every step of Finn's recovery.

What if I can't do it? What if I don't have the guts to follow through? What if I choose the easy route again and cause more damage?

'Listen to yourself, Finn. You were the highest scor-ing scrum half for the Swans and nothing spooked you. Not the endless taunts from the other teams. Not the crappy refs. Not the stupid commentators. Not the prick of a coach who dropped you. You held your head high and pushed back. You fought tooth and nail to get up-right after the accident. You went skiing against every-one's advice. I'm not saying it's going to be easy. But you'll do it, Finn. Because you can't not. Because having that boy and his mother in your life is far, far better than the alternative.'

For once his brother was right; having them in his life would be so much better than knowing they were out there somewhere and that he was missing everything. First day at school. First wobbly tooth. Teaching his boy how to ride a bicycle.

How had their own father managed to cut himself off from his own boys? *God*, Finn had only known Lachie a week and he couldn't wait to see him again.

He made his excuses and said goodbye to his brother, then flicked to the last message trail he'd had with Sophie. Was it too soon to contact her again?

He didn't care.

How's Lachie?

What he really meant was, *How are you both?* But he didn't want to freak Sophie out by coming on too strong or being too personal with her, crossing a line that couldn't be uncrossed.

His heart hammered as his phone lit up.

Tucked up in bed and asleep, which is where I will be very soon. Big day. Long week.

He thought back to Monday, when he'd been oblivious to the existence of his son. Or of her being so close by. He flicked her an answer, deliberating over every single word. Not too pushy. Not too flippant.

Huge week. Thanks for today. Sorry I bailed so quickly.

His phone lit up again.

It's okay. I understand. We need to take things slowly, introduce you gradually.

He didn't have the patience for all that—he had a lot of time to make up.

How about one evening this week?

Immediately he regretted that. Too pushy. She wouldn't want to see him again so soon especially after he'd almost kissed her. Had she noticed or been too distracted by the snake? Had she felt the same tug of attraction?

But his phone chimed with her reply.

There's a thing at Nursery on Wednesday. A sort of family bring-your-own-dinner open evening with wine. I'll sort the food. You bring wine. White, preferably. Meet me at my work. Six o'clock. We can walk from there. It's not far.

That was quickly followed up…

I didn't mean anything by that last bit…

He smiled. At some point everyone in his life would stop overcompensating for his lack of leg…but not yet, it would appear.

I know. It's okay. Stop overthinking. I ran a five-mile race last weekend. I can walk around the corner. You don't have to tread on eggshells. I don't hop on them… See, I can even joke about it.

I like a man with a sense of humour!

He imagined the sweet turn-up of her lips as she smiled, the gentle sound of her laughter, and he sent her his immediate response:

I like you.

Damn. Why had he said that? They'd been getting along just fine.

There were a few minutes' silence and he figured he'd blown it. But then…

Going to bed now.

He imagined her dark curls on a white linen pillow-case. The soft noises she'd make as she slept. Her scent of apples and vanilla and something flowery in the air. He flicked her another message:

Sweet dreams.

A quick reply came back.

Oh, I'm sure they will be.

Interesting…

About…?

That's my secret…

His heart picked up. His skin prickled. His gut tightened.

Sophie, tell me more…

Finn...

He grinned. This was just being friendly. And funny.

Should I guess...?

Not a good idea. See you on Wednesday. Goodnight.

Slumping back against the sofa cushions, he grinned. He was going to see her again, and very soon. It would be a very good night indeed.

CHAPTER SEVEN

WAITING FOR WEDNESDAY was giving Sophie heartburn.

There was something about Finn she couldn't resist. Couldn't help being playful around him. Couldn't help reacting to his charm with some flirting of her own. And she wondered whether the silly texts had given him the wrong impression.

Or the right one.

He was due at the clinic in twenty minutes and she could barely concentrate on her job.

Which was wrong for so many reasons. Because for this to work between them all there had to be no emotional ties between her and Finn.

Tonight was going to be an introduction to Lachie's nursery and routine, that was all. Nothing more. So there was no point being all silly and giddy. All she had to do was write up her notes, put on some lipstick, grab the food she'd prepared and she could go.

A sharp rap on her office door made her jump. It was Evelyn, the clinic receptionist, her face set in a grim line. 'Jackie Campbell's in Reception with her kids. She said she needs help.'

'It's late. She knows our hours… We closed thirty minutes ago.' Sophie's heart rate kicked up and she scolded herself. Jackie was trying to pull her family up from a life of poverty; she was a good woman who'd had a lot of knock-backs and a tough ride in life so far. Sophie felt inherently sorry for her and her three children. Given they were all under the age of five, they were all her concern. 'What kind of help does she need? What's wrong?'

Evelyn shrugged and shook her head. 'She wouldn't say but she looks rough. And scared.'

It was wrong of her, she knew, but Sophie glanced at the clock and her heart sank. Fitting an unexpected client in now would make her late.

What would Finn do?

Now, that was a thought she'd never expected to have.

He would move Heaven and Earth to help someone in need. He'd already done it for her, so he'd understand if she was running a little late. 'Tell her I'll be out in a minute. I'll just finish up here. Can you grab the kids something to eat and a drink if they need it?'

She heard them before she saw them. But it wasn't just Jackie and her three children; it was Billy now too. A hard man with a history of addiction, he was swaying and not quite focused as he shouted at his wife, 'Get yourself back home and bring them all with you.'

'No. This is the last straw, Billy. You said you wouldn't go drinking again and look at you. You're a mess and you're scaring the kids.' Jackie stood and faced him, pushing her youngest, Billy Junior, behind her thin pale legs. It was May in Edinburgh and in no way warm, but she wore only a thin, creased T-shirt and a short denim skirt that had seen better days. The two other children were in the toy corner playing quietly but glancing over at the action. The saddest part was that they seemed to be used to this kind of scenario.

Sophie took a deep breath and walked towards them, remembering her negotiation skills training and trying to appear neutral. 'Hey there.'

Jackie whipped round, her shoulders sagging the moment she saw Sophie. She had dark shadows round her eyes and her skin was sallow, cheeks hollow. 'Sophie. Thank God. Can you do something about him? I've had enough. Can you sort out a restraining order or something? I don't want him near us when he's drunk.'

'Don't be stupid, Jax. You don't mean that.' Billy swayed forward onto the toes of his ragged black canvas shoes and then back again, face contorted into a grimace. He was similarly dressed in unsuitable unseasonal clothes, covered only in a T-shirt and jeans. At least the children were all wrapped up warmly, Sophie noted. Jackie always put the kids first even if it meant she went without things for herself.

Sophie found what she hoped was a non-judgemental smile and remained as calm as she could be. This was going to take longer than she'd thought and would require delicate handling. 'We can talk things through, sure.' She turned and faced the wiry man. 'We just need to make sure everyone's safe, Billy, and that we all know the score. You know that. You know how it works. Yes?'

'You! You keep away from my kids,' he snarled, nostrils flared. 'Keep away from my wife.'

Sophie's heart kicked into overdrive. All well and good looking calm and in control on the outside, but inside she was shaking. 'She came to me, Billy. She wants some help and I'll give it to her. I can help you too if you want.'

'I don't need your help. You can't keep me away from my kids. I love them.'

'I know you do, Billy.' Today he looked rough and

on edge but she'd seen him on good days, on his hands and knees giving the children rides on his back. Seen him besotted with love and in tears after the birth of each child. Heard him apologise over and over for the way he seemed to lose grasp of his self-control. Like right now when he had anger in his eyes and tension thrumming through his body.

Sophie raised her hands just a little and indicated she was on his side. On everyone's side. Glancing briefly over to Evelyn, she nodded so minutely no one else would have noticed. But Evelyn nodded back and activated the silent alarm system. Just a precaution. 'We just want to make sure the kids are okay. And Jackie too. You want that, right? You love them and you want them to feel safe.'

'You even think about taking them anywhere but my house and I'll kill you. You got that?' Billy took a step towards her. Then another until he was an inch away from her face. He smelt of booze, fresh and stale. And unwashed clothes. And sweat. Cords of veins stood out in his neck as he pointed a very shaky finger right into her face. Sophie stood her ground, determined not to be intimidated even though her hands were shaking as much as his were and her breathing was far too fast. If she jumped now or moved too quickly he could curl that hand into a fist. He was wiry but he was strong.

She breathed out slowly. 'Billy—'

'Get your hands away from Sophie. Now.'

Finn. Great. Let's add another alpha into the mix.

She fought against her raging heartbeat. *Stay calm.* Keeping all senses alert to Billy and any sudden movements he might make, she half turned to Finn, pushing her palm downwards over and over, indicating him to back the hell off. 'It's okay, Finn. We're working this out, aren't we, Billy?'

Any other day Sophie would have appreciated how damned magnificent Finn looked with his eyes blazing and his muscles primed. She'd even have noticed the way part of her yearned for those taut arms to hold her, the way her heart kicked up just seeing him. Never mind the soft blow to her solar plexus that he was here, protecting her, no matter how misguided she thought him to be.

But right now she was so damned angry that he'd barged in as if she was helpless, she only noticed the prickle of white-hot anger in her gut. *How dare he try to take over?*

One look at Finn, chest all puffed up, jaw set and with his rugby physique making him twice the size of Billy, the drunk man took two steps back. Three. 'I didn't… I wasn't going to…'

'No, you weren't going to, pal. Sit down.' Oblivious to her irritation—or just plain ignoring it—Finn stepped across the room towards the man and stood close until Billy sat down in one of the plastic chairs. 'Has anyone called the police?'

Evelyn raised her hand from behind the desk where she was now feeding the little ones some sandwiches and distracting them by pointing to things out of the window. 'They're on their way.'

'No.' Billy's face creased up. 'They'll lock me up for being drunk and disorderly.'

'Again. You might as well move into Edinburgh jail.' Jackie sat down next to her husband and took his hand. 'Why, Billy? Why do you have to do this?'

'Can't help it.' Billy shrugged and slumped further in the chair, head in his hands as huge tears slipped down his cheeks and onto the linoleum floor, the aggressive drunk phase moving into the morose drunk stage.

Jackie seemed unmoved by the tearful display. 'Benefit day and you have to waste it all on booze. We've been waiting on that money for days. What about the kids? Food? You promised me. *This* time it was going to be different.'

He looked down at his dirty shoes and shook his head. 'Sorry, love. I couldn't help it. I just couldn't. But I won't do it again.'

Sophie's heart went out to them both. She'd followed the family after the births of each of the children. Times were hard for them, but getting him back on track was going to need work. So many times he'd promised to get help and he'd never even made the first step. 'Look, we can get you some food for over the weekend. The food bank's still open. If you come back and see me on Monday morning we can take things from there. Okay?'

Jackie looked up, wiping a hand across her tear-stained face, and smiled wearily. 'Thanks, Sophie.'

'And we need to work out how to help you, Billy.' Finn sat down on the seat the other side of the man. Finn's bravado had been replaced by something akin to conciliation. Understanding. Although he definitely still held the authority. 'Life sucks sometimes, eh? You feel like you're sinking and you can't find a way out.'

'Yeah.' Billy shrugged and ran a hand over his jaw. 'Tell me about it.'

Finn's fingers went to his own chin and he rubbed too. 'You feel like you have to be the man and it's hard. Everyone looking at you for answers and sometimes you just don't have them, right?'

'I can't get a job. I can't pay my way. I can't look after my kids. I was just walking past the boozer and I saw a sign for a barman's job. Popped in to ask about it. But then I couldn't stop myself having a pint. Then another…'

'And then you feel even worse. It's a spiral.' Finn kept his eyes ahead, not looking at Billy, and nodded. Sophie wondered whether he'd had negotiation training too. *Don't hold intense eye contact because it unnerves the aggressive client. Listen. Empathise. Mirror movements to gain trust.* Either that or he was just an innate listener. 'You don't have to carry all this, you know. You can get help. There are people, places who can help and you know what? It takes a big man to realise he needs help. An even bigger one to go get it.'

Billy turned to look at Finn, eyebrows raised. 'Have you…you know…?'

Finn sat forward, elbows on his knees, hands clasped and kept looking forward. 'There was a time. Things got pretty bad. Not drinking, but I felt as bad as you do now. Worse.'

Sophie's chest constricted as she wondered how dark things had got for Finn. How he'd managed to fight his way back to the man he was now.

Billy flicked a glance at Finn's expensive-looking leather jacket and huffed. 'Dinna look like you had it bad.'

Now Finn turned to catch Billy's eye. 'Lucky for me, someone helped. You want help, Billy? Before you lose your family completely? Your wife? Those lovely kids. They need their dad. They need you. But you've got to be in a better state. They deserve that. You want help, just say the word. But you've got to mean it.'

'Nah.' Billy rubbed his trembling hands down his thighs. 'I can manage this.'

Finn nodded. 'Like you did this afternoon?'

'That was different. Just a slip-up.'

Finn nodded again. No judgement, no opinion. 'You have them a lot?'

'Yes, he does.' Jackie looked defeated. 'And I'm sick of pointless promises. I've had enough. This is it. I'm finished with it all. He can go to hell for all I care. In fact, I'd prefer it if he did, then we could get on with our lives without him messing them up.'

Finn shook his head. 'This is a big deal, Billy. I'd say by the looks of her she really means it. Is it worth losing your family—everything—for?'

The man sat for a moment, looking at Finn, then he turned away and looked at his hands. The floor. His wife. The kids. And he nodded slowly, cheeks more hollow, eyes more desperate, saying what Sophie had heard him say so often but never with such determination and meaning. 'Help me, man. Now, though, before I do more damage. Can you sort it?'

'I will. Stay here.' With that, Finn stood and went outside. Made some calls. A siren alerted them to the police arriving, but Finn headed them off.

Sophie watched the faces of the family as relief filled the room. No restraining order. No broken hearts. No broken family—at least no more broken than it was already. When he headed back in, Finn walked straight to Billy and took him back outside. A taxi arrived and took Billy away.

Jackie watched him leave and breathed out slowly. She'd get a reprieve at least and Sophie could work on more strategies to deal with Billy when he came back. 'Thank you. I love him to bits but he drives me insane.'

'Come on, Jackie… I'll give you a lift to the food bank and then we can get those bairns to bed.' Evelyn bundled them all out with a cheery wave and an appointment reservation for first thing on Monday morning.

Which left Sophie and Finn alone with a whole lot of displaced and confusing emotion. Because, no matter what he'd been through, he'd still barged in and tried to take over and he needed to know there had to be boundaries in both their personal and professional lives.

He wandered back into the clinic as if he was meant to be here. 'Right. That's that sorted. Are we going to the nursery now?'

'No, we are not. Not yet.' She willed herself to calm down. After all, this was supposed to be a unifying night, not a breakup one. But she couldn't contain her irritation. 'Who do you think you are, Finn? You can't come charging in like the damned cavalry and rescue me like that. Especially when I don't need rescuing.'

His eyes widened. 'He threatened you, Sophie. You don't expect me to stand by and watch that happen? Do you? Really?'

No. Yes. No. She was annoyed that he had, but also flattered and impressed he'd felt strongly enough to act. 'I was sorting it out, Finn. He would have calmed down, if you'd given me the chance to talk to him.'

Finn raised his palms. 'Okay, I may have overreacted. But he just about had his hands on you. I thought he was going to hurt you.'

'I have a panic button which Evelyn pressed the moment we sensed things turning sour—we managed that by eye contact and prior agreement and it's part of our clinic policy. Obviously, I had Evelyn there too—we're never alone if we can help it. I also have a telephone in easy access and I've had a lot of training in dealing with these kinds of things. This is my job, Finn. I know what I'm doing.'

Finn shook his head, eyes adamant and assertive. 'He was two inches away from your face. I'm not going to watch someone I care about being threatened. Never.'

'He's drunk and scared and angry with himself more than anything else. Not me.'

Someone I care about. Something shifted in Sophie's chest and the space filled with a warm glow. But she wasn't going to let it affect her job. She just needed to work on keeping the glow alive in non-work environments. She went over to the play corner and started tidying the toys back into the huge red plastic box.

Finn watched her, came over and sat down heavily on a chair, started handing her some of the displaced toys scattered around his feet. 'Now he's got a place at the Rose Clinic he'll get the help he needs.'

She stopped tidying. The man was crazy. 'The *Rose* Clinic? That's a private place. He can't afford that.'

But he smiled. 'They have a couple of spots they do pro bono. I know the guy who runs it. He owes me a favour.'

Now the crash started to hit on the heels of the adrenaline rush. She started to feel just a little shaky so she sat down next to him and wrapped her arms across her chest. Finn had done a good thing. Maybe she was the one overreacting and being all independent to prove a point. 'Thank you. You did well. I shouldn't be angry. He'll get the help he needs there. Hopefully.'

'I can't imagine how he must feel with the threat of having his children taken away.' Finn frowned. 'I'd... I'd feel like killing someone too.'

He sounded beaten up, taking this very personally. 'Wow. This has really affected you, hasn't it?'

'Of course it has. The whole scenario is nuts. He's got a beautiful family and he's messing it up. If he doesn't sort himself out they'll live with the fallout for the rest of their lives.'

She knew enough about Finn to realise he wasn't just talking about Billy, but about his own father too. He was also talking about himself. Realising what he needed to do as a dad—and yes, it was overwhelming and intense but also incredibly satisfying and beautiful to watch a child grow into a man and he wanted that chance.

She looked over at him and realised her impression of him was changing. He wasn't the charmer so much now—although that was still a part of him that appealed—he was much more than that. Deeper, complicated, damaged—better somehow. Time had changed him, although she guessed his experiences had been the bigger factor. Every day she'd looked at her son and tried to ignore the parts that were Finn, but she couldn't ignore them any more. Didn't want to.

She ached to touch him. But she knew that would take them down a route she shouldn't go. 'What did you mean when you said you'd had dark times?'

A shoulder lifted. 'It's nothing. Just stuff I had to deal with.'

Without thinking, she put her hand on his left thigh. 'Your leg?'

'Er… Yes.' She thought he might reject her touch but he put his hand over hers and squeezed gently before lifting their hands from his leg. 'Boring stuff. I'm over it now.'

'Er… Liar. I imagine all those surgeries and all that healing took its toll. But I'll let it go because you clearly don't want to tell me.'

'Really, no.' He shook his head. 'Why ruin what's going to be a nice evening?'

He was still holding her hand and she was still gripping his and her heart was tripping crazily and her focus seemed fixated on him. Just him and the sensation of skin against skin. His warmth. His scent.

She wanted to know everything about him and she resolved she'd ask him about his dark times again some other time when he wasn't all about showing how good he could be. Developing relationships was about sharing the bad things too.

But they needed more time. Things were happening very fast here and she wasn't sure her head could keep up, never mind her heart. 'Okay, well, don't think you can keep waving your magic wand and solving all my clients' problems.'

His eyebrows rose and he smiled. 'Sophie Harding, you really do seem a little obsessed with my magic wand.'

'I am not.' Okay, she might be a little intrigued. After all, she'd experienced him before and knew what would be in store.

Lust crackled through her at the memory and she should have pulled her hand away from his but she didn't. She should have leaned away from him too, but she stayed exactly where she was, breathing in his scent and enjoying the tingles prickling through her body as he ran soft circles on the back of her hand with his thumb.

He shifted in his seat so he was facing her, lacing his fingers with hers. 'You keep talking about it.'

She laughed. 'I do not.'

'I've met up with you twice and my magic wand has come up both times.' He jiggled his eyebrows up and down and she laughed even more. 'Excuse the pun… But at least I made you laugh and now you're not angry with me any more.'

'Who says I'm not?' She was still a little bit angry but also turned-on and laughing. The whole gamut of emotions wrapped up in response to one package: Finn Baird. She couldn't take her eyes from his face.

Something, the Arctic breeze coming off the Highlands probably, had blown his hair a little awry and she ached to put her fingers just…there…and straighten it. Even though she knew a Baird's hair never did anything it was told to do. She had a feeling it wasn't just their hair that was stubborn and belligerent and just a little wilful.

His eyes sparked a deep intense blue and his mouth— oh, that mouth—was close enough for her to lean in just a little and press her lips against. Need scuttled down her spine, tightened her limbs, made her insides warm and molten.

What would he do if she just kissed him?

But he tilted his head to one side and the distance between them grew and the moment, the opportunity, was lost. 'Is your job always as intense as this?'

Thank God he'd taken things back a step. She breathed out more heavily than she'd intended but didn't have the resolve to slip her hand out of his. In fact, she wanted to touch more of him. It was crazy. She was crazy. Because there was nowhere they could go with this, too many reasons.

But she didn't let go of his hand. 'It's a mixed bag, which is why I love it so much. It's very rewarding. I see a lot of lovely babies and gorgeous children and I see parents across the spectrum, from families in desperate need to families who are coping just fine, and all of them just want the best for their kids in the end. Some days are lovely, some are intense, some are difficult.'

He gave her a soft smile which reached down to her belly and tugged. 'Today was difficult.'

'Yes.' She finally found enough willpower and slipped her hand from his, stood and picked up her bag. 'And it's not finished yet. We should go.'

'Not yet.' He caught her arm and tugged her to sit back down and she did, so close. Too close. 'Sophie—'

'Finn.' She put her hand between them, onto his chest—to push him away and, yet, to touch him too. To feel his heart beating fast and sure and hard. And for a second neither of them moved. Their eyes locked and she knew that they were on one single trajectory unless one of them was brave enough and strong enough to pull away.

But she knew it wouldn't be her, because she'd just used up the last of her willpower and this was a chance she might never get again.

He reached a hand to the nape of her neck, this time tilting his head towards her. 'Tell me to stop and I will.'

'Don't.' She shook her head.

The pressure of his fingers lightened and he inhaled sharply. 'Don't?'

'Don't stop.' Unable to resist any longer, she breached the distance between them and pressed her mouth on his. Gentle at first, slow and searching, relishing the feel of him, committing him to memory. Because the first time they'd kissed she'd believed they were at the beginning of something. So she hadn't known how important it was to remember the feel and the taste of him. This time, she knew, could be the last. Should be.

Don't stop.

He opened his mouth and she melted against him, climbing onto his lap and wrapping her hands around his neck. He tasted so fine: something fresh, something male, something intense and beautiful. One of his hands still clutched the back of her neck while the other cupped her face, fingers spanning her cheek. Claiming her as his.

And God, yes, she wanted to be, all over again. Even though he overstepped and overreached. Even though he'd disappeared out of her life. Even though…he kissed like a demon. Like a god.

She pressed closer as he slid his tongue into her mouth. Heard a guttural moan escape her throat. Melted at the smooth stroke of his hand down her arm and the smooth slide of his tongue against hers. She pressed closer still, desire spurring her on. She wanted him. Like this. In her bed. She wanted kisses that never stopped. Wanted his hands on her body.

Urgency deepening the kiss and blurring her thoughts, she ground against him, pushing her fingers through that unruly hair. Gasped as his hands ran down her side, under her T-shirt.

Aching for him to touch her breasts, she arched her back.

Then the shrill buzz of her phone cut through the soft moans and kisses and her senses returned.

Lachie.

They were supposed to be at the nursery, not making out like teenagers in an empty clinic.

Lachie.

He was waiting for them. They should be there playing families.

She pulled away. Jumped off Finn's knee. 'Hot damn, Finn. What the hell are we doing?'

CHAPTER EIGHT

'ISN'T THAT OBVIOUS?' He was making a joke, but she was definitely right. They'd got carried away. She wasn't listening as she snapped up the phone from her bag.

Meanwhile, he was barely capable of movement at all. Arousal had shot through him the minute she'd covered his hand and hadn't abated; in fact it still continued to flare inside his gut, his groin, his head. He wanted to take her there on the floor. Wanted to feel the soft weight of her against him. Pressure against his heart. In his heart. Wanted to be inside her.

Dumb idea. But the best one he'd had in a long time.

Now, here they were with the best kiss of his life wedged between them, feeding her anger at him and herself. And he still wanted to do it again. And again.

'Yes. Hi. Sorry, got caught up in things at work. We'll be there in five minutes. As quickly as we can.' She threw her phone into her bag, dived behind the back of the reception desk for a carrier bag filled with plastic boxes and started towards the door, straightening her skirt and smoothing down her hair with a palm. Pity. She suited being ruffled. And he had barely started to ruffle her. She shook her head as if reading his thoughts. 'Come on. Come on. We're late. Not a good impression at all.'

Well, at least she wasn't overcompensating for his leg. She seemed to have forgotten all about it.

Good.

Which was not how he was feeling right now.

He caught up with her and stepped outside the front door. 'Sophie, just calm down a minute.'

As she locked the door and activated the alarm he saw the shake in her hands. He'd felt that when he'd held her before. She was anxious, turned-on, maybe a little scared. Not of him, but of the idea of *them.*

God knew, she had good reason to be. Things hadn't exactly worked out well before. She was right; they needed to take a step back and regroup. But it didn't have to be quite so knee-jerk.

She was tapping her foot as he retrieved the bottle of white wine from the car. 'Are you ready now?'

'Sure. It might not be cold enough, though.'

'I don't care. We're very late, Finn. This is not how I operate.'

'We could tell them we were developing cordial relations between mother and father. Surely they couldn't complain about that?'

'This is not funny.' She stormed down the path and onto the pavement, took a sharp right turn and headed off ahead of him.

'It's the truth.' Although things had spiralled a long way from cordial, judging by her reaction. 'So we're running there, is that it?'

'I'm in a hurry. I don't know about you.' She pulled up short and glared at him. Her cheeks were still pink, her lips bruised and swollen from the kiss. Her hair was awry, despite her efforts. He didn't think he'd ever seen her looking more beautiful. 'We can't do this, Finn. Okay?'

'What? Go to the nursery?' He didn't understand. Things hadn't suddenly become so bad she suddenly wanted him completely gone. Had they?

'No. Us. The kissing. Flirting. Any of it. Because if it doesn't work out between us two, what would that mean for Lachie? He needs stable parenting. God knows, I never had it. How would he feel to be in the middle of a sour relationship? It's not fair on him.'

'We'd never do that. Whatever happened, we'd always be civil and never put Lachie in shooting range.' He started to walk. He had no idea where they were going but it felt better to be moving.

She fell into step with him. Although hers was a whole lot smoother than his limping gait. 'Trust me, people say that all the time and then do the opposite. I know. I see it a lot.' She turned her head to catch his eye, he presumed to make sure her point was hitting home. 'I also see separated people who co-parent well. People who put their children first and their own needs second.'

'Is that what you want us to do?'

She pursed her lips. 'It keeps everything simple. No mess. No fallout. Don't you think it'd be for the best?'

'I think kissing you all over again would be pretty damned good, to be honest.'

'Finn! Would you stop joking for a moment?'

'It's not a joke. It was a good kiss. Okay, okay, sometimes I say things to make you laugh. Sometimes I just say things to make me laugh. God knows, life can be very tough otherwise.' But she was right and they needed to work together to make this acceptable and pleasurable for Lachie. He didn't need to be brought up in a battleground, he needed a family. Family wasn't something Finn had ever planned on, especially after the accident. Family meant people relied on you day after day, they invested. He didn't want her investing in him. 'But okay. We stepped over the line. Got a little too carried away.'

'So we're good?'

He sighed. 'Sophie, we're very good. That's the problem.'

'I bet you say that to every woman you sleep with.' She shook her head.

'There hasn't been anyone since you.'

'Oh.' Her head whipped back round to look at him. 'You expect me to believe that?'

'Up to you. But it's the truth.' He hadn't had the strength of character to bare himself to another woman and risk seeing the disappointment in her eyes as she looked at his leg. Hadn't the confidence in himself to find someone and then be unable to give her what she needed—his focus and attention and time. But, also, he hadn't been attracted enough to anyone to try, until now.

They'd reached the nursery, a detached white bungalow a little back from the street. *Little Acorns* was emblazoned across the gate in bold, bright primary-coloured letters, across the front of the house, across the windows and on a huge banner outside the front door. Finn narrowed his eyes. 'Great-looking place, didn't catch the name?'

She nudged him and seriousness leached from her. 'Behave.'

'I am doing.'

'Finn's in the zero to two room. Squirrels. Be warned…it's loud.'

She pushed open a door and he was hit by a wall of noise. Babies crying, adults talking, glasses chinking, a soundtrack of high-pitched kiddie music. He strained for a glimpse of his boy. 'Where is he?'

Sophie grinned and he could see pride glowing from her. 'His favourite place to hang out is the sandpit. He likes the diggers and trucks they have to play with in there. He's got a couple of friends he plays alongside with.'

'Alongside with? Does that mean he's not great at sharing or something?'

'Finn, he's one and a half. He's not at the mixing and mingling stage yet. At this age they just all play on their own, together. If that makes sense. Look, there he is.' He watched as she spotted Lachie, knee-deep in sand in the far corner of the room, and waved. Everything about her changed in an instant. It was as if someone had indeed waved a wand and she'd transformed. Smiling, vibrant. Bright. 'Hey there, wee man.'

Lachie dropped a blue truck and held out his hands to his mother with a grin, identical to the one he'd seen a lot of recently on Cal's face, that lit his features.

She picked him up and covered his face in kisses and whispered something to him. Lachie grinned more and nodded.

She pointed to Finn as he wandered over to meet them at the sandpit. 'Look, Lachie. Here's Finn. He wants to say hi. Can you say hi?'

Lachie turned his head towards Sophie's armpit and rubbed his forehead against her chest.

'He can be shy sometimes.'

Finn dug deep and waited. *Please say hi.* No matter how much he told himself it didn't matter if Lachie didn't take to him straight away, it did matter. A lot. Silly to set so much store on the little guy. But he couldn't help it. Didn't every dad want his kid to like him?

Sophie repeated, 'Say hi to Finn, Lachie. Look, he's saying hi to you.'

'He did it so well at the clinic when I gave him the stickers. He can do it again now.' That was the thing; the boy had seemed blissfully unimpressed or bothered when Finn had met him the first time. But now, did he somehow sense this was a big deal? A father and son moment that he didn't want?

Sophie looked over and nodded, eyes silently saying something he didn't quite understand. But Finn gently tickled the boy's ribs with one finger and said, 'Give me a high five, Lachie? Like last time?'

He stopped short of bribing him with more stickers just to get an acknowledgement. But slowly Lachie turned to face him and raised his little fist.

He did it.

'Yo. High-five, dude.' Finn fist-pumped the boy very gently, showing him what to do.

Geez. First thing to teach him: how to be gangsta. He'd never live it down.

'Hi, Sophie. You made it.'

Finn swivelled to see an older woman in a very prim jacket and tweed skirt peering over.

Sophie smiled. 'Hi, Elaine. Yes, we had a bit of drama at work. Sorry to be so late to the party.'

'Not a problem. As you can see, we're nowhere near finished. Your boy's pleased to see you. He's had a good day today. Ate all his lunch and tea and played very well.' Elaine laughed at Finn, who was still stuck on high five variations. Making Lachie laugh too. He was making his boy giggle and chuckle and ask for more! *More!* Finn felt the woman's eyes on him a little longer and then she asked, 'And this is…?'

Sophie caught Finn's eyes as he stopped playing.

What would she say? She opened her mouth, cheeks burning. She surely must have thought this through? He stuck out a hand and said, 'Finn. I'm Finn. Nice to meet you.'

'Hello, Finn.' Her handshake was exactly as he expected. Firm.

Sophie explained, 'You'll be seeing Finn around a bit from now on. I'll make sure he fills out all the correct forms in case I need him to pick Lachie up or do drop-off or…'

'I see.' Elaine looked over to Finn again and he wondered if he measured up to her standards. 'If you come through to my office some time before the end of this evening we can go through it all then. Just routine.'

And with that she turned on her low heels and went to talk to some other poor bloke. 'Is she the headmistress? Because she's a bit Professor McGonagall.'

'Oh, yes. She keeps the parents on their toes.' Sophie grimaced. 'I'm sorry. I didn't know how to introduce you. Lachie's starting to repeat things he hears. He probably wouldn't understand the words but…'

But I'm his father.

'You don't want him to say Dad and get used to the idea until I prove I'm going to stick around.'

'Two outings isn't a lifetime commitment, Finn.'

'I'm trying here. I can't suddenly fit everything into ten days. Tell me what more I can do.'

She looked up at him and her gaze softened. He could see the struggle in her eyes. The memory of the kiss. The wanting. The knowing it was stupid to go there, but wanting to do it again anyway. He understood that she was torn in so many directions and that, for her, the hardest choice was to start to trust him.

She'd be wise not to.

He wasn't that reliable guy who would be there when needed. He had form, history of choosing himself over others.

'I know this is out of left field for you, Finn. You got up last Monday morning with no idea your life was going to change so much.' She put her free hand on his arm and leaned a little closer to speak, her scent bombarding him, stirring the desire again. He wished they were alone. Wished they didn't have this barrier between them. He wanted to start again with the kissing. And this time to not stop. Her breath feathered across his throat. His concentration was shot whenever she was around; he couldn't focus on the important things. Well, other than kissing her—that was very important. 'I know you're trying hard, Finn. I can see that. And you're handling it well.'

He'd handle it a lot better if he didn't like her, didn't want her. 'I'll go fill out those forms. I know there'll be sections about my relationship to the child. You need to know I won't lie.'

'I don't want you to. But I'll ask them to keep the knowledge low-key until Lachie understands. Okay?' She nodded. Decision made. Everyone at the nursery would know he was Lachie's dad even if Lachie didn't. It felt like fireworks were going off in his chest. 'We'll be waiting here for you. Oh—do you think you'll need my help with any of the information?'

He patted his jacket pocket where he had the picture Lachie had drawn for him back when he was just the nice guy at the clinic. Finn's gut tightened that he needed a piece of paper to know the intimate details of his son's life. Details he should know by heart, have lived through. 'I'll be fine.'

'Yes. You'll probably just need to fill the bottom section of my form.'

'And you'll probably need to sign to say I'm legit or something.'

'Okay, do what you need to do and I'll get this boy settled in the reading corner. Which is…' she pointed to an area with low white bookcases and beanbags '… over there.'

When he returned from Elaine's scrutiny he found them curled up on a huge green beanbag, holding a book between them. Lachie was turning the pages and Sophie was saying the words in a sing-song voice.

His chest expanded and filled with light.

Soft idiot. This scenario had never been on his radar. Not once in his life had he wanted this. Rugby, mud, glory, beer, messy uncomplicated sex: that had been his life for so long. Then the hard route of recovery and wondering if his life was over.

This. *Wow*. This was altogether new. He hadn't realised what he'd been missing. But, hell, he'd missed the best part of living.

She turned and smiled. 'Hey. You found us. We're reading a story. How did it go?'

'Elaine's just waiting for your signature to say I'm trustworthy.'

'Did you get the headteacher beady eye?'

'She's a tough nut to crack, but when I said I was Lachie's dad she actually smiled. She didn't ask me much though.'

'She wouldn't. She's the height of good manners.' Sophie wriggled off the beanbag and said to Lachie, 'Mummy's going to talk to Elaine but guess what? Exciting! Finn's going to read you a story. You can choose which one.' She winked at Finn as Lachie stayed exactly where he was and didn't cry out for his Mama. 'Winning, see? If you slide your hand the other side of the beanbag you'll find I've poured two glasses of wine. Lifesavers when he wants you to read the book for the tenth time and you're bored out of your skull. Just a life hack from someone who knows.'

He watched her walk away, watched the swish of her curls, the sway of her backside and wanted to run after her and drag her into the store cupboard and kiss her senseless. *Stop it, man. Close yer mouth.* It wasn't right to think such things with a bairn close by. Was it? 'Right then, Mr Superhero. Which book do you want to read?'

Lachie pointed to the one Sophie had left on the beanbag so Finn picked it up.

But Lachie kept his distance, watching Finn holding the book. *Geez,* if he thought he'd had a breakthrough with the high five game he was certainly wrong.

'Come here, Lachie. We can read it together.' Finn held his breath as the boy shook his head and dropped his gaze to his shoe. He hit the trainer and it flashed. He looked back at Finn. Waiting. For?

Finn caught up. 'Ah. Your trainers. You remember I like them?'

The boy still didn't say anything. But he hit his shoes again and they flashed red. He looked up at Finn.

Finn's heart nearly exploded. His kid didn't know what to do or how to act either, but he wanted to make this man smile. 'Yep. Superhero trainers. I remember.' He had an idea. Stupid, maybe. But it was worth a try. At some point he was going to have to breach this issue; it might as well be done now as part of play.

Glancing round to make sure no one was looking, he rolled up his trouser leg and exposed part of the carbon fibre pylon attached to his prosthetic foot. 'Look at this.

Half man, half robot.' He tapped the pylon and gestured to Lachie to do the same. The boy frowned and wiggled his fingers over Finn's shoe and slowly tiptoed them to touch—so carefully—Finn's artificial leg.

'Tickles!' Finn drew his leg away. Feeling nothing, but feeling everything just to see his son interested and giggling. Lachie reached out and touched it again.

'Gentle. I'm very ticklish.'

Lachie snatched his hand back, eyes huge. Then gingerly reached out and patted Finn's leg again. This time Finn let him explore a little more.

It took a few minutes but Lachie's interest gradually waned and he seemed keen to read the book. So Finn encouraged him to come sit next to him and they opened the book together.

One step nearer. And yet Finn felt as if they'd conquered Everest. Lachie had taken it all in his stride and had even been so unimpressed he'd got bored. If only adults could treat his amputation the same way instead of making it a big deal.

This was the big deal: his son in the crook of his arm, the sweet baby boy scent, the cute curls, the profile of the little nose and long, long eyelashes. The concentration as he followed the words and nodded at the cadence. The next generation of Bairds. His son. Real live flesh and blood and, as far as he could see so far, brave and empathetic too. Sophie had done a great job, but now it was time for him to step up too.

This was real.

The lump in his throat almost cut his words off. But he forced them through. He was reading a story to his son, who seemed entirely happy to be here. All he needed now was Sophie on his other side, wrapped against him, and things would be perfect.

And now he was really in Dreamland. Because not only was it the furthest thing from her mind, it was also the most ridiculous thought he'd had. One kiss did not make a family; one kiss had, in fact, put a wedge between them.

Pity, because given another chance he'd do it all over again.

CHAPTER NINE

SOPHIE WATCHED AS Lachie tapped Finn's artificial foot then work his way up the carbon fibre pole and chuckle. It looked like something from a sci-fi movie, all black and silver and shiny with a skin-coloured foot encased by a shoe. Any adults seeing it would've been hard-pressed not to stare but Lachie seemed to be taking it all in his stride. But kids were like that; they accepted differences, barely even noticed them. Her heart stalled. This was the breakthrough Finn had been hoping for.

She craned her neck to have a better view of his prosthetic, then thought better of it. It wasn't her business. Instead, she watched them settle down together and then Finn turn the pages and say the words. The way he looked at his son almost broke her heart in two. He was invested and trying hard. That was something. A beginning.

The kiss had pushed everything from her memory back into reality. The past and the present were getting dangerously blurred. He'd tasted exactly as she'd remembered. And even though she'd only spent one night with him she remembered the way he kissed too. Remembered the way he'd made her feel.

Even though she was enjoying his company, she

couldn't help feeling panicked that this was all happening too quickly, that they needed to slow things down.

He seemed to be aware she was watching, turned and waved, which made Lachie look up and come running over and the book reading was abruptly over. 'Sorry, I didn't mean to disturb you.'

'He likes me.' Finn looked as if he'd been given the best Christmas present ever. 'I think.'

'Of course he does.' How could he not? 'I told you it was just a matter of time. But don't be put off if he starts to gravitate to me again. He's tired and likely to get clingy.'

'And kids always want the familiar when they're tired, right?' But she'd broken the spell for them and now Lachie was stretching his arms out to be picked up by her.

Finn twisted to get himself out of the beanbag; for most people it would have been an easy manoeuvre, but for him it looked difficult. She should have thought about that and chosen a more comfortable chair. But then he'd have hated that she was thinking of concessions for him. She turned away so as not to be seen watching.

Once he was upright he laughed. 'Everything is so much easier with two legs. If only I'd known before. Can I walk home with you guys?'

She tried to crush the uplift in her heart. It wouldn't do to get too involved. But she seemed unable to stop it. 'Sure. But your car's still over at the clinic.'

'It's not far; I'll walk over later and get it.'

'You can do the boots and bars tonight then.' She added an evil-sounding laugh. 'My first night off. Ever.'

'I'd love to. Anything to help.' Again with the Christmas present smile. Which did nothing to calm down the hitch in her heart and the desire to be with him, to spend time with him, no matter how much she knew it was a very bad idea.

She grinned, knowing the hullabaloo waiting for him with the boots and bars. 'You won't be thanking me later, trust me.'

They were home in no time and it felt surreal and yet somehow right to be showing Finn how to bathe and get his son ready for bed. How easy it would be to allow herself to fall into a kind of dream here. The perfect family.

Until he changed his mind.

Finn was laughing as he poured water over Lachie's head and rinsed away the bubbles. 'What a waterbaby. You just love it, don't you?'

Sophie took a step back and, with mixed feelings, watched the bond between them tug tighter and tighter as he lifted Lachie out of the bath, all dripping wet and covered in soap bubbles, and wrap him up in a warm towel. 'Right then. What's next?'

'Boots and bars, then bottle and then bed. It's a regular routine, same thing every night, then he knows it's time to sleep. No messing.' She handed him the warmed sipper cup of milk and as their fingers touched their gazes met over Lachie's head.

'Thanks, Sophie.' Finn smiled softly. 'I mean it. Thanks for this chance.'

'Don't thank me yet. You haven't done the boots and bars.'

His fingers curled into hers and longing wove through her, deep inside, making her lean towards him. Wanting him. Feeling too many things: a chance to find bone-deep happiness in his kisses, however fleeting, a threat to the status quo she'd worked so hard to achieve as the only parent to her adorable son. She didn't know the answers—if there even were any—but she'd bet that mooning over Finn wasn't part of the equation. She breathed out, let go of his hand and went through to Lachie's room and waited for them to follow. 'We usually sit on the floor for the boots and bars; it's easier.'

'Cool room.' He glanced round, eyes wide. 'Did you do all this?'

She felt a stab of pride as he noticed the pale grey and light blue paint on the walls and ceiling, the jungle-themed mural with a lion and giraffe keeping watch over Lachie's white wooden cot, the dip of branches from a tree heavy with grinning monkeys. 'Yes, it was great fun doing it. I knew I was having a boy so my friend Hannah and I decorated it before he was born.'

'It's exactly what I would have chosen. Although I don't have an artistic bone in my body.' He clambered down to the floor, left leg sticking out rigid as he leaned onto his hands, then twisted his body down. Everything he did required extra effort and forethought. That had knocked out the immaturity in him, for sure. But it hadn't diminished him in any way.

She tried not to look at the strength in his arms and upper body, tried not to imagine those hands on her face, on her skin. Or that smiling mouth on parts of her that hadn't been kissed by anyone but him for years. She picked up the boots and bars and handed them over. 'Right then, do your best.'

'Dickers.' Lachie tugged at his mum's arm and pointed to the drawer she kept them in.

'If you're a good boy and sit nicely, you'll get stickers.'

'Me?' Finn pointed to himself. 'Excellent. I love stickers. I can sit very nicely and I can be a very good boy...'

She knew he could. And a deliciously bad one too. 'Finn Baird, I swear—'

'Dickers. Mine.' Lachie's bottom lip began to tremble.

'Oh, dear. This may turn ugly. He's a bit fractious. It's quite a bit past his bedtime.' She grabbed the stickers and held them out to Finn, pushing back the memory of the teasing in his eyes. Trying not to recall the way he tasted. 'Right, boots and bars on then you can choose a sticker.'

Lachie shook his head.

'Lachie, mate. Boots and bars first, then stickers. I won't have any, they're all for you if you're a good boy.' Finn held out the boot for Lachie to slip his foot into. At least she didn't have to go through the motions of showing him how they worked.

'No.'

Sophie made a face. 'This is what it's like. One day he's great with them, one day he isn't.'

'That's toddlers for you.' Finn shrugged. 'Go pour the wine; I'll stay until he does it.'

'Are you sure?'

'Rough and crunchy or smooth and silk, it's all part of it. I'll sit here and wait all night if I have to. Go. Go put your feet up.'

'Really? Wow.' And boy, that was the last time she had to be asked. This was a glimpse of how different things could have been; a shared load, shared life. But she'd decided she wasn't going to dwell on that any more. She was just going to take advantage while she could. 'Okay. I'm out of here. Don't take any cheek and don't give in. The Chardonnay will be ready when you are.'

As it was she'd only polished off one glass of wine before Finn appeared in the lounge. 'I'd give anything for him not to have to wear those boots.'

'I know. Broke my heart at first too. You want them not to have to struggle. The endless plaster casts were a challenge too.' She tapped the sofa for him to sit and then handed him a glass of wine, which he took with a smile. It felt altogether strange, good and weird, that they were doing this. 'Only a few more years and he'll be fine.'

Finn's eyes blazed. 'He *is* fine.'

'You know what I mean. You want them to be…' She didn't want to say the word because it didn't describe what she really meant, but he guessed anyway.

'Perfect? No one's perfect, Sophie. I mean, not even me…damned close but…no dice. Or, rather, no left leg.' He used his humour as a shield, she could see that now. Always making fun of himself, to put others at ease. Getting the words in before anyone else had the chance to.

'I didn't mean perfect. I meant…it's hard for me to watch the other kids running around with no issues when we have this rigmarole every night.'

He shrugged. 'He probably won't even remember when he's older. He's hitting milestones, you say? He'll just be one of the boys. He'll rise above it all and achieve great things.'

'Is that how you feel about what happened to you? That you've risen above it? Got over it?'

Finn shook his head. 'I'm not one of those who thinks it's a good thing in the end that I lost my leg and that I see life differently now, that I appreciate things more. Like those people who say, *My life is better because of it. I really grasp every second now.* I was always grasping at everything, Sophie. I did grasping like a pro. I took everything for granted, the fact I could run and jump and grasp and grasp again at success, at life. Now I just have to grasp further and hold on tighter.'

'I can see you doing that. You're different to when we first met. More intense somehow. Same…same but different.'

He shuddered. 'Ugh. Sounds depressing.'

'No, actually. I think you're remarkable.' *God*, she sounded like she was his number one fan. She realised things were going down a mutual appreciation route she didn't want to take so she quickly changed the subject. 'Where do you live now? I don't remember you being from Edinburgh; weren't you just visiting? From near a loch somewhere?'

'I was born in a tiny village called Duncraggen at the tip of Loch Lomond, did most of my physiotherapy degree in Glasgow and then completed the rest by distance learning when I moved to Aberdeen to play for the Swans. The day we met I'd travelled here with the team for a game.'

'And you found me to keep you company while they went on to a club.' And they were both struggling with the consequences. 'So where do you live now?'

'Heriot Row. Ground floor apartment.'

One of the better places in the city. 'Very nice.'

'Not affordable on a physiotherapist's salary, but I did earn decent money playing rugby before the accident. I'm not rich, but I have more than enough.' He became a little more animated. 'I want to talk to you about that. We need to talk about financial support for you and Lachie.'

She didn't want to know where this was going. 'I don't need anything. I haven't got the authorities chasing you up for maintenance payments or anything.'

'I want to help out. I have money. I want to give you some. For Lachie. For you.'

'We don't need anything. We're fine.'

'You said you wanted a holiday. To travel. I could pay for that.' He was really excited by this.

It would make things easier, but she didn't want to be beholden to him. 'We're fine.'

His voice deepened and he frowned. 'You may be *fine* but everyone wants something. The only thing I want right now is to provide for my child.'

'I don't want your money. I didn't tell you about him because I wanted your cash. I told you because it was your right to know him.'

'He's my child. I want to support him. How do you think I'd feel if you won't let me get involved at all? It's what people do.' Not letting him contribute was a challenge to his manhood, to his male pride, she could see.

'It's what *couples* do, Finn. People who've had a relationship breakdown. We didn't even have that. It was one night.'

'Whoa.' He jerked back in the seat as if she'd slapped him. Things were deteriorating. Fast. But instead of snapping back at her he took a couple of beats to compose himself. 'Yes, and that was because of my oversight. I need to make amends here. I can't make up for the last two years but I can make the next ones easier.'

'You have to stop trying to overcompensate for what happened. I haven't even thought…it's all so complicated. Jumping ahead. Too far ahead.'

'I'm not going to let you fob me off on this one, Sophie. I'll set up an account in his name and put something in every week and I'll set one up for you too and put money in there and you can use it for whatever you want. Holidays—that's what you want, right? He needs to have sun and sandcastles and buckets and spades. Ice cream for afternoon tea and fish and chips out of paper.' She could see the longing in his eyes as he said those words. He wanted to do that too. Because his father hadn't been around to do that with him and his brother. He wanted to do all those things his father hadn't done, to give Lachie everything he hadn't had.

He was shaping himself to Lachie's life, to his heart and to his love, and she was suddenly terrified and awed at the same time.

Would he be the one taking Finn away? From her?

Would she be left behind? She had never considered being apart from her son, had never missed one night of his life. She couldn't bear the thought that she might miss him doing something fabulous, or something just mundane or silly or…being left on her own. Or being beholden to someone financially, having to take them into account with her decision-making. She was losing control. Losing a little of her relationship with her boy possibly too.

Tears sprang to her eyes and she fisted them away.

But Finn caught her in the act. 'What's wrong?'

'Nothing. I'm just tired.' And overwhelmed. She couldn't say any more. It wasn't her place to deny her son a fun time—to deny him the things she couldn't give him—but it didn't mean it hurt any less.

They sat for a moment in silence and she wondered how they could navigate through this and make things better. Time, probably. Maybe a contract would be a good idea. Her brain was muddled, mainly by the intensity of her attraction to him. By her desire to do right by all of them, and also by the threat to the independence she'd forged that meant she could call the shots about what happened to her and her son. 'I just want him to be happy.'

'Me too. We'll work it out.' Finn turned to face her on the sofa and took both her hands in his. 'I can see you love him so much. I just want to do the same.'

'Lucky boy.'

'You don't want to share him?'

He could see right through her. 'I'm scared what that means. For me.'

'He can love us both without one diminishing the other. Sophie, I know you didn't have the best time growing up without your parents, but we don't have to be like them, or like my own useless father. We can make this work. I'm not out to hurt you. Far from it.'

'I know.' He didn't want to hurt her but someone would be hurt.

'Let me show you.' He tipped her chin up and pressed a soft kiss on her mouth. And instead of pushing him away she wrapped her arms around his neck and pulled him closer. Seeking comfort from his heat. And that was the thing; she could be frustrated and angry at him and yet also deeply connected to him.

It was as if they'd been set on a predestined trajectory that nothing and no one could stop. He tugged her close and she could feel the heat of him. It didn't seem to matter that they'd agreed they couldn't do this. Neither of them could stop. She wanted to be here with him. She wanted to fit into his arms, to mould herself to the shape of him, and into his heart. Just for long enough.

However long that would be.

As long as Lachie didn't get hurt. She would never let that happen.

At the thought of her beautiful son sleeping upstairs she pulled away. If she wasn't strong enough to stop this for herself, she could be strong enough to stop it for Lachie. 'This is too complicated, Finn. We agreed. I can't see anything clearly at all. Nothing. I want you in ways I didn't imagine, but I'm too scared to go there. I want you in Lachie's life, but not at a cost to me. Or to him.'

'I want all those things too. I also want to kiss you again. For a long time. I want you, Sophie. So badly it's like an ache that won't go away.'

This was too much for her to deal with. Bad enough she wanted him, worse that he wanted her too. But lust was like a shiny new present, easily dulled over time by overuse and familiarity. True unconditional love took time to grow and came from mutual trust. 'We agreed we shouldn't.'

'We can un-agree it too. We make the rules.'

'Don't make this harder than it already is, Finn.' She shook her hands free and went into the kitchen, switched the kettle on, kept busy. Because not being busy with Finn around was far too much temptation. 'I think we have to be firm with ourselves. If we keep giving in to this then one of us is going to get hurt. Or all of us. Because, be honest with me…do you see a long-term future thing here? Or has your head not worked through all that yet? Because it's all very new right now, but trust me, getting up in the middle of the night to a sick child, not being able to go out when you want, having to pre-think about every potential eventuality is damned hard.'

'You don't think I have to think about every eventuality? You think I can just jump up and dash out the door without planning ahead?' He shook his head. 'You don't know me at all, Sophie. You still think I'm the immature guy who's going to run, don't you? You don't think I can do this long-term. That I have some fantasy idea about being a father? That I can't do it.'

'No. I just—'

'You just don't trust me. Right?'

She didn't know how to respond to that. Because she wasn't there yet, but she was learning to let go, learning she had to. 'I want to trust you.'

Hurt was written in the lines around his eyes, in the way he took a deep breath and shuddered out the exhale. In the swift turn of his body away from her. In the grip on the table top to steady himself. In his voice and his words. 'Glad that's clear then. I'll be in touch about access to my son.'

CHAPTER TEN

Truth was, Finn didn't trust himself either. So, in many ways, she was right; they needed to keep this all above board with rules and guidelines so they both knew where they stood. Something to bind them all together, which was what he was doing now at the end of a busy shift. A week since Finn had left her house and he hadn't contacted Sophie, apart from a daily text asking about Lachie. Nothing else. No flirting. Nothing.

It was killing him. But it was the right thing to do.

'Bad day?' Ross stood in the doorway of Finn's office as he did every evening, assessing, checking in.

'Just getting a few things sorted out.' He still hadn't mentioned his relationship to Sophie and Lachie to his boss; better to keep things quiet until they'd nutted out the details. He sent the email and closed his laptop, girding himself for the reaction he'd get. But it was what she'd been hinting at. It was a start, anyway, to making things crystal-clear between them. Maybe then they could start working on the trust thing.

Ross coughed. 'I said…pub?'

'Yes, actually. I do need a pint.' Having talked to clients all day, what he really craved was some alone time, but he knew it wasn't what he should do right now.

Being alone wasn't good for him. Cal would be proud he had such personal insight.

Ross grinned. 'Well, what are we waiting for? My round, and perhaps this time you'll actually turn up?'

'Try stopping me.' But as they walked down the hospital ramp and into the damp Edinburgh evening he couldn't help looking over his shoulder for a woman with caramel eyes and a heart of endless depths.

She wasn't there.

Two pints later he shoved the key into the lock of his house and dashed in out of the now lashing rain. His phone was buzzing with Cal's ringtone but he ignored it. What could he tell him? Things weren't working so well between him and the mother of his child. They'd muddied everything with a kiss. Two kisses. His self-control had let him down again.

He slumped onto the sofa, dragged off his prosthetic and liner and rubbed the pain away. Tried to.

The doorbell rang.

Damn. He'd expected a reaction, but not so soon. Maybe by return email. A grumpy text. Definitely not in person. He reached for the liner and fumbled to pull it on. Failed. Threw it back on the sofa.

'Finn! Open the door. I know you're there.'

The lights flickered and thunder crackled overhead. It felt like the thud of his heart. It felt like the end of the world, the beginning of hell. But they needed to go through this so they could come out better.

'Finn! I'm getting soaked out here. Open the door.'

He didn't have time to mess about with his leg. She'd have to take him as he was. He had no secrets. It wasn't as if she was going to see the scarring anyway; his trouser slipped down and over the stump.

Grabbing his crutches, he made it to the door by the time she pressed the bell a third time. 'Sophie.'

'Finally.' The caramel eyes were a dark fire of molten gold. Water dripped from her hair; she had no raincoat, no umbrella, just a sweatshirt that was soaked through and jeans that stuck to her like plastic wrap. Shivering, she dug deep into her voluminous handbag and pulled out printed documents and waved them at him. The rain beat down now, thick and fast, and the paper started to wilt in her fist. 'What the hell is this?'

He moved aside and let her into the hallway, skin prickling just at seeing her, heart beating triple time, and it wasn't because he was worried about her reaction. He was worried about his own. How could he find an angry woman such a turn-on? He tried to focus on more important things. 'Where's Lachie?'

She glared at him. 'In bed. At home with Hannah. What the hell is this, Finn?'

He needed to stay calm. 'The start of negotiations. I just got a lawyer friend to mock something up so we could start setting out what we expect from each other.'

She shook her head. 'I can't afford to pay someone to do this. I thought we could talk about it one-to-one. An informal agreement. Why did you have to do this?'

'Because if it's written down then maybe you'll believe I have Lachie's long-term welfare at heart.'

She pointed to a paragraph she'd highlighted in orange and held it towards his face. 'You want him to stay over at your house? Here?'

'Yes. When he's ready. When I'm ready. Only on occasion. I'm not asking for joint custody or anything extreme, Sophie. I just want to see him.'

Her nostrils flared, her eyes blazed. Her mouth screwed up. 'I'm so damned angry with you.'

'I can see that.' *God*, she was magnificent. Heat prickled through him, made him hard. He wanted to absorb all that energy of hers in a kiss, in passionate lovemaking. He wanted her more now than he'd wanted anything in his whole sorry life. 'This is what you wanted, Sophie. This way you can hold me to my word.'

I've missed you.

He felt it resonate through him.

He'd missed her and he wanted so badly to hold her, kiss her. To give in to the need that misted everything when she was near. Even when she wasn't. He wanted to let that need overtake them both, give in to it and stop fighting.

'No, Finn. Oh—' Only then did she seem to realise he was standing with a crutch shoved under his armpit. She looked at his trouser leg and shook her head quickly. 'This isn't what I want.'

So that was it. The heat seeped out of him. She was angry. She was scared. She was repulsed. The trifecta of doomed relationships.

Leaning on his crutch, he stumbled through to the lounge, expecting her to follow. It wasn't a pretty way to move, but he had to get her out of the cold hall and into the warm open-plan lounge-diner. They needed space. Walking over to the dining table, he flicked the top of a whisky bottle and poured out two fingers for each of them. Handed her a glass and leaned against the heavy wooden table. Steady. Belying his raging heartbeat. 'What do you want, Sophie?'

Her gaze caught onto his as she took a sip of the honey-coloured liquid and put the glass back on the table. 'I want to scream at you so damned loudly, Finn, for doing this.'

'Go on then. Scream.' He probably deserved it.

'No.' Eerily quiet, she crumpled the paper into a ball and threw it to the floor. He caught her arm, tugged her to face him. Her breathing was ragged. Despite the cold, heat radiated off her. This wasn't about the contract he'd sent her. Not at all. This wasn't about his leg. It was about the need between them.

'What do you want?'

'You've turned my world upside down. My head's all muddled. I thought it could be straightforward. I want it to be.'

'Which is why I've found someone to help us clarify everything. I don't want emotions getting involved in our decision-making, not where our son is involved.'

'Everything I do for that boy is chock-full of emotions. I can't see clearly where he's concerned. He's been my first and last thought and almost every thought in between every single day for over two years. He's part of me, Finn. He's my everything. But you're…well, this is the bit I struggle with. I was angry with you for so long and I didn't expect you to be like this. I didn't expect to feel the way I do.' She put her hand to Finn's chest. 'So I don't know what I want. I don't want to be confused and angry, that's for sure. I don't want us to communicate through lawyers. I want us to talk. I want—' Her fingers curled into the fabric of his shirt. 'I want—'

'I want you.' She'd described exactly how he felt— even after such a short time of knowing he was a father— confused, muddled and too attracted to Sophie that it made his head hurt and his heart ache. The emotion in her voice was thick and raw and it seemed to reach deep inside him. It took all the strength he had to ignore it. 'But that's not good for either of us.'

Her fingers relaxed against his heart. 'I know you'd make me feel good, Finn.'

'I can't give you what you need, Sophie. I can't make a whole load of promises for ever and ever. I'm not that man. You almost said it yourself. You can't trust I'll be there for you. Hell, *I* can't trust I'll be there for you. Not long-term. Not happily ever after.' If anything showed up his weakness and lack of self-control it was her. This need. Now.

'Maybe this is the way forward. Maybe it isn't. But I don't think we can do anything but go with it. Tonight. Now.' Her mouth was inches away from his. Her eyes sparked a dare and a promise. Her tongue ran along her bottom lip and that almost undid him. 'Now, Finn.'

I want you.

Unable to resist any longer, he tugged her close, slid his hands around her waist. For one short moment he gave her time to pull away, saw the hesitation in her eyes, then the hunger. Saw the moment she stopped fighting. Then he pressed his mouth to hers, branding her as his.

She tasted elemental, of tears and rain. Of something new and fresh and yet so familiar it felt as if she were part of him. The kiss was soft at first, exploring, relearning. Then, as need unravelled inside him like ribbons of silk, they kissed harder. Deeper. Her fingers gripped his hair as her tongue danced with his in a messy open-mouthed kiss. Finding each other again. Searching new places. Feeding an insatiable hunger. He didn't know how long they stood entwined together but he didn't want it to end.

'God, Finn. Yes, I want you. I don't want to. But I do.' Her breath came quick and fast as she fitted her body against his. He felt the damp press of her breasts and his hands found their way there. Over her sweat-shirt, then under. Sliding his fingers under the straps, he unclipped her bra, palmed a nipple and groaned at the pebbling under his fingertips.

She shivered under his touch. He shifted against the table so she could step in between his thighs. Moaning, she rubbed her core against his hardness but then she suddenly stopped kissing him and pulled away. 'Are you okay here?'

With the lack of leg? The subtext was glaring.

He closed his eyes against the rage of shame firing through him. No one had ever asked him if his body could handle this before. No one had asked if he could manage the act, or even make out. He fought back the strangling irritation in himself. He looked over at the sofa and the cast away pylon, the liner, and felt inadequate. Why the hell had he taken them off? She wouldn't have seen him as anything less if he was standing on two legs, even if one was false. He tried to keep the tension out of his voice, but knew it was still there. 'I'm fine.'

She looked up at him and smiled. 'You're making me very hot, Finn Baird, but I'm soaked through and starting to shiver. Can we…can I…? Where's your bedroom? I need to get out of these wet things quickly and under covers before I catch pneumonia.'

Touchy bloody fool. 'I thought…never mind.'

'Finn.' She followed the track his eyes had made and she sighed. 'You think I won't find you attractive?'

'You don't want me to screw up your life, Sophie. I can't give you what you need.' Therapy had taught him that his missing leg was an external metaphor for the missing internal part of him. The part of him that had made him choose his friends over his mother, made him fight his brother just to prove he was right. *That* was unattractive.

But she palmed his erection and all logical thought was lost. 'I want you, Finn. You. Not select parts of you. I want all of you.'

He needed her to be sure. 'When we first met I was in peak condition, Sophie. Plus, I had two legs.'

'Pretty good condition, as far as I can see. Besides, I have stretch marks now; I've changed a lot too. People do, over time. You said no one's perfect, Finn. You hold that standard up for just you? Because from where I'm looking you're the closest to perfect I've ever seen.' She ran her free hand over his pecs. 'Will it hurt you in any way?'

Hurt? This was paradise. Her hand was still rubbing his erection and he was so hard he couldn't string two thoughts together. 'I don't know. No. I can't see how.'

She pinged the button on his trousers, slowly tugged down the zip. The anticipation of her fingers on him made lights flash behind his eyes. Then reality hit and the firmness of her hand around his naked flesh had him muttering soft curse words. It had been so long and he was too damned hard—it'd be over before it began. He moved her hand away. 'Give a guy a chance. Sophie, please. I want to kiss you everywhere first.'

He bent and gently caught her bottom lip between his teeth, then slid his mouth over hers again. Somehow he managed to strip the sweatshirt from her damp skin. Threw the bra to the floor as she peeled his shirt from his back.

'Just look at you.' She dragged her mouth from his and kissed his collarbone, his pecs, sucked in a nipple and made him shudder with white-hot lust. 'Bedroom?'

'Too far.' Grabbing his crutch again, he walked to the

sofa and with one motion of his forearm swept everything to the floor. From the arm of the chair he grabbed a thick tartan blanket and wrapped her in it and laid her on the cushions. Perching his bad leg on the sofa and taking all his weight on his good one, he wriggled the wet jeans from her legs, leaving her naked except for her panties. Goosebumps dimpled her flesh. But, God, she was beautiful. 'I'll kiss you warm again, Sophie Harding.'

'Do it. Do it now.' She threw the blanket over him too and giggled, wrapping them close and hot.

He didn't need two legs to give her pleasure. Pressing her back against the cushions, he kissed a trail down her throat as she arched against him. As he reached her breasts she moaned soft and low and he nuzzled there until she was pulsing against his leg. Pleasure sparked deep inside him, spurring him on, making him drunk on lust, on the taste and the feel and the smell of her, melding her indelibly in his brain and in his heart as the connection tugged tighter into a desperate, ragged insatiable need.

His trail went lower until he reached her hip bones, kissing across the delicious dips and curve of her pubis. With one flick of his hand the panties were discarded and his fingers probed into the soft, wet depth of her core. He ran small strokes with his thumb over the tight hard nub and felt her contract around his fingers.

'Finn.' Her upper body lifted from the cushions as she thrust her fingers into his hair. 'Finn. I can't… Don't stop.'

'I'm not going to.'

'Oh. Oh… I need you inside me…' He felt her fingers grow slack, her head fall back and her core clamp tight as she moaned loud against the pillow. She enslaved his thoughts—his body was hers—and he knew that whatever she commanded he'd do it, willingly.

She'd never felt so desperate, so turned-on. A couple of moments, three, she was sitting up and tugging his face towards her for a greedy hot kiss. Then her hand travelled south again, slipping his trousers off, then his boxers. As his erection slipped free he groaned into her mouth. He was so hot. So hard. And she couldn't wait another second for him to be filling her. 'Condom?'

'Wallet.' He reached backwards and grabbed his wallet from his trouser pocket. From this vantage point she could see the side of his left leg. The missing space.

When he turned round he caught her looking. He shook his head and twisted so she couldn't get a direct line of sight to it. 'Don't. Just don't, okay?'

'You're beautiful, Finn. Magnificent.'

'Don't look at it.' He tugged her face so she would make eye contact with him. 'I want you, Sophie, so damned much. And I want you to want me. Don't spoil the moment.'

'Finn, your body turns me on. *You* make me feel so much. Too much that I'm scared. The way you survived your accident and what you've achieved since makes you more of a man, not less. Let me in.'

She clamped her eyes shut and fought the way he'd sneaked under her skin, through her bones and into her heart and wondered whether he'd ever feel the same about her. Whether she was making another mistake by being here with him. But she couldn't do a damned thing about it; she was in so deep. She couldn't help but be honest; this wasn't a time for holding back so she kissed him, opening her eyes and looking only at him, at the bright shimmering blue of his eyes, at the face that had melted her resolve that first night and still did so today. At the man who was the father of her son, a part of her life. A piece of her heart. And she told him through that kiss exactly how much he turned her on, what she felt.

By the time they drew breath he was hotter and harder and his breaths came in gasps. 'Are you sure?'

'Hell, yes.' She pulsed against him, trying to assuage the need between her legs, the sexual frustration rumbling through her body as it ached for his touch. Then he was sheathed and above her and his eyes were burning and yet misted and she could see the same out of control desire she felt mirrored there.

She shifted her hips and felt the hard length of him fill her, whip her breath away and fill her with heat and light. She clenched around him and he gasped again, pulling out almost…almost…then thrusting into her again. She matched his rhythm, hooking her legs around his thighs and pressing her body full against his so she could feel the solid fast beat of his heart and inhale the masculine scent of him.

He groaned into her mouth and she felt him shift sideways and the pressure lessened. Another stroke and the pressure mounted again—he was playing her like a musical instrument, building to a crescendo she didn't want to wait for.

'Can I…? Can we…?' She wriggled out from beneath him and sat up, then straddled his thighs, positioning herself over him.

The mist in his eyes cleared and for a moment she thought he was going to stop.

But she found his mouth, caught his gaze then slid over him, rejoicing in the way he filled her like no man ever had. 'Don't you remember? Last time?'

'How could I forget?' His smile was all sex as he tugged her legs around his waist until she was sitting on his thighs, her face touching his face, her breasts touching his chest. Skin against skin. Mouth against mouth, until she didn't know where he finished and she began. He rocked into her. Harder and faster. She could barely form words, definitely not thoughts, as pleasure tightened deep within her, threatening to burst her heart wide open. 'Oh my God, I can't…this is…perfect.'

'Yes. You are.' He held her face as he crashed into her over and over. He held her gaze as his eyes widened and he groaned loud and strong, her name over and over. Sophie felt wave after wave of light thrumming through her as they reached the peak together. And she knew that whatever happened next, however their lives unfolded after this, she would never be the same.

CHAPTER ELEVEN

FINN LAY BACK on the couch with Sophie wrapped over him and tried to catch his breath. Tried to make sense of the swirling emotions in his chest.

So much for him having changed, having wrestled his self-control into submission and being the big guy who thought of others first. No matter how mind-blowingly brilliant making love with Sophie had been, this had no doubt thrown them into more confusion. But, even so, he wouldn't change a thing; this time with her was a gift.

She pressed kisses along his collarbone and up his throat and sighed against him. 'Well, that wasn't what I came here for. But I'm very glad I did.'

'Me too.' He kissed the top of her head and squeezed her closer. 'I need to get you angry more often.'

'No, thanks. I prefer to keep my blood pressure within normal limits.'

'Mine's sky-high right now. The things you do to me.' He kissed her again, then latticed his fingers with hers as she rolled off him and settled against his side. He was drawn in by the golden hues in her eyes as she smiled at him. Satiated. Breathless. Beautiful.

Lachie had his eyes. Her smile. The best parts of them both. They'd created something so perfect and now this…her. Reaching heights he'd never thought he'd go to again. A solid heat settled under his ribcage and his mind cleared. For the first time in a long time he felt complete. As if, in this very moment, he had everything he needed.

How long would it take for him to blow it? 'So, why did you choose Lachlan out of all the names in the world? Is it your dad's name?'

She shuddered at the thought. 'No way. I wouldn't name him for his grandfather. Lachlan means from the land of the Lochs. Warrior. It was used to describe the Vikings when they invaded. I thought Lachie may need to be a warrior one day; having a strong Scottish name would be handy. I also—' she stopped '—nothing.'

Finn was more than intrigued. 'What? What were you going to say?'

'Nothing.' She kissed him again and he wondered how it was she knew exactly how to turn him on. How to fill the need and stoke the fire at the same time. It was as if she had a direct line to his very core.

'Don't think you can fob me off with mind-melding magic kisses.' He stroked her hair, unable to remember a time when he'd chosen to lie with a woman and just talk…except the last time with Sophie. 'Tell me what you were going to say.'

She smiled. 'Okay… I remembered you said you were brought up near a loch. It seemed fitting.'

Fireworks lit up his solar plexus. 'You named him for me?'

'In a roundabout way, I guess. Loch boy.'

Even though she'd been angry and confused and hurt, she'd clearly been determined not to pit her son against his father. She hooked her leg round his good one and the rub of bare skin made him prickle all over with heat. One look, one touch had him burning with desire. He was destined to want this woman for ever.

'And Spencer? What's that about?'

'Don't laugh, but my grandma had a cat called Spencer when I first moved here. I loved him the minute I met him. He let me do those horrible things kids do to their pets, like dress them up, or carry them like babies. He was very tolerant and very calm and I hoped Lachie could be a little like that too. Calm, but wise. A warrior when necessary, but also quiet when needed.' She laughed. 'He's got a fair bit to go yet. One day, maybe.'

'He's named after a cat?' Okay, so now she was a little crazy, but he loved it.

'It's his middle name, but yes. Why not? A lovely cat with an awesome temperament and he was brilliant at catching leaves.'

Yes. Crazy. 'Good call, then.'

'You wouldn't have called your son after a cat?'

'Hey, I had a cat back in Duncraggen called Fidget, not really the name for a boy.'

'Actually, the perfect name, but I think he might get ribbed at school for it.' Her stomach growled and she rubbed it, laughing. 'Oops. Sorry.'

'Hungry?'

'Ravenous. I missed dinner somewhere between getting your email and waiting for Hannah to arrive to babysit. I was too angry to think about eating.'

'Like I said. I should get you angry more often.' He slid out from underneath her. 'Stay right there.'

'Yes, boss.' She gave him a salute and collapsed back into the cushions.

The goosebumps were back on her arms, her hair still damp and forming little curls that framed her face and made her seem younger somehow. He tugged the blanket around her. 'I'll put your clothes in the tumble drier. Should be dry by the time we finish eating.'

She sat up again, the blanket wrapped around her breasts. Still modest after everything they'd done. 'But I can do it—'

'Sophie—' he cut her off '—it's just food and washing. Simple. How do you think I manage day to day?'

Turning away from her, he reached out and picked up his liner and prosthetic and dragged them on, hoping she couldn't see what he was doing. Then he pulled on his trousers, bundled up her wet clothes and got the hell out of the room. It wasn't that he was being helpful so much as it was a good excuse for some headspace.

She'd called their son after him, even though she'd been angry and hurt and confused. They'd kissed each other naked, shared the most intimate of lovemaking. But even now he needed to take his time before showing her his leg and she felt embarrassed with him seeing her naked.

All the desire and need in the world couldn't make up for the depth of intimacy time brought with it. They'd taken steps into the unknown here tonight, but they were still new to each other in so many ways.

His head was whirling as much as his chest. Too much too soon? Unspoken promises he didn't know if he could keep?

Once he'd finished piling things onto a tray he steadied himself and balanced it in one hand while he used the crutch for his other.

She was still sitting up when he came into the room, still wearing the blanket as she eyed the food greedily. 'Finn Baird, you're a domestic goddess.'

'I try my best.' He set the tray down, then went back to the kitchen for a bottle of wine and two glasses. The half-full whisky glasses twinkled in the light, catching his eye as he walked past the table. Had that only been an hour before? So much had happened between them since she'd stormed in all wet and fierce and he'd thought he might lose her altogether.

He poured the wine and slid onto the couch, the tray between them as they tucked in to olives and French bread and cheese.

'This is exactly what I needed.' She wiped her mouth on a napkin and sighed. 'How long will it take for my clothes to dry? I should really think about going soon.'

His gut tightened. He wasn't ready to say goodbye yet. 'I wish you could stay longer. You wouldn't stay the whole night last time either.'

'Finn Baird, you know the rules. You never sleep over the first time.'

'And you wouldn't let me take you home.'

She shrugged a shoulder and tore off a piece of bread. 'Taxis are always easier. Trust me, I didn't want to leave. I just thought I should.'

He should have made her stay and spent the next day with her too. Things would have been so different. 'I remember feeling two distinct ways as you left—empty and lost that you'd gone. And so excited that I had your number and would see you again. You made me happy for the first time in months. I just wanted more of you. Of what we'd shared.'

She put down the bread and nodded for him to continue talking. 'So walk me through that next day. What happened?'

It had been an idle reminisce; he hadn't meant to turn the conversation down this route. 'It's ancient history. Boring.'

She shook her head. 'It's filling in the gaps for me,

Finn. I often wondered why you didn't call. You stood me up. You pissed me off. My whole life changed. So tell me...so I can fit the pieces of the puzzle together properly.'

She had a point. He owed her an explanation. 'I think I told you a bit about my mum when we were in the bar. That she'd had a stroke and died a few months before you and I met?'

'Yes. You were really cut up about it when we started to share our sob stories over too many shots of tequila.'

He laughed. 'A sob story. That's one way to describe it.'

Sophie's eyes softened and she covered his hand with hers. 'You really loved her.'

'I did. But not enough. In the end.'

'That's not who you are. Why would you ever think that?' She had a way of asking that seemed to promise she wouldn't judge. He wanted to tell her. Tell someone. Sometimes he felt as if he was carrying a huge weight in his gut and maybe talking to Sophie could help with that.

'When I first started to play for the Swans I was the golden boy. Everything I did worked. On and off the pitch. Everyone loved me. The team, the boss. Women.'

She flicked her free hand at his. 'I do not need to know that.' She pigged her eyes. 'Was I a groupie, Finn? That's what you thought?'

He laughed. 'You can't be a groupie if you don't even know who the guy is, Sophie. That's not how it works.'

'Oh. Okay.' She shrugged again. 'That's a shame. So tell me about being a golden boy; maybe then I can be a real groupie.'

'Oh, I think you could be now.' She was trying to make this easy on him, but he didn't deserve that. His gut clenched tight as he talked, guilt infiltrated his bones. 'I played well, scored a lot of tries, did everything right and loved the praise. I'm ashamed to say, I got a little cocky and narcissistic.' *A little?* 'One night I was playing close to my old home so I told Mum I'd be round to see her. She was so excited. But I got distracted with my teammates. We'd won a game and I was all cock-a-hoop and we were celebrating hard. I kept looking at my watch and promising I'd leave in a minute. But I never did. We went to a nightclub and my phone kept buzzing and I just ignored it.'

He shook his head. How had he thought he'd feel better giving voice to this?

'Finn…you were just a kid caught up in yourself.'

'Not such a kid, really. It was less than three years ago, Soph. Turns out she'd had a stroke in the kitchen. She'd made my dinner, set the table. Then she'd collapsed and wasn't found until the middle of the night when the neighbours saw the light on and the curtains open. If I'd been there I may have been able to help her so much more quickly. Worst case—she had the stroke because she was so upset I hadn't turned up.'

'You can't carry that on your shoulders, Finn.'

The weight in his gut travelled to his chest and pressed down. Hard. 'I can and I will. I was selfish and stupid and self-centred and should have kept my promises to her. Instead, I chose to get drunk with people who I couldn't rely on when I needed them. I lost my mum because I couldn't give her what she wanted, couldn't put her first.'

She lifted the tray and put it on the floor beside them then edged closer to him, stroking his back. 'You're different now.'

He wished he was, but he was so stuck in getting by,

getting on, he still wasn't sure he had enough space for anyone else. 'How would you know? When have you had to rely on me? When have I had to give you anything? You refuse money. Time with Lachie is managed. And trust...?'

'I trust you can do things for him, Finn. For us. We need to get to know each other better. Like this.' Her voice was soothing and silk to his raw one. 'Tell me about that night.'

'I'd rather not. I'd rather talk about you. Or, even better, I'd rather...' He reached for her and pulled her onto his lap. 'I'm done talking for tonight, Soph.'

She put her hands on his shoulders and pressed him back against the arm of the couch. 'Finn Baird, you are strong and wonderful and funny, but there's a part of you that's still lost in the dark and needing light. I know there's a bruise on your heart and I want to rub it clear away. But the only way you can help is to let it go. I'm here, it's okay. Let it go.'

She wriggled closer and kissed him deeply. And again. Kissed him until he couldn't think straight. The only thing he knew for certain was that he wanted to be inside her all over again. And he knew she wanted him there too. He thumbed her bottom lip. 'I'd much rather do this.'

She shook her head. 'We're honest, you and I. That's just one thing I like about us. Don't hide from me. Let me in.'

He kissed the tip of her nose and then tapped his heart. 'You are in.'

The smile she gave him at that admission had a direct line to his chest. 'So talk.'

'Not tonight.'

'Then I'll go. Are my clothes dry, d'you think?' She edged away.

'No. I doubt it.' He took a deep breath and blew it out slowly. She wasn't going to let him get away without offloading some of his story. If keeping her here meant talking, then he'd talk. 'Mum's death was just the start of things going wrong. I was grieving and angry and made some bad calls on the field. The harder I tried, the worse things seemed to get. I went from golden boy to water boy in a matter of weeks. And the guilt over my mum's death seemed to grow. I couldn't talk to Cal about it. I couldn't talk to the boss because it wasn't the kind of thing you did. So it started to eat me up from the inside. Then I met you. The one shimmeringly good thing about those few weeks.'

'You didn't tell me this at the time, though. You just said you knew how I felt about my grandma dying.'

He smiled, remembering how much he'd wanted to impress her that night in the bar. 'Hardly the greatest chat-up line: *I think I killed my mum*. Besides, you actually seemed to like me. I didn't want to jeopardise all that. You were amazing. This shining golden star in the midst of a whole lot of crap.'

'But you kissed me goodbye, said you were going to be busy and you'd call me in a couple of days. You never did. I take it you saw Cal the next day and did the hike?'

'Yeah. We'd planned it a few weeks before. I think he wanted to check how I was. He's always kept watch on me, like a father figure. I guess, being the older brother, he felt it was his job. Still does. We both wanted to climb Ben Arthur again. So we set off. I was in a foul mood. And tired.'

She grimaced. 'My fault.'

'Not at all. Seriously. I think I was just completely

wiped out by all the guilt and emotion. We trudged to the top pretty much in silence. I was going to tell him everything—I wanted to—and I'd just about got the courage up when it started to snow. It went from clear skies to a whiteout in a matter of minutes. We lost our bearings and started to argue. I lost it. He lost it. Two angry men filled with grief and testosterone and pride. Not what you want at the top of Ben Arthur in a storm. He wanted to go in one direction, I wanted to go the other. Both of us believed we were right.' Finn hauled in air. Two stupid pig-headed men.

'Not ideal.'

'He was shouting at me. I told him he didn't have to think he was always right. That if I wanted to do my own thing I could. So I started to trudge down one way in the snow. He came after me and told me to grow up and that we had to stick together. Things got bad. I told him he was jealous of my success. I said some stupid stuff that I'd been bottling up—all the anger poured out of me, towards him and towards myself.'

'You were hurting, Finn. Sometimes we lash out when that happens.'

'He said he would never be jealous of me. That I was an idiot and he'd had enough of looking out for me. Sibling stuff. Nothing important and yet…'

He drew in a deep breath. 'I see things differently now, but in the heat of the moment when I was hating myself I thought he hated me too. I thought everyone did. I thought I'd killed my mother, let the team down and in a blinding flash of clarity I thought things would be better for everyone if I didn't exist.'

'But you'd just spent the night with me. You knew I didn't hate you.'

'Logic says yes. I couldn't stop thinking about you

on the drive out to the mountain. But by the time we were lost up there all the good vibes had gone and I was cold, hungry and angry with big brother. So, Cal's next to me, grabbing my arm, trying to pull me to go his route. I'm pushing him back and I can see the edge of the mountain looming up towards me. And beyond that it looked like there was nothing there. Just nothing. And for one minute that was what I craved. Nothing.'

She looked at him, open-mouthed. The pain he felt deep inside was written in her features. 'What are you saying?'

'That I still don't know whether I lost my footing or whether I stepped out into thin air on purpose.'

'Oh, darling.' She took his face in her hands and kissed him hard and it felt like some kind of forgiveness. Absolution. 'I can't imagine how that felt.'

'Trust me, you don't want to be there.' He couldn't even put it into words. 'I woke up on that ledge, dazed and confused and shivering and in so much pain. Everywhere. And my brother talking non-stop to keep me alive. I knew then it was what I wanted more than anything too. I've been fighting my way back ever since.'

'Thank God you survived. Look at you. You're magnificent. You can do anything.' She paused and thought for a moment. 'But when I found out I was pregnant I searched for you everywhere. I looked online and I never saw anything about you and the accident...'

'I insisted it was kept low-key, out of the news as much as I could. No names.' He looked at what was left of his leg. 'You think I wanted this broadcast to everyone?'

She ran her hand down his thigh and to his knee. Then over his knee to where it stopped. 'Does it still hurt? Phantom pain, that kind of thing?'

He took her hand away from his knee. 'I get it occasionally. I still forget I don't have the damned thing from time to time too.'

'Can I see it?'

He closed his eyes. Exposed both inside and out. And some of that old exhaustion bit him again. 'Why?'

'Because it's part of you. Because I want to prove to you that I think you're amazing, whatever your leg looks like. That I know you can do amazing things.'

'Another time, eh?'

'Finn. It's me. We've just shared something… I can't even describe it. My heart feels so full.'

'I know.' He cupped her face and kissed her. But he wasn't ready to open himself up to such scrutiny yet. 'Not today, Soph. I can't.'

She shivered and dropped her gaze to her hands. 'Okay. That's okay.'

But he knew he'd disappointed her. 'Another time. I promise.'

'It's okay. Honestly.' The invisible lines tugging them closer were starting to fray and if showing her was the only way to mend that, he'd do it. He began rolling the trouser leg up but she stopped him. 'No. You're right. I'm pushing you too much. It's all happening too fast.'

'It's okay. Look. Let's just get it over with.' He bent towards the trouser leg again.

But this time she shook her head and pulled his hand away. 'Stop it, Finn. I don't want you to do it like this. I'm sorry.'

He didn't know what to say or do as the warm bubble around them popped, covering them in a confetti of awkward silence. 'So. You want more wine? More food?'

Her phone buzzed and relief flickered across her

eyes. 'That's probably Hannah thinking I've got lost or something. You know what? I really should go.'

'I'll drive you.'

'No. It's stopped raining. I need the fresh air and exercise.' She leaned in and kissed him. Squeezed his hand then slipped off the sofa, wrapping the blanket like a shield across her body. 'Don't get up. Text me later. We can arrange another time to get together. If you still want to?'

'Sophie, don't get the wrong impression; of course I do. I just don't want to do a show-and-tell right now, okay?'

Showing her meant opening himself up to his absolute most vulnerable. It wasn't about the way it looked. Okay, it was…but it was also about the way it made him feel. A symbol of all the stupid decisions he'd made. She was one of the better ones and he didn't want to risk what they were growing. Although he had a feeling it might be too late.

She came back into the room a few minutes later, dressed back in her jeans and sweatshirt. She waved as she left. No more kisses. And his heart began to stutter.

Truth was, it wasn't Sophie who had problems with trust. It was him.

CHAPTER TWELVE

Sophie was trying to concentrate. But everything seemed so muddled today. Ever since she'd left Finn's flat two days ago she'd been out of sorts. He'd bared his soul and she'd got all sniffy and tried to push things instead of letting him take his time.

Texts back and forth had been friendly enough but she knew she'd overstepped and it seemed as if the emotional reaction to having him in her life had become physical; she couldn't stop her heart from racing and her hands from shaking. Which was difficult when she was writing up the results of a hearing test on a toddler.

She looked over at Jackie Campbell and smiled reassuringly at the anxious-looking mother. 'The glue ear is all healed up and Billy Junior is doing just fine.'

Relief shone on the woman's face. 'So he's not deaf?'

'All the results today are within normal limits. He may get glue ear again, but we'll keep monitoring him. If it does come back and starts to affect his learning or speech, we'll have to think about inserting grommets. But that's down the track.' The shaking wasn't going away and now it was accompanied by a thumping headache and a raw throat. Not a physical reaction to Finn, after all. Still, she had enough of them to keep her body on alert. She tried to focus on Jackie. 'So, how are things at home?'

Jackie smiled, the most relaxed Sophie had ever seen her. 'Better now we've got a good routine sorted out and money to spend on food.'

Something going right for someone. Good. Jackie deserved some happiness. 'How's Billy? Have you heard from him?'

'He's doing okay. He's called a couple of times, when he's allowed to. It's hard for him, but he's committed. I've never heard him sound so determined.'

'That's good.'

'Can you thank that man again for me?' Jackie stood and beckoned to her boy to come over and take her hand. 'If he hadn't sorted out that place for Billy I don't know where we'd be.'

'Finn? Yes. I will.' And there she was, thinking about him all over again. Trouble was, she couldn't stop and it was getting in the way of everything. 'Have a nice evening, Jackie.'

'Thanks. You too. You look a bit pale. You okay?'

'Just tired, I think.' Sophie waited for her clients to leave, then pulled out her phone and did a quick check of her face in the camera app. Her eyes were glassy and her cheeks bright red. *Ugh*. Not a good sign.

A sharp rap on the door had her stuffing the phone back into her bag. 'Come in.'

'Sophie? Ready to go?' Finn stood in the doorway and her heart raced in a *pleased-to-see-you* tattoo.

'Hey there. Yes, I'm done.' And strangely, physically, she felt it too. Completely done in. 'Let's go get the boy.'

But he didn't move and there was a strange look on his face. One she couldn't read. Was he having second thoughts about what they'd done the other day? Was he feeling backed into a corner? That wasn't a conversation she wanted to have but they had to broach it.

He gave her a kind smile. 'Having another difficult day?'

'No, actually, it's been okay. Jackie said to say thanks for getting Billy a place at the Rose Clinic. He's doing well.' She ran a hand round the back of her neck, suddenly feeling hot and cold at the same time.

'Yes, I saw her on the way out. You okay? You look… how best to say this without you taking it the wrong way?' He came into the room and held his arms for her to step into. 'Very beautiful, but tired.'

'I'm fine.' *Beautiful.* She felt far from it. She felt befuddled and confused. She laid her head against his cool chest and wrapped her hands around his back. Nothing felt better than his arms around her, holding her… holding her *up* today. But she couldn't hide from reality for ever. 'Finn, we need to talk. About the other day.'

'Ah.' She sensed rather than saw tension capture his jaw. He shook his head. 'I was an idiot.'

'No, you weren't. I've been thinking—maybe we should slow things down a bit.' She unfolded herself from his arms, feeling the swift bite of space and cold away from his heat.

He took a step back, palms raised. 'You want to stop this…?'

'No.' Not with one cell in her body, but her brain had other ideas. 'But we can't fit the last two years into two weeks or even two months.'

'Okay. I can do slow. I like slow…slow kisses, slow dancing, slow sex…' Relief flickered across his eyes. His fingers played with the hem of her top and then tiptoed underneath and up towards her bra. She curled back into his touch. She didn't want to be apart from him, from this. 'I'm enjoying getting to know you.'

'The feeling is very mutual. But we need time. I shouldn't have pushed you.'

'Sophie, I was more than happy with everything we did. And, for the record, whenever you want a rerun just say the word.' He backed her against her office desk. 'In fact…are we the only ones here?'

'Yes.' She arched against him, pressing herself along his length as his hand covered her breast, wanting him inside her—her body hot for entirely different reasons now. It was so inappropriate to be doing this in her office, but she didn't care. And cared even less as his mouth found hers.

It was the kind of kiss that branded her as his. That wiped all sensible thought and made her legs woozy and her brain even dizzier. But she managed to drag her senses back when she clunked her elbow against her work computer and scattered papers across the floor. She pulled away, reluctantly. Hesitantly. 'We really need to stop doing this here.'

He straightened her top and smoothed down her hair. 'Yes. Lachie needs picking up; we don't want to be late again.'

The thought of her son had alarm bells ringing in her head. Or maybe that was the fog of headache that seemed to be getting worse, despite all the best kisses in the world. 'I think we shouldn't do this kind of thing when he's around. You know, the holding hands thing or kissing. Am I being presumptuous that you even want to do that?'

'Still protecting him?' Finn didn't answer her question, she noticed, as he gathered together all the scattered papers and piled them on her desk.

She should have filed them or something, but she didn't have the energy. She needed what little she had to get her point across to Finn and then whatever was left to walk round to pick up her son. 'I'll never stop protecting him. But I don't want him getting confused. Until we know where it's going.'

He tipped her chin up. 'Where do you want it to go, Sophie?'

To bed. For ever. To be in those arms, to kiss him and never stop. To feel the roughness of his jaw against her skin, to bask in the heat of those eyes. To soothe his grief. To share his worries. To raise him up. To share the wonders of their boy.

She wanted the works: everything he had to offer and more. But she knew what he had to offer might not be enough. That he was still healing. Knew, too, that fairy tales didn't happen, families didn't always end the way they started and that no amount of wishing could make dreams happen.

Mostly, she didn't want their son caught up in a war. 'I want Lachie to be happy and feel safe.'

So both of them could avoid the difficult questions. Another thing they had in common.

'So no holding hands or kissing in front of…anyone? That's what you want.' He ran his thumb across her cheek and anyone else would have thought he was on board with the idea but she could see he was stung by it.

'It is. Now we should go.' As she stepped forward the room blurred then eventually caught up, making her nauseated. 'Ugh.'

His arm slid round her waist. 'You okay?'

No. In so many ways.

Her head hurt and her heart didn't know how to act. 'Just a bit dizzy, you know. Nothing.'

'You're very pale.'

'A bug, I think. My throat's cracked and my head's pounding. I hope you don't get it too; I shouldn't have kissed you.'

'Oh, yes, you should have.' He fitted his hand into hers and walked slowly with her to the door. 'It's because you got wet the other day. I knew I should have undressed you sooner.'

'Yes, you were a bit slow on the uptake.' She couldn't help smiling at that. 'Really, I'm around littlies every day with their snotty noses and coughs. Lachie's at a nursery where every week there's a note about some bug or other going round—I think I've had just about everything in the book.'

'Maybe this is a new edition.'

'It's probably a twenty-four-hour thing. I just need painkillers and an early night.' She grabbed hold of the wall as the room swam in front of her eyes again. 'Whoa. Dizzy. Hang on.'

'I'm driving you home right now and you're not getting out of bed until I say so.'

'But Lachie needs collecting from Nursery.'

His eyebrows rose. 'Well, here's my first chance at being the pick-up dad. Do I look like I'd pass Elaine's inspection?'

'Yes.' He looked pretty damned eatable. Very determined. And a little out of focus. 'But I can—'

'I'm not taking no for an answer. You stay in the car while I nip in and collect him, then I'll do the bedtime routine. Okay?'

She'd miss reading her boy a story. Miss the cuddles. Miss the endless scuffle over the boots and bars.

Was this the beginning of the changes she was so afraid of?

Finn winked. 'Don't look so worried. I'll manage.'

'If you need me, you'll ask, okay?'

'We won't need you; we'll be fine.'

That was what she was afraid of. She bent and got into the car, let him pull the seat belt across her and closed her eyes to stop the world tumbling around her. He was being thoughtful and kind and exactly what she needed.

But not necessarily what she wanted. Oh, she wanted him with a force she didn't understand. But she didn't want a Finn-sized complication in her life. He was going to take over. He was going to be the last person her son saw tonight. He was going to reinvent the sweet routine she'd worked hard at creating. He was going to be with her boy and she wasn't, and she didn't have the energy to disagree.

Bath. Bottle. Boots. Bed. That was what she'd said the last time he was here. Or something like it. She'd made it sound so easy, but how did you do the kitchen thing without bringing the kid downstairs with you and all the problems that entailed? Conversely, how did you leave him upstairs on his own?

Finn had put his hand up for this without thinking it through.

Story of his life. Plain and simple: he hadn't a clue what he was doing.

His brother's face appeared on the phone screen. 'Morning. Evening. Whatever it is where you are. Not like you to call me. What's up?'

Finn shook his head. Yeah, phoning his brother was a surprise to him too. 'How do you make up a baby's bottle?'

'It says on the side of the tin.' Cal scratched his

head. He looked weary. Unshaven. 'Wait. Are the bottles sterilised?'

Finn looked around the kitchen and didn't see anything that looked like a steriliser. Or a tin of milk powder. 'He's one and a half…do they need to be sterilised? Does he even need a bottle? I think he had a cup the last time I was here.' He should have paid more attention instead of goofing at Sophie. Right now he'd give anything to be goofing at Sophie—goofing with her instead of trying to work out a puzzle of his own making. Every thought he had seemed to be directed at her. She'd shifted space in his chest and stepped right in, but now he was walking into thin air and falling. 'Actually, yes, a cup. It was…plastic…yes. How long in the microwave to heat milk?'

Cal shrugged. He was in his own kitchen, across the world, shaking cereal into a bowl and splashing milk over it. 'How do I know? Look it up on the Internet.'

'Right. Yes. Good.'

Cal's laugh rumbled round the kitchen. 'You're looking after Lachlan on your own? Have you been dumped? Or just dumped in the deep end?'

'Sophie's sick. She looks terrible.' He was surprised by how the raw instinct to look after her had sprung out of nowhere. How, even after the confusion of the last few weeks, he still wanted her with a ferocity that took his breath away. The microwave beeped and he swivelled round to switch it off so as not to wake her. Twisted his leg. Bit back a shout. He didn't have time to be precious about his stump right now. He had other things to focus on. 'I'm being Dad. And not a very good one.'

He wanted to be everything she wanted him to be. She couldn't say it in words, but he saw the wistful look in her eye. Knew enough about her past to guess she wanted the happy ever after thing.

More than anything he wanted to promise her that, to make her happy for ever. But he didn't know if he could do it. He was still working on happy right now.

Cal laughed again. Heartily. 'Finn, you'll be fine. Just go with your gut feel.'

'Which is to hide in a wardrobe right now, exactly where my son is, refusing to do his nightly treatment for his feet.'

'Crawl in with him then.'

He shook the milk, tasted a bit to test the temperature. Tried not to heave. Hot milk. *Ugh.* 'I've left him upstairs. There's a gate on the bedroom door so he can't get out. There's nothing there that can hurt him… I checked and triple-checked. But I need to go back and deal with him.'

'Bring me upstairs with you. I've got to see this. You with a bairn. Plus, I want to meet my nephew.'

The stairs in this house were lethal. Steep. Narrow. Finn edged up them as quickly as he comfortably could and found Lachie exactly where he'd left him: in the wardrobe playing with wooden trains. Finn put the cup down and crawled in with him, then showed him Cal's face on the phone screen. 'Say hi to Uncle Cal. Do a fist bump.'

'He's only one and a half, Finn.'

'So? He's very advanced for his age.' Pride bumped in his heart as his boy lifted his hand to the screen and touched his uncle's fingers. 'Good lad. Now show Uncle Cal your stickers. Lachie gets them when he's a good boy.'

'Like now? He's being a good boy now.' Cal's voice changed from gruff Scots to a gentle burr Finn didn't even know his brother had. 'Show me your boots and bars, clever wee man.' And just like that Lachie tore open the Velcro on his boots and he slipped them on.

No arguments. No curled lip. No tears. 'See? He's very advanced for his age.'

'Precocious. Like his father.' Cal's eyes danced as he watched father and son. 'Nah, he's a good kid, Finn.'

Finn crawled out and beckoned to Lachie to come with him. Together they hopped across the floor to the cot. Man and boy with dodgy legs and crooked smiles. A pair from the same mould. Something deep and feral surged in Finn's throat. 'I'm going to read him a story.' If he could get the words out. 'So we'll go now.'

'No! Don't hang up. I want to say goodnight.' So Cal stayed with them through the bedtime story and even sighed as Lachie slipped off to sleep. 'I never thought I'd see the day where you thought of someone other than yourself, Finn.'

Ouch. But he was right. For the first time in his life Finn's first thoughts weren't of himself or his day or his future, they were filled with pride and excitement at seeing Lachlan and his mum. With trying to work out ways of convincing her that somehow he could be in their lives all the time instead of having to wait until the designated rendezvous day. And, always on the tip of his tongue, convincing her that spending another few hours in bed with him would be a very good idea. 'I think I'm falling, Cal.'

'Fallen, mate. A goner, I'd say. Not surprising, he's very definitely a Baird.'

I mean Sophie.

'Not just Lachie, though.' He tried to find the right words, deliberated, and decided to just say what was worrying him. 'She wants to see my stump.'

'So? Show her.' His brother's eyebrows raised. Nonchalant. No big deal.

'Just like that?' He made it sound so easy.

'It's who you are.'

'That's the problem.' He had to say it before he imploded. 'She might not want me then.'

'Ach, one day you'll realise you are so much more than what you believe yourself to be.' Cal looked at him through the screen, those Baird eyes as intense as that night in the snow when his big brother had convinced Finn to stay alive. 'Just stop fighting everything. You seem to think the accident was a penance for being a bad lad or something, but it wasn't. It was just an accident. You need to put your energies into other things now. Your boy, your family. Let yourself fall for them, Finn. Enjoy the ride instead of analysing it.'

Family. Was that what they were? Was that what he wanted? Just the thought of it made him hopeful and panicked at the same time.

'I can try. I want to. Thanks.' One day Finn would have the guts to tell his brother about the night their mother died too. One thing at a time. A pint together in the same city would be nice. A pat on the back, a shared joke. For once the distance between them seemed too big. The floorboards in the room next door creaked and Finn's attention was diverted. 'I can hear her moving around. Got to go.'

His brother grinned. 'Aye, okay. Love you, honeypie.'

'Back at you, ya bampot.' Finn laughed and rolled his eyes. Things were starting to even out between them. About time too.

One problem solved. Now he just had to work out what to do about Sophie.

* * *

There was something cool on her forehead. Someone sponging her neck. Then a lot of shivering. Blackness.

Someone climbing into bed and holding her close, stroking her back, pulling the covers over her when she was trembling with cold. Stripping them off when she was too hot.

Someone tugging off her damp T-shirt and helping her on with a fresh one. Giving her sips of water. Holding her steady as she fumbled her way to the bathroom.

Someone kissing her forehead and telling her to go back to sleep...not to worry.

A lot later she was aware of light filtering through the curtains, an empty space next to her in the bed. And an ache for those arms round her again. She sat up, her head less muzzy for the first time in what felt like weeks.

The door creaked open and Finn stood there, a tray in his hand and a smile on his face. 'Hello. You're looking a lot better.'

'My headache's not so bad now.' If ever there was a remedy to illness, just looking at him smiling at her was it. But there was a piece missing. *Oh, God.* What had she been doing, sleeping in bed when she should have been taking care of her son? 'Where's Lachie?'

'Having a nap. He's fine. He's missed you, but we've managed.' Finn settled the tray on her lap. Opened a napkin and pointed to a bowl of something hot and steaming that smelt divine. 'Some chicken soup for you.'

He was surprising, this man. At every turn. 'More domestic goddess goodness. You made me soup?'

'Let's not break the spell with the truth.' He perched

next to her on the bed and handed her the spoon. 'Not made exactly; I heated it up.'

'Packet?' She looked at the pieces of chicken in the thick broth and didn't care where it had come from, only that he'd thought enough of her that he'd done this.

'Organic and homemade, it said. Nice?'

She tried some; it tasted of garlic and rosemary. Of comfort and home. 'Yes. Delicious. Just like my grandma used to make.'

'You mentioned her a couple of times while you were sick.' He picked up the photo she had on a dresser. 'Tell me about her.'

'I miss her.' She took the photograph and ran her finger down the black and white image of her grandma, taken in the back garden of this ancient house, dressed in an old jumper and thick woollen trousers, spade in hand and smiling warmly at the camera.

Sophie's heart lurched. Maybe it was because she was still sick, but she missed her more today, not less. She had a feeling her grandma would have known what to do about Finn. She'd have told her not to be scared and to have an open heart. That Lachie had a capacity to love both parents equally. That loving one didn't mean there wasn't enough left for the other. Her grandma had had that capacity too; having already brought up two daughters on her own, she'd made a home for her granddaughter and never once made Sophie feel she was a burden. But Sophie knew that love could stop short. That wanting someone to love you and knowing they didn't was the biggest heartbreak of all. 'She taught me about unconditional love.'

'I'm sorry your parents didn't, Sophie.' He stroked her hair. 'She must have been very special.'

'She was. She was wise and funny and strong.

She tried to protect me from the damage my parents wreaked, but you can't protect kids from everything.'

'Though you want to try.' He meant it, she could see. He was living it. 'Sounds like she was a good woman.'

'She never said a word against them, but she supported me, listened to me, made me believe what I was feeling was legitimate.'

'Sometimes that's all you can do.' He fitted his fingers into hers and held her hand gently, and that gave her encouragement to talk.

'The first time they arranged to see me I sat in the lounge and waited for them for five hours. They never came. I got up the next day and waited again. My grandma never said a word, just fed me and made sure I got to bed. But on the third day I bawled. *They weren't coming.* She said they must have got caught up with something important. *What about me?* I screamed. *Aren't I important?* I heard her talking to them on the phone, insisting they come. But they didn't. It happened time and again, and if they ever did manage to come they'd be in and out in a matter of hours. Like I wasn't enough to keep them there. And each time they left it broke me a little bit more. I went from being this super-confident kid to a...weak one.'

She shivered. It was the worst thing. That and believing that if you wished hard enough for someone to love you then they would, in the end.

He tipped up her chin so she could look into those blue-blue eyes. 'You, Sophie Harding, are far from weak. You are formidable and strong and God help anyone who gets in the way of you and your boy. You love fiercely and that's not a weakness. That's the greatest strength there is.'

There was something missing from his words. His

expression told her he wanted to be that. To have that capacity to love someone else. But he didn't think he could do it, she understood that now.

He didn't think he could, but love was in his actions, in the way he looked at Lachie. He loved his son fiercely already; he was just scared to let himself relax into it all.

They were matched in that then. 'Lachie's the reason I get up in the morning. My life's shaped around him.'

'You give him everything you didn't get from your own mum and dad.'

'I try to.' But she was still struggling to work through the ramifications of Finn being in their lives and how they could, or even if they should, shape things around him too.

'Now, eat.' He made sure she ate every drop of the soup. Gave her a glass of water and made her drink it all. Then he slid down next to her and tugged her to him, his breath whisper-soft on her cheek. 'You had me worried for a while there.'

'Sorry. I was completely wiped out.'

'We coped, me and the boy. It was touch and go with the bedtime routine, but we got through. Lucky I'm a fast learner.' His gaze wandered over her face, settling on her eyes. He smiled and every cell in her body hummed for his touch. He leaned closer and pressed a soft kiss on her mouth, sending shivers of desire through her. It was exactly what she wanted, but he pulled away too soon. 'I needed that. Right, close your eyes and get more rest.'

She wasn't going to argue. Her bones still hurt. She lay back against the pillows and wished he was in here with her. Had she dreamt he'd climbed in and stroked her back? Or had that been wishful thinking? 'Yes, boss. What about you?'

'I have chores to do.' He picked up the tray and her heart stuttered. 'A man doesn't get to be a domestic goddess by sitting around chatting.'

CHAPTER THIRTEEN

THE BEDROOM WAS in darkness the next time Sophie woke. And she was alone. The old house was making its usual little night-time creaks and groans and she should probably have stayed in bed, but energy rippled through her and she needed to stretch and move.

Slipping out of bed, she tiptoed to Lachie's room and found her boy fast asleep in his cot. She kissed the tips of her fingers and pressed them gently to his head, unerring endless love spreading through her as he cooed and turned over. Her boy was safe. He was well.

Thanks to Finn.

She needed to see him, to say thank you. And more.

The lounge was lit by the orange glow of a lamp on a side table in the corner of the room. Finn lay fast asleep on the sofa, wearing a T-shirt and dark cotton jersey shorts.

Had he been sleeping on her couch the whole time? Had she dreamt his hands on her back?

At some point he'd been back to his house and gathered some things together: a small overnight bag with neatly folded contents, his crutch propped against the sofa arm. His prosthesis lay discarded on the floor, his damaged leg exposed. Heart pulsing at her throat, she stepped closer, tiptoeing so as not to wake him. Wanting to look. Wanting to get over the hurdle he seemed to think was insurmountable.

It was a leg that stopped just below the knee. That was all. With fading stitches and a neat fold. It was what it was. A leg without a foot. Not pretty, not ugly. Just what it was. She looked deep within herself, measuring her reaction. There was nothing. No emotion, apart from a deep sense of sadness about what he'd endured and that he was still dealing with the fallout.

He shifted on the cushions and seemed to sense she was there, even in his sleep. He sat up; immediately his hand went to his leg. He dragged a throw over it. 'Sophie? What's wrong?'

'Nothing. Nothing at all.' Her son was safe and asleep. She was feeling better. Finn was here, in her house. Everything was almost perfect. The one thing that would make it wholly so was him sharing her bed.

Sharing her life?

She was scared as hell about that.

He relaxed. A little. 'So, you're awake and it's the middle of the night.'

She knelt next to him, not looking at his leg or the prosthesis, just looking at his face. And wondering how just looking at a man could give rise to so many emotions. 'Yes. I'm wide awake. I feel like I've been asleep for years.'

He nodded, hand still on his leg. 'Three days, actually. You missed the whole weekend and a day at work. But you were clearly very sick. I almost called the doctor out, but you settled. In the end.'

'Three whole days?' Time had been a blur. 'Were you here all that time?'

'Of course. I phoned in sick for you this morning. And my boss is very understanding, although he was a little shocked when I told him about Lachie being my son. I've taken carer's leave today.' He was wearing it like a badge of honour, his back straighter, pride etched through his features. 'Didn't even know there was such a thing. How do you feel now?'

'I feel better. Cooler.' Determined to face the one thing between them, she pushed the cover off his leg and laid her hand on his stump. 'See. Cool.'

He twisted, his hand hard over hers, his voice a warning. 'Sophie—'

'I've already seen it. And you know what?'

'What?' His whole body stiffened. Guarded. Defensive. And it damn near broke her heart. This was a man who deserved so much and yet flinched at anyone getting close. He just had to let go. Let her in.

Let me love you.

The thought thrummed through her, unbidden. Uninvited.

No.

Loving him was a step too far. Loving him was a sure-fire way to breaking her heart.

She blinked as tears gathered behind her eyes. He was generous and funny and smart and a domestic goddess. How could she not love him?

She didn't want to love him. *But she did.*

Oh, hell. When would she ever learn? She loved him and he didn't want her to.

He didn't want to share his fears, his scars. He didn't want to let her in. Sure, he wanted to be a father to Lachie. He wanted to be part of this, but he didn't trust himself enough to be able to take that leap wholeheartedly.

Her mind whirled, trying to make a plan and to reconcile her thoughts and her emotions. She had to show him he could do it.

'It's just an amputation, Finn. That's what it is. And you're magnificent with it.' She'd liked him with two legs; she loved him with one.

Although, she doubted he wanted to hear that. She didn't want to believe it herself.

She placed a palm on his chest, ran her fingers slowly down to the soft arrow of hair on his belly that she'd seen when they'd made love. She felt him harden at her touch. 'I've run a bath… You want to come and share it?'

Hunger flared in his eyes but he shook his head. 'No. I'm great here. You go.'

Her body ached through to her bones for him, like the sickness she'd just been through: systemic and utterly consequential. The only way of recovery was through his touch, his kisses. 'Come with me, Finn. Let me in.'

Let me love you.

Refusing to take no for an answer, she pulled his face to hers and kissed him. Hard. Felt him hesitate then give in to the rush of raw arousal that was spiralling between them. Hot and hungry.

Eventually he pulled back and captured her gaze in his and she felt naked and exposed and beautiful. His fingers cupped her face and his next kiss was sweet and sexy and languorous as heat and need flared inside her.

Let me love you.

The words were on her lips and she fed them to him in snatched breathlessness until she felt him relax.

Let me love you.

She pulled his shirt over his head and pressed against him, fitting herself to him. Body to body. Heart to heart.

He stripped off her T-shirt and her foggy memory reminded her of a blurry time during her illness where he did the same to the soundtrack of soothing words. She didn't want comfort now. She burned for him. She wanted him on her, in her. Now and always.

His hand was on her breast, then his mouth sucked in a nipple, and the only sound she heard was his name on her lips. The only scent in the air was of them. Of us.

She writhed against him, impatient and desperate. 'I need you, Finn. Please. Please. Come with me.'

His assent was more growl than words, but it was enough.

This wasn't happening. At least, couldn't be. Shouldn't be.

Finn was too drunk on need to resist. She drove him wild, made him want to do things he'd be better off not doing. Like this—sitting on the edge of the bath with her straddling him. Her hot mouth on his. Her damp core writhing against his erection.

His leg in plain sight. In all its messed up glory.

One minor shift in position and he'd be inside her. It was the only thing he could focus on.

But she stepped off his thighs and climbed into the bath, then took his hand as he turned and slid into the warm water to face her. Her kisses slowed, her touch became less frenetic, more reverent as she scooped water into a cup and let it flow slowly over his head, like an anointment. The soft touch of her fingers in his hair as she massaged added a surreal sensation of relaxation and intense arousal. Only Sophie could do that to him. Only Sophie…

He tried to take the cup from her so he could wash

her too, but she stopped his hand and rinsed the soap away. 'This is for you, Finn. Lie back.'

Leaning in to kiss him, she ran soaped hands down his chest, across his belly. Down his thighs. Then she kept her eyes on his face as she slowly massaged down both legs. Inching closer and closer to his scars.

His gut twisted in anticipation and fear.

Stop. He tried to move away from her touch, but she shook her head, taking his left leg in her hands and kissing from knee to stump. He couldn't move without the risk of slipping or drowning. Hell, he was already drowning in her eyes, in lust with her. She paused. 'Does it hurt?'

'A little.' It was reddened by lack of rest but he didn't care. He'd done what he'd had to do and been father to his son, helper to Sophie. *Lover.*

It was all he wanted, he knew that now. But after she examined his leg…he didn't want to imagine the fallout. Cal said he should let go. But Cal didn't wear these scars inside and out every day.

But maybe his brother was right.

Holding his breath, Finn hardly dared watch her expression as she reached the scar site. Saw no revulsion as she ran her fingers so gently across the bumpy skin, no grimace, no pretence of affection. She wasn't turned off. She didn't turn away. She accepted him.

Accepted him.

Hell, at least one of them did.

In her eyes he saw only genuine compassion. And need. And something he was not going to give name to because it was too soon, too intense. Even though he felt the same emotion flare in his chest.

He wanted to run. He wanted to stay. He wanted her.

Sophie's pupils were flecked with a shimmering gold as she smiled at him.'I want to kiss the pain away.'

He wished it could be that easy. 'I think that would work a lot better further up, honey.'

She laughed. 'Incorrigible.'

'Just being honest.' He pigged his eyes at her and laughed with her. 'A man can try, right?'

'I know exactly what you need.' Lifting his leg from the water, she kissed from stump to knee. From knee to thigh, eyes greedy and dancing and laughing and teasing. Hot waves of lust fired through him as her lips closed in and she took him in her mouth.

'Sophie,' he groaned as his fingers curled into her hair. It was almost too much. 'Sophie.'

He should have told her to stop. But the words never made it from his throat.

She didn't stop. She sucked him in, and again, and he couldn't stop his back arching as white light flared deep inside, building and building.

He was on the edge. So close. Her mouth so hot on his skin. Warm water soothing and arousing. Her breasts against his thighs.

But then she stopped, reached across to a cabinet cupboard, hands back to frantic as she fumbled with a packet. 'I want you inside me.'

'Trust me, there is no place I'd rather be. Ever.' He sat forward and pulled her to him, face to face, body slick against body. And she slid over him, moaning as she did so, rocking on him hard and fast. Then crying out as she rose and rose, taking him with her.

He crushed her against him, held her tight and let himself fall with her. Fall deep and hard and completely. His broken body, his heart, his everything.

* * *

It was late when Finn woke, entangled in bed sheets and Sophie's languid limbs. She was fast asleep, curled into his arms. The fever had definitely gone now and her chest rose and fell slowly.

His heart stuttered just to look at her. On her breasts he could see faint stretch marks. Tiny silvery lines that told of a woman who'd carried his child. Who'd fed their baby.

Geez. He wished he'd been around to see that. Now he had to make up the time.

He glanced at the clock and smiled. They were going to be late for work and he didn't care. He wanted to do this all day and all night.

Her eyes flickered open and she sleepily whispered, 'Look at that. We managed a night together.'

'Rule-breaker.'

'I never thought I'd be called that.' She wriggled close and kissed him. 'Did you ever think this would happen? You and me like this again?'

'Never in my wildest dreams.' That was what this felt like: a dream. Any time now he was going to wake up and be alone and filled with self-loathing for the person he was.

But dreams didn't come with sound and smell. Dreams didn't come with the benefit of touch. He ran his hands over her silk-soft skin, running circles over her thigh and higher as she snuggled against him, moaning against his shoulder. Her floral shampoo scent filled the room as she kissed him with a need that matched his and, just as things started to get very interesting, the silence was crashed by loud wails coming from the room next door.

'Uh-oh. No rest for the wicked.' Sophie shrugged and moved away. He could see she was torn between her own needs and her son's. But he knew damn well she would always put her son before anything else. As would he. Now and for ever. Her hand trailed along Finn's thigh and she flashed a smile full of promises. 'I like being wicked, just so you know.'

Then she shimmied out of bed and pulled on a dressing gown.

Finn sat up and swung his legs over the edge of the bed. Still not wanting her to see what he didn't have, but feeling as if something monumental had changed for him last night. Sure, he didn't want her to see him like this, but he knew he was the only one who cared. She'd made it very clear she liked all of him and not just the physical.

Besides, he didn't want a minute without seeing her or his boy and if that meant his scars were visible then so be it. He reached for his crutch at the side of the bed. 'I'll get him if you like—give me a minute?'

She stopped at the door and thought. 'Okay. We normally have cuddles in bed first thing in the morning, but this *Mum and Dad under the covers* scenario might be confusing for him. Bring him downstairs? I'll get the milk ready. And bacon sandwiches. You've done enough waiting on me; I need to return the favour.'

'Excellent.' So this was what a family was. His heart bloomed as desire made room for excitement, rubbing along with a deep feeling of being…happy. She made him happy. Sophie made his life so much better. He blew her a kiss. 'Have I ever told you how much I—?' He clamped his mouth shut to stop the words pouring out of him. *How much I love you.*

Hot damn.

Did he love her?

He wanted to. More than anything.

But it was stupid to think he could love her so soon. That kind of thing didn't happen. Not to him. Not to Finn Baird, who didn't know how to love anyone but himself.

'How much you love…?' Her eyebrows rose and uncertainty flickered across her face as she gripped the bedroom door handle. Uncertainty and longing.

Which almost shattered his heart. He couldn't promise something he couldn't give. 'How much I totally love bacon.'

'Doesn't everyone?' She breathed out and her gaze slid away for a second then back to him. 'Oh, and Lachie likes to manage the stairs himself. You just need to stand in front of him and let him slide down on his bottom.'

'Yeah. We've been doing races.'

'Of course you have. Men!' She rolled her eyes. 'Thanks for watching him. I'll make a start on breakfast.'

'I'll make a domestic goddess out of you yet,' he called after her, laughing.

'Takes one to know one,' her voice floated back as she disappeared.

Love was such a small word for a big deal. A huge deal. These two people were a big deal. This family.

He didn't know if he loved them yet, but he wanted to. After the accident he'd believed he was unlovable and incapable of loving anyone else, but she'd made him rethink that. He'd done some stupid things, shown nothing but egotistical pride and selfishness, and he'd paid a hefty price. Even so, she accepted him as a father to Lachie and as a lover. And God knew, he'd do anything…anything…for them.

That was a huge deal. A lot like love.

Still smiling, he walked through to Lachie's bedroom and helped him out of his boots and bars, then, balancing half on his crutch and leaning heavily on the cot sides, Finn lifted him out of the cot. Lachlan smelt of sleep and was probably still half in Dreamland as he clutched little fists round Finn's neck and cuddled into his neck. They'd come so far in such a short space of time. They had so many good years ahead of them but he couldn't wait. He wanted it all now.

He held the boy against his chest and whispered, 'Hey, good morning kiddo. Time to get up.'

'Finn.' Lachie grinned and put his finger on Finn's chest. 'Finn.'

'That's me.'

Daddy. One day he'd hear the word, when the time was right. He was okay with that; he knew who he was to his son, so Finn would do for now.

Nappy changed and standing on the carpet, Lachie held his arms out to be picked up again, but Finn shook his head and walked him to the top of the stairs. 'Nah, wee man, get your slip-slide on down the stairs. Mum's cooking. Come on, I'm starving.'

But Lachie stamped his foot and stood on the top step with his arms outstretched. 'Finn.'

Oh. Trouble on the horizon. What kind of a dad should he be? Authoritative? Stoic? A pushover? A friend? Would he ever stop asking himself that? Did anyone? 'On your bottom, come on, Lachie.'

'No.' His little arms stretched further as he tiptoed up towards Finn. The bottom lip started to curl and big fat tears started to roll down his cheeks. 'No.'

'What's the deal here, eh? The last two mornings you've wanted to race. Why not today?'

As if a toddler had any rhyme or reason for being contradictory.

'Okay, mate. Calm down.' The boy was still half asleep, and maybe he was getting his mum's bug. Who knew? Finn couldn't do anything but give in to him. The pull to inhale his boy's sweet scent again was too much. He picked him up and shifted him onto his right hip. 'One cuddle, then we're going down on our bottoms. It's not safe any other way.' He nuzzled against Lachie's head and felt emotion clutch his heart. He was besotted. For sure. 'We're on our way, Mummy. Get the bacon ready,' he called down.

'Finn!' Lachie pressed his hands to Finn's face and laughed, tears just a memory.

Unbelievable. He was too cute, this kid, and he certainly knew how to play the heartstrings.

'Right, time to sit down.' But as Finn bent to put Lachie down, the boy wriggled in the opposite direction, clinging to Finn's neck and scrambling up over his shoulder.

'What are you do—?'

Spinning off balance, Finn twisted sideways and forwards. Tried to catch the top step with his foot.

His goddamned *not there* foot.

Missed.

Tried again.

No. Hold the boy. Save the boy. Hold him.

And once again he was falling into thin air.

CHAPTER FOURTEEN

A SICKENING CRUNCH had Sophie running towards the stairs. The pained groans had her heart racing. Too fast. 'Finn? Lachie? Lachie?'

No. She didn't want to look, to know. Air stalled in her lungs, she couldn't breathe.

'Lachie? Finn?' Relief made her limbs weak as she found her little boy sitting halfway down the stairs, eyes huge and glassy, lip trembling. But whole. Then panic again, seeing Finn face down across the stairs, head and shoulder at a funny angle.

No. Her heart hollowed out.

Who to comfort first?

Finn made the decision easy. His voice, though muffled, was determined. 'Get him. Quick. Is he okay?'

Lachie's eyes were big and scared but he wasn't crying. Yet. 'I think he's in shock, but he looks okay. What happened?'

Finn slid himself upright onto the floor at the bottom of the stairs. He groaned and rolled his shoulder back and forth. She could see he didn't want to admit what had happened. To say the words.

'Did you fall or something?'

'Is he okay?' He groaned again as he shuffled up the stairs to check on Lachie. His hands ran over the boy's body, head, face. Checking. Worrying. Assessing. 'Did he get hurt? Are you okay, mate? I'm so sorry.'

'He's fine.' Thank God. She shouldn't have left them alone. But they'd been okay while she was sick. What the hell happened? This time she infused assertion into her voice. 'What about you? Are you okay?'

'I'll live.' He shook his head.

She didn't want him to just live. She wanted him to be the happy-go-lucky man he'd been ten minutes ago. The one who'd kissed her to sleep. She wanted him not to hurt. 'You don't look okay.'

'I'm fine.'

'No, you're not. Just admit you're hurting and we can sort it out.'

He turned away and checked his stump. Closed down and froze her out. Just like that.

'Finn. Look at me. It was just an accident.'

He carried on checking his body, rolling his shoulder. No words. Nothing.

She put her hand on his shoulder. 'Finn. Talk to me.'

'It was my fault.' He finally looked at her with hollow eyes and the burden he was carrying was almost palpable. 'Take him and give him something to eat. He's hungry and he's going to start grizzling.'

'But—' She stopped herself from pushing him for more. He was angry and sore and no amount of mollifying words were going to help, she knew that about him now. She picked up Lachie and squeezed him close. Kissing his face. Then bent to Finn. 'If you won't let me help...' *Or let me in.* 'Then at least tell me what happened.'

He huffed out a long breath and shook his head. 'Just take him away. I'll be through soon.'

But he wasn't. In the end she gave up waiting and fed

Lachie. Managed to force a couple of mouthfuls into herself. Got her son ready for Nursery and gathered her things for work. On autopilot.

She was in the hallway clipping Lachie into the push-chair when the sound of a bag zip flared a warning deep in her gut. Finn was leaving.

Of course he was; he'd only moved in to help her. But she'd allowed herself to believe beyond that. Idly wished he might just move more things in.

Slowly, she walked through to the lounge and found him sitting on the sofa surrounded by the bits of his life he'd brought with him. He stood up as she walked in. 'It happened so fast, Soph. He wanted me to carry him downstairs, but I refused. I was trying to put him down so he could slide down. I'm not used to the way he can wriggle and shift his weight. I couldn't compensate for it.'

'He can be very wriggly.' She tried for a smile. Couldn't find one.

'I shouldn't have been holding him at the top of the stairs. It wasn't just stupid; it could have been deadly. I could have killed him.'

'But you didn't. You're both a bit shocked, that's all.'

'I was taught how to go downstairs. I was taught how to fall. But not with a bairn in my arms.' He paused. Shook his head. 'I can't do this.'

Pain caught her under her ribcage. Where was this going? She didn't want to imagine. But, soul-deep, she knew. Panic had her gut twisting. 'Stuff happens, Finn. You can't always plan for everything.'

'Can't I? Don't you get it? I know what my limita-tions are. I know where I end and the false leg starts. I know how easy it is to lose balance. But I did it any-way. Because I wanted to hold him. Because I'm his dad and I can't get enough of him. Because I can't see further than what I want. I wanted to hold him. I wanted to feel his weight in my arms.' His eyes became dark and held little hope. 'It's not about my leg, Sophie. It's me putting myself first. Again.'

'It was an accident, Finn.'

'No. No.' She didn't want to know what was coming next. 'Doesn't that tell you I shouldn't do this?'

'Do what?' All the happiness she'd felt over the last few weeks started to dissolve. She'd been a fool to think she could find someone to love and for them to love her back. To want to stay.

Even so, she wanted to walk into his arms and hold him because she had enough belief for the both of them.

But he turned and picked up his bag. 'It's best I take a big step back here. It's all going too fast. Yeah. Maybe it'd be better if I ducked out. Obviously I'll make sure you're looked after.'

'Geez, Finn. Really? One setback and you're out?'

'I don't want to wait around for another one; it could be a lot worse.'

'We'll just be careful and put plans in place.'

What about me? She wanted to scream at him. Didn't he want to stay for her? Couldn't he make it work? For her?

'You were right all along, Soph. I can't do this. I can't be around him if I'm going to hurt him.' He closed the distance between them. Put his bag on the floor and pressed his palm to her face. 'You're amazing. And wise. And beautiful and funny.'

So stay. For me.

'Back at ya, Finn Baird.' She wanted to tell him she loved him. The words hovered on her lips like the butterflies they'd seen together...fleeting, beautiful, ethereal…but she couldn't say them and risk him stamping on them.

But he gazed down at her and she saw the love shining there in his eyes. He was running scared, he was doing what he thought he should do. Because, whatever excuses and false truths he told himself, he had feelings for her and they went soul-deep. 'I should have listened to you in the first place, Soph. I should have stayed away.'

'I didn't know what I was talking about.' She held his wrist to keep the contact between his hand and her cheek. She didn't want to let go. 'You're very different to how I thought you'd be.'

I love you.

He shook his head. 'It was like a dream. A lovely dream where we were a family. But that's all it was. Reality is a whole different ballgame, right? Let's quit pretending it could work when there's too many reasons for it to fall apart. It's better all round if I stay away.'

The pain under her ribcage intensified. 'I know you're rattled. I know you think it's for the best—'

'It is for the best.'

He was trying to do the right thing; she got that. What he believed was right. Such was his honour and depth of feeling for his family. But while he didn't want to hurt his son, he was breaking her heart. 'Finn—'

'Mama!' Lachie's wail reached her heart and tugged. And here she was, torn between the two of them again. Torn between what she wanted and what Finn thought was best. Torn between making him stay and letting him go.

Her mothering instinct cut straight in. She could survive being heartbroken but she was not going to let Lachie suffer that. 'Finn. Do not leave. Do you hear me?

If you go now then that's it. Over. You can't play this game of being in his life one minute and then not the next. It's the worst thing you could do. You're either here for good or gone for good. Okay?'

'I'm sorry, Sophie.' He picked up his bag and walked to the door.

'You're really going to do this? Break my heart? Break his?' She pointed at Lachie, who was completely oblivious to what was happening. But he wouldn't always be like that; one day he'd dream of having his father in his life. One day he'd want that more than anything else.

Finn was at the front door now. 'I am taking responsibility. For the first time in my life.'

This wasn't about the fall. It was about him not believing in himself. He still thought he was unreliable and untrustworthy. 'Families deal with things, Finn. They don't break when one thing goes wrong.'

'They do the right thing.'

'They look after each other.'

He shrugged a shoulder. 'I can't be relied upon.'

'You can say that again.' Anger pushed heartbreak out of the way but still love fluttered around the edges. Because even now she loved him—loved him for believing in his own convictions, no matter how furious they made her feel.

Fists clenched by her sides, she watched him leave but she didn't run after him and beg him to stay. Wouldn't have been able to get the words out through her closed-over throat.

He loved her, she was sure. He just didn't want to. And she was so done with loving people who didn't want to love her back.

Why the hell had she trusted him? Why had she let

him into their lives and into her heart? Into Lachie's? What a fool to have been so concerned Finn would drive a wedge between her and her boy. Fool to think he wanted the same things. Fool to love him. To believe an idea of them together could be possible.

She knelt and wrapped her boy in a hug, tried not to let him see the tears landing on his coat. 'Okay. We'll be fine, little man.'

In a while. They'd build a life together and they'd be okay. It would be a wonderful life—she'd make damned sure it was—but Finn would always be there in the shadows somewhere.

Breaking her heart all over again.

'When I said let yourself fall for her I didn't mean it literally.'

'Quit the jokes, Cal. I'm not in the mood.' Why had he bothered to call his brother? Stupid idea. Finn massaged his temple. Looked out of the car window into the hospital car park. Watched the rain sluice the windscreen. *Geez*, the weather was as bad as his mood. 'You're making things worse.'

'I'm trying to get you to lighten up, Finn. So you're both okay? Apart from the bruised ego?'

'Physically. Yes.'

'So let me get this straight—you fell and you stopped Lachie from being hurt by taking the brunt of the fall yourself?'

'Uh-huh.' He'd somehow managed to twist himself to make sure Lachie had a soft landing, at a cost to his stump and his shoulder. 'The X-rays say I just have soft tissue damage. Nothing that can't be fixed by time and a wee dram.'

Unlike the heaviness in his heart. No amount of time

would fix that. And alcohol would only be a temporary balm.

Loving Lachie was as natural as breathing, and he'd make sure he would always have contact and be in his life, somehow. And he could, legally, morally and emotionally: he was his father. Blood. Family. And nothing could ever change that.

The real ache in his heart was for Sophie. It had only been three hours since he'd walked away but he regretted every single step. He'd thought things would feel better once he'd made the break but they didn't. Everything felt worse.

He loved her, more than anything, but he couldn't bear to be the cause of the anguish he'd seen on her face. The blinked-away tears. The panic. The fear. Never again.

He'd been the reason she'd given up her travel plans. The reason she had to work full-time and be a single mother. He didn't want to *be* any more reasons to hurt her.

He had to protect them all, didn't he?

Cal was still talking. As was his wont. 'So you saved the boy then really? He was going to get hurt but you made sure he didn't?'

'Cal, stop. Okay? It was my fault in the first place.'

'Ach, kids get into all sorts of mischief. Adults do too, right?' Cal waved his hand. 'And we can protect them as much as we can, but sometimes stuff happens. Trust me, I know this; clearing up after stuff is my job.'

Stuff happens. Sophie had said the same. 'Stuff seems to happen a lot when I'm around.'

Cal's eyes narrowed. 'Oh? What else? And don't go mentioning the accident because we both know it was a mixture of a lot of things neither of us could have predicted.'

'I shouldn't have stepped out into nothing. I wasn't thinking straight.'

'I know.' Cal closed his eyes and looked as if he was reliving the whole episode again. 'I shouldn't have been pushing you.'

'You didn't push me.' He remembered a bit of shoving during the argument, but nothing like an intentional push over the cliff. *Hell*. His brother loved him; he knew that well enough. Not that they liked to show it.

Cal's fingers steepled on the ambulance station's white Formica table. 'I knew you were suffering, Finn. I knew you were in a bad place but I still goaded you.' His brother gave him the kind of smile he'd give to his baby daughter: tender. Tenderness from Cal Baird. It made Finn's heart clench. 'You're too hard on yourself. You want to take the blame for everything. You need to stop and look at how far you've come. Not only did you recover from the accident but you're working full-time. You love your boy enough to protect him at a cost to yourself. You want to save Sophie from hurt because that's what you think you'll give her.'

'Because I don't know if I can do anything other than that.'

'Why not?'

'Because I'm a selfish idiot.' The truth of it.

Cal nodded. 'You're talking about Mum now, and that's something else altogether.'

'How do you know?'

'I'm your brother. I know.'

If it hadn't been for Finn's stupid selfishness his son would have a grandmother to dote on him now. He had to get it out in the open, once and for all. Then Cal would understand why he'd had to back away from Sophie and Lachlan. 'I was the reason Mum had the stroke. I said I was going to go see her and I didn't. I stressed her out. I should have kept to my word, but I was all gung-ho and immature and didn't think.'

Cal shook his head and rubbed his jaw. 'Thing is, Finn, she'd had a run of small strokes before; she begged me not to tell you in case you barrelled home and missed out on your game time.'

What the hell? 'You knew she was sick?'

'The docs said it was probably a matter of time before she had the big one, even though she was taking meds. Her blood pressure was out of control. Yes, she was sick.'

'And you kept this from me because?'

'Because we wanted you to make the most of your chances. Like I do now. Still.'

'Wait…so she was sick and you didn't tell me? How could you do that?' His mind went off at a tangent. If his brother had told him their mother was sick he'd have made sure to visit her. If his mum hadn't died he wouldn't have been so hard on himself, wouldn't have fallen into a bad run of form in his rugby, wouldn't have met Sophie.

So many ifs.

'I'm sorry. I didn't realise you'd taken it so much to heart and blamed yourself. You have a huge capacity to love people, Finn. You've just got to believe in it.' Cal leaned forward, made sure to make eye contact. 'Do you love this woman?'

Whoa, back to Sophie again. He didn't hesitate. 'Yes. Absolutely.'

'Do you want to make a go of it with her?' Cal paused for a beat then added, 'I don't want a speech or justification of why you can't. Do you *want* to? Just yes or no will do.'

Again, no hesitation. 'Yes.' More than anything.

'Assuming she wants you. And I have to say she needs her head checking on that score. But…' Cal grinned '…you have a chance to have a family, Finn. Don't stuff it up. Go back and tell her you're sorry and you're going to make it work. Or I will.'

'You wouldn't? Please back off from my life, Cal.'

His brother laughed. 'As soon as you stop stuffing it up I'll back right off. Okay? I don't want to see your sad ugly face here again until you have good news.'

'I'm a grown man with a son. I have a responsible job and a heap of sporting medals. Will there ever be a time when you're going to treat me as your equal and not your baby brother?'

'I doubt it.' Cal shrugged in the way annoying siblings did. 'So deal with it.'

Looked like he was going to have to. And he was going to deal with the Sophie situation. Right now.

Sophie checked her phone for the millionth time. No messages. No missed calls. Nothing.

Although she didn't know why she was torturing herself by checking. He wasn't going to phone. He'd been determined to leave.

Cursing, she threw the phone down next to her on the couch and flicked through the TV channels. Nothing worth her attention there either.

She picked up her phone again. Dialled. Breathed out when the call was answered. 'Hannah. Hey. Yes, I'm fine. He's fine. Listen… I need a distraction—tell me about that hen night you went on last Saturday.' When Sophie had been comatose and Finn had looked after her. Pain hit her in the chest. When would she stop thinking about him? 'Fun?'

'As ever. And so much gossip.' Hannah paused.

'Spill the beans.' *Make my thoughts stop.*

Her friend coughed. 'You want me to talk you down, right? Has he rung?' The best thing about friends was that they didn't mind when you called them at work and cried your eyes out. They took you out for lunch and made sure you ate something. And they listened for the nth time about your fractured love life.

'No. No calls. No texts.' And he'd only left this morning. Nowhere near enough time for either of them to gather their thoughts properly. All she knew was that she ached to see him, to hold him. And that that ache wouldn't go away for a very long time. 'It's been a crappy day.'

'If I ever see him can I personally tell him what I think?'

'No. Yes.' Sophie smiled. She had people she loved and who loved her; she was glad of that. Somehow they'd pull her through this. 'Okay, Rottweiler. You can do your worst.' Which was fairly bad; Sophie had seen her in action before.

A sharp knock on the door made her jump—made her heart jump too. 'Er...there's someone at the door.'

'Is it him? Quick, go look. Through the curtains or something.' Hannah breathed heavily. 'If it is, pass the phone over to me so I get my chance.'

Sophie dragged herself from the sofa and to the front door; her body ached from the wonderful things he'd done to her last night. She didn't want that particular ache to ever go. 'It'll be someone selling something; it always is.' She pulled the door open and froze. 'Oh.'

'Is it him?'

'Yes.' Rain dripped from his hair, flattening it to his head. Little rivulets ran down his cheeks, over his nose. His eyes sparked determination and so many other emotions it made her dizzy to see them. Because they were all directed at her: love, fear, passion. 'Finally found something to tame the Baird hair, then?'

He ran his hand over his wet head. 'I don't want anything tamed when I'm around you.'

What did that mean? She wasn't going to allow herself to hope. 'Did you forget something? Why are you here?'

'Can I talk to him?' She'd forgotten Hannah was on speaker phone. Her voice was loud and piercing.

He took the phone out of Sophie's hand. 'This is Finn.'

'I hope you're pleased with yourself? That's twice you've hurt her. She's a sweet, lovely woman and she deserves better than you.'

He looked at Sophie again. Captured her heart with his gaze. 'I know she does. Oh, and you forgot sexy. She's sexy and clever and funny. And I love her.'

'Sorry, Hannah, got to go.' He *what?* Sophie grabbed the phone and clicked it off. Stepped aside to let him in out of the rain, even though he deserved to be in it for a good time longer. Then she hauled up some of her friend's inner Rottweiler. 'You can't come here and say things you don't mean.'

'I mean every word.' He took her hand. 'I stuffed up, Sophie. I hurt you and I'm so sorry. I realised that by walking away I was making everything ten times worse. It's not about my leg, is it? It's not actually about dropping Lachie, in the end, because a man with two legs could do that—that was just an accident. It's about believing in myself—in my heart and my love for you.

It's about knowing I will do the right thing and choose you two before me, every time.'

'Damned right it is. I was willing to do that for you.' But then she'd always chased the love she couldn't have.

'When I walked away from you I was putting myself first. I was choosing not to work with you to find answers and solutions. That was beyond selfish. I was being Billy and choosing to go for a pint instead of finding help.'

'But you can't yoyo in and out of our lives, Finn. It's not fair. You have to be sure and you have to stay.'

'I know.' He was starting to shiver from cold. His hand shook as he smoothed down her hair. She felt love in his touch, in the way he looked at her. 'I know you waited for your parents to come home. I know you packed your suitcase and cried when they didn't come. I can't be that person who does that to either of you.'

'But you did it already.'

He closed his eyes, took a breath. 'Sometimes it's overwhelming. All of this. You. Lachie. Being a father. Being an amputee. I got lost in it all. I'm so sorry, Sophie. So sorry. I won't get lost again. I want to stay here with you, my anchor, my everything.'

Hope bloomed in her chest, in her heart. He understood her. He understood himself and that was most of the battle. With that they could move forward. They could love. She stepped close to him, wrapped her arms around him, felt the steady beat of his heart, his strength. Strength he hadn't known he'd had until he was tested. And tested again. This man had been through so much and survived, and she loved him for that with every cell in her body. 'If you start to lose your way, just say so, Finn. Let me help you. I want to do that…not because I don't think you can manage, but because we're a team. Believe me, there will be days I need to lean on you too.'

'Any time. All the time. Every day, Sophie. I don't want to be apart from you and Lachie ever again.' He reached into his pocket and pulled out a box. Then he was letting go of her and kneeling down. It wasn't a pretty kneel but it was a beautiful Finn one. 'Sophie, will you forgive me? I love you. Will you make a family with me? Marry me?'

Tears pricked and she didn't fight them. She was done with trying not to love him. All she could see was a man who had captured her heart and her soul, who made her happy, who made her world complete. And a beautiful ring that signified his love for her. Their love. 'Yes. Yes, of course. I love you too. So much.'

She kind of wished she'd kept Hannah on the phone for that bit.

But then he was standing up and hauling her to him and kissing her as if his world was complete too. When he pulled away he was breathless and shining. 'You know what makes me sad the most?'

'What's that?' She didn't want to think of him being sad.

'If I hadn't been like this I could have loved you longer. Both of you.'

'Well, today is the beginning of the rest of our lives. We just have to love harder from now on to make up for it.' She tugged his damp shirt from his pants, laughing at the quick upturn of his mouth. Loving the feel of him against her. Loving him. 'If you don't want to get sick we need to get you out of these wet things super quick.'

'Yes please.' He kissed her again. And again. 'If you insist.'

EPILOGUE

Twelve months later

'DADDY! DADDY, COME and see the big boat!' Lachie ran back along the lakeside path towards Finn, grabbed his hand and tugged him to see the great old-fashioned steamboat on Lake Wakatipu. A warm summer breeze caught up the boy's hair, tugging his curls in every direction.

Daddy. That never got old. Finn picked up his boy and swung him onto his shoulders so he could better see the deep blue lake and the fancy boat and steam. 'Look at that! And see the ducks there.'

'Whoa! Careful.' Cal frowned at him the way big brothers did and reached a hand to Lachie's back to steady him. 'Sure you're okay doing that move?'

Irritation rankled, but Finn forced it back. Time here was short and he wasn't going to let old arguments bite. 'It's fine. I've perfected it. We know exactly how to do it, right, Lachie?'

'Yes, Daddy. I have to stay very still.' His foot rocked against Finn's heart, stamping on it little impressions of love. 'We can do it 'cos we're a team.'

'Never thought I'd see the day you were settled. But you're full of surprises, Finn.' Cal's hand had left Lachie's back and was now clamped on Finn's shoulder, making Finn's chest contract unexpectedly. 'I think it's time I backed off the bossy bit now. You're on your own.' He laughed. 'But if you need me—'

'I know.' Finn exhaled. 'But thanks, anyway. You were a great stand-in dad, even though you should never have been put in that position in the first place.' He owed Cal so much. One visit to the other side of the world was not going to be enough to pay him back.

Lachie tugged on Finn's hair and giggled. 'Where's Mummy?'

Finn turned and caught sight of Sophie, swinging little Grace between her and Cal's wife, Abbie. She looked up and saw him watching her and she waved, her mouth forming the words, *Thank you.*

He hung back a little and waited for them to catch up. Managed to get her to himself for one minute. 'Thank you for what?'

'For bringing me here to New Zealand. For helping me live my dreams of travel. For loving me.' She snuggled against him, caught Lachie's foot in her hand. 'Before it's all too difficult.'

Finn pressed his hand to the tiny belly she was growing. A new life. He couldn't believe he could be this lucky. 'Life will never be difficult. Not with you. Did I ever tell you how much I love you?'

'Yes. Every day. At least three million times.' She stood on tiptoe and kissed him. 'Don't ever stop.'

'Not a chance.' And then he told her again, just to make sure she knew.

* * * * *

MILLS & BOON

Coming next month

ONE NIGHT WITH DR NIKOLAIDES
Annie O'Neil

"Cailey *mou*. I've always felt we had a connection, you and I. Don't you know that?"

She shook her head against his finger, fighting the urge to open her lips and draw it into her mouth. Any connection they'd had had been more master and servant than anything. She'd grown up working in his house. Scrubbing, cooking and cleaning alongside her mother, who had spent her entire adult life serving as the Nikolaides housekeeper.

She'd thought that kiss they'd shared all those years ago had been a dare. A cruel one at that. For it had been only a day later when she'd overheard him telling his friends he'd never marry a housemaid.

She was surprised to see him looking hurt. Genuinely hurt.

"Not in the strictest sense," she whispered against his finger.

"We're peas in a pod. You must know that. And today, working together, wasn't that proof?"

"No. It only proves we work well together. Our lives… we're so different."

She wanted to hear him say it. Say he'd held himself apart from her because of her background.

"You *are* different from me," he said, lowering his head until his lips whispered against hers. "You're better."

Before she could craft a single lucid thought they were kissing. Softly at first. Not tentatively, as a pair of teenagers might have approached their first kiss, more as if each touch, each moment they were sharing, spoke to the fact that they had belonged together all along.

Simply kissing him was an erotic pleasure on its own. The short walk to Theo's house had given his lips a slight tang of the sea. Emboldened by his sure touch, Cailey swept her tongue along Theo's lower lip, a trill of excitement following in the wake of his moan of approbation.

The kisses grew in strength and depth. Theo pulled her closer to him, his lips parting to taste and explore her mouth. The hunger and fatigue they'd felt on leaving the clinic were swept into the dark shadows as light and energy grew within each of them like a living force of its own.

Undiluted sexual attraction flared hot and bright within her, the flames licking at her belly, her breasts, her inner thighs, as if it had been waiting for exactly this moment to present itself. Molten, age-old, pent-up, magically realized and released desire.

Continue reading
ONE NIGHT WITH DR NIKOLAIDES
Annie O'Neil

Available next month
www.millsandboon.co.uk

LET'S TALK
Romance

For exclusive extracts, competitions
and special offers, find us online:

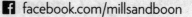 facebook.com/millsandboon

@millsandboonuk

@millsandboon

Or get in touch on 0844 844 1351*

For all the latest titles coming soon, visit
millsandboon.co.uk/nextmonth

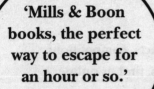